1/7

Th

SEX

DIARY

of a

Metaphysician

by Colin Wilson

Ronin Publishing, Inc. ● Box 1035 ● Berkeley, CA 94701

Published by
Ronin Publishing, Inc.
Post Office Box 1035
Berkeley, California 94701

Sex Diary of a Metaphysician
ISBN: 0-914171-59-3
Copyright © 1963 & 1988 by Colin Wilson
(first published in the USA in 1963
by The Dial Press under the title
The Sex Diary of Gerard Sorme)

Second Ronin printing 1994
Printed in the United States of America

Ronin Credits
Project Editors: Sebastian Orfali and Beverly Potter
Editorial Consultant: Peter Beren
Cover Design: Brian Groppe
Cover Photo: Oswald Jones
Typography and Production: Ginger Ashworth

With Love to Joy and Sally

Introduction

by Timothy Leary

The Sex Diary of Gerard Sorme is my kinda good read. High aims and low-down deeds. It's a psych-probe satire that gives you insights into the human realities of a specific culture from the down-and-dirties of daily life to the up-and-atom frontiers of science-philosophy.

Now, the scope of *The Sex Diary of Gerard Sorme*, is by no means as grandly epic, as what James Joyce wrought in *Ulysses* or Thomas Pynchon in *Gravity's Rainbow* or William Burroughs in his *Western Lands* trilogy, but the angle of approach is similar. Colin Wilson has written us an amused, tender guide to the sects and sexual situation in London in the late 1950s.

Yes, I know, it's boring to keep on deploring the British National Sex Wound — the horrid effects of the harsh, sin-whipped public-schoolmanship which makes it chronically impossible for the educated British male to relate to women, wogs, or commoners. All of whom are, apparently, genially patronized as colonial victims to be conquered and exploited.

But Colin Wilson's novel is no gloomy recital of sexual disappointments. It's the bouncy journal of a young, introspective writer who hungers and trembles to realize his neurological potential, to activate his throbbing, swollen mind, to evolve to a higher state.

Gerard passionately wants to become an evolutionary agent. A creative participant in the updating and product-improvement of new life forms. "I am talking about human engineering... evolution made conscious. I am trying to help life forward, or in its struggle upward."

Gerard has convinced himself that through intense sexual

experience he can illuminate and mutate. His lustful glands smile in agreement. Thus the first half of the book is a witty recital of his varied, often harassed genital encounters. I found this section charming and mildly arousing. We experience: Gerard's climax when a plump woman in a crowd presses against him; the bland, emotionless loss of his virginity with an irrepressibly steamy virgin waitress; his continuous shuttling of compliant ladies, actresses, maids, shopgirls, in and out of the always available beds. Then there's the tender post-romp scene of the girl lying naked on a misty lakeshore, still quivering from orgasm, quoting Baudelaire.

There's much intrigue, some adultery — but almost no emotion. At times the tone is eerily flat, like that of Brett Easton Ellis in *Less Than Zero*. I did this. I thought that. I want to sleep. Smooth satire, it is.

But then there's the Dark Side.

References do keep cropping up about sex murders and evil obsessions and satanism.

Eventually, on page 111, we are introduced to one Cardoc Cunningham, an enormously industrious sex magician closely based on Aleister Crowley. The book suddenly becomes a detailed, step-by-step, clinical description of the unremitting attempts by Cunningham to possess and control the lives of those around him.

How? By invoking the paraphernalia and pedantic rituals of Victorian Age occultism. Pentagons. Incense. Incantations. Invocations. Drugs. Animal sacrifice. Colorful costume changes. Oodles, my dear, of simply scandalous pranks! Woven together with group hypnotic spells — all of which work like, well, just like magic with the docile, horny, bored, unsophisticated observers!

One is reminded again of the thermo-dynamic power of British Calvinist Puritanism to build up erotic steam pressure to churn to thrill-wheels of naughty desire and schoolboy rebellion. And, we understand why restless Eton grads, before 1960, bored to frenzy by the tired pomposities of the staid protestant rituals, responded so enthusiastically to the smoking psychodramas and hilarious reenactments of ancient pagan and voodoo scenarios.

Colin Wilson's satire represents Cunningham and the narrator, Gerard Sorme, as slightly comic emblems of the two sides of the prepsychedelic spiritual search.

Cunningham evokes and exploits the spiritual potentials which all of us contain within. But, as a dutiful product of the factory society, he does it for power. And spiritual efficiency. This is what "magic" meant in smokestack Victorian England. Power and control. Gung-ho spiritual engineering to exploit supernatural resources. Cunningham is like a madcap Monty Python industrial manager, a frenzied John Cleese frantically organizing assembly-lines of sexworkers in the satanic mills.

The literary Sorme seems bored with the complications of power. His is the sincere quest for personal enlightenment. When he attains illumination he will, of course, write several serious books about it. Sorme ends up in a proper writer's cottage attended to by a loyal, dependent, loving wife.

Cunningham, unnaturally, ends up in California forming a new religion.

I was impressed to note that this book was published in the ancient, dim past of the year 1963. Thus it was written prepsyche-delia and pre-Women's Lib. Before Werner Ehrhard and Carlos Casteneda and Jim Jones and Jim Bakker. Before Shirley MacLaine. Before, even, the Sexual Revolution and the sexual marketeering of Hefner, Guccione, and Larry Flynt. And, of course, pre-A.I.D.S.

I have admired Colin Wilson for decades. To my regret I have not yet met him but he appears to me as a thoughtful, good man. *The Sex Diary of Gerard Sorme* is a thought-provoking, good book.

Preface

by Colin Wilson

It gives me little pleasure to recall the early history of this novel.

As incredible as it may seem to readers of the 1980s there was a time about three decades ago when sex was practically unmentionable in a novel, and the word "fuck" had to be printed as an "f" followed by a dash. James Jones broke new ground by printing the complete word in *From Here to Eternity*, and then, in 1960, *Lady Chatterley's Lover* was cleared for publication by a British court, and became an instant bestseller. In Paris, a small publisher that traded under the name of Olympia Press — printing "pornographic" books for sale to British and American tourists — suddenly received international recognition as a result of publishing Vladimir Nabokov's *Lolita* — or rather, as a result of the sudden notoriety that descended upon Nabokov when Graham Greene declared that *Lolita* was one of the best books of 1955, and an hysterical newspaper columnist accused him of helping to sell pornography. By the early 1960s, Maurice Girodias — owner of Olympia Press, and publisher also of the Marquis de Sade, Henry Miller, and J. P. Donleavy — had ceased to be regarded as a peddlar of pornography, and achieved the status of a hero of the avant garde.

He quickly realized that this placed him in a far more powerful position than that of an underground publisher of "dirty" books, and that if he took his stand as a defender of the right to free speech, he was practically unassailable. And I suspect that it struck him that if a book had some literary merit, or could lay claim to intellectual seriousness, then the author could be as sexually explicit as he liked. This may be why, in 1962, Maurice Girodias approached me and asked if I would care to write a novel for Olympia Press.

The idea delighted me. I had always been irritated by the

prudery of Anglo-Saxon publishers. A good writer is obsessed by
the urge to describe life precisely as he has experienced it, and this
urge has been the driving force of literature — particularly the
novel — for the past two-and-a-half centuries, since Samuel
Richardson's *Pamela* — a lengthy account of the attempted seduction of a servant girl — became a European sensation in 1740. The
Pickwick Papers may not strike us as very real, but as Dickens was
writing it, he must have felt that he was capturing "life" as no one
had ever captured it before. And Sinclair Lewis must have felt the
same as he wrote *Main Street*, and Joyce as he wrote *Ulysses*. And
when, at the age of eighteen, I began to write my first novel, *Ritual
in the Dark*, I also had the feeling that I was describing life exactly
as I saw it — trying to give the reader an idea of what it was like to
be inside my skin. I felt I had captured with precision what it was
like to live in a furnished room in Camden Town, to eat cheap meals
in a workmans' café, and to get around London on a bicycle. But
what I was *not* allowed to describe was the obsession with sex that
every normal young male experiences, the feeling that he would
happily spend the rest of his life deflowering virgins at the rate of
twenty a day. At that age — and for many years after — every girl
in the street represents a delicious mystery. I remember once
spending the night with a girl in a flat borrowed from a friend, and
the friend asking me the next day: "What kind of panties did she
wear?" I rather admired his honesty in asking the question, for it
was at the back of my own mind every time I talked to an attractive
girl. A year or so later, another friend confided to me that his wife
had left him after she found his secret "sex diary," and discovered
that he was an incorrigible Casanova. But what really upset her was
not the tale of endless casual seductions, but the minute detail in
which he described undressing the girl, the colour of her bra and
panties and pubic hair, whether she helped him introduce his penis
or let him do it unaided, whether she moved her pubis up and down,
whether she simply kept her legs apart, or wound them 'round his
buttocks... The approach struck her as horribly clinical — whereas
for my friend, each girl was as unique as a bottle of ancient
Burgundy to a wine connoisseur, and deserved the same kind of
detailed entry in his "cellar book."

In its final version, *Ritual in the Dark* contains two or three
fairly explicit sexual episodes, but as I wrote them, I felt they were
pathetically inadequate; *that* wasn't what it was like at all... I envied

Henry Miller, who had been able to describe his own sex life with total honesty because the book was being published in Paris. But then, when I read *Sexus* or *The Tropic of Capricorn*, I felt that Miller had totally wasted his opportunities; instead of trying to tell "the truth" about sex, he had merely produced a kind of compendium of schoolboy smut.

But what exactly was this elusive "truth" about sex? It was easy enough to see that, until *Lady Chatterley*, no major novelist had been allowed to include the all important sexual element of human existence. But to me, the relationship between Lady Chatterley and Mellors was as unreal as the relationship between David Copperfield and Dora. Lawrence was not actually dishonest, but he had only covered one small aspect of the relationship between male and female. He had said nothing about that violent and apparently unassuageable desire that every normal young male feels towards every potentially beddable female — the desire that made the hero of a novel by Kingsley Amis remark that the sight of the words "Girl, 20" in an advertisement was enough to give him an erection. In an earlier version of *Ritual in the Dark*, I caught something of the essence of this male obsession in an episode in which the hero, Gerard Sorme, has spent an afternoon making love to Caroline in a basement flat. After seven orgasms he feels totally drained; he feels that the sexual delusion has finally lost its potency. Then he goes out to the basement area to fetch the milk off the doorstep, and catches a glimpse up the skirt of a girl who is walking past the railings; instantly, he experiences a raging violence of desire...

This, it seemed to me, was the truth that no one had ever attempted to express about sex. The Georgians and the Victorians had simply told lies about sex; to read Jane Austen or Thackeray, you would think that all a young male wanted from a pretty girl was to lay his eternal devotion at her feet and beg permission to support her for life. The result was the development of an industry in pornography, full of seduction, rape, and incest. But pornography did not even attempt to tell the truth about sex; all its tales of "forbidden pleasures" were outrageously unrealistic. Pornography was merely the "dirty-minded" reaction to the artificial "clean-mindedness" of Victorian bigots, just as Sade's horrifying excesses are a reaction against the hypocrisy of a society that kept throwing him into jail for indulging in a few harmless perversions.

In the late nineteenth century, a few bold spirits decided to risk the consequences and try to tell at least a little of the truth about sex. Nowadays, as we read Strindberg's *Marriage*, Zola's *Nana*, Sudermann's *Song of Songs*, we find it hard to imagine what all the fuss was about; but in their own time, these writers were denounced as vicious hawkers of obscenity whose real ambition was to bring about the ruination of society. By 1909, the situation had improved enough to permit H. G. Wells to portray a middle-class young girl — Ann Veronica — who offers herself to her schoolteacher and becomes his mistress; but only six years later, D. H. Lawrence's harmless *Rainbow* was banned by a court in which no one had actually read the book. But for many years after their publication, *Ulysses* and *Lady Chatterley's Lover* were seized and burned by the British and American customs authorities.

All of which explains why I was delighted to accept Maurice Girodias's suggestion that I should write a book for Olympia Press. It seemed to me that, even by 1962, no one had tried to tell "the truth" about sex. Nabokov was an honorable exception. I was not much concerned about whether Nabokov himself was a pædophile or not; but I felt that he had made an honest attempt to talk about that whole "forbidden" side of sex, and that by making Lolita a ten-year-old girl, he had turned her into a symbol of the sexually unattainable. At the same time, by making his hero a pædophile, he had diverted attention from the real issue: that in our society, sexual desire has somehow outstripped the possibility of its own satisfaction. So I felt there was still room for an attempt to tell the plain, unadorned truth about sex in the twentieth century.

At first, it began to look as if I might have been exaggerating the difficulties I might encounter. When I told my London publisher that I wanted to write a book for Olympia Press, he said that he would like the opportunity of seeing the typescript. And when, in due course, I sent it to him, he told me that, as far as he could see, there was nothing in it — except one short episode about a masturbating machine — that might cause problems with the law, and that he would offer me a far larger advance than Girodias... Soon after this, the book was accepted by Dial Press in America.

Then the problems began. The original title of the book was *The Man Without a Shadow*, a reference to the hero of Chamisso's story *Peter Schlemihl*, about a man who loses his shadow. (If Musil had not already used it, I would have called the book *The Man Without Qualities*.) Dial Press insisted in changing the title to *The Sex Diary of Gerard Sorme*, which they felt wold ensure a larger sale. Worse was to come. I had written a book called *Origins of the Sexual Impulse*, an attempt at an "existential" analysis of sexuality. When Dial learned that Putnam's intended to publish this in the summer of 1963, they rushed the publication of the *Sex Diary* in an attempt to get it out first. Instead, the two books appeared simultaneously, and most literary editors decided to review them together. Inevitably, one book "killed" the other; even the conscientious reviewers found it too much to read one book immediately after the other. Typical of the reviews was one in the *Chicago Sun-Times*, headed "Chronicle of a Nasty Boy." It read: "This outpouring by one of the first of England's 'angry young men' might best be described as the dreamworld chronicle of a nasty little boy who matured only physically. The perpetrator (a lame word, but a better one than protagonist in this case) is apparently an aging juvenile who hopes to solve all the great puzzles of existence, particularly the mysteries of life, sentience, and consciousness, while experiencing the sexual climax. His *Diary* is a recording of mean, grubby little affairs, casual liaisons, and his association with a childishly unregenerate Faust named Caradoc Cunningham — a man who can see around corners, practices magic, and is the epitome of evil. The *Diary* — even at best a most unfortunate vehicle for the novel — also is overly larded with pseudo-intellectual and five-drink philosophy. Often the language is that of the pool hall or the men's room of a third-run movie theatre. This 'angry young man' has not written a novel, really. He has merely indulged himself in a sexual orgy of literary narcissism."

The only consolation of this kind of review is that it might send some readers rushing out to buy the book. Indeed, it did just that. But when I finally came to receive my royalties, they were infinitesimal. The reason, it appeared, was that a Boston librarian had decided to sue the publisher for obscenity. The case was dismissed — the judge remarking that although he thought the book had no literary merit, it was certainly not technically obscene. But a clause in my contract — which I had sadly overlooked — stated that the author should bear any legal costs. So the few thousand dollars the book had earned in royalties went into the pocket of lawyers.

My own reaction, on reading the book after more than twenty years, is that I overlooked the major problem of trying to "tell the truth" about male sexuality: that literature is less about telling the truth than telling a story. Most readers who open a novel want to be entertained. In the preface to the British edition (which Dial Press insisted on dropping on the grounds that it was "too intellectual") I made a plea for the novel of idea — works like Lawrence's *Women in Love*, Wells's *World of William Clissold*, and Huxley's *Point Counterpoint*. But I was forgetting that these novels have never had a large audience of admirers — certainly not as many as *Sons and Lovers*, *The History of Mr. Polly*, or *Brave New World*. I had hoped that the subject — sexual experience — would make the ideas palatable, but I suspect that most of the people who bought the original edition skipped the ideas and looked for the "dirty bits."

Yet if I push aside these objections, it still seems to me that it was a worthwhile attempt to do something that had not been attempted at that time: to analyze the fundamental paradox of male sexuality. There is an episode near the beginning of the book that goes straight to the point. Sorme has gone into a shop that sells women's underwear to buy his girlfriend a pair of stockings; as he stands waiting at the counter, he turns casually, and catches a glimpse of a woman in one of those dress cubicles, pulling her skirt over her head. He experiences an instant shock of intense desire, and then becomes aware of the absurdity of this response. He can see that this is a middle-aged woman. In a few hours' time he will be watching his teenage girlfriend taking off her clothes; yet he will not experience anything like this surge of excitement. The conclusion seems to be that human sexuality is nine-tenths imagination, and that reality plays only a small part in it... More than two decades after writing the *Sex Diary*, I continue to be preoccupied with the same problem — in fact, have just made one more determined attempt to get to the bottom of it in a book called *The Misfits*, a study of "sexual Outsiders." So in spite of its failings — due, as the *Sun-Times* reviewer pointed out, to the diary form — I still feel that the *Sex Diary* is a creditable attempt to use the novel as a medium of philosophy.

A brief explanatory note for readers who are not acquainted with the hero's previous exploits in *Ritual in the Dark*. Gerard Sorme is a young man in his early twenties who lives alone in a room in London. In his early days, he has worked in a City office, and found it unutterably boring. In those days before Social Security, most people had to work for a living. Sorme daydreams of having a tiny income — just enough to be able to rent a cheap

room and spend his days reading, writing, and listening to music. Under these conditions, he imagines, he would be ecstatically happy. In fact, a small legacy enables him to give up his office job. And now he has been able to realize his ambition, he discovers that he feels curiously bored and dissatisfied. The human capacity for freedom is not, apparently, as great as he has imagined... At this point, he makes the acquaintance of a wealthy homosexual named Austin Nunne, and of Austin's aunt, a Jehovah's Witness called Gertrude Quincey. As he pursues Gertrude (and her drama-student niece Caroline) he gradually begins to suspect that Nunne is a sadistic killer of prostitutes. He finds himself confronting a moral — and "existential" — dilemma. Although he likes to think of himself as a metaphysician, he is aware that he would, given the opportunity, deflower every virgin in Camden Town. In spite of our romantic pretences, sexual desire is basically impersonal. So can he really blame Nunne for carrying this recognition to an extreme, and treating people as "throwaways"? (In recent years, the problem has been dramatized by cases of mass sex-killers like Dean Corll and Ted Bundy.)

In fact, Sorme is brought face to face with his own inability to understand sadism when he is take to the morgue to see the corpse of one of Nunne's victims; suddenly he recognizes that, in spite of his own sexual obsession, he would be incapable of committing a sex crime. In spite of this, he still refuses to betray Nunne to the police. The book ends when Nunne is committed to an asylum for the criminally insane. And Sorme's inability to solve his own moral dilemma is underlined by his inability to give up either Gertrude or Caroline.

Ritual in the Dark was begun in the early 1950s, when I was living a life not unlike that of Gerard Sorme — except that I could never escape the necessity of working for a living. One day I decided that *Ritual* was overloaded with ideas, and that I ought to throw most of them overboard — or rather, explore them in a work of nonfiction. This became *The Outsider*, and when it appeared in 1956, it had the effect of rocketing me to overnight notoriety. Together with John Osborne, the author of *Look Back in Anger*, I was labeled an "Angry Young Man," and we received an unprecedented amount of publicity in the popular press. At this time, I was living with my girlfriend Joy (now my wife). When her parents — highly respectable members of the British middle class — found out about this, they burst into my flat one evening, and accused me of being a homosexual and having six mistresses. Joy's father was waving a horsewhip, but made no real attempt to use it. But while I was telephoning the police to request them to leave, one of our dinner guests (a villainous old pouf called Gerard Hamilton — the original of Christopher Isherwood's Mr. Norris) notified the press, and within half an hour, there were a dozen or so reporters and photographers on our doorstep. Joy and I sneaked out of the back door and fled to the west country, then to Ireland. It was the worst thing we could have done. As soon as the British press was able to track us down, they pursued us — even *Time* magazine featured the story. Joy's father handed my journals — which I had offered to let him read — to a newspaper, which printed long extracts. When we finally returned to London, my publisher advised me to go and live quietly in the country, and try to live down the scandal. We did as he suggested — and have been living in Cornwall ever since — but the after-effects of the episode were as disastrous as my publisher had feared, and when my second book, *Religion and the Rebel*, appeared later that year (1957) it received a universal panning.

At least I made use of the "diary scandal" in the present book, although autobiographical elements have been diluted by fictional episodes from the life of Gerard Sorme. It will be unnecessary to inform modern readers that the character of Caradoc Cunningham is based on Aleister Crowley, the "wickedest man in the world"; I never met Crowley (and on the whole am glad I didn't), but heard a great deal about him from people who had, such as John Symonds and Richard Cammell. He still strikes me as the liveliest character in the book.

There is little to add, except that in 1969 I completed the "Gerard Sorme" trilogy with a novel called *The God of the Labyrinth* which is still one of my favourites. One day, perhaps, they will be published together in one volume. Meanwhile, I am delighted to see my alter ego Gerard taking on a new lease of life.

AUTHOR'S NOTE

*   *   *   *   *   *   *   *

In the late December of 1956, at the time of the "Cunningham scandal," a reporter managed to bribe his way into a flat that I had recently occupied in Spitalfields, and walked away with five volumes of my journals concealed in his pockets. These journals were then quoted, without my permission, in certain articles on Caradoc Cunningham that appeared in a daily newspaper. They were described as my "Sex Diaries" and "Black Magic Journals," and I was even misquoted as having written that I wished that I had committed the Whitechapel murders.

Although I was advised that I could sue the newspaper for libel, violation of copyright and illegally obtaining possession of my journals, I preferred to allow another newspaper to print long extracts from these journals, so that the various quotations that had already been made could appear in context. I assumed that this would be the end of the matter, although I was aware at the time that both newspapers had photostated the journals. Over the next two years, I heard periodic rumors that the "sex diary" (i.e., the second notebook, as printed here) was being circulated in typewritten copies, and that these copies could be obtained, on payment of a large deposit, from certain dubious bookshops in the area of the Charing Cross Road. I made inquiries, but was never able to verify these rumors.

A fortnight ago, however, I had definite information that an admirer of my work in New York had paid $2,000 for a photostated copy of the "sex diary." Its source could not be traced, but I gathered that there was a fairly brisk trade in these photostated copies in the United States.

This decided me to accept an offer from The Dial Press to publish these notebooks in full. At first, I was inclined to publish only the parts dealing with Caradoc Cunningham (i.e., the "Black Magic Journal"), but this would have the double disadvantage of leaving the "sex diary" to circulate in pirated form, and in rendering parts of the "Black Magic Journal" incomprehensible, since it refers back so frequently to the earlier notebook. Besides, I have been told that the duplicated copies of the "sex diary" were abridged—that is, everything that would not appeal to the public that gloats over these things was cut out. These included, of course, all the "metaphysical discussions of sex" that were for me the main point of the diary. It is hardly surprising that the book has acquired a reputation in certain circles as high-class pornography. I think it will be seen, from the present edition, that the intentions were anything but pornographic—that, in fact, the book owes more to Gabriel Marcel's *Metaphysical Journal* than to Frank Harris.

The journals, as printed here, are unabridged and completely unaltered, except for correction of spelling mistakes, an occasional rearrangement of words and the addition of a few footnotes. In two places, I have been advised to omit a sentence; where this has happened, I have left blanks in the text of the same length. (These can be found on pages 66 and 108). I have also begun this journal with the final pages of an earlier notebook, for reasons of continuity that will be apparent. I have resisted the temptation to divide the journal into two parts—before and after I met Cunningham—because this would seem to be an apology for its lack of unity, whereas, on rereading it, I feel that it nevertheless possesses a certain unity of idea and intention.

One extremely difficult problem arose in connection with this book—the question of persons other than myself who are treated in it. My original intention was to change all names so that most of the people could not be identified. But in certain cases—Oliver Glasp or Robert Kirsten, for example, this would be nonsensical, since their names are too well known and their identities too obvious. In other cases, the problem was whether I had a right to publish certain details of the private lives of the persons concerned. Public figures may be regarded to some extent as public property, but this is certainly not true of "private persons" who prefer to remain private. So in a very few cases in this book, I have changed names and an occasional personal detail, to obscure the identity. However, it is obvious that too much of this would defeat the aim of publishing this journal by giving the pirated copies a kind of scandal value. I therefore wish to thank many of the people concerned for their permission to publish the passages in which they are mentioned.

Finally, I wish to thank my wife for her patience in typing out these notebooks, and the publishers for their help and encouragement.

Corrib Cottage, Moycullen
GALWAY

The Diary

* * * * * * * *

Oct. 20. Today I feel a strange state of excitement and anticipation—there is a heavy, Christmassy atmosphere, the kind of thing I haven't experienced since childhood. This is no doubt due to a heavy cold in the head that started two days ago. Last night I drank half a pint of whisky before I went to bed; my nose and throat were blazing, and my left eye felt as if it was hanging out of my head. I also took two aspirin. I slept like a rock, and woke this morning without a hangover, but feeling a strange and pleasant detachment from reality. My head is still thick, but the world feels as if I were looking at it through the long end of a telescope. The cold insulates me. I feel like Proust. I remember a line of Maurice's: "The dusk is gray with longing." It expresses the almost musical nostalgia I experience as I write this.

Curious. I wish I understood myself. What is it that happens in these moods—in terms of emotional chemistry, I mean? All my life I have fought the present. I simply don't like existing "here and now." Unless the world is richer—unless it has other depths and dimensions, I loathe it. My attention is like a gramophone needle; in the normal course of events it is confined in a narrow groove of the present. Things are too obtrusive. I open my eyes; I am *too* aware of the things I look at; they edge their way into my consciousness and push me backward. Today, all that is changed. The world is covered with a pearl-gray mist; reality is cushioned. When I look out of my window, what I see doesn't press itself on me, like an annoying stranger on a train; it keeps its distance, respectful, discreet. And I can be aware of all kinds of other things. Or I could compare it to listening to music. If music is too loud and stupid, it isolates you, like pain. But there *is* such a thing as good background music, that only makes conversation more pleasant, or forms a pleasant accompaniment to reading.

This is what the world ought to be—background music. Then that other world—of feelings and memories—gets a chance to express itself. I wonder why a bad cold releases so many memories? I can sit here, on my bed, a large mug of strong tea beside me, and this notebook on my knee, and cast my mind to almost any period of my life. Usually, the images I am able to evoke are shadows or abstractions. Today they come up like heavy incense; every memory brings its distinct atmosphere.

I believe that the brain is full of well-worn paths, rather like the scratches on a gramophone record that *always* make the needle jump several tracks. Under normal circumstances my mind, fueled mainly by my intellect, is driven along paths of associative thinking. In this mood, I am freed from the "scratches"; I can sink into my own being, leaving my conscious self sitting contentedly here on the bed, ignored, while I clamber down a rope into the mineshaft of myself. I used to be fond of comparing man's being to an iceberg, with only a third (the consciousness) above the waterline; but this is nonsense; the part above the waterline is actually a tenth—perhaps a hundredth or a thousandth. Why. . . .

Blast that phone.

That was Caroline. I told her I had a lousy cold and that she hadn't better come over for fear of catching it. I wish there were some other way of writing that was quicker than this. My thoughts move too fast; they're like fireworks today, leaping, blazing, exploding, and my body feels an extraordinary sense of catlike comfort. My body's normally such a fucking nuisance; it won't let me go far without clamoring for attention, so that writing and thinking is a perpetual struggle with it. I understand why Socrates told Phaedo that the philosopher spends his life trying to escape the body.

Today I feel free even of sexual desire. This is something. I'm afraid that, ever since my childhood, I've been oversexed. I sometimes wonder about this. As far as I can determine, it

was born in me, for I can recall sexual excitement long before
I learned the "facts" about sex or began to think of sex with a
certain morbid excitement. One of these days, I must try to
write fully and honestly about sex . . . but it would be necessary to buy a separate notebook, and also to buy a box that
will lock. I'm sure Carlotta reads my manuscripts and letters
and I wouldn't put it past that nosy cow of a landlady to read
anything she can find.

My sexual desire is undoubtedly connected with this
normal "confinement in the present." This warm, hazy nostalgia I feel today is exactly like sexual fulfillment.

Oct. 21. Gertrude called and I had to break off yesterday. But
I shall use this new notebook for the purpose I mentioned—a
kind of "sex diary." This morning, I picked up a small chest
in the local junk shop—the sort sailors take to sea—and
bought a heavy Yale lock. It's strange—the effect of being
secretive, the joy and stimulation of it. I now feel as if I want
to go on writing non-stop for ten years. Why shouldn't I fill
a thousand pages? I wish my shorthand were better, though;
I'd like to keep a diary in shorthand, but can't read it back.
I wonder if Pepys could read *his* diary back—almost certainly not, I imagine. Bertrand Russell used to keep a diary
in English, but written with Greek letters. A long job. I
often wonder why I dislike Russell's mind so much. I suppose it is because we could both be called "inductive ex-
istentialists." All my work is existential in the sense that it
badly wants to stick to living experience; but it's inductive
because it wants to reason from the *particular* to the general.
Russell's mind is also inductive, but it's certainly existential,
because he's always writing about marriage, education, etc.
And yet somehow the two never quite manage to connect.

There I go. That is also my problem; I'm too much an
intellectual to stick to the "basic facts," like sex. . . .

Yet, since I've begun, I should try. I still feel this sense
of distance from reality, although no longer so strongly; I am

getting back to the "world" I normally live in. I didn't stay with Gertrude last night; not merely because I had a cold, but because this strangely distant mood makes me feel already as I occasionally feel after an orgasm—serene and awake, as if the power of my thought had been magnified tenfold—or perhaps merely that my bleeding nuisance of a body is temporarily satisfied. I wonder if it will become less of a nuisance as I get older? I recall one occasion, eight years ago, when I experienced this total serenity through sex. Donald Baumgarten had invited me to go with him to Birmingham one Christmas; he was working with another Jewish bloke called Morrie, selling all kinds of things in the market. I enjoyed it all; I liked the crowds and the excitement, and the lights in the market late at night—even the cold in the air. At one point, I was standing in front of the market stall, jammed forward by the crowd. Behind me stood a girl—probably a young married woman, on the plump side. She was watching Donald over my shoulder, and her thighs and belly were pressed very tight against my behind. After a few minutes of this, I began to feel an intense sexual excitement. But the delightful thing was that time seemed to have stood still—or rather, my desire stood still, quiescent, neither vanishing nor overflowing. She couldn't have been pressed more tightly against me if I'd been lying on her in bed. I could feel the hardness of her garters against my legs. She must have been wearing a thin dress, because I was soon conscious of her warmth against me. The curious thing was that she kept making very slight movements, each one of which made my excitement rise like the mercury in a thermometer. I still don't know whether she was aware of my excitement, and experienced it herself, but her movements seemed calculated—a tiny wriggle that convinced me that I could actually feel her pubic hairs against me. After what seemed about a quarter of an hour (but must have been less) I could bear it no longer; I pretended to make a movement to get a handkerchief out of my pocket; this pressed me against her even more tightly and also pressed my overcharged loins against the table in a continuous friction. I am sure she must have felt the slight convulsions of the climax; as if in response, her whole body pressed tight against me. I stood there, very still, watching Donald selling off a case of alarm clocks at what he claimed was a fraction of their market value, and feeling as full of sweetness as a barrel of treacle. It lasted all the time I stood there—only a few minutes longer, because the selling stopped and some of the crowd dispersed. The woman behind me went. I didn't turn to look at her—I suppose I felt ashamed. And yet I felt no guilt, not a shred—and all the way home that night, driving in the lorry and watching the cats' eyes coming out of the dark, there was the same complete serenity inside me. I was a virgin then; I sometimes felt guilt about masturbation (although never much); but this was different; it had taken place out in the real world, and yet it was like a sexual daydream. I always feared that the world of imagination and the "real world" would prove to be completely incompatible, would simply never connect, so that I'd be doomed to a lifetime of ironic frustration. This occasion seemed like a promise of something better, of fulfillment. It also raised the question: How far are men capable of absolute fulfillment? Of expressing *everything* they have in them? More of this later.

I found it curiously difficult to write the above paragraph —as if I were writing dirt, I suppose. No doubt I *was,* by certain standards. And yet are our sexual experiences to remain perpetually confined to this limbo? Either never mentioned at all, as in Trollope, or mentioned with an awful degraded gloating, as in Sade or Frank Harris?

An hour later. Gertrude came in and brought me a small bottle of rum, which she insisted on heating with lemon and sugar and watching me drink. This kind of thing worries and embarrasses me. I *know* that by normal standards, I'm a swine. I also know that if she found out I was still seeing Caroline, she'd never forgive me. Yet I can't quite convince myself that

I'm in the wrong. I feel obscurely that there's something I should learn from all this.

I'm sometimes astounded at Gertrude's capacity to close her mind. For example, when she speaks about Austin,* she mentions him casually, as if he were a member of the family who is away in another country. My attitude, I know, is morbid. And yet I can't help brooding about the women he killed, and trying to make myself feel as if I were the murderer. Austin's father came to see me a few weeks ago. I'd never met him, never heard from him before. He turned out to be a curious man—very tall, like Austin, with a bald head and thick lips, and an unpleasant air of power—ordinary material power, mostly used for evil. Gertrude tells me that he is one of England's six richest men, and that he gives a lot to charity—with one eye on a peerage. That may be true, but I know that in an enlightened country, his kind would be exterminated, quickly and painlessly. His ostensible excuse for coming to see me was to "thank me" for standing by Austin, and to give me a check for £250. (I know I should have refused this, but when you've been living on £5 a week for two years, it represents so many luxuries that you'd almost forgotten.) What he really wanted was to find out if I was Austin's pathic, and if I shared Austin's taste for beating people. I think that, in a way I can only sense, Austin fascinates him. Are all these men—the power-men— driven by a kind of sadism, I wonder? He can't help feeling— I *know* this—that in a funny sort of way, Austin has "made good" by becoming a sex killer. He tells me, incidentally, that Austin has become far more openly "dotty" since he's been under confinement, and that it is difficult to make him take any interest in anything. God knows how much it's costing him

* Austin Nunne. Between July and November, 1955, Nunne murdered seven women in the Spitalfields district of East London. A homosexual with strong sadistic tendencies, he was certified insane at the request of his own family and interned in a private mental home near Ascot; the murders were officially "unsolved" at the time the above was written.

to keep things hushed up. The newspapers haven't mentioned the Whitechapel killer for two months now. I would have thought this kind of thing was impossible. Or perhaps he's not really having to exert influence; perhaps the police and the newspapers have come to a kind of agreement not to refer to the case "for the public good." I read that an old lady in Bow had committed suicide because of the murders.

And yet, in a strange way, I can't help envying Austin the experience of murder. No, I don't mean that I want to commit a sex crime (and I'd certainly have no interest in committing any other sort of murder). And yet I wish my imagination was powerful enough to tell me exactly what it would be like to commit a murder. Why are we such miserably inefficient machines? I am perpetually aware of my tremendous limitations. For some odd reason, it suits the gods, or destiny, to have us inefficient. I often feel as if I'm driving a car with the brakes on when I try to use my imagination to solve a problem. Or as if I'm trying to light a fire of wet wood with damp matches. The resources of the brain are enormous. It is undoubtedly the most complicated machine ever invented. In comparison, all other machines are incredibly childish. It can store a hundred languages, knowledge of literature, music, mathematics, science, philosophy. And it can do all this simultaneously. Sherlock Holmes was talking rubbish when he told Watson that he couldn't care less whether the sun goes around the earth or vice versa, because the mind can only store a limited number of facts. The brain *could* hold all the knowledge of all the libraries in the world, and a human being could still live a full sex life and social life, without losing an atom of human sympathy or physical well-being. All this I know. In occasional moments of vision, I have *seen* that there is no reason why a man should not be a god.

And yet what actually happens? I sometimes wake up at midday, make tea, try to write, and fail, try to read, and lose interest, do the shopping, get a meal, and feel totally exhausted by six in the evening. Why? Because in some way my body is

working at minimum efficiency. Imagine that a tribe of ignorant natives finds a motor car, and decides that it makes an
ideal storage room for food. So when they set out on a journey,
they load it with food, attach ropes to it, and pull it through
the jungle as if it were a cart. One of them, fiddling about inside it, discovers the hand brake and releases it. Immediately,
they find the car much easier to pull. They congratulate the
discoverer, tell him he is a genius, and convince themselves
that they *now* know the purpose and use of the car.

This is how I feel with my body. Occasionally, as I am
dragging it along, it accidentally gets into gear; there is a roar,
and the engine starts for a moment. Then, just as quickly, it
cuts out. But I *know* that this body is not merely designed for
this boring, irritating, two-dimensional life that so easily becomes a burden to me.

This, I suppose, is the reason for my sympathy with
Austin. Since last year, I've read books about various sex
killers—Heath, Christie, Kürten, and they repel and horrify
me. And yet I still feel that Austin was dimly, vaguely trying
to follow his own deepest nature to some unheard-of form of
self-expression. It is strange that he always makes me think of
Nijinsky. . . .

All of which brings me back to the sexual problem. There
have been moments when I wonder whether all romantics—
and I am essentially a romantic—are completely mistaken in
their basic assumption. They all feel that they only need the
"key" to life, the "way"—and that man will be able to turn
on at will these tremendous moods of exaltation and power.
But consider a dray horse, or that poor old red setter they
keep chained up next door. The lives of these animals are
very boring indeed; no one pretends that the animal is
"completely fulfilled." He isn't supposed to be. He is supposed
to be useful to his master.

An evolutionist would argue that man's limitations are
a necessary part of his low position on the evolutionary ladder.
He is not so far above the monkey and the cave man; why

should he expect visions? I see this point of view. And yet there are moments when I am convinced that man is actively *impeded* from climbing higher by some force that finds him most useful in his present position. It wants us to live like cars with their brakes on; it wants our consciousness to remain so narrow and absurd that we never learn to put two and two together. It is true that I have never had the least doubt of my own genius. But what is that genius in the scales of what man could attain? It merely means that I have one less spanner in my works than most people; the "force" has done a slightly less efficient job of wrecking me.

And yet I'm not a pessimist. Because there *is* something in me that drives me on. Whatever the force that holds us down, I don't think it is malign—not entirely so, anyway. We are not mere sheep waiting for the butcher, being fattened and exploited.

Of one thing I am certain. The sexual force is the nearest thing to magic—to the supernatural—that human beings ever experience. It deserves perpetual and close study. No study is so profitable to the philosopher. In the sex force, he can watch the purpose of the universe in action.

This is my most important conclusion about sex so far: there is no such thing as sex for its own sake. The libido is a myth.

Later. I recall the earliest impressions ever made on me by sex—by sexual knowledge, I should say, for I was always aware of the force of sex. It was somehow a powerful and obscene force that demanded a definite "descent," a loss of pride and dignity. I recall an old joke I heard at school that expresses this aspect. A newly married husband was too shy to touch his wife, so she guided his hand to her sexual regions, then said: "Now do something dirty"—so he emptied his bowels. I am sure that most of us at school thought that marriage was an ideal kind of state because it was a way of legalizing "something dirty." Again, I think of a red-haired boy called

Barrett who talked of nothing but sex. One day, I heard two of his friends laughing about him. They had been to the theater the night before, and had picked up three girls in the balcony. Barrett disappeared into a back street with his girl; when his friends went to look for him, he was fucking her against a dustbin. They called to him, but he was apparently unable to stop. The boys imitated his motion obscenely, jerking the hips back and forward like a dog with a mechanical motion. This stuck in my mind for a long time—sex as the force that turned men into dogs. The worst of it was that, even so, I envied Barrett.

And yet compare this to Bill Payne's attitude to women. I know that he actually finds the sexual act a letdown after the pleasure of seduction. There's something delightful in his perpetual enthusiasm, the way he says: *"Women, Gerard, women. They're delicious."* I honestly believe he could devote his life to the pursuit of women, like Casanova, finding in each one a new universe. He's an example of the sexual illusion at its most intense—and in many ways, at its best.

And yet consider my own case at the moment. I am involved with two women simultaneously. From Bill's point of view, the fact that Caroline is Gertrude's niece makes it only more piquant. I could sleep with either of them tonight. And yet this knowledge destroys the excitement and the desire. Somehow, the value of sex is in its *life-enhancing* value, not in the sex itself.

For example, Caroline has been in her flat for three months now, and I spend a lot of time there with her. Madeleine, the girl she rooms with, obviously has an ambivalent attitude to me. I think she envies Caroline her sleeping partner, yet at the same time, feels she ought to be shocked. The other night, I took Bill around there for supper, and then we got rather happy on burgundy. Finally, Madeleine, claiming that she had to be up early, went off for a bath, and then got into bed. But we all went into her room, and had a last drink. Then Bill and Caroline decided that we ought to get just one more bottle of wine before the shop closed and went off together to get it. I simply stayed on Madeleine's bed, kissing her. She opened her mouth and let me excite her; I started to kiss her neck, then went lower, and finally pulled down the top of her nightdress and began to kiss her nipples. She simply lay there, with her eyes closed, looking as if she were listening to a heavenly choir, and would obviously have let me go on all night if Bill and Caroline hadn't returned. And yet as soon as they came into the room, she pulled the sheet around her neck and started talking as if nothing had happened. And this is the girl who told us a few days later that she intended to keep her virginity for her husband.

Still, I must confess that the situation appealed to me more than any of its individual elements explains. I like lying there in the morning, watching Caroline get out of bed and get dressed. She has no self-consciousness, and usually asks me which panties I think she ought to wear, then wanders in and out in her underwear until she's made tea. (I suspect this may not be as uncalculated as she'd like me to think; very few mornings have gone by when I haven't pulled her back into bed and undressed her again.) Gertrude never lets me watch her get dressed; she always vanishes into the bathroom in a dressing gown and appears fully clothed.

Usually I stay there when Caroline and Madeleine have gone out—Caroline to her drama school, Madeleine to her office. I stare out of the window at the warehouses opposite, and nearly always have a kind of wrestling match with my consciousness. I think: "Here I am, in a situation that ought to delight me, in the bed of a pretty blonde. Tonight I shall be in another woman's bed. And yet I stare at these warehouses . . . and they are *meaningless*. Why? Why does this experience mean so little to me?" I am like a man dying of thirst who has found a spring—but it flows only in tiny drops, so that he has to wait five minutes for each drop to fall. Most of us hunger for experience, for life. Our whole entertainment industry is built up on this naïve hunger: the shopgirl who wants to identify herself with Norma Talmadge being carried off into the desert by Rudolph Valentino.

The other night, on my way to see Caroline, I remembered that she wanted some stockings, and went into a ladies' shop in Kensington High Street to get them. As I turned around from the counter, I found myself looking into one of those cubicles where women try on dresses. The woman hadn't bothered to draw the curtain, and was pulling a dress over her head. Since she was blinded by the dress, she wasn't aware that I was looking at her—and I took care to look my fill before the dress came off—and then she realized that she was standing in front of a man in exactly the same clothes that Caroline wears to make the tea in the morning. I pretended not to have seen her, of course, and heard the curtain hastily drawn. But I practically had to limp out of the shop. I was in an appalling state of sexual excitement—due to the unexpectedness of it, I suppose. I was burning from head to foot with lust. But the trouble with it was that simply hurling Caroline onto her bed wouldn't necessarily have satisfied it. It was its *lack of object* that shattered me. The woman—as I had time to notice—was middle-aged; her figure was good, but not startling. Caroline is in every way a better candidate for lust. If I had found the woman in my bed, I doubt whether I'd have been able to summon the appetite to take her. And yet I recognized that the intensity of desire I felt could easily drive a man to murder and rape. I am, I hope, incapable of either, and yet I was trembling with excitement—an unhealthy, burning excitement that does no good. As I passed other girls in the street, women returning from offices, I felt: All these women have the same capacity to arouse this feeling hidden below this opaque outer layer of clothing. Our society is sitting on a sexual powder barrel. Is it any wonder that the rate of sex crimes is going up? As men go, I think I'm capable of a fair degree of self-discipline and self-restraint. But if other men are less restrained than I, God help them. And God help civilization. We only need a war to prove how thin "civilization" is. Men go in for rape and sadism as if they were born to it. I remember how a man came to talk to us at school, and told us about how he had been in a train wreck, and had helped the rescue workers to release trapped people in spite of his own injuries. But I still recall that my main feeling was sexual excitement at the thought of unconscious women in railway carriages who could be quickly violated before being dragged to safety. I wonder how many more of the boys who heard him had the same thought. I never told anyone; I would have been too ashamed, and even schoolboy sexual frankness seldom goes to that length. And yet what stability can we expect of a civilization built on this kind of basis? Unless, of course, I can comfort myself with the thought that I am completely abnormal, and other men never entertain such daydreams.

What conclusions do I draw from all this? I believe that, far from being "abnormal," the intensity of my sexual impulse is a part of the total intensity that makes me what I am—an intelligent being, responding with unusual directness to the problems of modern civilization. I watch my sexual impulse at work with a kind of amazement. *I* may not know why I'm alive, but something inside me does. Sex is the only power I know that can defeat the awful pressure of the present. The world looks blank and meaningless, gray, pointless, mocking my brevity and hunger with its permanence and serenity. Only when sexual desire blazes in me can I overcome its indifference; the desire turns on it like a flame thrower; my body suddenly carries a current of thousands of volts, surging from some main down in my subconscious; I become realer than the world; harder, intenser, *more lasting.*

I know that this power exists in me for other purposes than sex. Sometimes it can be evoked by music or literature or ideas. Something like it flows in me now as I write this because I am writing with excitement, enjoying being able to pin down these ideas into words. I feel like a detective cross-examining the world, trying to trap it into admissions of purpose. I know bloody well it exists—an immense power and purpose. So why am I left outside? This damned lying cheat of a world. I don't know yet why I exist. I feel superfluous, like a gramophone in the middle of the Sahara desert. And yet there are times when I *almost* get plugged in, when some of my plugs find their sockets, and there's a whisper of power in my nerves. I predict there will be a day when all man's purpose will be on the surface; he will know, he will understand, instead of living in this blackness of ignorance. Instead of having to strain his ears to catch murmurs from his own depths, he will have a clear conscious understanding of his purpose.

And yet I am always aware that the central problem is the problem of my body, my stupid, intractable body. My body is my despair. How can I achieve the kind of things I want when my body is so unutterably stupid? I am like a carpenter who is asked to build a house of rotten, worm-eaten wood, or like a dressmaker who is asked to design clothes for a queen out of dyed sugar-sacks.

There have been so many occasions when I have felt that the time wasted in sleep is an indignity, and have tried to keep myself awake half the night. My eyelids close against my will, and I lie down with a sense of defeat, realizing that it is barely twelve hours since I got out of this same bed. And yet there are other times, when I've had little sleep, when a book or an idea interests me; suddenly I notice that it is four o'clock in the morning, and I am still not tired. My body responds badly to bullying, and yet allows excitement to *charm* it into obedience. If only I had the secret of charming at will. It happens unexpectedly, or takes twelve hours of continuous mental struggle to produce a few hours of serenity. But in these hours of serenity, the body is at last working with decent efficiency, *and I understand what life would be like if I knew the secret.* Is life bound to be a losing battle with the body, a struggle against its sheer insensitivity, in which our artificial allies—alcohol, drugs—only lend their aid at ruinous rates of interest?

Can any of us fail to be interested in this fight against

the body? I know of no one who is worth tuppence who hasn't
tried to beat and torture his body into obedience. Bill Payne
once starved himself for a week, and told me he began to
experience visions, to feel a strange lightness, as if the body had
finally surrendered. Oliver Glasp slept naked on the bare wires
of his bed. I have a photograph of his picture of Matthew
Lovatt in the room now—the man who tried to crucify himself
in Geneva. I think it probably his best painting; every stroke
of the brush shows the intensity of his involvement with the
subject. Only such men deserve any consideration; all others
are weaklings and dupes.

Oct. 22. Caroline interrupted me last night. This was probably
just as well; I felt tired, but resented my inability to keep on
working.

    She wanted to talk to me about dropping Gertrude. I
didn't quite see her point. At the moment, I don't give a
damn—I'd drop Caroline *and* Gertrude without a qualm.
Gertrude is an emotional blackmailer; she takes care to be
undemanding and generous and attentive, then allows me to
see that she's unhappy and unsure of me. I never leave her
without feeling guilt. I'm fond of her—I respond instinctively
to affection. But it's all so bloody irrelevant at the moment.
Whenever I leave her place, there seems to be a mist of irony
hanging over London.

    I wish I could explain this more fully. It's worth explain-
ing. When I first met Gertrude, I was puzzled by her apparent
independence; she seemed to have come to terms with herself
and with some kind of belief that made her independent of
close relationships. This fascinated me; I wanted to know
what it was that gave her this strength. When I got to know
her better, I realized it was ordinary reticence—a refusal to
confess to loneliness. At first, there was a strange charm about
the affair. I didn't particularly like being fed and plied with
drink; it made me feel too dependent. But I liked the way
Gertrude started to come here and turn out my dirty clothes

and lug them off home to wash them. (She has a machine that does it all in a quarter the time it would take me.) I also like the curious way in which she surrendered herself. I can still remember the excitement I felt about very minor things. This, for example. One evening, I started to kiss her on the settee. She doesn't like being undressed downstairs; she feels it's not respectable. After a few minutes she began to get excited, and I started to get her skirt up around her waist. At this moment she sat up, and told me she had to go out to the lavatory. So I had to contain myself. In the meantime, I made sure the curtains were properly drawn and the back door locked. She came back in and lay down, and I started to go through the preliminaries again. When I got my hand under her dress, I discovered to my astonishment that she had taken off her panties, and had apparently rubbed some kind of cream on herself that made entrance very easy. As I think back on this, I can still recall my shock of surprise on discovering that she had no pants. It was so unlike her. She prefers everything to be in the dark, and the ritual has to be strictly observed. She prefers to get dressed and undressed in the bathroom; but if, for some reason, she gets undressed when I'm in bed, she takes care never to take off her clothes in their natural order—apparently feeling that this would somehow place her on a level with a strip-tease artist. She loosens her bra, eases her pants down under her slip, then does a curious little wiggle that brings the whole lot down around her feet; then she makes a leap for the light, and hurls herself into bed in one movement, the idea being that I should see as little of her as possible without clothes.

Caroline is amusingly different. She doesn't give a damn about whether she's dressed or not, and her attitude toward sex is sometimes so Rabelaisian that it shocks even me. She said to me the other day: "No, you can't fuck me now, there's not time. Masturbate when I've gone." The other day, I went with her to a fitting for a dress in the play she's doing; she'd unexpectedly spent the night here, and wasn't wearing a petticoat.

Apparently she had to take off her skirt so they could get the measurements. I asked her who took them, and she said: "Oh, a middle-aged queer and a rather nice young boy." I asked her if it didn't embarrass her to stand in her pants in front of two men (she admitted she didn't *know* that either of them was queer). Obviously, this idea had never entered her head. Sex is something nice you do in bed with your clothes off; it never strikes her that the sight of a girl in her underwear might excite a man.

Why, under the circumstances, Caroline should want me to drop Gertrude, I don't know. I'm certain she even takes a pleasure in feeling that we're deceiving Gertrude. Brooding on this, and recalling various hints dropped by Caroline, I conclude that she has marriage in mind. God knows why. I suppose she has the usual female desire for security. I don't think it's *me* in particular she wants, although she thinks she's infatuated with me. She admits that there are two film actors she's crazy about, and that she'd probably leap into bed with either of them if she got the chance. . . .

Later. I've been reading a paperback I picked up yesterday, *The Protagonists* by James Barlow, which, according to the jacket, is the story of a sex crime. It is a very good novel, but is certainly not the story of a sex crime. It is about a shifty ex-RAF type who sees a beautiful red-headed girl in a shop and goes to enormous lengths to seduce her, persuading her that he's unmarried. He strangles her when she tells him she's pregnant. In this case, all the sex took place *before* the crime, which was no more "sexual" than any robbery with violence. The author has done a good job of portraying a certain type of criminal, the confidence trickster, the dishonest Romeo. This type is far more common than the real sex criminal. It's impossible not to feel that his misdeeds come under the heading of *miscalculation* rather than crime. Criminality implies an acknowledgement of and a respect for society. You cannot imagine a Beethoven or Bernard Shaw committing crimes because neither cared enough about society. This means that "master criminals" are rare, because when a man has enough vitality to become a master of anything he has too much sense to waste himself and his evolutionary potentialities on an anti-social act. It is amusing to imagine a man of "noble mind" de-liberately setting out to be a criminal, but impossible to follow the idea to serious lengths because the first characteristic of a man who has any touch of greatness is an inability to hurt anybody. This is what I never realized about Austin—until almost too late.

But reading Barlow's book makes me aware not only of the essential stupidity of the criminal, but also of the essential silliness of the seducer. There is a girl at the tobacconist on the corner whom I'd love to screw, and the way she wears tight skirts and sweaters and smiles seductively convinces me that it would be possible. But I think of the sheer boredom of the consequences, of her proximity to this place, and drop the idea without a qualm. If I could offer her five pounds for an hour in bed, and no "consequences" I'd take it like a shot. And yet I could never bear the idea of a prostitute, and am sure I'd be a total failure if I ever found myself in bed with one. . . .

Strange, the amazing amount of energy men waste on seduction. I suppose it's one of the most basic mechanisms of the healthy male—looking at a girl, trying to imagine what she'd be like undressed, and then the thought: "I *must* have her." Even if it takes ten years. Or costs a fortune in expensive meals and theaters. Or involves marrying her. This latter, I suppose, is the biological explanation for the mechanism. Otherwise, why should Barlow's murderer go to such absurd lengths to screw a girl, just because she's red-headed and looks innocent? Is one cunt any different from another? I *know* it's not. I recently woke up in the middle of the night and made love to a girl I assumed to be Caroline, then went to sleep again. (Caroline doesn't mind being screwed unceremoniously at any hour.) In the morning, Gertrude was reproachful be-cause I'd had her without going through the usual ritual of endearments. Reduced to its physical basis, the sexual act is about as unexciting as driving a car is to a salesman. The emotions and delusions count for everything. Bill told me an amusing story from his days as an RAF policeman in Hamburg. A German photographer made his living selling dirty pictures, in which his wife was his chief model; he would photograph her in all kinds of positions with a big Greek sailor. He was also subtler than these fellows usually are; he made a fortune from a series of pictures showing the sailor hiding behind a curtain and watching the wife get undressed, and then knocking her out and raping her. But Bill told me that the partnership broke up one day when the photographer observed that the sailor was moving more than was strictly necessary for the photographs, and that he had an orgasm inside the wife. This was strictly infra dig. The physical act in itself meant nothing; what mattered was that the sailor was putting his emotions into it and not treating it strictly as a matter of business. The photographer proposed Bill as the sailor's replacement; Bill, unfortunately, was not attracted by the wife.

An interesting concept emerges from all this. *What exactly* was the sailor "putting into" the act when he allowed himself to have an orgasm? Emotion? No, too vague. Desire, lust, excitement? All too vague. What he was really putting into it was the same quality that makes an African savage die of sheer nerves when a witch doctor puts a spell on him. Or —and this is nearer to it—what makes a good Catholic believe that the host is Christ's body, etc. A quality of inner content, meaning. If a fly settles on my face, I try to squash it instantaneously, as a pure reflex. If someone pulls my hair, I lash out at him with a pure reflex of rage. In both these cases, the act is *saturated with meaning;* my interest, my desire, my vitality, fill the act as I might fill a glass with water at a tap.

On the other hand, in the days when I worked in an office, this quality of meaning was exactly what was missing from my days. Sometimes, on my way to work, I would wonder if I'd shaved, and I'd have to put my hand to my face to find out. The act was so ritualistic, so devoid of meaning, that I had no memory of it. After six months in that office, I had got so used to this ritualistic half-life that I fell into a kind of emotional paralysis, an emotional counterpart of sexual impotence. Music ceased to move me; I could still think, but no real feelings or intuitions drove my thoughts. This total boredom didn't vanish until I was on holiday at Marden, in Kent, and I suddenly thought how nice it would be to destroy Western civilization, and all the shits who can live these rotten half-lives in their meaningless offices without going insane. The hatred got me started again. . . .

I wish I could think of a word to describe the meaning-content that distinguishes a *vital experience* from the ritual that constitutes about 90 per cent of living. I suppose it's sheer vitality, since to the really vital, everything is interesting.

I feel all the time that vital purpose has become *muffled* in modern civilization. If only we knew exactly what we were doing, exactly where we're going. I hated the office job because I knew that the purposes to which I was devoting my day were mean and trivial; knowing the limited nature of the purposes, the vitality in me refused to respond. It is true that when I try to squash a fly on my face, I am also aware of the limited nature of the purpose; but this is an instantaneous physical response. Only sex surprises me all the time by filling the act with a vitality that seems to rise of its own accord.

Here is an example of what I mean. Carlotta rather attracts me—she has the healthy, shapely body of a German country girl. I am pretty sure she once had ideas about me. I never tried to follow this up, because I could see the hopelessness of having a mistress on the premises—especially one who can walk into my room at any time on the pretext of cleaning it up.

About two months ago, I heard the kettle upstairs whistling, and went rushing out of the door. Carlotta was on the landing, on top of a stepladder attacking the cobwebs, and I cannoned into her before I could stop myself. She unbalanced

and put her hands on my shoulders, and I took her weight and helped her down on to ground level again. Her wide skirt got caught on the top of the ladder and she had to mount two of the steps to unhook it. In the meantime, I had time to admire her legs—which are by no means spoiled by the thick black stockings she wears to work—and her behind, which was visible enough. (I can never understand why girls bother to wear panties that might as well be made of pink cellophane.) When she got unhooked, my reaction was completely automatic; I simply pulled her to me and found myself shamelessly pressing my loins against her so that she could have no doubt whatever of the precise physical nature of my response. She looked very pink, but not at all displeased. I said "God, Carlotta. . . ," and then had to stop myself from saying: "For Christ's sake let's get into bed." She didn't even try to disentangle herself, and I sensed that she'd probably agree—or at least promise to come back later—and I remembered that Caroline was due to come around. So I just gulped half a dozen times, kissed her, and rushed upstairs without looking back. When I came down again, I said rather lamely: "You shouldn't do things like that. You'll get raped against the banisters." She just laughed and said: "I didn't do anything," which was obvious enough anyway. So I said: "If you intend to climb stepladders, you ought to wear ballet tights." She looked pleased at the implied compliment to the seductive nature of her underwear, and I escaped into my room. When Caroline came an hour later, I screwed hell out of her, but my mind wasn't on her. I wonder if these mental infidelities in the act of intercourse are frequent, and if Caroline imagines that she's being embraced by one of her favorite film stars.

This Carlotta episode really makes me feel I'm a Jekyll and Hyde. Oh, I know I'm fairly sexually excitable, and I take account of this in my conscious idea of myself and my motivation. What shattered me, as I stood upstairs in the kitchen, was the *force* that was making my hands tremble as I tried to lift the kettle. Hector asks Shotover how long he can think of a subject without its being branded in his brain for the rest of his life, and Shotover answers "Half an hour." Well, I think that I shall still be able to evoke the sight of Carlotta's legs, the area of white between the top of the stocking and the panties, the garters stretched tight between them, the shadow of pubic hair showing clearly through the thin nylon, to the end of my life. I felt as if an elephant had trampled over me. Above all, I found myself asking myself: "What is it in you that is opposing this overwhelming and simple desire to pull Carlotta into your bedroom and undress her?" An animal would have no such self-division. I suppose this is what we call "the spirit of man," the imagination, warning me that if I screw the girl, I'm going to have to leave this house within a month. And I like the place.

I am aware of certain things about myself with absolute clarity, all the time. And the most important is this: just as my body is perpetually subject to the force of gravity, so my "spirit," my mind, is subject to a kind of spiritual gravitational pull. It is a *depressing* force, exactly as if someone had attached hooks to my clothes and hung weights on them. I can imagine an angel, someone ideally strong, as powerful as lightning, with a spirit like fire. And I can imagine such a being, who could never know the meaning of weakness, failing to notice that human beings are unhappy, because after all, life surges on, in cities as well as in the jungle. And I ask: Why am *I* not like that? Who has attached these hooks to my spirit, to my imagination, and hung great weights on them? For what reason are we so weighted down? The Catholics say Adam sinned, but since Adam never existed, this is unlikely. *Why?* WHY? I want to know. It is not an abstract question. I *feel* it with all my being, for every moment of my life. Who has tied this tin can to man's tail?

I'm not entirely defeatist about this. I think I'm fairly strong. I'm certainly stronger than the Graham Greenes and Aldous Huxleys and the rest. At least my intellect can get the problem into focus, which is the greatest step towards solving it. Added to which, there have been the moments of insight. . . . I suppose that I'm a "stranger to revelation" if by revelation you mean something like the experience of St. Paul. But there have been other moments—when my whole being seemed to overflow with power, when I could see new areas of myself, when the possibility of getting rid of the tin can and becoming a god did not seem too distant. Hence the importance I attach to sex. I think of that scene in Wedekind where Jack the Ripper murders Lulu. The Ripper staggers out of her bedroom, his eyes bulging, his chapped red hands (with their bitten nails) dripping with her blood, panting from sheer excess of relieved sexual tension, and mutters: "I was always a lucky fellow. . . ," knowing that the human spirit is not confined to the flat earth of consciousness, but can also rise vertically, as if in a helicopter.

I have also known these revelations in sex, and I despair when I think of the inability of my language to fix their meanings. Yet it can be done; we can create new language, and language and sex will become allies, language clarifying and purifying the sexual impulse, sex powering language to achieve a new complexity.

Oct. 26. Today is one of those irritating, dull days when my brain and my feelings refuse to co-operate; I don't know what I want to do or where I want to go. I look at all the books on my shelf; nothing attracts me. I stare out of the window, then look through my records; I play a Schubert quartet, but after two minutes, my attention wanders, and then the music begins to irritate me. My consciousness hedges me in. I wish I had some kind of an explosive rocket to launch against this blank wall, to smash it down and free me from this prison of boredom. There must be a way. For two days now, I have intended to go on writing in this diary, but for some reason, the thought repels me. However, I see no other solution but work. If I obeyed my boredom, I would sit down and try to read a few pages of about twenty books, make myself tea I don't really want, try to sleep, and succeed in wasting the day completely, as I wasted yesterday.

I thought I would like to write about Mary and my first

experience of sex, since it is undoubtedly true that no subsequent experience ever achieves the same importance. (Caroline tells me that all women keep a corner of themselves for the man who takes their virginity, even if they subsequently sleep with a man a night.) And yet I feel less than garrulous about it all. . . .

Mary, then. . . . I cannot remember her face as I write, except that it was oval, and rather pretty. She was fifteen, I was nearly nineteen at the time. It was too long to wait to lose my virginity. I remember reading somewhere that most of the great Elizabethans lost theirs at about the age of twelve, and no one thought anything of a girl having a baby at thirteen. Maybe that is what's wrong with modern society, and the reason for the overemphasis on sex. I know *I* should have had my first sexual experience at thirteen, when I became aware of my body. The six-year wait was too long. I sometimes wonder if I shall ever be sexually healthy, or if I shall always have a slightly "morbid" approach to sex because of that long wait when it seemed to me that I was doomed to a lifetime of frustration.

I also remember my teens as a time of miserable shyness, when very small social embarrassments could throw me into agonies that made me writhe with self-loathing for months afterward. Like farting once in front of a girl I rather liked, or merely stumbling in my speech and mispronouncing a word. I mention these things because they help to explain how sexual desire could become magnified until it became unhealthy.

I met Mary at the first dance I attended after my National Service. I was not particularly attracted by her; her hair had been soaked by the rain and hung in rat's tails, and she looked about ten years old. At all events, I danced with her, then persuaded her to come with me into a pub, and later walked her home. She was in no way at all my "type" of girl. She worked as a waitress in a dirty little workman's café near the bus station, had no interest in books or ideas, and had never been to the theater. I was even puzzled why she should be attracted to me; she admitted later that I wasn't her type either. I should add that I had no thought of sex with her. Or rather, I had, but only in a vague, hopeful sense. And I felt guilty because I was going out with a girl I didn't particularly like, simply because I might use her body. I felt like a murderer. That first night, I kissed her good night, in a chaste kind of way, and walked back home feeling a fool. The next day, I went to the café for lunch, and we agreed to meet the next day. (She was not allowed out that evening—her family was strict with her.) The following afternoon, a Sunday, we took a bus out into the country, walked for a few miles, had tea in a café, and finally lay down in a haystack. We began to kiss—rather long, frustrating kisses. And suddenly, to my astonishment, she opened my lips and darted her tongue between them. I found this interesting, but not exciting. Similarly, as we walked home and she placed my hand on her breast, I felt that I ought to be excited, but wasn't. But as we kissed good night, she could feel my sexual excitement, and raised it several degrees by rubbing herself against me in a way that suggested we were experiencing precisely the same desire.

The following evening—it was midsummer, and uncomfortably hot—we again took a long walk, and ended in a rather deserted park in a nearby village. We lay in a hollow and kissed, and pressed together as we had the night before. I had no thought of allowing my hands to stray—I was afraid it might upset her. Finally, we sat up and talked, but there was a curious, unstated frankness between us; she was aware of my excitement and I of hers. We kissed again, sitting up. Suddenly, she pointed to a darker spot on the gray of my flannels, and said: "Oh, look!" And with a candidness that staggered me, she unzipped me, and plunged her cool hand to the source of my excitement. The episode was not as exciting as it sounds here. I felt a little apprehensive that someone would approach us, although we were sitting in a way that concealed what we were doing; besides, she examined my member critically, and commented upon a certain freckled appearance. Some children began to play ball close to us, and we decided it was time to leave. All the way home on the bus, she kept my hand pressed tight into her lap (except when people walked past our seat).

The following week was frustrating. I saw her every day at lunchtime, and two or three evenings. There were feverish hours in local parks, and an even worse evening in a local cinema. Although I have been told that a great deal of sex goes on under cover of darkness in these places, I could not bring myself to believe that we were not under the supervision of the whole row; when Mary placed her hand in my lap, a woman sitting next to me got up in a marked manner and went to the end of the row. So we finally went home, without even seeing the film out to its end.

But on the following Sunday, we decided to spend a day in the country, and accordingly packed up a great deal of food and drink, and took a bus for ten miles. We found ourselves a pleasant spot at the side of a stream, under some trees, opened the food, and stood the bottles of lemonade in the water. And finally, after half an hour of looking around for mushrooms, we drank some dandelion wine that my grandmother had given me, and lay down in the most sheltered spot we could find. Mary always tended to take the lead in these sexual exercises; within about five minutes, she had me almost completely undressed. I now, somewhat shyly, thrust my hand inside her dress, and worked it inside the elastic around the leg of her knickers. (She was wearing the blue things that schoolgirls wear.) She giggled and said: "Aren't you naughty." At this point, I was frustrated. I knew absolutely nothing about female anatomy, and had always imagined the vagina to be situated further forward; she had to reach down and guide my hand. I was interested to observe my own reactions; I felt very little excitement—certainly not the maelstrom of ecstasy I had always expected. After a while, I tried, rather awkwardly, to move into a position more suitable for mutual contact; I was clumsy, and she moved away, ordering me to

lie on my back. Then, to my amazement, she sat astride me,
grasped my overheated member as if it were a door handle,
and in a rather businesslike way, lowered herself onto it. At
this point, her face twisted with agony, and she gasped: "Ooh,
don't move!" So I obediently lay still, aware that I had penetrated her—or had been used by her for penetration—and
thought: "So this is what I've spent six years speculating about?
This is the great experience?" Although I felt enough excitement to maintain an erection, I was otherwise curiously detached. The feeling of her vagina, closed around me, might
have been a warm glove, or my own hand. If I had been more
of a romantic, I might have felt like crying: What about the
ecstasy? In about five minutes, she had begun to move on me,
and I was aware that I had to worry about pregnancy; so I
asked her to move quickly. We then ate and drank, dozed a
little, and continued in the same manner for the rest of the
day—seven times in all. After the second time, it no longer
hurt her, so she allowed me to assume the normal position;
after the sixth time, she complained of soreness. In the late
afternoon, feeling very tired, we walked out of the field, and I
felt as though half my life had been passed there. I was not
disappointed. On the contrary, the elation I felt had little to
do with sex. I think my feelings could be expressed like this:
"At last I have no more reason to be curious about women. I
also have no more reason to suspect that destiny intends me
for a life of frustration." About the sexual experience itself, I
felt: "So that was all," and felt the kind of elation we feel
about certain kinds of disillusionment.

After that, the affair with Mary ran a fairly smooth
course, except for quarrels. We met two or three times a week.
I inquired among relatives about baby-sitting, and got into the
habit of taking Mary with me. As soon as we were left alone, I
produced contraceptives, and we both stripped and lay down
on the rug. She probably enjoyed sex more than any girl I
have ever known. She would often say: "Don't move, don't
move," and then lie completely still, groaning: "Oh God, that's

lovely." After five minutes like this, when she had controlled her feelings enough to avert an imminent orgasm, she would allow me to move a little, still groaning.

Even then, I was struck by the difference in our responses. Mary, like Caroline, enjoyed sex; she enjoyed the act itself in a straightforward way. The desire was apparently attached to its object in a simple relationship. I soon noticed that my own excitement was more complicated. She bought herself some more adult underwear, and took pleasure in walking around in it; I soon noticed that this excited me more than seeing her naked. Why? It is probably tied up with the male-conquest impulse, as well as with a conditioning that connects our sexual impulses to underwear advertisements. One day, she bought herself a garter belt. I watched her dressing, her panties pulled just below her buttocks while she hooked it up; the sight instantly provoked me to take her again, with an urgency so great that I would not even allow her to undress. And yet this puzzles me when I think back on it. I suppose seeing her like that gave me a sense of seeing something forbidden, and this added to the desire. (I doubt whether Mary ever felt this.) This immediately connects sex with all the 19th-century romanticism about black magic, etc. It also reminds me of the joke about the man who cured himself of impotency by repeating "She is not my wife, she is not my wife," before climbing into bed with his wife.

Again—I digress from Mary, but the subject is worth pursuing—I notice that Gertrude, in certain ways, evokes stronger sexual emotions than Caroline, simply because she always allows me to feel a sense of violation. This came to me strongly a few weeks ago; she warned me there was no point in staying the night because she had the curse. I decided to stay anyway, and we got into bed; Gertrude was wearing a sort of sanitary belt under her panties. Halfway through the night, I woke up in a state of excitement. And *because* I knew that she would consider it horribly indecent to attempt to make love under the circumstances, I tried to, very cautiously. Luckily, she is a heavy sleeper; I, in any case, was in such a fever that I reached my climax long before my cautious maneuvers achieved their object. Again, the forbidden has this power to raise ordinary sexual excitement to an extraordinary pitch.

To return to Mary:

After a few months, and two or three pregnancy scares, I no longer felt the same excitement. It would be untrue to say that I tired of her; I was never in love with her, or even very emotionally attached, and we had very little to hold us together except the pleasure of going to bed. That August, just before our final quarrel, we went on a holiday together to Wales. One windy afternoon, we climbed a hill near Leominster to look at an old ruined tower, and managed to get inside it and climb the stairs. On our way down, it started to rain; we took shelter in a wood, lay down between two ground-sheets, and stayed there for half the afternoon, until we both felt exhausted. Finally, the rain stopped, and we made our way back toward the youth hostel. The wind was terrific; it prevented us from walking direct down the hill; the ground-sheets, which we were wearing as capes, acted as sails, and threw us along in the wind. I looked at the line of hills on the other side of the Severn, and felt an almost mystical satisfaction and certainty. The life in me seemed to swell and rise to the surface —more than it ever has in sexual excitement. I felt as if I were close to Captain Shotover's seventh degree of concentration. I felt with certainty that man is on the brink of a new phase in his evolution, that life is about to make another important concession, and give man one more degree of freedom from the perpetual imprisonment in half-consciousness. It seemed to me that I was very close to discovering a secret—another small piece of knowledge about the controls of the machine. It may be only a tiny concession—how to release the hand brake, how to turn on the headlights—but it will be a step closer to godhood. Such moments as these seemed to justify the long misery and boredom of my teens, as if an unknown power had whispered in my ear: "Carry on, you're doing well."

A month later, Mary and I quarreled; she went off with an engineer she met at a dance while I was in London, and accepted him when he proposed to her. By that time, I had already met Geraldine, so I didn't pay much attention.

The chief thing I remember about the Mary affair was my feeling of triumph during those first few weeks. I suppose, after six years of wanting sex and trying to imagine what it would be like, I suddenly had a great deal of surplus mental energy at my disposal. For years I had thought and analyzed obsessively, but never really enjoyed being a "thinker," suspecting that it separated me from life. Mary's effect on me, oddly enough, was not to make me exult in my body, but in my mind. The sex provided long holidays from introspection; I went back fresh and full of new ambition. I also felt as if I had unmasked a confidence trickster; I felt: "Never again shall I sweat and lust after a woman." At first, this was true. After making love to Mary, I would look at women without desire, no longer curious about what they'd be like in bed, *knowing* already what they'd be like.

This did not last. I thought the affair had blown away all my cobwebs, dried out all the damp spots of morbidity in me. It didn't. The life force won't allow us to learn much from our sexual experiences. . . .

Besides, as I realized with Geraldine, sex is by no means my deepest impulse. There were times when I felt like raging against my body, shaking the bars of my cage. Sex can give us momentary release, but almost immediately the enormous oppression of the body descends again; we are released from one prison cell and promptly locked in another. I gain a few hours release in music, and then discover that I'm hungry; I eat, and discover that I'm now drowsy and inclined to indigestion. Always a new oppression to make up for the momentary sense of escape.

And yet this is not wholly true. When I work well and

think well, I have a sense of release; the opposing army is forced to retreat, and has not time to regain its lost ground while I'm asleep; I wake up with a feeling of well-being and vital excitement.

I wonder how many other disciplines there are for contacting this powerhouse? I have experienced it once or twice listening to music, particularly Wagner. *Tristan* was the great love of my teens. I remember hearing some of it one evening on the radio—unexpectedly; I listened with total concentration, trying to keep in my mind the whole idea and feeling of the drama, the love potion that is stronger than either of them, the illusion of touching heaven in the garden. My brain began to feel *hot,* as if it were an engine being run properly for once, and suddenly, time stood still, the past and the present became identical, *as if time were a confidence trick of my body,* and I had seen through the trick. I am sure that power over the body resides in the brain. If only the brain could work at a certain intensity, the intensity it may accidentally achieve in reading some book, listening to music, the body's power to oppress the spirit would disappear, and the body itself would become to the spirit like an instrument in the hands of an expert performer. This intensity is achieved too infrequently, and I do not have its secret, *except effort,* non-stop, day-by-day effort to attain power over the body. Van Gogh must have achieved this kind of intensity many times in his painting; it is visible in "The Starry Night" and "Road with Cypresses." I myself achieved it many times in the days when I wanted to be a ballet dancer—the days when Nijinsky was my chief symbol of the powerhouse—usually when dancing to music I associated with Nijinsky—the Faun, the Sacre, the Firebird.

Oct. 27. This morning, in the second-hand shop in the Hampstead Road, I picked up a copy of Gorki's reminiscences of Tolstoy. I have never written about this, incidentally, the intense pleasure I get from pottering around second-hand bookshops. It is not merely the bookworm's delight. These places are like churches in the middle of this stupid civilization; outside there is business, money-making, the commercial jungle where everything is devalued; inside, another world that plots the secret overthrow of the world of money. I still remember my excitement on picking up a tattered copy of the first volume of Schopenhauer, and walking up the Kentish Town Road reading it, and feeling as if I'd found one of the secrets that would free me; life is all surface, hard, polished, screaming for attention. The world is like a bad-tempered and imperious housewife who wants to keep her husband under her thumb, who never ceases to nag him, make him feel in the wrong, assure him that he could go further and fare worse, etc. She also plants in him an immense guilt feeling about feeling attracted to other women. Then one day, he meets another woman who is totally unlike his wife, gentle, good-tempered, intelligent, and perfectly willing to give herself. In five minutes he feels that the whole world is changing, feels that his wife's fits of jealousy, self-righteousness, hysteria, are completely intolerable, and that nothing but timidity and force of habit have made him endure them for so long. This is the taste of freedom. . . . I look for it in bookshops.

I find on the title page of the Gorki this comment by Tolstoy: "The flesh rages and riots, and the spirit follows it, helpless and miserable." This was the first thing I saw when I opened the book, the subject that has been foremost in my mind for days. Are these things chance? They incline me to believe that the world has its own secret motives and intentions.

On the first page of the book, I find this remark: "He is like a god, not a Sabaoth or Olympian, but the kind of Russian god who 'sits on a maple throne under a golden lime tree,' not very majestic, but perhaps more cunning than all the other gods."

I sympathize. We all want to create gods, to believe in godlike men. This book shows Gorki's struggle to romanticize Tolstoy, to see him as a god, and his continual disappointment that he was only a human being—until, after Tolstoy's death,

Gorki can at last drop his image into the saturated fluid of his own mind, and bring it out encrusted with crystals.

Yes, I know this desire to believe that men can be like gods, that Shelley's old Jew, "wiser than God," really lives somewhere in his sea cavern "mid the Demonesi." I experience it now as I turn my head and look at Nietzsche's works on the shelf. When I bought them—found the set in a junk shop that didn't realize their value—I brought them back greedily, stood them on the shelf and then stared at them as if I'd found the key to my salvation, a man who used language like a scalpel to cut the truth out of his own heart. And then I thought: But Nietzsche died insane. This man whose thought is so powerful and clear, whose step is so purposeful, seems to know exactly where he is walking; it is impossible not to believe that he can lead the human race out of its moral wilderness. But he died insane.

Oct. 28. Dennis Paulham came last night, bringing with him a bottle of some peculiar cocktail that someone had given him; I was feeling tired, so to discourage conversation I gave him the sex diary to read. He read avidly without saying a word for an hour. Dennis is a curious little man; he must be nearer fifty than forty, and yet looks like a willful schoolboy, with his round face and snub nose. And yet at his age, his sex experience has been negligible. He was particularly excited by my account of the woman who excited me by pressing against me in a crowd, and told me that he had once had a similar experience, but that it had led to some unpleasantness.

He then told me a number of things that struck me as so interesting that I set them down here. His most amusing story was about a prostitute in Notting Hill. Dennis saw an advertisement on a board near the station, the usual "Attractive girl wishes to do modeling work." He phoned her up, and went over to see her. He said she was horribly unattractive, with a face like a horse and a figure that suited it. He felt embarrassed, and took her out for a meal. Afterwards, they returned to her room; he wanted an excuse to go home, but couldn't think of one. As soon as they got in, she stripped off her clothes and climbed into bed, and he reluctantly did the same. But it was useless; he simply felt no desire. After she had tried to excite him, without success, for ten minutes, she said that she had just the thing for him. She went to a cupboard, and took out a machine! He said it had a large wheel and various electric wires that ran to two small leather straps. The girl buckled the straps around his limp member, and turned the handle. Immediately, small bolts of electricity shot through him, and achieved the desired effect almost immediately. She hastily unbuckled the straps, and leaped into bed, but by this time, his interest had vanished and he had subsided again. Once more she buckled the straps and turned the handle; once more Dennis demonstrated his manhood; but as soon as she unbuckled the straps, the excitement vanished. After a few more attempts, she gave up. He left her some money and promised to return the following day, but never did.

I asked him if he had had any more experience with "machines," and he launched into a rambling story about a homosexual he knew, who had taken him to a kind of Turkish bath somewhere in East London, where he was astonished to discover that a large proportion of the clientele were big, athletic-looking men who might have been army drill instructors. Apparently the most extraordinary things went on under cover of a blanket of steam. When Dennis revealed that he was not particularly inclined for these exercises, the proprietor offered to let him try a "machine." Dennis was a little vague about the nature of these machines, except that they were ostensibly "massage machines." He looked at one of these, and complained that it was filthy, showing very obvious signs of the use to which it had been put. At this, the proprietor looked surprised, and explained that his clients insisted on their being filthy, that they would simply refuse to make use of a "clean" machine. Dennis grabbed his clothes and excused himself. . . .

Again, this problem of the association of sex and "dirt." And yet I am not sure that it is a "necessary" association. I read a case recently of a young burglar who slashed the armchairs with a razor and pissed on the carpets. The burglary expressed a power complex; it was obviously a kind of "rape" of a rich person's flat, and the rape would not be complete without this kind of indignity. The sense of *freedom* in a strange person's flat had to express itself in some form of destruction. In the same way, we may associate sex and "dirt" as two things that are forbidden.

And yet it is the powers inside ourselves which are "forbidden," which we know nothing about, and yet which we have a *right* to know about. There is no reason why sex should be associated with destruction. I think of Harry Thomas who worked with me once at Golders Green. (I met him again a few nights ago in Tottenham Court Road.) He had every reason to be fairly happy; he was a good-looking man in his thirties, with a pretty wife and two intelligent children, a comfortable little house in Hampstead, and a good job. And yet he never seemed happy to me; his eyes always looked strained, as if he were suppressing nervous tension. He used to come and talk to me when I was spraying toys in the shed outside the factory, and tell me how he longed to escape. (We once planned a whole trip across Europe and North Africa on his motor bike, but it never came off.)

But what interested me most were his symbols of freedom. He talked to me about fighting in the Western desert against Rommel. He had a special friend named Ginger. One day, in a bombardment, Ginger looked over a heap of sandbags when a shell exploded; his head rolled to Harry's feet. Harry said he went insane; he jumped on top of the sandbags, in full view of the enemy snipers, and began screaming at them and firing his rifle. He said he didn't care if they shot him; he hated them so much that he wanted to kill every German with his bare hands.

Harry also told me about the bombardments, and the

tremendous noise the guns made when they opened up. He said that all the guns along the line would begin to fire together, at a given signal, and go on without pause for an hour or more. The explosions were so continuous that they lit up the sky as if it were daytime, and the noise was simply a non-stop thunder that left everyone deaf for days. But Harry told me about this with a kind of exaltation. He said: "It was like Hell let loose," but he said it with so much feeling that the cliché expressed some of his amazement, almost an admiration, for the racket.

But the story of Harry's that impressed me most was about a girl he met when he was training in some town in the North of England. Harry is always a little apologetic about his lack of education, and he's a non-stop reader. He is also a fine sportsman. One evening, he and a few friends were playing cricket in a park, when some men stopped to watch the game. Afterwards, an old colonel came over to him and asked him if he'd like to play cricket in his team. Harry was delighted —it got him off a great many duties. He met the colonel's daughter, and was immediately dazzled by her; she'd just returned from a Swiss finishing school, and was apparently rather beautiful. Harry knew that he might be moved abroad at any moment; this gave the love affair a wartime urgency, and within a few days they were lovers. They had to keep it secret from the colonel, and used to meet late at night, after the cricket practice. Harry told me how one night, they went into a park, and had sex at the side of a lake. It was a warm, starlit night. After they'd finished their lovemaking, neither of them bothered to put their clothes on immediately. The girl apparently liked to take off most of her clothes. Harry told me that he lay there at her side, while she sat up, and he looked at the shape of her breasts outlined against the sky. He said that she suddenly began to recite poetry in French—at least, he thinks it was French—a poem he thought was about the stars.

Harry told me that story on at least three occasions.

Obviously, it represents something to him—a dream that will always make him dissatisfied. They never saw one another again after he left the town, and he heard later that she had married an officer. (Harry was a sergeant.) He told me that he would never forget the outline of her breasts against the sky, and the sound of her voice spouting Baudelaire or somebody of the sort. It symbolized a kind of fairy-tale fulfillment. When he told me these stories, I could understand why he was dissatisfied in his job, with his excellent wife and pleasant home. As to me, I'm sure he'd have been even more unhappy if he'd married the girl. And yet the thought remains his symbol of freedom.

How much unfulfillment there is in all modern society! I am not now speaking about the unfulfillment of the poets and potential artists who dream of a world of Wagnerian ecstasy, but about men like Harry, about the working-class boys who go to sea hoping for an "adventurous life," about the shopgirls who get starry-eyed about a nonsensical musical film in which the dashing hero is played by a film star who is known to be a homosexual and a drug addict.

I have two photographs that fascinate me. One is in a book on German films. It shows Hans Albers, who was apparently Germany's most popular film star in the thirties, dressed for dinner, and walking down a broad staircase with several beautiful girls on either side of him. I am told that Albers always played the part of the bellhop who marries the princess, the poor boy who marries the boss's daughter, etc. This photograph symbolizes all the longing of shopgirls and factory boys for the life of grace and money.

The other photograph is of Douglas Fairbanks playing in *The Iron Mask*. I suppose he is D'Artagnan; he is dressed in leather boots and an open-necked shirt. He stands on picturesque looking flagstones that immediately evoke the Paris of *The Vagabond King*. One hand rests on his hip, the other holds the hilt of a sword whose point touches the flagstones. He has a tiny pointed beard as well as a moustache, his head is thrown back, and he smiles with total confidence. Everything about his pose suggests immense vitality; I have never seen him in a film, but I can imagine him leaping out of windows, stopping runaway carriages, clambering over battlements and fencing with ten men at the same time. He symbolizes the other daydream—the life of action. Albers is grace and the glamor of riches; Fairbanks is unchallengable, undefeatable vitality, a man who can never be hurt or discouraged, who looks at all life with the same confident, handsome smile. "Pooh, it's easy when you plunge into things with one tremendous leap. . . ."

The two dreams, and a society sick with longing for both of them, like Harry and his naked girl reciting Baudelaire. . . .

Later. While I'm on the subject of Harry, a few more points about him that interest me. Sexually, he is exceptionally successful, and always has been. He told me once about his first sexual experience. He used to go to the cinema a great deal. One day, an attractive woman sat next to him—he was about ten at the time—and allowed her hands to roam. Harry had no thought of stopping her; in fact, when he got over his first astonishment, he helped her by unbuttoning himself. In the interval, she took him to a café upstairs and bought him ice cream and lemonade, then sat next to him again and continued to fondle him. I asked Harry how he felt about this —alarmed or perhaps a little shocked. He said: "Oh no, I enjoyed it." He made no attempt to return the caresses, and after the film, never saw the woman again. His theory was that her husband was impotent or unsatisfying; I would suppose it was some kind of neurosis uncommon in women. (There are hundreds of men who would like to do the same to little girls, but few women who feel any interest in young boys.)

Only one more of Harry's stories stays in my head. He told me how, as a child, he climbed over a railway embankment, and saw two small girls engaged in sexual play, poking twigs into each other!

All this helps to explain his nostalgia about the Baudelaire girl. His earliest experiences of sex were of a fairly degrading kind—a mere physical titillation. From some of his confidences about his extramarital relations, I gather that they continue to be rather unidealistic—brutal adulteries in parks and so on. He is so obviously handsome, in the Douglas Fairbanks manner, that women often take the lead in seduction, and offer themselves frankly. The one thing, therefore, that his sex life has always lacked has been the element of glamor, the "great love." And no matter how unromantic a man might think himself, there is always a corner of him that envies the Tristans and Lancelots; he secretly longs for sex to cease to be a pleasant but animalistic activity; he wants it to become part of the driving force for his greatest ambitions, his need to live more fully and intensely.

Why is it that these romantic ideas never cease to exercise their influence on us? I can never read the passage in Dante about how Paolo kissed Francesca's mouth, "all trembling," without feeling that shiver of longing. The music to which Zandonai sets this scene in his opera seems to me some of the greatest in the world. And why do we feel such a response when Tristan and Isolde drink the love potion, then stare at one another in silence, until the orchestra takes up the opening phrase of the Prelude in a whisper? When finally she sings "Tristan," and he sings "Isolde," I feel a ripple through my hair and a shiver down to my fingertips. It is because of the idea that love is a force greater than either of them, and that from now on, nothing else can ever matter to either of them but that total absorption in one another. We live boring and dissatisfied lives, never feeling much contact with another person. My "sex life" is adequate, but my "love life" is an ironic absurdity. I suspect Gertrude of being possessive in a kind of suppressed-neurotic way; Caroline, I know, might go to bed with a handsome drama student any day—and I wouldn't even feel jealousy. I would like to believe that the Tristan-Isolde love *can* exist, and can transform my being.

Oct. 29. Sitting in this room, drinking endless cups of tea, there are times when I wonder whether I have not somehow chosen a completely false direction. Should I not rather be in another city, struggling for existence? I disgust myself. A few years ago I thought that I would like to spend every day in the reading room at the British Museum, like Butler and Shaw and Wells. Now, I sit here within half an hour of the place, and cannot overcome my laziness.

I go back over my calculation to see where I've gone wrong. It goes like this: Animals are feeble creatures; they are thrown down into the world, guided by a few instincts. They have no freedom; they do nothing that the body does not order them to do. Man is also an animal, he also finds himself in an environment, with various pressures to determine the direction of his life. But he has discovered a number of methods of increasing his minute powers. His memory is almost nonexistent, a mere candle flame. He learned to use language to preserve his knowledge. A transformer is a device that can turn a low voltage into a high voltage. Language is man's memory transformer; his memory has the power of a mere flashlight battery, but language multiplied it until it becomes a power station, capable of holding the knowledge of hundreds of years. But language was not his only "transformer." He also developed imagination. This meant that man was no longer confined by his environment. He can be born into poverty and dirt, but through imagination, these cease to be absolutes; he can nourish his mind on beauty and idealism. Surely imagination is the greatest power ever discovered by man, greater than oil, electricity, atomic energy. With imagination he leaves the realm of the animal and enters the realm of the god.

This is astounding; to an animal, it would seem a kind of black magic. Yes, undoubtedly, imagination is freedom, a new dimension for human beings. Imagination is the power of the absurd; it is nothing less than an antigravity device that can cause man to rise into the air like an Indian fakir. Everything may be against him; he may, like Blake, be a total

failure in every worldly sense, without money, without reputation, his paintings dismissed as untalented, his poems described as the work of a madman; and yet, with every "natural" disadvantage to push him backward, he defies the laws of physics and moves forward.

Man, then, is a flea who has invented devices that enable him to lift mountains. Yet then I open Shaw's *Caesar and Cleopatra,* and find Caesar refusing to save the library of Alexandria because "It is better for the Egyptians to live their lives instead of dreaming them away over books." If it were as simple as that! Life versus dreams. But it isn't. Man is awkwardly poised between god and animal. I sit here, surrounded by the devices that taught me freedom in my childhood—books, gramophone records, writing materials, and I place my trust in them to achieve still more freedom. But it's an uphill struggle; my body would rather go and get drunk, take a run over the fields in a high wind, rape the first pretty girl I meet in Camden Town; it doesn't like all this study and her breasts, and very obviously enjoyed it.

Then she added

Oct. 30. I took my own advice yesterday, and went over to meet Caroline after school. She wanted to look at the site of the Christie* murders, so I took her along to Ruston Close. A nasty area. We went into a café and drank tea; it was a grimy little place with oilcloth on the tables. While we sat there, two women came in who might have been Christie's victims. Perhaps it is the associations of the Christie case, but this district always seems to me to reek of sex. I watched this poor, sluttish looking woman of forty come in and buy tea and ten Woodbines; fat behind; her slip hanging crookedly below her lopsided skirt. She sits opposite, looks out of the window at the kids playing rounders in the middle of the

---

* John Reginald Halliday Christie, a multiple sex murderer. Sexually impotent with conscious women, he murdered and violated at least five women at his home at 10 Rillington Place, London W. 11, between 1940 and his arrest in 1953. He also killed his wife in December 1952.

road, then looks curiously at Caroline. Caroline looking very blond and pink and pretty and well-dressed in a red skirt with large gold buttons, and asking me with morbid curiosity if I can understand how a man could violate dead bodies. When I reply Yes, I think I can, she shivers. I imagine Christie staring out of this window, and dreaming an Eastern despot's lurid daydream: being given the freedom of all women. Beckoning to that thirteen-year-old girl playing rounders: take off your skirt. Then to that girl in the green coat who is swinging a handbag that is too big and too glossy: raise up your dress to your waist and let me see if you attract me. This is my "transformer," magnifying sex until it fills the world. Because sex isn't really all that important. . . .

Caroline wanted to go and see *Cyrano de Bergerac* with Jose Ferrer. I enjoyed the first half, then got sick of his feeble defeatism. I think I prefer Christie, who wants to seize girls like an animal, to this fool who thinks Roxane a goddess.

Afterward, we went and drank cider in a pub behind the BBC, and somebody put on some gramophone records— Trenet singing "La Mer"—and I suddenly felt superbly sentimental and happy and looked at Caroline and thought that it's a pity this isn't a real love affair, just an affair. These moments give a love affair a kind of immortality.

In the night, I kept thinking about Madeleine in the next room; I knew she had the day off today. The other day, she came into the kitchen and caught me making tea in my underpants. She pretended to be very shocked—in fact, made such a fuss about it that I could tell her indignation was drawing strength from some other emotion. So this morning, when Caroline had gone to school, I made more tea, went into Madeleine's bedroom with two cups, and climbed into bed with her. She ordered me to get out, but without much conviction, so I simply sat there and drank my tea. We talked in a funny, embarrassed, casual way. I was sorry to see she was wearing a nightgown with a high neck. I didn't expect much from her, but was curious to see how far she'd let me go. The conversation was deliberately casual, even a little prim. Then we lay down, I put my arm around her, and we talked some more. Then she let me kiss her and caress her breasts through the nightgown. I cursed the bloody thing; it came all the way down to her feet, making it difficult to raise without bending down—which would be the ideal opportunity for her to stop me. Seduction should be able to proceed by tiny stages, like sliding down a slope; any sudden steps are likely to stop it for good. However, after kissing her for twenty minutes and getting indecently excited, I knew I either had to go on or get out of bed; besides, I'd managed to raise her nightgown by pretending to caress her behind. So I grabbed the bottom, pulled it up above her waist, and went to work kissing her and pressing myself against her. She didn't put up any defenses, just opened her legs. I expected it to be impossible, but tried anyway. To my amazement, I managed to get in without much trouble, but it obviously hurt her like mad. She insisted on lying perfectly still; I deliberately cooled my excitement by thinking about something else. After about half an hour, I could move without hurting her too much; finally, I had to withdraw quickly. We then got up and made tea. She seemed rather resentful about the whole thing, saying contemptuously: "Is that all sex is?" I assured her that no one ever enjoyed it the first time. She said: "If that's all it is, I don't think I'll bother to try it again." After breakfast, she gave me a little lecture about how important it is that Caroline never find out. (I don't think Caroline would give a damn. I think she'll enjoy looking at Caroline and feeling that she's one up.)

Now I try again to remember how the conjurer performed the trick. Because it *was* a trick. I didn't really want Madeleine. It was just the usual male desire to enter one more moated castle. When I use the bathroom, and see Madeleine's underwear drying in the bath, I don't like to think that it represents a world that is forbidden to me; now I can think instead: That belongs to another of my mistresses. But what does this mean? I feel like saying to the Life Force: why don't you trust me, why don't you take me into your confidence instead of *cheating* me into doing what you want? I'd be only too happy to know *why* I'm serving, how the purpose can be achieved.

My mind manufactures considerable power. It struggles, it doesn't allow itself to be imposed on, it analyzes. But not *enough* power for certainty, for knowledge of purpose.

Yet despite this sense of stagnation, things are not so bad. Today I read Borchert's play *The Man Outside*. Powerful, beautifully written—but its defeatism bores me. In Louis Vertrand, I find this comment: "Even so is my soul a desert, where on the brink of the abyss, one hand stretched towards life, the other towards death, I utter a despairing sob." This strikes me as balls. At least we're no longer as feeble as that. I don't stand between life and death and sob despairingly. I have no doubt whatever which I prefer. I may not quite know what I want out of life; I may fornicate and then feel cheated. But at least I have no doubt at all that death is an evil stupidity. Most people live on the surface of life; they can be brushed off like flies. My roots are a little deeper, and every day I try to push them deeper still. *That's* why we die: we don't want to live enough. I remember that Polish student in Birmingham who could make himself burst out into the most awful pimples and boils when he got upset. We don't yet understand the strange power of the mind. But one day, someone will discover how to use that power to live twice as long as at present, and how to avoid the present dreariness and lack of direction.

An interesting speculation occurs to me. Austin once told me that Sweden is a country of fornication, where one of the catch-phrases is: "Let's go to bed and see if we like one another." And yet Sweden also has the world's highest suicide rate. This is my theory: when a man and woman get into bed together, they imagine they are going to titillate one another; *there is no one else,* just the two of them. But this isn't true. *There is a third.* In the very act of sex, they are performing an incantation that arouses the sex god, whose business is to drive the world in the direction of evolution. If the two are performing the sex act in a spirit of boredom, he loses his temper and punishes them.

Yes, I remember it now, the sensation I experienced after that first night with Caroline. I remember lying beside her, staring at the light on the opposite wall, and feeling an immense exultation, *as if I were a magician who had just succeeded in raising elemental spirits*. It was a feeling that there are other forces in the world besides the ones of which we are aware, forces that hide below the surface, but are fully cognizant of everything that goes on. These forces inject meaning into the world. The world is meaningless without them, like the scenery stored in an empty theater.

I find this difficult to explain, but I am sure that meaning is like a conjurer's cloth, an invisible cloth that the invisible conjurer drops between us and "reality." I look out of my window at the Kentish Town Road. It fails to arouse any response in me; it is "meaningless." Suddenly a very old man walks below my window; he has a white beard, a filthy overcoat that brushes the pavement, and his dirty gray hair hangs halfway down his back. Instantly my attention is "caught"—and I imagine that this is because meaning has obtruded itself into my universe, reached out and hit me. But this is an illusion; it is something *in me* that imposed meaning on the old man. Perhaps he reminded me of Tolstoy, or aroused some idea of the "romance" of being Outside Society, refusing to fit in. Or I put a Beethoven piano sonata on the gramophone; it fails to interest me. I make an effort, and think about Beethoven's life—the arch-rebel shaking his fist at the thunder, etc., and the music immediately becomes meaningful. But it is I who have imposed the meaning on *it*.

But where sex is concerned, the problem is more mysterious. The violence of my responses convinces me that this is no autohypnosis. For example: two years ago I went to visit a friend in the hospital. When I came out, I took a walk around the hospital grounds, then took a short cut between two buildings. I saw a porter standing against a corner, obviously trying to conceal himself, and looking out across the road; when he saw me, he turned round, and looked guilty. When I drew level, he winked at me, and said: "Look at that." Twenty yards away, a girl was sitting on a doorstep—I imagine she was a student nurse, from her cloak—with her legs wide open. The porter, a slobbery looking man with thick glasses and a dripping nose, said: "She's been on show like that for ten minutes." "I don't suppose she knows we're watching," I said. "Oh yes she does. Watch this." He walked from behind the building, and went along the road, in front of the girl, taking a long look between her legs as he went past. She pretended not to see him, and went on staring abstractedly ahead of her. I must admit that, left alone, I felt considerably excited. Somehow the presence of the porter had acted as a brake before —as if it would be a kind of self-exposure to be excited in front of him. I found it incomprehensible that the girl should be sitting like that, her panties on view to the world. If she'd been ugly and sex-starved, I could have understood; but she looked about seventeen, and, as far as I could tell, was pretty. After a few minutes, the porter returned back down the road, this time keeping his eyes focused between her open thighs; he stopped near her and said something; I saw her nod, and he walked on, and came round the corner of the building.

"I asked her if she was feeling OK," he said, "and she said she was." He had tried the only explanation that seemed fairly likely: that the girl felt ill, and was not aware that we were watching her. The porter said: "Walk by like I did. She won't move. When you get close up you can see the hairs on her fanny." I wanted to, but would have felt ashamed; it was too obvious. I also wanted to talk to her. After all, she *might* be advertising a desire to lose her virginity. But again, I felt unsure of myself. Finally, realizing that I was only torturing myself—because from twenty yards, I could only see a blur of pink where the white of her thighs ended, and it was absurd to keep staring, as if longer exposure would re-

veal more—I turned and went home. This episode has stayed
in my mind ever since, and recurs frequently—particularly
when I feel sex-starved, when I daydream of what I *might*
have done if I could have got her into a bedroom. Yet when I
turn my full attention on it, the meaning vanishes. Why was
she exciting? Because she aroused in me a whole response of
secret lusts, far more violently than Caroline will arouse them
tonight when she undresses in front of me. It is not that a
girl's body is exciting in itself; the conjurer threw veils of
excitement between my eyes and the girl. (On considering
this episode, I am now convinced she did it as a "dare"—that
the other nurses bet that no girl would dare to sit on the doorstep with her thighs open, and that this girl probably replied:
"Nonsense, what does it matter if men *do* look up your skirt?
It doesn't do you any harm." . . .) All the secret repressions
of civilization rose up, all the girls who walk past in summer
dresses.

It may seem that in writing like this I am only indulging
in a kind of intellectual onanism; but this would be to miss
the point. *There is a point.* I keep trying to break into reality
with this crowbar of reason. I don't try a "systematic" attack,
like a philosopher or a theologian; I don't want to "explain"
the world, like Thomas Aquinas. I want to keep *jabbing,* in
the hope that the point of my crowbar will find a crack
in the stones and be able to lever them apart. In a way, this
diary is the ideal way to try and do it. My method of attack
is the same as that of Nietzsche, Kierkegaard, Wells: frag-
mentary, yet this is necessary. I make short, violent attacks
on the faceless reality in an attempt to take it by storm, driven
wholly by an intuition, not by reason. And sex is the ideal
driving force for my pneumatic drill; my mind may get tired
and bewildered brooding on the problem of how we ought
to live; I think of sex, and feel a shock, as if I've touched a live
wire. Something is revealed. And what I want to try and get
at is this inconsistency in the sexual impulse. I feel as if I'm
an accountant who has caught Life trying to fiddle with the

books. Because when I climb into bed with Caroline or Gertrude, I may or may not feel excitement; but it is not that
magic that the strangeness of a woman evokes. The women
who stay in my mind are the ones I never had. I remember
a girl on the beach at Felpham; I lay behind a breakwater,
watching her dress, watching the way she wrapped herself
carefully in a bath towel before she shed her bathing costume;
every single move was calculated to outwit the staring males.
But a point came when she had to concede a certain amount,
because it was almost impossible to pull on her panties without exposing something. I can still remember, with awful sick
excitement, the sight of her standing there quite boldly, her
dress raised for a moment above her waist, her legs very
straight and braced apart to balance herself. And the longing
is not merely sexual; it is also social. I don't merely want to
rape her. She looks healthy and beautiful; I want to meet her,
talk to her, take her out. But she walks off the beach with her
parents, and a man of about her own age who might be her
brother or her lover or even her husband (but I think not; she
seemed somehow unmarried) and I curse Fate, that has
dangled this goddess in front of me but offered me no opportunity of making her acquaintance. Of course, she might not be
a goddess . . . but even that would be a triumph. I remember
once, when I was about thirteen, I sat on the bus behind a
girl who had marvelous hair. I tried hard to see her face; she
half-turned once or twice, and I saw that she was pretty. In
the twenty minutes of that bus journey, I fell horribly in love,
and was assailed by daydreams as endless as the Arabian
Nights. My stop came; but I decided to stay on, and watch
her for just a few minutes longer. Then someone she knew
got on the bus, and shouted: "Allao, Sheila luv, 'ow are you?,"
and the girl in front of me replied in exactly the same voice,
the noisy, high-pitched yawp of the Midlands, as devoid of
tone as cats making love. I hurried off the bus, my adoration
in fragments—and yet perversely glad to be free again, glad
not to be a slave of daydreams.

And yet it would be untrue to pretend that a girl of this kind could not be as desirable as any debutante with a carefully modulated voice. Shaw is right when he says of Anne Whitefield: Give her a cast in one eye and strike all the aitches out of her speech, and she will still make men dream. I know this to be true. I remember once observing one of these "suburban Cleopatras" in Birmingham. I was waiting on a street corner; she was talking to a boy in overalls on a bicycle; she was not particularly pretty, although she had a good figure; she kept twisting and turning as she talked to him, as if with a kind of impatience; possibly she was aware that I was watching her with admiration. Her manner was definitely coquettish. But there was something indefinably vital about her as she stood there, shifting from one foot to the other, patting her hair, lacing her fingers together. I could hear her voice; it was what you'd expect of a Birmingham working-class girl. I think she probably had a turned-up nose; she might have had a cast in one eye, and it would have made no difference. She was like an incandescent lamp, and I think most men would have taken her on any terms. I envied that stupid looking mechanic with his face smeared with grease.

So this is sex—an appeal to something inside us of which we know nothing. It is like a spy signaling from the coast during the war; there are flashes from out there, at sea, and answering flashes from inside your own country—and yet you don't know where the spy is.

Another point that struck me the other day, thinking of Christie. Why do murderers kill certain women, yet not others? Heath murdered two girls with sadistic cruelty, yet another girl with whom he spent the weekend between the two murders didn't even suspect that he had sadistic leanings. What was it about her that made him gentle to her? Landru murdered a whole string of women, including one who had no money; yet he was also living with a girl with whom he had been having an affair for a year, and who had no suspicion that he was a killer. Kürten killed some of his female victims, yet

other women who were ill-treated by him continued to go out
with him without even suspecting that he might be a killer.
What was it about his victims that incited him to kill them?
What was it about his wife that made it impossible to treat
her badly? Surely the answer must be: the same curious
vitality that made my "suburban Cleopatra" so desirable.

So there is the problem, the discrepancy in the books
kept by the Life Force. Yet no, I can't believe that the vital
excitement is an illusion. It is a glimpse into the possibility of
an intenser form of existence, a life where there is no unsatisfied desire.

There is, of course, the opposite of this intensely-focused
desire. For example, a communist tart I met once, and the way
that all my sexual desire drained away when I was in bed with
her, as if she'd pulled out a plug. Why? Partly, of course, because I felt her to be worthless, a neurotic bitch with whom
it would be dangerous to get involved; perhaps my instincts
were reacting more perceptively than my conscious mind. Also
because she lacked mystery. I remember Bill Payne telling me
about the time when he was sleeping in the same flat as a girl
who attracted him violently. He waited until everyone was in
bed, then crept into her bedroom, where she was still reading
with the light on. When he came in, she looked up and smiled,
then threw back all the bedclothes. She was naked. He said
his desire simply evaporated at the sight of that nakedness; it
was too open, too honest. He turned and fled back to his own
room; he told me that that was exactly what she had intended
him to do. (I would have supposed her movement to be an
invitation, but Bill denied this strongly.)

So all that we know as greatness is connected with the
opening up of horizons. Why do we all love a story about
a frustrated man or woman who succeeds in realizing some
dream? It is because we are all frustrated, trapped in this
prison of a body. This is why I cannot believe that the lust I
felt for the student nurse, for the girl on the beach, was somehow an illusion, a response intensified by frustration. Certain

ideas, certain works of art, evoke for me the absurd, ecstatic, metaphysical mystery of life. Van Gogh's "Starry Night" does it; so does Beethoven's last quartet, so does that picture of the three old sages around the Well of Life in Korea. These things are not illusions; they are glimpses into a *possibility* that might become a reality at any moment. Surely the same is true of sex? It presages a freer, cleaner existence, without endless obstructions and perplexities. And I've felt this often through sex. For example, that first night I slept with Caroline. After she'd fallen asleep, it suddenly seemed to me that I'd been making a much better job of life than I realized. It was like a stock-taking when you realize that you're a great deal better off than you thought yourself.

If I had to define the belief that drives me to torment myself, to bully my body, to drive myself instead of drifting and "taking life as it comes," I would express it in this way: At any moment it is possible that we shall make the "break-through" in consciousness, that consciousness will suddenly leap to a higher level and turn us into something more like gods. With this intenser consciousness would come far more energy—or rather, I would know the secret of the source of my energy. Why do I feel as if life has somehow not yet begun, as if I am still a child, as if when I die, it will be as if I have never lived? Why did Yeats call life a long preparation for something that never happens? This I believe: we are still in the chrysalis stage; we live in a kind of daze, an oppression. And yet this I believe: we *could* go on developing, growing, so that our present "adulthood" at the age of twenty-one would seem no more than the first milestone on a hundred-mile journey. If we could discover the secret of the *next stage*, of getting past that first milestone, at which the human race has now been stuck for thousands of years, we would also have discovered the secret of living beyond our present seventy years.

Yes, we are *attacking* reality with our weapons of logic and language. The world induces a "conditioned reflex" of *blankness* in us, like a snake staring at a rabbit—a weird paralysis; we merely accept it, without asking for its credentials. We do not ask why we are born and die; we do not ask why we suffer, or why "destiny" carelessly throws us hours of silly bliss. We ought to ask, to refuse to accept anything without knowing the reason. I refuse to be hypnotized or to sink into a state of blank nausea. I place myself in circumstances where I can be most easily attacked, where I am most exposed —alone in this room, making no attempt to distract myself, only trying to look without blinking at the problem: What am I doing here? The world is a clever swindler; it robs us of our lives while it distracts our attention. It is like a dishonest jailer who is paid an allowance for the upkeep of the prisoners, but who pockets the allowance; then, when the governor pays a visit and asks "Any complaints?," somehow hypnotizes or bullies them into saying "No." And what is this "allowance" of which we are being robbed? I believe that, if we had the key, we could get past that first "adulthood," become real living beings instead of the stupid, deluded, petty creatures we are. We have a right to become more godlike than we are; we have a right to more knowledge than we possess; we have a right to know what it is all about. Once human beings catch a glimpse of that new level of maturity, they will refuse to be robbed by the jailer any longer; they will fix their eyes on it and demand it.

Sometimes, when listening to music, I catch a glimpse of it. For example, if I listen to certain things with deep concentration—the *Liebestod,* the final dance of the Firebird— time is destroyed, and I am suddenly back ten years, when I first heard them. That kind of conquest of time is a movement towards the godhead I speak of.

Later. Caroline came and interrupted me. She talked about marriage again, in a rather vague way; and I, to distract her, talked about her future success in the theater. That's Caroline's trouble: like most of us, she can't believe in her future; or even in her past. Only in the present.

She is curious about this diary. I went out of the room to put the kettle on; when I came back, she was looking at it, and to my horror, was looking at the page about Madeleine. I took it away; I don't think she had time to read it. Certainly, she didn't show any of the signs of having read it.

Oct. 31. A stupid thing happened last night, and makes me wonder if I shall ever get any sense. Caroline left at about eleven; she had early classes this morning; I settled down to fill in my diary, and decided to drink some wine. I took a bottle of Spanish burgundy out of the cupboard, and opened it standing over the bed. To my astonishment, as the cork came out with a pop, the bottom half of the bottle simply dropped away, soaking the bed with wine. I don't know whether the glass had a fault, or whether I'd somehow cracked the bottle, and wrenched it in half. Anyway, I was more worried about the state of the sheets and the mattress than about the wetness of the bed, so I rushed down to Carlotta and told her what I'd done. She came upstairs and whipped off the sheets and the blanket next to the mattress; the mattress wasn't too badly soaked, and I don't see why the landlady should ever see it. Carlotta said that the stains would come out of the sheets if she washed them right away, and I kept apologizing like a fool. I ended by going down and offering to help. Then I got the idea of opening the other bottle of wine. I stood around in her kitchen for ten minutes, getting in the way, then said I'd leave her the wine and go back upstairs; she immediately asked me where I was going to sleep. I said that the wine stain didn't make much difference; I'd cover it over with newspapers. She then said she hadn't any clean sheets, so I said I'd sleep between blankets. At this, she offered to let me sleep downstairs. I agreed; I suppose I half wanted to sleep with her anyway. Then she stopped washing, and we drank the wine, and she found some German station on her radio playing old records of Willy Frisch and Marlene Dietrich and Maurice Chevalier, and she began to sentimentalize about Munich. Finally, when we'd finished the wine, and she had asked me all kinds of personal questions about Caroline and Gertrude (which I answered truthfully), she said it was time she went to bed, and asked me if I'd be comfortable on the settee. I said yes and went upstairs to get my blankets, and switch off my fire and light. When I came down, she was in bed, and told me that if I'd promise to be "a good boy" I could sleep with her. I suppose this was what I'd been wanting—and not wanting. Temptation is very difficult to resist when it actually waves itself under your nose.

Of course, I didn't sleep a wink. She got into bed in a bra, petticoat and panties. I asked her if she always slept like that; she said no, she always slept naked, but didn't want to lead me into temptation. Then followed the usual conversation about sex; she admitted she wasn't a virgin, but said it had only happened once, and that she didn't want it to happen again. I asked her why she trusted me; she said she knew I had self-control from what happened the other day!

Finally we turned back to back and I tried to sleep. Naturally, I couldn't. I wanted to say: Stop play-acting and take off those pants, since I presume that's why you invited me into your bed. Then I dozed for a bit, and when I woke up, she was taking off her bra. I naturally took this as an invitation, and tried to kiss her, but she pushed me away, and said she was hot. So finally, rather irritably (I can't stand teasers) I went to sleep. I woke up at about six this morning, and took advantage of her sleep to start kissing her. She let me do that much, but very firmly grabbed my wrist when I tried to go further. My hands were allowed anywhere above the waist, but below it was strictly taboo. She even allowed me to kiss her breasts, and very obviously enjoyed it.

Then she added insult to injury by giving me a lecture about trying to make love to her when I was supposed to be in love with Caroline. I knew she wanted me to protest that I wasn't, but I was so irritated that I didn't. Finally my sexual tension exploded harmlessly, and I was immediately pleased that she was still a virgin as far as I was concerned (sex is a selfish business anyway). At seven o'clock she told me I'd better get up to my own room because the landlady might choose this morning to call in. She has a damnable German coolness and a tendency to lecture, so that I was in a rage with myself for being fool enough to sleep with her. I hate these girls who pretend to offer their bodies, and then reveal that what they *really* want is to stuff their personalities down your throat, make you acknowledge them as *minds*. It makes me thing of that splendid poem of Heine to an ex-mistress who wanted to carry on the relationship on a "spiritual plane," which ends:

> *Your body's love I still desire*
> *For it is young and fair.*
> *Your soul can go and hang itself,*
> *I've soul enough to spare.*

So in a bad temper I came up here and made myself tea, and am now writing this at eight o'clock—the earliest I've been up for years!

All the same, the night wasn't wasted completely, for my annoyance and rejection of her has left me aware of the things I ought to be thinking about. I now open Jean Paul's *Fruit, Flower and Thorn Pieces,* and feel excitement. Yes, the romantics of the 19th century were right; man ought to be more than man, more than a social animal. Too much association with people sickens me. This is not because I dislike people; on the contrary, I like them too much. And yet social intercourse is one thing, real "exchange" another. I don't mean intellectual exchange, but any kind of "giving." This girl Carlotta is not herself a particularly happy person; that is, she's not a particularly fulfilled person, not a grown up person. If she didn't have a desirable body, I wouldn't dream of having any but the most casual relation with her.

Because—this, I suppose is the problem—I can't help

feeling, in certain ways, a kind of "spiritual aristocrat." Pride and egoism, no doubt, but it still has its element of truth. I can sympathize with snobs like Wilde and Yeats in a way, because I transpose their social snobbery onto another level. Hell, all philosophers are snobs. Schopenhauer devoted a lot of space to railing against the mob and declaring that people who made noises should be dealt with sternly by the law. . . .

Nov. 1. A typical November day; drizzle and fog. I love such weather. So do all true Englishmen. (Strange, I suppose, that I think of myself as an Englishman; yet I have a genuine love for England, and a kind of love for Germany, and a loathing for the French, who are a feeble lot.) Why? Because, I suppose, such a day as this is already halfway towards Dickens's foggy nights with the shops filled with holly and Christmas turkeys and Scrooge on his way home through the icy rain.

Last night, suddenly impatient and bored, and also afraid that Carlotta might come and knock on my door, I cycled down to Fleet Street and went into the usual café. Bill Payne came in with another Bill—Bill Fletcher, whom I'd never met. They made an odd pair. Bill was in one of his periodic moods of contempt for all humankind, and even went so far as to advocate dropping hydrogen bombs "to liven people up." His friend Fletcher was a curious type—tall, very good looking in a clean-cut kind of way, with gentle manners and the eyes of a poet. (But he is an engineer—and a successful one.) This man struck me as one of the types I ought to introduce to Gertrude. A pure idealist of a rather tough kind. I mean that he doesn't seem to shrink from life; yet his theories are the most airy-fairy I've ever heard. At one point, he said: "The world is like a brass band marching by, with everybody trying to make as much noise as possible—just a blaring. The music of the spirit is gentler, like the music of violins. . . ." He finally invited us back to his studio, where he spends his evenings painting, and we went (both rather dubiously—neither of us has much sympathy for painting and painters). He has a pleasant studio at the top of a house in Northumberland Avenue. But the paintings were more disconcerting than anything I'd expected. To begin with, all were in very pale pastel shades. Secondly, they were all very symbolic, with lots of weird angelic figures hovering in the air. The one that gave me most of a jar was a picture of a little clerk leaving his home on his way to work, carrying a brief case, wearing his pin-stripes and bowler hat. Above him hovers an angelic figure, with her arms around his neck.

I could see what he was getting at—that the "mystic presences" hover behind the world. What Blake meant when he wrote:

How do you know but every bird that cuts the airy way
Is an immense world of delight, closed to your senses five?

All right, so perhaps there are lots of spirit violins playing inaudibly in Regent Street, and guardian angels hovering over Piccadilly Circus; but all this feeble spirituality irritates me. Fletcher also offered to play us some of his own music. (He seems to be a man with many talents.) He sat at the piano and played us several pieces—all very slow and pensive. Afterwards, I asked him who his favorite composer was, and he said Delius—as if I couldn't have guessed. What baffles me about him is that he's no "sensitive plant," no maladjusted life-hater, but an apparently contented man, married, with a child. Bill and I couldn't make him see that all this "sweetness and light" made his paintings look like soap advertisements, and that no painter ought to stick symbolic angels into his canvases and still call it painting. He just didn't see my point of view, said Cézanne had no "spirituality." Bill got very excited, and started explaining that what the human race needs is torture and crisis, not sweetness and light. He seemed to be against Fletcher's spirituality rather as the Communists used to be against the Salvation Army—because it holds off the true revolution with false hopes and inadequate half measures.

Bill declared he would launch his new magazine with an article entitled: "Bring Back the Rack," a counterblast against the anti-capital-punishment people! He said that if man won't make voluntary efforts to achieve greatness, then he must be driven with a whip, and that the Hitlers and Stalins are the greatest friends of humanity because they have the moral courage to recognize its feebleness and drive it ruthlessly. He calls this "ultimate compassion," and likens it to a surgeon amputating a gangrenous leg.

Poor Bill Fletcher was horrified—he doesn't know about Bill's Welsh habit of stating his case in somewhat rhetorical terms. It was amusing to see them together, but somehow futile, because they had no language in common. Anyway, Bill is too impatient to bother much about language—he would call it hair-splitting to stake out definitions.

We left around midnight, having drunk a dozen cups of poisonously strong tea. Bill's first comment was "What's the use of talking to weak people?" I didn't point out that he had been doing most of the arguing—I'm too lazy when I feel I can't communicate easily. We were both too wide awake to go home, so we went back to the Fleet Street café and sat there until three this morning, talking about the need for a new literary age, and speculating on whether it would help if we assassinated John Lehmann and Stephen Spender. After talks like this, I feel better; it seems to me that even if I'm cooped up in this room for another five years, at least I'm doing something active about changing things—planning a revolution. Probably it's as well that I remain unknown as long as possible.

I cycled to Caroline's flat and let myself in with my key. She didn't even wake up when I got into bed.

I forgot to mention that I asked Bill Fletcher to come and meet Gertrude.

Nov. 2. Complications continue. Carlotta came up to my room last night to ask if I was annoyed with her. When I said I wasn't, she asked me down for supper. I refused, claiming I'd eaten (I hate "having supper" like that—too sociable). But she came up at about eleven with some German drink—Steinhager, I think she called it—and she sat around talking to me about her family. As I felt bored and sleepy, I finally suggested that she get into bed. She said she wouldn't, that it would be silly with her own bed downstairs, but made no move to go, so I simply undressed and climbed in, and after a few more hesitations she did the same. I don't know why, because she was still sternly virginal—kept on her slip and pants as before. I suppose she may be afraid of sex, because she's happy enough to be kissed and caressed. Or perhaps she wants to get her claws in deeper before she gives way. After half an hour of frustrations that were as shattering as braking violently in a car, I turned over and went to sleep, and was asleep when she got up this morning (one advantage of staying on my home ground!). She actually brought me coffee at half past nine, and sat on the bed, and behaved more affectionately than when undressed and in bed. I shall never understand women. Again, I am face to face with this stupid conjuring trick of sex. This morning, after she'd gone, I reread my entry about the time she fell off the ladder. I can still recall my excitement at the sight of her legs. Why, then, don't I feel anything analogous when I watch her taking her clothes off to get into bed? I remember when I first read *Wuthering Heights* I was irritated by the narrator's confession of his emotional capriciousness—how he fell violently in love with a girl at a watering place, but as soon as she obviously returned his affection, lost all interest in her and fled. This seems to me childish and boring. I cannot bear such people when I meet them—and I'm always meeting them. (The other night, for example, in the café with Bill, some mincing queer called Denison came over; great expert on ballet—he thinks—and contemptuous when I said I thought Nijinsky was important in other ways than as a dancer. Anyway, this Denison struck me as the arrogant, immature, capricious type, and I loathed him.) And yet in spite of my hatred of emotional capriciousness, I find this physical capriciousness deep in me, and I can do nothing about it. Again, I suppose it's the abstract feminine that allures us, and the personal contact spoils it. The personality blankets the sexual drive in rather the same way that sex is less satisfying wearing a contraceptive. (I recall an interesting instance of this. When I first went to bed with Caroline—before she visited the birth-control clinic —she insisted on my wearing a rubber, and I saw the sense of this. And yet one night, as I was making love to her, I felt irritated by it, and by maneuvering my hands—which were under her bottom—I managed to get the damn thing off without her knowing; I then experienced a tremendous excitement as I continued to make love to her, feeling as if we were now *really* having sex. The feeling was so strong that I felt a compulsion not to withdraw. I realized this was stupid, that I didn't want her to have a baby; yet my response to this thought was: So what? It cost me an enormous effort to do the sensible thing—like Ulysses hearing the Sirens' song. This seems like a plain case of the Life Force trying to persuade us to perpetuate the species; yet I wonder whether the motive of the confidence trick was as simple as that?)

Nov. 3. I spent most of yesterday at Gertrude's, helping her redecorate the bathroom. It was another windy, rainy day, and after lunch we lay on the settee in front of the fire, listening to the rain—the pleasantest occupation I know—and ended by making love. She's funny. She obviously finds it incredibly wicked and exciting to do it downstairs in the daytime. This makes it seem quite different. She also took off her dress. Afterwards, I refused to give her the dress and her pants until she'd put on the kettle for tea. She went off into the kitchen, but some tradesman rang the doorbell, and she came flying back in as if the day of judgment had arrived. Incidentally, she tells me that the Jehovah's Witnesses suspect her of sexual immorality, and Brother Robbins gave her a grave little sermon on the subject the other day.

She told me she had a letter from Oliver Glasp;* apparently he's in Lancaster. I can't imagine what he's doing there. Gertrude says he's got the Preston art gallery to give him an exhibition, and they've bought two of his paintings. He inquired about Christine, but not about me. I asked her not to mention that I've brought Christine here. He'd probably suspect my motives! It's a pity that Christine's father stopped her coming to see me; she's one of the brightest children I ever met. There was even a time when Gertrude thought of adopting her and sending her to a university.

We had a curious evening. I had asked Bill Fletcher to come over to meet Gertrude. But she told me she'd agreed to let a Yugoslav friend use her sitting room for a meeting. There was nothing for it but to sit through the meeting. This proved to be unexpectedly interesting. Fletcher arrived at half past seven and had supper with Gertrude and me. Finally, the Yugoslav came, a man called Georgi—I can't pronounce his surname. Apparently he is changing houses this week, and can't hold the meeting in his own place. He was a middle-aged man, obviously Jewish, with a gentle, broad face, brown eyes with the liquid expression of a spaniel, and a large waistline. He was thrown out of Yugoslavia years ago for Red sympathies, then out of Germany in the thirties. He seemed to love music, which recommended him to me, and we immediately got into a discussion about Bruckner and Mahler. At eight o'clock, the rest of the meeting began to arrive—all very young men, and a couple of girls; pleasant, naïve young chaps, but they didn't strike me as particularly bright. Finally,

* Oliver Glasp, the well-known painter, had also been a friend of Austin Nunne and of Gertrude Quincey. In 1954 he met the girl whom I shall call Christine, who was then ten years old. His curious emotional relationship with her led to a nervous breakdown, and he left London suddenly in November 1955. At the time of writing, I had heard nothing from him for over a year.

we settled down to the meeting. Georgi talked of tolerance and universal love, and advocated complete anarchism, with everybody "doing as they pleased." The young men all listened with complete seriousness, their chins in their hands. After half an hour of this kind of thing—all very vague—we had coffee, and Georgi threw open the discussion. Bill Fletcher started in, very enthusiastic, by asking about the role of the spirit in this ideal community. He got the shock of his life when Georgi scornfully dismissed the idea of spirit as a trick of the priests. (It was obvious they were talking at complete cross purposes.) Georgi now launched into a lengthy denunciation of religion, calling priests "black vultures" and scavengers, and declaring that the free man can live without such illusions. Fletcher gently insisted that he meant "spirit" in the sense in which you would talk of the spirit of Beethoven or Mahler. Georgi retorted that in that sense, they would do better to discuss Beethoven's music—or better still, listen to it—rather than talking as if "spirit" were something that could be sold in bottles for the nourishment of his Utopia. (At this point I got rather tired, didn't feel inclined to sort out their beautiful linguistic tangle, and sneaked off into the kitchen to have a little of the kind of spirit that comes in bottles.)

When it was all over—well after midnight—and we were in bed, I asked Gertrude what she thought of Georgi's denunciation of religion. She said mildly that she thought he was a "good man," so it didn't matter much how he expressed himself; she then turned her attention to lovemaking. I'm convinced that, like all women, her world is "personal"; she wants love and security, and she'd cheerfully fix her affections on the devil if he could give her these.

But I left here this morning feeling irritable and oppressed. What do I care about Georgi and Fletcher and their silly wrangles that spring out of a desire to talk and be sociable rather than any need to arrive at results? I'd like to be away from here—at least away from this area. I think of Oliver with a kind of envy, remembering his old room in Whitechapel, his obsessed pictures; he somehow succeeded in living like a monk. I want to live like a monk in theory. In practice, I keep getting overdoses of people, which is rather like getting yourself blind drunk on rum. The taste of it stays with you for weeks afterwards, and the mere thought of its taste is enough to make the stomach lurch. You can make yourself sick on an overdose of almost anything. Well, I've got people-poisoning at present, and I've been suffering from a mild case of it for what seems years.

I sit here, in this room, and the problem seems at once immense and nonexistent. Life is a desert of freedom; but because it is a desert, we are too free. It is like being suspended in a total void, with no gravity; because you can do anything, you do nothing, and every effort to change your position costs immense energy because there's nothing to brace yourself against; try to move your arm backward, and your whole body turns, leaving the arm in the same position. I sometimes used to wonder how certain writers could spend their whole lives in an unchanging state of despair or feebleness. Now I know; they imagine that the chance position into which freedom has flung them is a law of the universe.

Nov. 4. Things are coming to a head sooner than I expected. These complications bore me.

Last night, I met Carlotta in the hall and asked her to come and have a drink. She knew what I had in mind, and came up with her Steinhager, and we drank some wine and she cooked me some frankfurters with spinach. At about midnight, without even asking her, I undressed and got into bed. And without any comment, she went out. I assumed she had gone back to her own room; but she actually went to the bathroom, and came and climbed into bed just as I was dozing off. I woke up and tried kissing her, but a hand on her thigh got firmly pushed away. So I decided to make the best of it; I said good night, turned over, and went to sleep. After half an hour or so, her movements woke me up; evidently my indifference didn't suit her either. So I turned over again, moved on top of her (which she doesn't mind, provided I restrict myself to kisses) and allowed myself to get excited. Although she was wearing a slip, it was above her waist. These girls puzzle me. She is in bed with a naked man; she is wearing nothing but her pants, allowing him to lie on top of her and get her into a state of sexual excitement—and yet for some weird reason of prudery or virtue, she denies him the "final privilege." I carried on like this for about half an hour, then finally reached down and pulled aside the leg of her pants. She still showed no sign of objecting, so I hastily carried on. However, I'd barely achieved my objective when the accumulated tension of half an hour exploded and I was forced to withdraw ignominiously. I decided this irony was too much, and turned over and went to sleep. I woke up again a few hours later, but didn't feel the faintest inclination to take advantage of my new status as her lover. I realized, to my dismay, that somehow I didn't *want* this to turn into another "regular relationship" of the Caroline type.

She slept later than usual. Suddenly, I was awakened by Caroline entering the room. My first relief at seeing Carlotta was gone vanished when I saw that her skirt was still on the chair; a few moments later, she came in in her slip. Caroline was just looking pointedly at the skirt, and starting to ask me whom it belonged to. They stared at one another with hostility; Caroline merely said: "I'll see you later," and went out. Carlotta only said: "I'm sorry, but she's bound to find out sooner or later, isn't she?"

I only turned over to the wall, thinking: "Damn all women." I didn't ask either of them into my life; why do they have to start behaving as if they'd bought me?

Later, Carlotta brought me coffee, and got into bed herself to drink it. This was obviously by way of consolidating her position; I found I no longer had to resist a temptation to undress her; I didn't feel any inclination at all. She asked me if I was in love with Caroline; I said no, but I was fond of her, and didn't want to hurt her. Finally, Carlotta said: "Well, you'd better go to her then, hadn't you?," and got out of bed. I didn't call her back; I felt all this was a kind of blackmail, but it was passing over my head.

However, I went down to the coffee house to see Caroline (she works there two mornings a week now). To my relief, she didn't show any sign of jealousy, and was obviously perfectly ready to believe me when I said that very little had happened. I swore that I hadn't made love to the girl (I thought my abortive attempt last night didn't count), and said, truthfully, that I hadn't expected her to sleep with me last night, but that she'd climbed into my bed. Caroline declared that she had noticed a long time ago that Carlotta had "designs" on me, claimed that Carlotta always scowled when she opened the door to her, and said that I ought to move out of the place. I was so charmed by Caroline's good humor and lack of reproach that I agreed to look for a new place this afternoon. (Caroline said I could move in with her for a few days, but I thought of Madeleine, and refused.) So this afternoon, I took the tube over to Whitechapel, and spent the afternoon looking around. Just as I'd about given up, disgusted with poky rooms where the landlady's family have non-stop right of way and the house smells of cabbage, I had some luck. My friend the barber in Hanbury Street told me about a flat only a few minutes away, and I found the owner and looked at it. He wanted thirty pounds for "fittings," but the rent is 25 bob a week—five shillings less than my present room—so I wrote him a check on the spot and took it. It hasn't much furniture, and is at the very top of the house, but apart from that, it seems too good to be true. I rang Caroline at school, told her to meet me, and took her to see it.

There is only one minor problem. When I got back, I felt I had to go and tell Carlotta immediately—I would have felt too much of a coward otherwise. But as usual, I tried to soften it all I could, said I wasn't leaving because of her, and hinted that this room is too close to Gertrude. Dishonest, I suppose, but I detest hurting people. Finally, I said that I hoped I would still see her. Unfortunately, she immediately took me up on this, and has offered to help me move in! Luckily, Carlotta's tied up with this house a great deal and is afraid of the landlady, who lives only a few doors away and loves to drop in unexpectedly.

Nov. 5. For two days I've been involved in the loathsome process of moving and trying to get this place into livable condition. I decided I could move my stuff with the bike in about three journeys, but it actually took seven. Even then, Gertrude brought over a load of stuff in her car. I told her frankly why I was leaving—she got very upset at first—and now she seems reconciled to it, although she hates Whitechapel. I am now alone again, it is half past eight, and there are sounds of fireworks from the street; I passed a magnificent bonfire in the middle of a piece of waste ground two streets away. Yes, I think I shall enjoy living here; perhaps I can get more solitude in the midst of so many strangers. The district reminds me constantly of Austin and Oliver, but I suppose this will pass.

Strange, how a mere change of environment seems to give you a better grip on living. Temporary, I suppose. For a person like me, life is bound to be difficult. Wells says somewhere that "we intellectual workers" are like the earliest amphibians dragging themselves out of the sea and learning to walk on land. Man's natural sphere is everyday life, action, movement, not sitting in a room, thinking. The amphibian on land naturally finds it hard work moving around on his flippers, and will continue to do so until he develops legs. I still have no legs. Besides, my kind of thinking is a kind that is foreign to the human race. We know how to think *objectively*, about mathematics or philosophy. But to try to force your own life into a strait jacket of thought, to see meanings in it—that is infinitely more difficult. When we used to play blindman's buff as kids, they blindfolded you, then turned you around half a dozen times to make you lose your sense of direction. Well,

life is like that, only a thousand times more so. You are
dropped into the world, turned around and upside down, hit
on the head, stupefied with noise and lights, and then told to
guess "what life is all about." Just to make it more difficult,
they repeat the bewilderment treatment every few days, just
in case you're succeeding. Or it's like Theseus' maze, where
you're continually crossing your own tracks. This diary, like all
my writing, is my own attempt to maintain a sense of direction
by a ball of thread; but it's not nearly so efficient as Theseus'
thread, because I cross my own track every few weeks, and
realize that a new "idea" that has excited me is only a slightly
different version of an idea I wrote in my journal two years
ago. Yes, this is the problem: we try to find a way in the maze
by thought, by applying the methods of science to actual living,
but so far, the results are not very spectacular.

Later. I've just had a curious experience. When I'd written the
above, my pen ran out of ink, and I discovered I'd left the
ink behind in Camden Town. So I went out and bought some.
Then I had a walk around, to stretch my legs, and eventually
found myself outside a public library. Naturally, I went in.
I found an interesting book on the Faust legend, and sat down
in a quiet corner to read it. From where I was sitting, I could
see across to the desk where the assistants stamp books, and I
couldn't help noticing one girl, dressed in red, who was returning books to their shelves. She wasn't particularly pretty
—rather bony, and in her late twenties—but something about
the way she was dressed and the way she walked aroused my
interest. It may only have been that her red skirt was rather
tight, but she made me think immediately of bed. As I watched
her, a man came to the bookshelves near where I was sitting,
and looked through the section on magic, ghosts, etc. He also
struck me as an interesting type—a big man, running to fat,
about 35 or 40, with a completely bald head. If he were an
actor, he's the sort I'd choose to play the mad scientist. This
man also glanced once or twice at the girl in red; then he took

a book, and came and sat within a few feet of me, on the other side of the table. I felt him looking at me, but pretended to be reading. After a few minutes, I heard him muttering something under his breath, and I looked at him cautiously over the top of my book. He had odd round eyes with a bulgy look, and he was staring at the girl who was now back at the desk. Suddenly I experienced a feeling of tension —the kind of thing you might feel if you went into a room where two people hate one another, although you've never met either of them before. Then, a moment later, the girl came over to our bookshelf, carrying a pile of books. The man looked away as she came toward us, then looked at her again when she had turned her back. Suddenly, she looked around, first at me, then at the man, wearing a startled expression, as if one of us had pinched her. Then an odd thing happened. I was watching her cautiously, sitting well back with my book propped on the desk. She stood staring at the man, quite openly, and went very pale, then very red. He was still staring back at her. Then she took a step forward, as if she wanted to hit him, then stopped and turned away. At this point, he said: "Excuse me, miss. I wonder if you could help me?" He had a heavy, actor's type of voice, rather rich, with a faint lisp. He got up and went over to her, then stood there, very close, talking to her in a low voice. I was fascinated by it, because for some reason, I felt certain she didn't know him, and that he had noticed in her exactly what I had noticed: a kind of sexual tension. He was standing there, facing her as he talked, but much closer than you would normally stand if you were asking a librarian an innocent question. Her back was toward me, so that I couldn't see what was happening, but I could swear he placed a hand on her breast. Then she said, in an odd, strained voice: "It's in the special collection, sir, in the basement. If you'd like to come this way, I'll show you." For a moment, he looked at me, and his look was as clear as if he'd winked at me and said: "You see, I've done it." As they walked away, he had his hand lightly on the back of her dress.

I sat there, trying to untangle the knot of lust inside me.

I've heard that certain animals perform a ritual courtship in public, but this was the first time I'd seen a man seduce a strange woman in a library.

About ten minutes later, they came upstairs, and he went out immediately. When I went out, I looked at her, and she looked back at me and blushed.

There may, of course, be another explanation. He may have been her lover; perhaps they had quarreled and he'd come to make it up with her. Or perhaps I was imagining it all, and he was really interested in the special collection. But I don't believe either of these explanations.

A Frenchman said "Women like to be violated." While ⌐n't think this is true, I *do* believe that certain women ⌐nate a kind of helplessness toward some men. This is the ⌐site of the come-hither sexiness of certain attractive ⌐en (Caroline, for example). I wonder if loneliness and ⌐al frustration can give some women a kind of *aura*, some- ⌐ like the smell given off by a female animal in heat? This ⌐what I seemed to sense about the girl in red as soon as I ⌐ her; something about her conveyed an invitation to take ⌐brutally, and I got the impression that the bald-headed man had done just that.

All this has made me unpleasantly excited, and unable to continue the train of thought that I started before I went out to buy ink. I shall try to sleep.

Later. I feel tired and depressed. My vitality has sunk so low that I can't even fall asleep. Why? I suspect that, somewhere down inside me, there's a knob like the volume-control on my radio, and it turns my vitality up or down. I wish I could find it. . . .

It's stupid. I have too much freedom. Consequently I don't know what to do or where to go. I'm now in a position I would have envied three years ago. I have a room of my own, enough money to live without working, and a few records and books. And yet I need to distract myself with seductions.

But there is always a good way of overcoming this "excess

of freedom"—that is, to make an exercise of recalling the worst moments in your life, or in other people's lives. When he was in front of the firing squad, Dostoevsky must have felt that he knew what life was all about. I often meditate on that episode in Lawrence's *Seven Pillars* when the Turkish leader has an old man thrown into a furnace, and then orders everyone to listen; there is a crashing noise, and the leader observes: "Their heads always pop like that." I imagine that I am standing there, waiting to be thrown into the furnace; all the life and power in me rises up, and suddenly I know a little about the *value of life.*

But what is it that actually happens in these moments? It is worth analyzing, because I suppose it is the whole subject of this diary, and of all my work. It is not that you *see* the value of life. It is more complicated. The *energy* in you rises up to meet the emergency. It is as if life said: "You are allowed only so many gallons of energy per day, but for special emergencies, you can draw upon ten times that amount." That immense flow of energy is vision. We usually put so little energy into living. Quite small inconveniences can make us think that it's not worth being alive, or at least, make us temporarily incapable of pleasure. We so easily relapse into a state of sullenness. "If life can treat me as badly as this, I'm damned if I'm going to put any energy into living." And, like angry children, we refuse to be made to laugh. Now if, at that moment, we were confronted with a real threat to life, that refusal to enjoy living would vanish immediately.

It seems to me that this refusal to enjoy living is somehow the basis of the whole problem—the biggest problem of all. Because what we are doing in this moment is *assigning a fixed value to life.* Most of us need much less than Job's suffering to refuse to make any further effort. We lie down in the middle of the road, like Ivan Karamazov's sinner, and refuse to budge. The woman in the local café has a fixed scowl of bad temper on her face, and even small inconveniences make her thoroughly impolite (nobody can bear the red-headed

bitch). Obviously, she is within the great gray shadow of boredom. A more precise name is needed for this bad temper, this devaluation of life, this decision that it isn't worth making any further effort, this area of human emotion where pleasure fails to arouse a smile (although we still object as vigorously to pain). I suppose it could be called the indifference threshold. *This indifference threshold is everything that is wrong with human nature,* and therefore corresponds to what the Catholics call original sin.

We accept pleasure as our right, as an animal basking in the sun accepts sunlight as its right. But there is no reason at all why our lives *ought* to be pleasant. If they are to be made pleasant, worth living, then it must be with infinite calculation —just as an animal's life cannot be pleasant because the sun goes in and the season of frost and hail arrives. "Natural life," "taking life as it comes," is death. We do not yet know how to live; we haven't even the faintest idea. But pain does make us think; and so it ought to: make us calculate how to avoid it. And then we learn that avoiding it is not enough, because a life without pain is not necessarily very satisfactory.

This, I would say, is about the point at which the human race has arrived at present—at least, our little Western bit of it. This idea that "freedom from pain is not enough" is now a cultural cliché; it has been said in a hundred different ways by a hundred different authors. In Shakespeare's time, a play about *boredom* would have been unthinkable. Now we have an extensive literature of boredom—a great deal of it Russian, beginning with Dostoevsky's *Possessed.* That is why we think Dostoevsky so great: all his work is completely preoccupied with these problems that are becoming the great problems for the human race. Kierkegaard was the first to give boredom its central place when he stated his principle "All men are bores" (and, therefore, are bored), and pointed out that there is only one satisfactory way of overcoming boredom: not conquering the world, like Alexander (or leaping into bed with different women, like me), but developing an inner concentra-

tion—Shotover's seventh degree of concentration. This inner concentration is what happened to Dostoevsky in front of the firing squad. It is also what happens in a sexual orgasm. I am actually aware that my inner being *contracts* and concentrates. It is like a large, diffused pool of light; the orgasm is like a magnifying glass that makes it concentrate into one tiny burning point.

But we're so horribly dependent on external stimuli . . . I scream at my energies like a sergeant major, trying to force them to form into ranks and concentrate for an attack; they're a sloppy bunch, and they refuse to stand together; they lounge around in corners of my being, smoking and telling dirty stories. The threat of death gets them together all right.

What, then, is the answer? I know one: we have to get used to using a lot of energy, to driving ourselves. Graham Greene's priest, about to be executed, reflects that it would have been so easy to be a saint. Well, it *is* easy. Yet this tremendous dullness blankets us.

The will is the compeller of destiny. Merely for the will to spring erect and *want something* is enough to set the wheels into motion. If we all realized this, we might will more. What deters us is the possibility of wasting our efforts. Kafka manages to catch an extreme sense of this waste of effort, this lack of connection between effort and achievement, so that whenever heroes set out to do something, it never gets done; he is abnormally aware of the feebleness of the human will power. (This doesn't make him a good writer; I can't stand him.)

The good moment comes when we ask clearly: What do we want, and how can it be achieved? Then we are in motion as human beings ought to be in motion *all the time,* every moment of their lives. They should encourage themselves to ask "What do I want?," to encourage the imagination to take greater and greater leaps into possibility. This is what human life ought to be; not this everlasting drifting and marking time. After writing these words, I look out of my window at the people in the street, and the sense of irony invades me:

that is, the disparity between what should be and what is. I can *see* something of what the human race is capable of. I am not speaking about the superman; all the talk for and against the superman is balls, missing the real point. I am talking about human engineering. *I am evolution made conscious.* I am trying to help life forward, or "in its struggle upward." I look at these shabby people walking past; they are nice enough, most of them good, decent human beings—amazingly decent considering the circumstances they live in; it's amazing there aren't more criminals trying to get their own back on life. But they aren't good enough. *Why are they like this?* Is it all a part of "God's will?" No, I can't believe it. Evolution is doing its best, in its fumbling way; it has taken a lot of trouble with the human race. Every one of us is more complex than a thousand electronic brains. But some of its best ideas have canceled each other out. Civilization, language and science were some of the best ideas it ever had, and they have poised man on a springboard from which he could become anything, a kind of god. But before man can go any further, he needs to develop a quite new faculty—the faculty I am trying so painfully to develop, sitting in front of this typewriter for days, a new way of *grasping* life. They say that certain fishes have nerves in their sides that register the pressure of every current that flows against them, so that if an enemy comes, they can sense him by the changed pressure of water long before they see him. Well, this is what we all need, a new sensitivity to living. It is not simply a more analytical approach to life, although that is a great part of it. These people in the street all take life as it comes. Tonight they feel drunk and happy; in two days' time, they might be completely miserable; but they never try to connect the two states, and ask which was the "right" reaction to life, or how far either of them are right. They crystallize their conclusions about life in a few convenient rules of thumb—a stitch in time saves nine, never say die, no use crying over spilt milk, and so on. They live from minute to minute, learning almost nothing. We must develop a type of man who carries analysis *in his sides,* like the nerves of the fish. He will overcome this immense obstacle to the human race, this original sin, this indifference threshold. The problem of why we die must be attacked as scientifically as any other problem of civilization. We developed the long-playing record because it was inconvenient to put a symphony on records that play for only five minutes a side. We must develop the long-playing life, because it is almost impossible to do anything worth while for evolution when the side comes to an end every 70 years. At the moment, this is unthinkable because people get fed up even with their mere 70 years. Even Shaw declared that he was tired of life and wanted to die. So the first problem is the conquest of boredom. For there will be no point in living longer until we can also live more powerfully, until my brains no longer feel like treacle when I get up in the morning and my body refuses to obey my mind, and my consciousness is like a pond that has been stirred up by cattle drinking and stamping in it. My mind is clear tonight because I've changed my lodging and have been stimulated by the change. But I must learn to make my consciousness clear at will, learn to defeat this sleepiness.

Nov. 6. A few of the disadvantages of this place begin to appear. I seem to have a madman below me who is a musician of some kind, and he plays the piano at all hours. At first I enjoyed it—he played a Beethoven sonata—but after 24 hours of the racket, even the singing of angels would become intolerable to a writer who wants to concentrate. I finally went downstairs and banged on his door, meaning to ask him politely if he could restrict his playing to the daylight hours, or at least stop before six in the morning. However, the playing went on, and no one came to the door, so I can only presume he's deaf. I have played my gramophone at top volume for hours by way of getting my own back, but to no effect. The only thing that occurs to me is to give a noisy party here that will go on all night, and make sure that everybody dances. When he protests, I can offer him a deal!

The main problem with this place is that it hasn't got a phone, so I'm more or less out of touch with Gertrude and Caroline unless I go out and phone them.

Anyway, I have a suspicion that Caroline is having an affair with someone at her school. Madeleine makes sly references to "Peter" and Caroline looks annoyed.

Still—on my central problem, which I must pursue in spite of these stupidities: why is the human memory so short? There is more truth than we realize in the Victorian cliché about "counting your blessings." I suppose the Life Force wants us to be perpetually unsatisfied, to get the maximum of work out of us. It's like a man who climbs a mountain because he hates the plains, but every time he sits down for a rest, he discovers that the ground is still there, right below him, and that it rises, like the sea.

It is easy to oversimplify this problem. Blake says that we must "love without the help of anything on earth." This is nonsense. Certain things are necessary. We have to breathe, we have to eat and drink. I would find it appallingly difficult to live without books and music, although I daresay I could force myself.

But we need to develop a kind of spring mechanism about reality, so that we can withdraw and then return with greater force. If my head is held under water for two minutes, the air tastes incredibly sweet to me when I can breathe again. If I hear no music for months, a Beethoven symphony can seem almost unbearably satisfying.

The mind is the "spring" that could hurl us back at the things we love so that their impact continues to be intensely satisfying. If the mind could be used properly, our love of life could be intensified tenfold. Unfortunately, the mind is a feeble spring that seems to be unable to move the weight of our emotions and reactions.

Yes, the strength of the mind must be intensified. At present, it is like a tiny engine in a monstrous and heavy car. We need artificial aids to keep up our appetite for life.

Later. When I had written the above lines, I decided that I needed the artificial aid of a bottle of beer to wash down my lunch, so I went to the pub on the corner. There I ordered a cheese sandwich and a Guinness. Sitting in the opposite corner, I noticed a man and a woman who immediately interested me. The man was obviously Jewish, wore very shabby, dark clothes, but had a good face—big forehead, the bulging eyes of a crank or an artist, weak mouth, yet something strangely attractive about him, perhaps because he reminds me of a picture of Mahler. The woman was delicious, but I can't describe her, except to say that she was dark, looked tired, and was obviously a great deal younger than the man. I found her so delightful that I kept watching them. They were eating sandwiches, and both drinking half pints of beer. Usually, I don't notice people, but I suppose the woman attracted me. From watching them, I gathered they were either lovers or married; he kept smiling at her with a kind of pity, then reaching over and touching her hand. Then he'd forget her and go off into abstraction; then, when she spoke to him, look at her as if he was surprised she was still there.

I finished my beer at about the same time that they did; as they got up, I also got up and followed them out. Then, to my surprise, they stopped in front of my door, and began searching for a key. I came up to them, and produced my own key, and asked them if they were trying to get in. It turned out that they live underneath me! I asked: "Oh, you're the man who plays the piano all night?" He smiled, as if I was paying him a compliment, but she looked embarrassed, and said she hoped it hadn't kept me awake. I am always a coward in matters like this; I said no. By this time, we had reached their door, and they went in. I'm glad now that I didn't start a quarrel with him.

No doubt they will turn out to be a couple of bores with commonplace minds. Still, she's delightful. I'd like to get to know them. . . .

Nov. 7. Gertrude came over to see me last night, and the evening turned into something like a quarrel—the first we've had. I'm not sure what she has on her mind, but I don't really care. Possibly she thinks I moved here to avoid her, or perhaps she suspects I still see Caroline. She was curious about this journal, which I carefully locked away when she arrived. I told her I was writing a novel about sex, and she immediately said she thought I was far too interested in sex. I suspect Brother Robbins has been preaching at her again. I didn't feel like arguing—it would be pointless. I refused to go back to Hampstead with her, we had a meal in a café across the road, and hardly spoke. Afterward, she said she had to get back home, and drove off. I was feeling pleased about this. I'd detest hurting her and making a move to break with her, but if she wants to cause the break. . . . Just as I was about to go on writing, she came back in tears, said she didn't think I cared about her any more, and I had to soothe her. Naturally, we ended in bed. When she left at about two in the morning, I sat looking out of the window at the streetlamp and thinking: "Fool, fool."

But I tried explaining to her that I can never look at sex as she does. For her, sex is either "lust," and therefore wicked, or an expression of a lifelong devotion. I don't care much about either. Lifelong devotion is all very well, but what does it matter when it means only a relation between two inefficient machines, both condemned to death? I have been reading Wells's *Star Begotten* today, and it strikes me that I am a "Martian"—one of those people who just doesn't seem to feel and think in the categories that make other people feel comfortable. (Camus wrote about the same idea several years later, but not nearly so excitingly as Wells.) It annoys me to feel that I haven't yet started living, simply because I don't know where to start untangling the mess of human life. I cannot understand why it doesn't worry other people. I feel like a motorist who notices a strong smell of burning and a grinding noise from inside the engine, and I want to stop the car and have a look. But everybody else drives along happily, ignoring the smell of burning and the grinding, apparently feeling that everything is as it should be.

Hence my absorption in sex. Because there are rare moments—not necessarily at the moment of orgasm, but often throughout the whole act—when the burning stops. Or, to change the metaphor, when some slight adjustment seems to set the whole being in tune—like turning the knob on a radio and suddenly getting a station with absolute clarity, without interference. This is what Yeats means:

> *What were all the world's alarms*
> *To mighty Paris when he found*
> *Sleep upon a golden bed*
> *That first dawn, in Helen's arms?*

These lines have always moved me. We contain within ourselves power to overcome all the degradations and irritations, to leave them behind as finally as an adult man leaves behind mumps and measles. The sexual act is an insight into power, a kind of invitation to greatness.

We know nothing about the movement of destiny. We are still children in the science of living. We live clumsily, by rule of thumb, wasting 99 per cent of our time and energy. And yet that moment "on a golden bed" promises a new kind of man.

It is true that sex cannot always bring this revelation. Yeats is right—it comes to a Paris who has gone to a great deal of trouble to get Helen into bed, to a Faust on his first night with Marguerite. I suppose we take sex too casually. But sex is an act of magic, an incantation of the unseen, the strangely intelligent and patient forces of evolution.

Later. The business of the man downstairs becomes more intriguing. I have discovered his wife's name—Diana. This doesn't suit her, as she doesn't look in the least like a queen and huntress, and isn't fair either. She has some of the loveliest eyes I've ever seen, and a curious, pointed little chin. I went out shopping half an hour ago, and when I came in, found her sitting halfway up the stairs massaging her eyelids as if she felt dizzy; a monstrous box of groceries—mostly cans—blocked the stairs. I asked her if I could carry it, and she looked worried and said she could manage it. I asked her if she felt all right, and she said yes, she'd found the box rather heavy. I found her quite stunning—she's the type who immediately arouses my protective instinct. I think she must have noticed this, because she looked embarrassed and tried to let me past. I insisted on carrying up the box anyway. She stood outside her door, key in hand, waiting for me to go, as if she was afraid I might see the inside of her room, so I came up. When I'd been in here five minutes, the woman from the flat above came down to ask me if I had a shilling for her meter (I think she really wanted to have a look at me)—a pleasant old thing whose husband works in the market. When I gave her the shilling, she stood at the door and talked, and told me that she thought the man downstairs was mad. She also hinted at something else—I don't know whether she meant drug addiction or simply alcohol, and I didn't want to press her. Apparently my neighbor is called Kirsten, and makes some kind of a living doing something or other for a music publisher. His wife has to go out to work to keep them going—she works in some small hosiery place in Sidney Street. She also hinted that the wife has admirers; I don't know whether she meant that she's actually unfaithful, but the old lady seemed to imply that she wouldn't blame her, since the husband is dotty. But she said that Kirsten thinks himself a great composer, which arouses my interest.

Nov. 7. Letter from Caroline this morning, explaining that an actor wants to marry her; she explains that she would rather marry me, but that she doesn't feel she should pass up this opportunity if I don't want to.

Nov. 8. Caroline came over last night to explain why she has to break with me. She seems to have an absolute obsession about getting married. Some small-part film actor has fallen for her. I told her that it would be insane of me to marry, since I haven't enough money for both of us to live. She immediately said that she wouldn't mind working. I was forced to do a noble act—tell her I couldn't stand in her way, etc. Finally, she said good-by, and that she'd keep in touch, and went. I got undressed for bed. Two minutes later, she came back, took off her coat and dress, and climbed into bed, saying: "Oh, well, I may as well stay till morning." We had such a splendid night that I felt like asking her to jilt the actor and marry me.

Still, she's gone now, and I feel rather pleased—I don't know why, because I was fond of Caroline, and expect I always shall be. There's something rather brave and decent about her. But Hesse is right; there's a magic in each new beginning, and in most ends too.

Oh damn all this stupidity. What do I care what impression I make on people? It's because we waste our lives caring about other people that most of us remain morons. The only thing I care about is this problem of consciousness. One of these days I'll crack it, learn to increase my consciousness as easily as I can turn up the flame of an oil lamp.

Later. I have just spent an evening with my mad composer and his wife. He's far more interesting than the old woman gave me to understand. I was playing Martinu's fifth symphony when he knocked on my door and asked me what it was! I invited him to come in and hear it. He obviously didn't much want to—seemed very shy. But I let him listen without trying to make conversation, and he insisted on hearing it all the way through.

I should mention that I had seen his wife, earlier in the day, walking along the Whitechapel Road with a flashy man in tweeds—looked like a bookmaker. I presume this is one of the "admirers" the old woman talked about. When she saw me, she looked embarrassed, and turned in the opposite direction.

Anyway, the husband vanished after I'd played him the record, hardly bothering to say thank you. I began to see what the old woman meant when she called him eccentric. I was just about to start cooking my supper, an hour later, when someone knocked on my door. To my surprise, it was the wife. She explained that her husband wanted to know if I'd like to join them for supper. When I said I'd be delighted, she looked embarrassed, came into the room, and then asked me if I'd mind not mentioning that I'd seen her with a man today! I assured her that I wouldn't dream of it. She then started to explain to me that nothing was "going on," that the man was an old admirer who wouldn't leave her alone, and that she simply didn't want to worry her husband. But she looked so guilty as she said it that I found it hard to believe her. Then she added: "You see, my husband is a very talented man, and I don't want to distract his mind from his work." I suspect she was a little resentful about having to ask me to supper, but I was too curious to get to know them to refuse.

I guessed that there wouldn't be much to drink, so I went out and got two bottles of wine before I joined them. I discovered later that I couldn't have hit on a better way of making him talk. When I went in, he seemed embarrassed, and asked me if I'd excuse him while he finished working. He was scribbling away on music paper (I gathered later that he was making a piano arrangement of some light opera by Reynaldo Hahn). His wife laid the table and hardly spoke a word. The place was fantastically untidy, and I began to wonder if I hadn't made a mistake in coming down. Then it turned out that she was going to produce fish, which didn't go with the red wine, and it really seemed that some fate was out to make the evening a fiasco.

For the first ten minutes of the meal, he hardly said a word, and she asked me polite questions about my writing. I began to wonder why they had invited me. However, we opened the wine—I needed it; Diana's cooking is excellent and I was hungry. Then we started to talk about Schoenberg, whom Kirsten had known in Germany in 1930; he drank a quantity of the wine, and suddenly became very lively. I find it difficult to describe Kirsten. A curiously weak, eager looking man—at least, that is the first impression. When he gets carried away by talk, the weakness disappears. He has fine eyes, like his wife, very deep, and almost round, with huge eyelids. A tremendous forehead, a small, thin mouth with a sensuous lower lip that would give an expression of cruelty to most men, and a yellowish complexion.

As soon as his wife saw that I was listening to him with attention, and didn't seem disposed to smile at some of his absurdities, she became far more friendly. I can see that she is certain that he's a genius; nevertheless, she finds it hard work being married to him.

The trouble with him is that he seems more completely "otherworldly" than anyone I've ever known. When I said I liked Beethoven's last piano sonata, he sat down and played it right through from memory, interrupting himself to make comments like: "Here he leaves the world entirely behind and soars into the clouds," or "I am convinced he wrote this variation with Plato's Philosopher-King in mind." (I asked him why; he thumped his heart and said: "I feel it.") At the end, he explained, with a curious, ecstatic expression: "This sonata presages the end of commerce and all forms of human selfishness. On the day when men turn into gods, they will play Beethoven's ninth symphony as a hymn of triumph. But then they will look back on man's long struggle, on the painful road, on the indomitable spirit that drove us on. Then they will play Opus 111 in a mood of reminiscence." All this greatly excited me; I found myself looking at him with a new feeling; it suddenly seemed clear to me that in spite of the inflated language, he was a remarkable man, a kind of prophet.

I asked him about his early life, and he gave me some details. He was born in Vienna in 1910, the son of a Jewish father and an Austrian mother. The whole family was musical. His uncle was a cantor in the synagogue; his father had known Brahms and Hugo Wolf. As a child he saw a great deal of Bruno Walter, and Kokoshka, the painter. His mother was a Catholic, and he was brought up as a Catholic. He started to learn the organ when he was about eight. When he was twelve he played, at short notice, the organ part in one of Bruckner's masses. He and several friends formed a music society, on the model of Schumann's Davidsbündler. (He has a vast admiration for Schumann; he told me that, when he could afford it, he liked to work on champagne, because Schumann worked on champagne, and that when he drank the first glass out of a new bottle, he always said: "To the memory of a divine man.") He said: "We ate and drank and breathed music; we thought of nothing but music." In the late twenties, his father got worried about Hitler; they moved to Prague, and the family fell on hard times. He had studied music in Vienna, but now had to take an office job. One of his sisters died—his favorite, he said—and his father began to drink too much. He said: "I was in despair. I was tempted to kill myself. And it was in this mood that I first realized that I would devote my life to music. One evening, the family were all out; I thought that if I intended to gas myself, now was the time to do it. First of all, I sat down at the piano, and played myself some Mahler— my own transcription of the Adagio of the tenth. Then all at once, I went into a condition of ecstasy. I had a vision. I thought that the ceiling of the room dissolved, and I was looking up into the heavens. I cannot explain my feeling, but suddenly I understood why the world has to suffer. I felt as if God leaned down to me and said: 'Don't worry. There will be an end to suffering. And when the end comes, all those who committed suicide, or died of discouragement, will want to die with shame. And the men who fought and refused to be defeated will know that they have saved the human race.' Then I started to laugh, and I played one of Beethoven's bagatelles —the third of Opus 126—and vowed that I would live as a pure artist, without compromise."

At this point, to my surprise, his wife broke in: "Is it possible to live without compromise?" He said: "I think so, my dear. I have somehow managed to do it." I felt like saying: "But your wife has to compromise." I suspect this is what she may have been thinking. However, he was in fine form by this time, finished the bottle of wine, and began telling me about Brahms. He said that Brahms once said to his father "The world will be saved by music." Then he played me some of Brahms' Handel variations with tremendous power and expression, although he struck the wrong key every other note. He explained that modern musicians had lost the great faith, and that, without exception, they all wrote a corrupt music of the nerves, compromising with the worst elements in modern culture. Berg's *Wozzeck* seemed to be his particular detestation, although he got nearly as irritable about Stravinsky, whom he called "a musical whore" because, he claimed, he changes his style to suit the changing taste. I asked him if there were no living composer whom he admired, and he said that the only one he cared about was Pfitzner, whose *Palestrina* is the greatest and most sublime opera of the twentieth century.

By this time, he had got me a little bewildered. I had begun by thinking him a crank, then swung to the opposite opinion, and decided that I'd found a genius; now every word he said propelled me nearer to my first opinion. I asked him why he had listened so carefully to the Martinu this afternoon; he said that it was music of tragedy, but that it was riddled with neurosis.

He then proposed to play me some of his songs—a cycle of short poems by one of his old Viennese friends. He sang a couple of these to me, and I liked them—they were rather Wolfian, and sounded well in German. But he then proceeded to praise this friend—a man called Schindler—extravagantly, and proposed to read me his own translations of some of Schindler's poems. At this point, the whole thing turned into absurdity. He produced a great ledger, and proceeded to read me the most awful drivel since the great McGonagall.* He was particularly enthusiastic about a long poem in praise of man, full of clichés like: "Thy spirit reacheth out towards the stars"; halfway through this thing (obviously inspired by Schiller's *Ode to Joy*), he placed the ledger on the floor, leaned back in his chair, and proceeded to recite from memory, staring at the ceiling, and sounding like some old ham from Drury Lane entertaining a theater queue. I glanced at his wife; she kept her eyes on her knitting, but she looked very pink. I could now understand why she hung around with a bookmaker type even though she thought her husband a man of genius.

Finally, he told me at length about an opera he is working on, to be called *The Spirit of Man,* and based loosely on Imre Madách's *Tragedy of Man* which, he told me, is the greatest Hungarian play. He even played me the overture to the opera, but apart from a few lively passages, it didn't strike me as in any way interesting. His wife fell asleep in her chair as he went on playing (the poor thing has to be at work at 7:30 in the morning), but he didn't seem to notice. He then proposed that I should write him a libretto for a one-act opera. By this time, I was half asleep, so I agreed. He said he wanted something about witchcraft. Finally, his wife woke up, and staggered off to bed, after muttering good night. He proposed he should come up to my room and listen to some Beethoven; I was half asleep, so said that I didn't want to wake the people above me. This view obviously struck him as completely eccentric, but he shrugged, and offered to make some coffee; I said I was tired, and went off to bed. He went on playing the Handel

---

* William McGonagall, Scottish poetaster of the 19th century. McGonagall's work was so atrocious that it became a popular joke; but as no one ever bothered to tell McGonagall why it was popular, he continued to believe himself a great writer, and described himself as "William McGonagall, poet and tragedian."

Variations, and I lay in bed thinking about his wife. She is certainly one of the most beautiful women I have ever seen, even though I would find it impossible to explain the reason. Her coloring is extraordinarily delicate, so that when she blushes she looks like one of those blossoms painted by Hokusai, and she moves with the grace of a dancer. Unfortunately, this life of overwork she lives makes her look pale and strained. Obviously, she appeals to me because, in some indefinable way, she is my "type." I could go deeper than this, but it would take me pages; besides, it would involve being immodest. . . . Yet I believe she knows how deeply I'm attracted to her, and accepts my admiration as she might accept a box of sweets. I'm not sure how far she responds to it.

Later. After writing the above, I suddenly felt an intense desire to see Diana again. As it was around midday, I walked along to Sidney Street. She had told me the name of the place she worked in, so I hung around until half past twelve, when the girls came out. Diana wasn't among them; I waited another ten minutes, then approached another girl who came out and asked about Mrs. Kirsten. She said that Mrs. Kirsten was inside, eating her lunch, so I asked her if she'd bring her out. A few minutes later, Diana came out, looking bewildered, and rather disappointed when she saw me. (I wonder if she expected her bookmaker type?) I said I'd hoped I could buy her some lunch in return for the supper last night. She actually looked scared, and said she always ate sandwiches for lunch. I asked her if she'd eaten them yet, and she admitted she hadn't, so I grabbed her arm and told her that today was going to be the exception. She protested—said it would make her sleepy to eat a full lunch—but I insisted, so she finally came with me to a place in the Mile End Road, where we got decent lamb chops. She wouldn't talk much. I noticed that her eyes are red today; I don't know whether she's been crying, or if it's just fatigue. At first I thought that she might be feeling guilty, eating lunch with a strange man, so I asked her if she thought her husband would mind my taking her to lunch. She

looked startled, and said: "Oh no, of course not," and actually
managed to smile, as if I'd at last said something really funny.

I even managed to persuade her to come into the pub
next door, although she'd only drink fruit juice. I asked her
point-blank about money, and she admitted that they often
live on four pounds a week. This is the real reason she eats
sandwiches instead of a full lunch. (She wouldn't admit this
—claimed that it was to do with her figure; but the poor
thing wouldn't be fat even if she expanded to twice her present
size.) Her husband makes a little money by orchestrating
various operettas and musical shows, and making piano ver-
sions of Oscar Strauss, Messager, etc. But apparently he
spends most of this on his "invention," a sort of organ, which
he keeps in a shop in Hanbury Street, and on which he has
now worked for five years.

I asked her how she'd met Kirsten. At first, she was unwilling to talk, but when I'd pried a few sentences out of her,
she went on of her own accord. I found it an interesting story.
Diana's father apparently made a lot of money in manufactur-
ing some domestic appliance. But being a domineering and
reactionary sort of man, the other members of the firm got
sick of him and somehow forced him out. He then wasted
most of his money in lawsuits against the firm. Diana, his only
daughter (there are two brothers, but the father hates them),
was at a finishing school in Switzerland at the time all this was
going on. Her mother died; she came back to England to look
after her father, who took out all his domineering instincts on
her. As he wasted money in lawsuits, they were finally forced
to live in a Liverpool boarding house. Her father went to terrific lengths to scare away young men who were attracted by
Diana; he was completely possessive, and would hardly allow
her out of the house without making her explain where she'd
been. Finally, Kirsten moved into the house, in the cheapest
room. The father apparently took rather a liking to him, although he made no secret of thinking him a poor fish. Also,
no doubt, he thought Diana was safe enough from Kirsten,
since Kirsten was so much her senior, and not particularly

attractive. However, Diana found herself much attracted by Kirsten's cranky idealism—it made a pleasant change from her father's unending preoccupation with money—and also felt a certain pity for him because he seemed so helpless, and would allow any shopkeeper to swindle him. This went on for about six months—neither of them ever speaking a word about being attracted to one another, but just talking for hours when the old man was asleep or out. Then one day, her father caught them talking on the stairs outside Kirsten's room. He flew into a rage, accused Kirsten of seducing his daughter, and demanded that the landlord should throw Kirsten out. He must have had a lot of influence with the landlord, for Kirsten was given notice. Diana knew he had no money. She had a little of her own—left by her mother—but not much. She tried to give this to Kirsten, and when he said he wouldn't take it, told him that in that case, she would go with him. The same evening, she eloped with him, and they were married two days later. Kirsten, apparently, would never have dreamed of making any advances himself! He didn't even tell her he loved her until after they were married.

She didn't say much about her married life, but I think I can read between the lines. She then discovers that leaving a tyrannical father, she lands herself with a husband who is a mixture of a father and a helpless and very selfish child. Apart from her finishing school, the poor girl never seems to have got any fun out of life.

She admitted to being born in 1932. That makes her 24 now, a year younger than I am, and 22 years younger than her husband.

I walked back to work with her, and watched her go into the miserable dump with a crowd of healthy looking cockney girls, all yawping to one another about rock and roll and Elvis Presley, and I realized that I feel very protective about her. I suppose that's halfway to being in love.

Later. Kirsten came and interrupted me as I was writing, and asked me if I'd like to hear him play the organ. I thought he

meant his curious invention; so, being anxious to get a look
at it, I went with him. However, we only went as far as the
local church. He seems to have some kind of arrangement with
the vicar, who allows him to play the organ on certain after-
noons. He is, as far as I can judge, an excellent player. After
playing me some Franck and Buxtehude, he finally did a Bach
Toccata and Fugue, and made it sound tremendous and quite
inevitable. He went on and on, for over two hours, while I sat
with him up in the organ loft (and consequently unable to
escape). There was no stopping him—Widor, Liszt, even
Brahms. His approach is rather fierce and square, but he is
so obviously absorbed by the music that you fail to notice the
imperfections.

We walked back here at six. (He remembered that his
wife hadn't a key, and that she'd probably be waiting.) However, she wasn't there, so I went in with him. More reminiscences of the Davidsbündler in Vienna, and of Max Brod in
Prague. He also repeated that he wanted me to do him a
libretto about witchcraft, so I said I'd go and see what they
had in the local library. I did this, and got out a couple of interesting books by Montague Summers. I took these into the
local pub, feeling certain that he'd invade my room as soon as
he heard me come in! He seems to have taken a great liking
to me, but uses me as a kind of tape recorder, to be talked at.
He insists that I call him Robert. And when I mentioned that
I'd taken Diana out for lunch, all he said was "I hope she
didn't allow you to pay for her," as if the poor girl were in
the habit of cadging lunches from his friends.

When I finally got home, I found Gertrude waiting for
me (I'd left my door open). She was in a rather gloomy mood,
and began asking me about Caroline, saying that Caroline's
mother was sure I was still seeing her, and that she was afraid
Caroline might get herself pregnant. I told her that I'd met
Caroline a few days ago, and that she told me she was getting
married to an actor. This seemed to reassure her. Someone
knocked on my door, and Diana opened it. When she saw

Gertrude, she looked disappointed, and said it didn't matter. I suspect she wanted to talk to me about something, and felt sorry I wasn't alone.

Gertrude immediately looked suspicious about her, so I had to tell her about Kirsten and his wife at length, and my project of the opera libretto. I saw the gleam of predatory interest in her eye when I talked about Kirsten. (There are times when I believe that Gertrude would like to collect a houseful of geniuses and devote her life to darning their socks.) As I don't particularly want to provide Gertrude with further reasons for coming here, I overcame the temptation to introduce her to Kirsten. Gertrude then proposed that we go back to Hampstead to supper. So we drove back—it was a pleasant evening, with a clear sky—and had supper at Gertrude's. There was a constraint between us most of the time, and it didn't improve when Brother Robbins dropped in about ten o'clock. He glared at me, and Gertrude seemed to be apologetic. I wanted to go home, but she took me aside and asked me to wait until he'd gone. But he showed no sign of going, and when it was time for my last bus home, I decided to leave. Gertrude looked unhappy, but I went.

A peculiar thing happened on my way home. I walked up Petticoat Lane, and stopped by the waste ground for a pee. While I stood there, a couple suddenly stood up from behind some stalls on the other side of the ground. From the way she was smoothing her dress, I imagine it had been around her waist. I walked behind them up the street. Then they passed under a lamp and I realized it was Diana, with the flashily dressed individual I'd seen the other day. I felt rather sick about this—or I suppose the correct word is jealous. If she's going to have sex with other men, why can't she go in for something more dignified than a piece of waste ground? There's always the park. I took a short cut through the back streets and got home before she did; I didn't want to see her. Her husband was playing Schumann when I came in.

Nov. 10. Have just returned from Bond Street where I found an art gallery exhibiting Oliver's stuff. I went into town this afternoon to look around Foyle's second-hand section, then thought I'd take a look at a book shop I know in D'Arblay Street. In one of those back streets off Bond Street, I found a small art gallery with a large notice: "Exhibition of Paintings by Oliver Glasp." I went in and inquired, but the man was very unhelpful. When I said I was a friend of Oliver's, he only gave me a resentful glare, and said he wasn't allowed to give any personal information about the artist. I was so irritated that I wanted to knock him down and stamp on his face—this kind of rudeness always sends up my blood pressure—so I shrugged and went out. Perhaps he thought I only wanted to borrow money from Oliver. Anyway, I presume this means that Oliver's back in town.

The weird thing is that as I started to write this down, I suddenly recalled that I had dreamed about Oliver last night, and I could swear that there was something about an exhibition in the dream. However, I suppose this is coincidence, not a proof of Dunne's serial time.*

The exhibition, which apparently opened yesterday, was very impressive; most of it seemed to be old stuff. The centerpiece of the exhibition was Oliver's picture of Matthew Lovatt.† The title in the catalogue only says: "A self-crucifixion."

Strangely enough, as I got off the bus at the bottom of

---

* J. W. Dunne's book *An Experiment with Time* deals with the possibility that we can have actual visions of the future in dreams; he developed a theory of "serial time" to explain his own dream-experiences of precognition.

† A shoemaker of Casale, Italy, who made two attempts to commit suicide by self-crucifixion. He constructed a machine that would lower a cross from a third story window overlooking the market place, and somehow succeeded in nailing himself to it. He died of self-starvation in an asylum. Oliver Glasp passed through a period when he practiced many self-torments; at this time he made several paintings and sketches of Lovatt's suicide attempt.

Commercial Street, I saw Christine walking on the other side of the road. I haven't seen her for a long time. So I ran over and caught up with her. She seems to have grown a lot since I last saw her. (I think she's nearly thirteen.) I didn't mention Oliver's exhibition. I didn't want to hurt her. I shall never understand why Oliver was so shattered when he found out that Christine had slept with her cousin. (Incidentally, she told me that this cousin has just been sent to a reformatory.)

I gave Christine my address, and she says she'll come and see me. But I somehow got the impression that she doesn't intend to.

Nov. 11. Diana came up to talk to me last night, but I felt too irritated after seeing her with the bookmaker type. She wanted to talk to me about Kirsten—whether I think he couldn't get someone to publish his music. I'm afraid I showed my annoyance, because after five minutes of lame conversation, she left.

I have decided to sketch out a one-act opera libretto about Major Thomas Weir, whom I've found in Montague Summers. It will give me a chance to make it a psychological study too. Weir was apparently known in Edinburgh as a Presbyterian of unusual enthusiasm, a highly respected soldier, an upright citizen. Quite suddenly, in his seventies, he started confessing to witchcraft, to incest with his sister, bestiality, adultery, and various other offenses. The respectable citizens to whom he confessed thought he was mad, and declined to act. But he was so persistent that they were forced to investigate. Finally, largely on Weir's own accusations, he and his sister were burned for witchcraft. His house remained uninhabited for many years after, neighbors claiming that they heard strange noises and saw lights. Summers claims that one man who agreed to take the house was almost immediately driven out of it by the devil in the shape of a calf. However, Summers seems to be a wildly imaginative writer, who manages to pack more inaccuracies into two paragraphs about

Jack the Ripper than most people could get into twenty pages.

The main charges against Weir were sexual. He slept with his sister Jane from the time she was sixteen until she was fifty (when he lost interest). He also slept with his stepdaughter and with several maidservants. He attempted to rape his sister when she was ten. He made a habit of having intercourse with mares and cows; on one occasion, he was seen by a woman in the act of bestiality with a mare, but when she reported him, no one believed her, and she was whipped through the town for slander of such a holy man! Weir was burned alive in 1670.

Even Summers, who seems to believe in witchcraft, makes very little attempt to present Major Weir as a sorcerer, and admits that the major charges against him were the sexual ones. Add to this that Weir refused to petition God for pardon, claiming that he was certain he was damned. All this, I think, indicates a case of overwhelming sexual guilt. Weir was obviously a man of intense sexual desires, born into a community where sex was regarded as sinful. The only parallel I can think of was the case of Peter Kürten, the Düsseldorf killer. Kürten also attempted to rape his sister when he was very young, and committed bestiality. I suspect that when sexual desire reaches this kind of intensity, it turns automatically to sadism.

So we have a picture of young Thomas Weir, born into a family of respectable Presbyterians about 1600, and later fighting with the Puritan army and being made commander of the forces in Edinburgh—a post that he owed to his reputation for piety as much as to his prowess as a soldier. But from a very early age, he is obsessed by sex; it haunts him all the time, so that there is hardly a moment of any day when he is not aware of an urgency in his loins. When his sister is 16, he succeeds in having intercourse with her. This could hardly be called rape, because if she had really objected, she had only to complain to her parents. But Weir also lives in a country where religion has assumed particularly nasty forms of superstition. He believes in the devil, naturally. But as he walks through the streets of Edinburgh, he is continually aware of a desire to grab every attractive girl he sees and heave her skirts over her head. This sense of strange forces working inside him must have convinced him that he was close to the devil. I take his bestiality to be a further corroboration of this idea. After all, what man in his right senses wants to have intercourse with a horse or cow? A moronic farm hand in a country district might do it out of frustration, or a shepherd who sees no one but his sheep for weeks at a time. But for most people, the idea would be as unattractive as eating the cow's dinner. Only a sense that it was wicked and forbidden could possibly stimulate a man's appetite to overcome his normal revulsion—particularly if there were women available, as apparently there always were for Weir (if only his sister).

It seems peculiar, but the idea of the forbidden has the power of channelizing and concentrating the sexual desires. In Thomas Mann, for example, there is an obvious obsession with incest between brother and sister; it appears in *Blood of the Walsungs* and again in *The Holy Sinner*. But why? Only because it is supposed to be forbidden. Imagine a country where it is regarded as highly moral to keep sex within the family, but horribly daring to touch someone else's sister! This is surely more like common sense? For after all, our own flesh does not excite us; therefore, someone else's sister is far more *strange*. Why do we take only the most casual interest in a girl dressed in a bikini, yet feel a tremendous twinge of lust if we happened to see the same girl in her panties and bra, although these may conceal far more than the beach clothes? It is this curious focusing power of the forbidden. So you get a fool like Baudelaire claiming that the element of sin must be kept in sex. To me, this is only to say that he believes sex to be entirely an illusion, and that the illusion should be preserved or even intensified. I'm not sure. There's a strong streak of original Rousseau in me. I can't help feeling that if the climate was temperate enough for us all to live as nudists, and if we were as promiscuous and as frank as the South Sea Islanders, we'd discover that the sexual impulse doesn't need intensifying by guilt and sin.

Anyway, to return to Major Weir. I imagine his final confession was almost a gesture of disgust with life, like suicide— a self-divided life when he could never feel completely at one with himself because he never felt he had a right to inner peace. And yet I cannot agree with Summers when he says that Weir was a monstrous hypocrite who used his acting abilities to deceive everybody. Weir didn't *have* to be thought more pious than anybody else; he didn't *have* to pray so fervently that people would come for miles to hear him extemporize. Plainly, he had a genuine talent for this kind of thing, for praying and talking about religion. He was an oversexed man; but in a less superficial culture, he might also have become a saint, since he possessed strong religious feelings as well as strong sexual urges. If he could have been franker about them, got into the habit of letting other people—if only a priest—know about them, he might have dared to allow his "opposing selves" to wrestle openly. He was like a frightened old maid who keeps her dog and cat in separate rooms because she is afraid they'll fight and disturb the other tenants; but in consequence, the dog and cat never have a chance to get used to one another.

I wonder. . . . If we could finally destroy the idea of guilt in connection with sex—if we could be completely open about our sexual desires—if the result might not be to release some of our mental blocks, hidden powers? When I think of those sexual infernos that seem the common experience of all teen-age boys, I'm surprised that far more girls don't get raped. This I take to be the real problem with Oliver and this child Christine. I doubt whether Oliver has had any sexual experience. He naturally has a masochistic tendency. Then he meets Christine, a girl who doesn't frighten or worry him. (I remember how awkward he was when he met Caroline —didn't seem to know where to put his feet and hands.) In fact, she obviously thinks he's something extraordinary. Unfortunately, she isn't suitable for romance, being only thirteen. Nevertheless, he is lonely, and allows her to touch dormant sexual feelings. Then she poses for him with nothing on, and the situation comes dangerously close to the explosion point. He won't admit to himself that what he really wants is to take a sweet girl of about sixteen to bed; Christine is just a substitute for this. Heavens knows how long it would have taken before he would have admitted that he wanted her in every sense, but before he can reach that stage, just while he is trying to hide from himself that he is sexually stimulated by her, he suddenly learns that she is not, in fact, a virgin. Most people wouldn't have felt particularly surprised by this. After all, in her kind of family, where several children often sleep in the same bed, and the facts of life are no secret from the age of five, precocious sexual experience isn't so unusual; neither does it necessarily do much harm. No doubt Christine was perfectly sincere when she said that her cousin had practically raped her, and that she hated him for it. (

　　　　　　　　　　） So why, under the circumstances, does Oliver go half insane and rush off to the other end of England, refusing to see the poor child again? Why on earth couldn't he be frank with himself, admit that he'd like to have sexual intercourse with her, but that at her age it would be impracticable?

　　How can we talk of sin and guilt, the world being what it is? The world is a confidence trickster—that is, it is careful not to allow its reality to appear to us. And what is its reality? This is the question I devote my whole life to studying. And yet I think I have more idea of the answer now than a year ago. Usually I feel almost nonexistent, as if I wouldn't even cast a shadow in the sunlight, like Chamisso's Peter Schlemihl or the man in Hoffmann's story. Yet I am learning to cast a shadow.

Nov. 12. It is the safe of *meaning* that I've got to crack, and I need a great deal more training in burglary. I've spent today like an absolute fool, staring out of my window, drinking tea, trying to read Huysmans' *Là-bas* and not being able to work up much interest in it. God this awful freedom. What are we to do? I spend my life trying to free myself from my conditioning, only to face this terrible lack of motive. Huysmans keeps asking why Gilles de Rais became a sadist and "ripper of children." He didn't understand that the desert of freedom is his answer. When a man has too much freedom, too many privileges, he becomes an utter fool. What could you expect from the richest baron in France? We all have an absurd compulsion to keep looking forward to things. We're incapable of sitting still. We have no will. We have to be driven on up the evolutionary scale, destiny sitting behind us and sticking a pointed stick up our arses.

The male confronts his boredom with a need to conquer, to penetrate, to achieve ecstasy by a kind of aggression. The female reacts to freedom with the cry: Come and penetrate me. Bring me ecstasy and sensation. But what training had a man like Gilles for freedom? A darling of destiny, flattered by the king and courtiers, a marshal of France in his twenties, the comrade-in-arms of Joan of Arc. The sadism follows naturally. Since the Life Force has turned sex into an act of aggression, has made us respond with desire to the notion of violating another's privacy with an erect penis, is it not inevitable that the sexual explorer looks around for new taboos to violate? Therefore, in some ways, the sex maniac must be regarded as admirable. The Life Force is like a stupid king, who drives his subjects to doing his will by forcing them to obey brutal morons. If a few of the subjects have the courage to revolt, so much the better for them. The Life Force appears to be incredibly stupid. It persuades us to perpetuate the species by implanting in us a kind of criminal impulse—for is not the desire to enter another's body similar to the desire to break into someone's house? When we were at school, we used to repeat a rhyme that went:

It's only human nature after all
To take a pretty girl behind a wall,
To pull down her protection
And to shove in your connection,
It's only human nature after all.

But note here the words "her protection," and its suggestion of leaving the girl helpless. (Presumably if she goes with you behind a wall, she is quite willing to have sex, so why the imagery of violating her?) Why? Because this is the rather clumsy device the Life Force has hit upon to stimulate man to take upon himself the boredom of fatherhood. Then, having planted in us this preposterous conditioned reflex, it relies on our timidity and cowardice to ensure that the children who get brought into the world have homes and families. A man who is free of this timidity will therefore go ahead and rape. The only reason he cannot be excused is that the stupidity of the Life Force doesn't justify us in doing the opposite. The means employed may be clumsy and silly, but the aim is valid. It is rather like a bad teacher who treats intelligent pupils as if they were small children, and irritates them by talking down to them; all the same, she *has* something to teach, no matter how unfortunate her manner. In the same way, life seems to rely on our timidity and need for security to keep us from wrecking society. Therefore a man who chooses to be a criminal might be admirable in the same way as the sex maniac. But the same objection applies to him.

Nov. 15. A hectic 24 hours. First of all, Carlotta came yesterday afternoon to bring me a letter. It turned out to be a note from Oliver, asking me to go and see his exhibition, and giving an address in the Hackney Road. Carlotta was in one of her teasing moods—turned away her mouth when I tried to kiss her (just a fraternal greeting!), then sat around on the bed showing her pants but behaving with the gravity of an alderman, and forbidding any passes. This was just as well. If she'd realized how easy it is to get hooks into me, she'd have stripped and got into bed immediately. Because I'm pretty certain that's what she had in mind. However, she succeeds in driving me into a state of suppressed irritation that has the effect of turning me into a monk. After ten minutes, it was obvious that this particular patch of human relations had got all snarled up, so I offered to take her out for a meal. She said she'd eaten. So I made the only other suggestion I could think of —that we go and call on Oliver. I didn't particularly want to do this: I know he hates strangers. But we went all the same.

Oliver's address is only a twenty-minute walk from here. We arrived at half past five, and found the door, but couldn't get any reply. So we went and had tea in the café opposite. Carlotta was being an absolute bitch—I don't know why she came to see me in such a mood—but I didn't really care, because I felt she was giving me an excuse for avoiding her in future. Kept saying she wished she was back in Germany, how she hated England, what swine Englishmen were, etc. Looking at her, I thought of that time she fell off the ladder, and my excitement, and thought what a damned swindle it is.

Then I looked up, and who should be walking into the place but Oliver. I called to him and went over. He looked older than the last time I saw him—he actually had some gray in his hair—and his face looked more skull-like than ever. Yet I think he looked happier than he did a year ago—there was no longer the same sense of strain hanging about him. I believe this must be the result of his success. He stoops just as much, has the same red stubble on his chin, and wears what appears to be the same paint-stained turtleneck sweater. His manner is also as abrupt and ungracious as ever—particularly with Carlotta.

As we went upstairs with him, he said: "I want to introduce you to a remarkable man." We went up to the third floor—up well-carpeted stairs (the house is several cuts above anything he's lived in before)—and into a room. Oliver said: "This is Caradoc Cunningham." And the man who came forward to shake hands was the big, bald-headed man I'd seen in the library a week ago. I was staggered. Cunningham saw that I looked astounded, and said: "Haven't we met somewhere before?" As I didn't want to bring up the library episode, I said I didn't think so. But afterwards, as we talked, I noticed that he kept glancing at me in a curious manner, as if trying to place me.

My first impressions of Cunningham in the library are verified; he is certainly one of the strangest men I have ever met. On the surface, he is something of an actor—big, rather fat, very tall, an almost hypnotic stare from eyes that seem to be round. I suspect that he deliberately cultivates a way of making his eyes bulge slightly to intensify this impression of will power. He has something of an actor's voice, with a faint lisp, and a booming way of talking. He also has various habits, like dropping his voice and narrowing his eyes when he says certain things, to give himself a sinister appearance. Altogether, the first impression he made on me was a bad one—of a charlatan, a man without self-discipline. But after ten minutes' conversation, this impression vanishes completely, and he seems to emanate a definite and rather sinister strength. There can be no doubt that his culture is very wide indeed, but it isn't used—as a charlatan would use it—to impress. For example, we started discussing Plotinus, and he began to quote Plotinus in Greek. I said impatiently that I didn't know Greek; he immediately dropped it, and didn't again revert to it.

Finally, he said to me: "Look here, won't you tell me where I've seen you?" Oliver said jokingly: "I thought your memory was infallible." "Not my memory," Cunningham said, "My insight." He closed his eyes, placed his hand on his forehead, and said: "Egypt, Athens . . . Alexandria." He opened his eyes, and looked at me in a puzzled way, repeating, "Alexandria." Then suddenly he looked pleased. "Alexandria, library! Of course!" He looked at me cunningly. "Yes, now it all comes back to me. You were sitting in the corner." I was disappointed in him. I was certain that he had recalled where he had seen me about ten minutes before, and had deliberately staged this little exhibition of thought-reading (or whatever it was supposed to be). And yet before the evening was out, I was convinced that I had done him an injustice. I will explain why in a moment.

Oliver tells me that he met Cunningham in the Lake District, where he was showing two rich young men the rudiments of mountain climbing on the east side of Helvellyn. (One of them nearly broke his neck, and went home rather hurriedly.) Cunningham liked Oliver's work, and offered to get him an exhibition. I don't know how he talked Oliver into it. However, the results seem to have been excellent; Cunningham showed me some of the notices, which were splendid, comparing Oliver to Münch, Vlaminck, Soutine and God knows who else.

Oliver's admiration for Cunningham is obvious. This is curious to see. Oliver naturally has a suspicious nature; I'd like to know how Cunningham won him over so completely. One more thing is obvious: Cunningham is using Oliver to make himself money. From something Oliver said, I gather that Oliver hasn't yet seen much of the cash from his pictures. And yet I am fairly sure Cunningham is no ordinary confidence swindler.

There was one curious episode that I find difficult to account for. After introducing me to Cunningham, Oliver said he wanted to go down to his studio (which is apparently on the floor below). Cunningham gave Carlotta a very long and quite unambiguous glance; he was obviously stripping her mentally. Carlotta bridled at this, and he grinned sarcastically. Cunningham then began to tell us that he had just returned from some mountain climbing expedition in Tibet, and talked about Tibetan Buddhism. It always irritates me to be lectured to on a subject I already know fairly well, so I lost no time in letting him see that he wasn't telling me anything new. He then went on to Tibetan magic; but as I'd just finished reading a book on the subject, I was able to checkmate him here too. (I derive an absurd and rather discreditable pleasure from these stupid episodes of one-upmanship.) At this, he became very friendly, "as between two brother adepts," and turned on all the charm and flattery. At this point, he suggested that we should have a drink, but after rummaging in a cupboard, could produce only half an inch of whisky. I had noticed a wine shop close by, so I offered to go down and get a bottle of wine. Cunningham insisted on paying, and handed me a £5 note—but made no attempt to go himself! This is somehow typical of him—he does everything with a kind of affected princeliness. He said to Carlotta: "You can stay; he won't be a moment," but she jumped to her feet and said that she couldn't trust me to buy decent wine! As soon as we were outside, she said: "I can't bear that man. He exudes the nastiest kind of sex." I pressed her to explain what she meant, and she claimed that, all the time he had been talking to me, she had felt an unpleasant sensation, as if she were naked, and he was running his hands very lightly over her. I said that I should have thought this might be pleasant, but she said it was no more pleasant than having frogs walking over you. We bought the wine—a fairly good Beaune—and returned to the room. Cunningham said we would have to warm it, and stood it in front of the fire. I wanted to go down to the bathroom, which is on the floor below, and he asked me to knock on Oliver's door and tell him there was wine. I did this, and Oliver immediately asked me: "What do you think of him?" I said that I wasn't yet sure whether he was a charlatan or a man of remarkable talent, and Oliver said excitedly: "That's how I felt when I first met him. But he has amazing powers—quite unusual." I pressed him to tell me what they were—thinking of the library episode —but he said that Cunningham would probably show them to me when he was ready. I decided to go back up again, remembering Carlotta's feeling about Cunningham, so I left Oliver to come up when he felt inclined. When I walked back into the room, I was amazed to see Cunningham bending over

Carlotta, apparently kissing her, with one hand quite definitely up her skirt. As I opened the door, he straightened up very casually and started pouring the wine. I didn't like to look at Carlotta—she was embarrassed; so I went past her to look out of the window; but as I passed her, I glanced down at her, and to my astonishment saw teeth marks on her neck. Cunningham is certainly the fastest worker I've ever met!

As we drank, Cunningham turned the conversation to the subject of Satanism. I made it fairly plain from my manner that I thought it a lot of nonsense. He asked me very smoothly how it was possible for a man of my obvious breadth and culture to take such a poor-spirited view. As by that time I'd had several glasses of wine (I had bought three bottles) and was feeling talkative, I tried to explain to him my true position: that 19th-century materialism is shallow nonsense, because although it acknowledged that 90 per cent of the world is a mystery to us, it still insisted that the world is pointless and purposeless, a matter of chance and blind physical laws. I said I was convinced that the world was made up largely of unseen forces—but that no amount of magical mumbo-jumbo would place us in contact with them.

At this, Cunningham seized my phrase "unseen forces" and became very excited. He asked me if I wasn't admitting that there are probably intelligences in the universe that are superior to our own. I admitted grudgingly that this was likely, but that I would have to define what I meant more precisely. But there was no stopping him now; he said that although it was probable that all the magic and alchemy of the Middle Ages was nonsense, this still did not mean that an educated modern man might not learn to tap the "unseen forces."

At this point Oliver came up, and we continued the argument in front of him. Suddenly, Oliver said: "Why don't you give him a demonstration?" Cunningham said: "Very well, I will." He then produced a pack of Tarot cards, all of them circular, and handed them to me. He told me to sit with my back to him, take one card at a time, stare at it, and concentrate on it. I did as he told me, with Carlotta standing beside me, and Cunningham on the other side of the room. I took one —a picture of a man hanging by his foot—and concentrated. Almost immediately, Cunningham said: "The Hanging Man," and described the card in my hand. I tried three more. The first two, The Juggler and the Nine of Pentacles, he got immediately. The third one—Three of Wands—he got wrong, saying it was the devil. He also got the next one wrong—it was The Pope, and he said it was Justice. At this point, he claimed that something was interfering with the transference —probably Carlotta being present, he thought—and suggested that we go down into the street.

Here, he showed either a remarkable ability at guesswork, or some kind of second sight. We walked down to a small side street, which he entered, telling me to stand on the corner and look along the Hackney Road. It was about half past six, and there were a great many people about. Cunningham told me to look at the people who approached along the pavement, and think hard about them. He himself stood about five yards from the corner—it was a blank brick wall—and closed his eyes. He then started to tell me who was approaching: "Two men, walking side by side, and an old woman. Now there is a young girl further away, and a child—I can't tell whether it's a boy or a girl." On the whole, what he said was accurate, but I couldn't tell whether it was simply guesswork, or whether he might have been helped out by some reflections in a window on the other side of the street. For example, there were two men approaching, more or less side by side, but they were obviously not together. There was also an old woman, further back, and there was a child in the distance. On the other hand, there were several other people between the old woman and the child, and he didn't mention these. At one point, he said: "There is a policeman approaching." I could see no policeman, but a moment later, a uniformed man came out of a shop only a few yards along the pavement, who might easily have been mistaken for a policeman if you looked at him casually. (He was actually some kind of a foreign naval officer.) As he became visible, Cunningham remarked: "Ah, his uniform misled me." On the other hand, if Cunningham was really reading my mind, then he had spoken about the officer *before* I actually saw him.

Oliver and Carlotta were standing nearby as all this went on, and were obviously both much impressed. But I couldn't help feeling that this proved very little. If Cunningham had drawn a chalk mark on the pavement and then said: "An old man is now crossing that mark," I might have agreed that he had second sight. But in a crowded street, it isn't difficult to make good guesses if you don't specify how close the people are supposed to be.

We went back up, and Cunningham promised another demonstration later if he felt like it. Carlotta hung behind with me, as Cunningham and Oliver went on ahead, and said: "I feel so ashamed of myself. But I think that man is really a magician. . . ." At this moment, Cunningham turned round and grinned at us in a most knowing manner, and Carlotta immediately shut up, as if he knew what she was saying.

After spending an evening with Cunningham and Oliver, there is no doubt in my mind that he's a most remarkable man —although I still can't decide how far he is simply an actor. He seems to be a great boaster, and talked casually about a yacht he sank off the coast of Africa, about mountain climbing records he has broken, about another magician whom he killed in a "magical battle" when he was in Marseilles and the other magician was in Paris. He told us all this in a nearby restaurant where we ate a pleasant meal, and since he had insisted that we were his guests, I didn't feel inclined to contradict him. There can be no doubt whatever about the man's generosity. When Carlotta said that she wanted to leave her present job, but couldn't afford to spend several weeks searching for another, he immediately offered to give her enough money to support herself, and offered her ten pounds on the spot! Carlotta, I'm glad to say, refused. (If she left Kentish Town, I'm afraid she'd spend most of her time at my place. At present it's too far for more than occasional visits.)

Cunningham paid me a flattering amount of attention—rather to Oliver's annoyance, I thought, although Oliver was also fairly obviously pleased to be able to show both myself and Cunningham that he had intelligent friends. Before the evening was over, I was pretty drunk; Cunningham, although I know he must have drunk at least three bottles of wine by himself, seemed relatively unaffected.

We left the restaurant at about ten, and walked back towards my place. I asked them if they'd like to come in for a drink, and they agreed. Then Cunningham agreed to try another demonstration of his "magic." This one was rather remarkable. He made us wait in a side turning, while he stood in the middle of the pavement, apparently looking in a shop window. There were a great many people around. An oldish man came along—looked like a senior clerk in a bank—and Cunningham turned round, and walked close behind him. The man was apparently unaware that he was being followed. Cunningham fell into step with him, and got closer and closer. We all walked along just behind Cunningham, who, by this time, was only about six inches behind the man, but in such perfect step that they didn't touch each other. Suddenly, Cunningham allowed his knees to buckle under him, and almost fell to the pavement. At the same moment, the old man, although apparently untouched, also stumbled, and almost fell. Cunningham caught him and said he hoped he was all right. The old boy seemed rather dazed, looked at the pavement, as if to see what he'd stumbled over, and muttered that he felt all right. Cunningham watched him walking away, and said: "You see, I didn't touch him, did I?" I had to admit that, although I couldn't actually see whether Cunningham had touched him, the old man would probably have said so.

As we walked down towards my place, I told Cunningham and Oliver about my insane musician. He showed little interest until I told him about Kirsten's "invention," the organ.

Then he asked me several questions, and when I said I knew nothing about it, said he'd like to meet Kirsten. So when we got in, we banged on Kirsten's door; oddly enough, he was out.

In my room, we opened another bottle of wine, and got into a rambling argument. Cunningham irritated me by explaining that he believes in total freedom—Blake's "Do what you will." I said I thought this was totally meaningless, and appealed to Oliver. To my surprise, Oliver said he agreed with Cunningham, and that he thought the chief problem is that too many people live as if they have no will power. He also said that he couldn't see why I disagreed, since I was so fond of quoting Mr. Polly's "If you don't like your life you can change it." At this, I tried to explain to them, as briefly as I could, exactly what I feel about human beings: that the trouble with men is not merely that they have no absolute standards built into them, but that they have almost no consistent standards at all. A nihilist or a hedonist can take this as an excuse to live for the moment. But the fact remains that, in a limited, animal kind of way, we do have permanent values. Even the most despairing nihilist will jump up if he sits on a pin. If we read a case of murder that is particularly silly and pointless, we feel that the murderer has somehow wasted his own life and that of the victim. Well, if we have a concept of "waste" inbuilt in us, then we must also have a concept of purpose. The real problem, I said, is the diffuseness of human consciousness. If only it could be concentrated—if only we could discover the secret mechanism in the unconscious that makes it narrow and focus—we could easily become gods. But "Doing what you will" isn't likely to help at all; on the contrary, it's likely to destroy self-discipline and diffuse the consciousness still more. I gave Aleister Crowley* as an example of this kind of thing.

* Labeled by journalists "the world's wickedest man," Crowley (1875–1947) was a curious mixture of charlatan and man of genius; he claimed to be a magician, and was the founder of a cult of "Crowleyanity." His life has been written by John Symonds, under the title of *The Great Beast,* and by Charles Richard Cammell; Symonds has also written a study of the magic of Crowley.

But it turned out that Crowley had been a close friend of Cunningham's (as if I couldn't have guessed) and Cunningham immediately launched into a defense of him.

Still, we got something good out of the discussion finally. I mentioned that the sexual orgasm has this power to narrow and concentrate the beam of consciousness, but that it appears to be done by some trigger-mechanism. No one who experiences an orgasm, and then tries later to produce the same intensity of concentration by ordinary will power, can deny that there *must* exist in the human mind some kind of a switch that can intensify the consciousness; a few men—like Sri Ramakrishna—learn the secret of this switch, and can plunge into a state of ecstasy at a moment's notice. But most of us never learn where it is situated, and have to rely on the sexual orgasm, or perhaps on the power of music, to re-produce it.

Cunningham now became very mysterious, and hinted that he had another means of producing this intensification of consciousness. Being rather drunk, I was in no mood to be polite, so I said I didn't believe anybody had such a secret—even if he *could* see around corners. My scepticism seemed to annoy him, and he declared that he had discovered the secret by means of "sexual magic"—various tricks taught him by Crowley. Crowley, he claimed, had introduced a completely new form of yogic discipline that involved all kinds of sexual practices. In its early stages, the devotee has to practice masturbation, and try to understand the way in which his "intensifying faculty" works. Cunningham likened a man having an orgasm to a man who suddenly sees a landscape below him, lit by a flash of lightning. If he sees the landscape often enough, and diligently tries to make maps every time he sees it, he will eventually begin to gain a real familiarity with it. Most human beings, he said, accept the pleasure of the orgasm without trying to analyze it. The devotee of "sexual magic" keeps his attention awake and concentrated while receiving sexual pleasure, and strives to develop a kind of phenomenology of sex. He used a rather good image. He said that we all find ourselves in this more or less dark and meaningless universe, but that each sexual orgasm is like a flare that can help us find our bearings. Unfortunately, even if a man had two orgasms a day, this still wouldn't mean that he can reckon on more than about thirty thousand orgasms in a lifetime. Thirty thousand flares sounds a lot—enough to explore any landscape—but it is really totally inadequate. For example, by the age of 25, most men have had at least five thousand orgasms. Yet how many of us can say that we understand life or sex any better after the five thousandth time? Life slips through our fingers; we learn nothing of its meaning and purpose, even though each orgasm gives us an overwhelming sense that it *has* meaning and purpose. Every work of art, every poem, every symphony ever written, is an attempt to try to prevent life from slipping away. And yet, with millions of books in the world, we still know as little about the meaning of life as the earliest human beings.

At this point, I heard the Kirstens come in downstairs, and Cunningham insisted that I ask them up. I went downstairs (feeling very drunk and very sleepy) and knocked on their door. They had apparently been out to a cinema, but they were also tired, and said they didn't want to have a drink. However, I persuaded them to come and meet Cunningham. I immediately felt sorry I had, because Cunningham took one look at Diana, and obviously formed ambitions of practicing sexual magic on her. And she was like a rabbit with a snake. Kirsten seemed to notice nothing. He protested he was tired, and finally accepted a small glass of wine. Cunningham tried to draw him into our discussion by recapitulating what he'd said about music as an attempt to stop life from slipping through the fingers, but it was no good; Kirsten refused to be drawn. However, Cunningham proceeded to flatter him in the manner I now recognized, having had it practiced on me; said that he'd heard from me about Kirsten's music, about his magnificent playing, about his intelligence, etc., etc., and that he couldn't wait for a chance to verify all this for himself. Finally, Kirsten said that he'd be glad to see Cunningham some other time, but that at present he couldn't keep his eyes open. He then went off to bed, leaving Diana with us. Cunningham immediately began to question her about her husband's invention; but either she knew nothing about it, or wasn't willing to talk. However, she invited Cunningham to call the following evening (today). Then, to my surprise, Cunningham said that he was tired too, and would go home. I had expected him to talk until five in the morning (and I'm sure he meant to before Kirsten came in—I suspect he has some reason for holding himself back—perhaps he wants to "save himself" for this evening). Cunningham also got Carlotta to go with him on some flimsy excuse—saying he thought his next-door neighbor would drive her home in a car. (It was now too late for the tubes.) So they went, at about midnight, and Cunningham borrowed the first half of my *Methods and Techniques of Self-Deception.* I have no doubt that Carlotta was instructed in the finer points of sexual magic. I didn't mind—I was glad Cunningham took her with him. (But she looked oddly frightened, as if she expected to be chewed up and swallowed.)

Diana went with them, and I immediately opened a window to let out the cigarette smoke, and climbed into bed. A few minutes later, Diana came back into the room, without knocking. She immediately asked me about Cunningham, and if I thought he could be of use to her husband. I said that he probably could, and told her about Oliver's exhibition; but then, being in a bad mood (or perhaps only jealous) I added that I thought Cunningham had been rather struck by her. She startled me by her frankness; she said she felt this as soon as she came in, and that it repelled her. I was curious, after the experience that Carlotta mentioned, and pressed her to elaborate. She said that she had felt a kind of sexual blow, just here (she indicated her solar plexus). But she hadn't had Carlotta's experience of feeling undressed in front of him— perhaps because his attention was elsewhere.

I must have been pretty drunk, because I asked her

bluntly if she'd sleep with Cunningham if it could help her husband. She looked offended, said I had no right to speak to her like that, and started to leave the room. So I then mentioned that I'd walked behind her up Petticoat Lane the other night, and seen her with her bookmaker type. At this, she blushed, but tried to put a bold face on it, and said that she didn't think this was any concern of mine either. I felt the time for frankness had arrived, and said that it only concerned me because I found her so attractive myself, and hated to think of other men having her. She said very primly that no other man had "had her"; but it was obvious that she wasn't annoyed any more. I even persuaded her to sit on the edge of the bed, and managed to take her hand. I said that if I wanted to pry into her relations with other men, it was quite straightforward jealousy. She said that I was obviously drunk; but for all that, she seemed disposed to be frank, and said that sometimes, living with a man like her husband was worse than living alone. His ideas were all very "noble," and she respected him as a great man, but she could never feel that she was essential to him. The bookmaking type, whose name, apparently, is Tom Drage, wanted to marry her when she was in her teens, and had come to live in the East End to be near her. She isn't even sure of his profession (she thinks he's an auctioneer), but says that he's generous and good-hearted. I said I appreciated all this, but that I couldn't be expected to approve of him much, since I wanted her myself. She said she'd have to go or her husband would wonder what was happening; I held both her hands and tried to persuade her to kiss me good night. She wouldn't, but didn't seem annoyed. When I let her go, she turned out the bedside lamp, then laid her hand on my forehead for a moment before she went out. As she stood in the doorway, I asked her to promise that she wouldn't go to bed with Cunningham; she said: "I promise," then closed the door. I felt that this was a long step forward, but went off to sleep in a state of frustration. Probably Kirsten was already fast asleep when she climbed into his bed. If she'd climbed into mine, I wouldn't have slept for several hours. This morning I felt very ashamed of myself—I must have been drunker than I realized.

Later. I thought I'd seen Cunningham's name on book jackets some time, so this afternoon I went to the British Museum to look him up. Sure enough, there are about ten volumes by him in the catalogue, mostly verse. I got them all out, and spent a couple of hours with them. He's an atrocious poet, who seems to possess no sensitivity to language, and shows no sign of having read anything later than Coleridge, except possibly Swinburne. There's a great deal of rather juvenile blasphemy, deriding of the church and religion in general, praise of whores, and all the other *fin de siècle* paraphernalia. It seems to me that he must be in reaction against an incredibly old-fashioned family who kept him firmly suppressed. But to me—and I haven't been to church more than 20 times in my life—all this is a fantastic waste of breath. Cunningham has this comment in one of his books: "Some people accuse me of flogging dead horses, but I can think of more interesting things to do with dead horses." (I think he's invented a new perversion there.) But flogging dead horses is exactly what he does for 90 per cent of the time in these books of his. There are, admittedly, a few pleasant lyrics. There was also a book of magic, purporting to be a translation from "Abrahamelin the Mage."

It's curious that a man can be as personally impressive as Cunningham, and yet be so obviously a show-off on paper.

Nov. 16. I was interrupted yesterday by the arrival of Christine, who wanted to tell me that she'd seen a picture of Oliver in a newspaper. I felt badly about this—I didn't want to have to admit that I knew Oliver to be in town. So I insisted on going out and buying some iced cakes while Christine made tea, and talked to her about other things, and generally did my best to make her feel "wanted." This, I think, is the root of the problem; it's not that she cares particularly about Oliver, but that she feels that a man she liked and respected suddenly turned on her and threw her out. My difficulty is that I can't really comfort her without telling her that Oliver isn't as "solid" as she thought him. I can understand her position. I gather that her family are a completely crazy lot, always having fights and getting drunk. Her father's a prison warder— and exactly the kind of stupid brute you'd expect to take a job like that—and one of her brothers has already got himself into serious trouble with the police and is on probation; her sister is married to a Pole who beats her up, and she comes and sleeps with Christine when her husband's in a murderous mood. But she's a decent little kid, and she *needs* a better sort of environment, and the feeling that people take an interest in her. Oliver gave her a sense of security for a while, and the kind of attention she needs, and then quite abruptly withdrew it. Naturally she's upset; she feels it's something wrong with *her*. But how can I tell her that Oliver was probably projecting into her something that didn't exist—a kind of primal child-ish innocence—a combination of wife, daughter, angel and good fairy?

While we were having tea, and I was explaining to her about the pictures of demons in the *Tibetan Book of the Dead* there was a knock on the door, and Cunningham arrived. He has quite a way with children. It was curious to see him chatter-ing to Christine, and then to think about his blasphemous poems and all his talk about sex magic. He was like a clever older brother. What's more, he seems to understand her psychology better than I do. He suddenly asked her: "Would you like me to tell you a story?" She said "Ooh yes," and he immediately launched into a fairy story about a giant and a dwarf who went into partnership to free a country of dragons. I would have assumed she'd feel herself too old for this kind of thing, but she listened with a fascinated stare, and didn't breathe until half an hour later. When she finally said she had to go home, he bent over and kissed her, then gave her half a crown, for all the world like a Santa Claus in some big store at Christmas. I found this an unexpected and most likable

side to his character. In fact I felt so warm about him that
I told him I'd been reading his poetry, and was hypocritically
complimentary about it. The delighted him—it was evident
that I'd touched his *amour-propre*—and he immediately
launched into extravagant praise of himself as a poet. I commented on his being born near Leamington, and he said: "Yes,
I have often thought it strange that Warwickshire should have
produced England's two greatest poets—for we must not
forget Shakespeare."

He hadn't been in the room for five minutes before he
declared he needed a drink. As I had nothing in the room but
a foul Spanish burgundy, he sent me out for some decent wine.
(I didn't mind playing errand boy—he was paying.) He stood
this in hot water to take off the chill, and we drank for nearly
an hour. He had some interesting things to tell me. When he
began to boast to me about his sexual prowess, I tried to jar
him by asking him bluntly how he'd obtained such a hold over
Oliver. He startled me by replying: "By saving him from suicide." He claimed that he was in the Preston Art Gallery, looking at a painting by Oliver, when he had a sudden overwhelming intimation that the artist was in danger. He was so urgent
that the authorities of the gallery gave him the address. He took
a taxi there, announced to the landlady that he was an old
friend of Mr. Glasp, and rushed up to the room she indicated.
Without even knocking, he tried the door, found it locked, and
burst it open with his shoulder. Oliver was asleep, and looked
amazed as his door burst open. Cunningham said he thrust
out a finger at him and said: "You are not to do it. I have
been sent to stop you." He claims that Oliver's immediate reaction was to collapse, and then to admit that he had been steel-
ing himself all day to the idea of cutting his throat, and had
just that minute decided that he would walk into the bathroom
and do it.

I have no idea at all whether Cunningham invented this
story, partly or wholly. All his stories about himself and other
people are somehow so much "in character" with the way he

sees things that he might almost be accused of being a novelist who invents his life in the act of living it.

And yet how otherwise can I explain the influence he possesses over Oliver? He told me that he made Oliver go out with him to an Indian restaurant, where he forced him to eat huge quantities of very hot food, washed down with wine. Oliver was so awe-stricken by this "messenger from God" that he did whatever he was told. Cunningham talked at him for two hours, and ended by getting him to sign a paper agreeing to let him arrange an exhibition at a London gallery and deal with the whole financial side of the venture.

I asked Cunningham what arguments he used to bring this about. "I didn't argue. I just staggered him with my insight into his condition. I told him that he felt as if he were sliding down a slope, but that he could arrest his motion at any moment." Cunningham now became very confiding and philosophical, but what he said excited me immensely. It went deeper than anything he'd said in his books, and made me wonder if he really does possess strange powers. He talked for more than half an hour, but what he said, in summary, was this: We all react immediately to pain and discomfort by struggling to be free of it. But the strangest thing about human beings is that when this negative stimulus comes to an end, they immediately devalue life by slipping back into boredom. Therefore, the "divine forces" (he either used this term, or simply "the Powers") have made stimulation-by-misery the secret of their method of driving men to become gods. The greatest sin is the attempt to escape this "goad" of the Powers by sinking into apathy. Men who have no reason whatever to fear pain or discomfort sometimes commit suicide from boredom.

There is only one way to escape the "goad" of misery. Not the Buddhist's perfect detachment, which is nonsense. Simpler than that. To go in the direction in which Fate is trying to goad you at such a speed that it can't catch up.

This was the essence of what he said, but he used a hundred illustrations (and I interrupted him to supply some of my own). He talked as if he were receiving inspiration (perhaps the wine). That we take all our moods and feelings for granted, as something "sent to us." In fact, we seem to assume that they *are* us. We are passive. We wake up feeling gloomy; we are contented to wait until Fate sends events to cheer us up. The desire for life is stimulated by a crisis, but subsides when the crisis is overcome, *and we are content to let it subside.* And yet we are always more detached from our feelings than we realize; otherwise, how could you feel "happy to feel happy," or even feel "happy to feel sad"?

Our first duty, he said, is to maintain a sense of gratitude for being alive. Any other attitude is a *sin,* to be immediately punished by the Powers. All those *fin de siècle* poets condemned themselves to death by refusing to be happy, by sitting around, gloomily waiting to be coaxed and patted into smiling.

Cunningham then, with immense conviction, went on to point to himself as one of those who are "loved by the gods" because he never allows a morsel of despair to settle anywhere on him. People like Oliver observe that he seems curiously favored by destiny, more vital, more magnetic than other people, and assume that Fate has been kind to him, while in fact, he simply lives according to the invisible law that states that boredom and lack of enthusiasm for what you are doing is a mortal sin. He doesn't worry about scrutinizing the universe for signs and portents. He said (and the image astounded me) that most men live as if they are the audience in a theater when they don't realize that they're actually on the stage, and the gods will throw things if they don't start acting.

I can imagine the effect that all this must have had on Oliver—especially Cunningham's conviction that you have to act and radiate vitality at all costs, send out waves of charm and enthusiasm, even when you can see nothing to be charming and enthusiastic about. "Such a man is a magnet to good fortune," he said. He went on to say that he never allowed himself to worry. He was born rich, and spent more than £100,000 in his twenties. Since then, he has had no regular income, and yet has probably spent another hundred thousand.

"For example, I spent a month in the Lake District trying to teach two rich young men the rudiments of mountain climbing. They got scared and went home, paying the hotel bill but leaving me without a penny. I did the first thing that came into my head—took a bus to Preston, and went into the art gallery. Now, within six weeks, we've made over two thousand pounds from Oliver's painting." This sum staggered me, but I couldn't help asking him how much of it would find its way to Oliver's pocket. "What does it matter if he never gets a penny of it? For a paltry two thousand pounds, he's learned the secret of greatness. He'd be dead if I hadn't stopped him." I had to admit that this reasoning seemed accurate. And yet I couldn't help thinking of the irony of the thing. Oliver may be a manic-depressive, but he also has genius. Cunningham has the vitality of ten men and the audacity of fifty, yet he can't write a line of decent poetry. This was not a subject I could discuss, after my extravagant praise of his poems. (Come to think of it, I suppose I owe his confidences to my praise!)

Before we left the room to go down to Kirsten, he said one more thing that stayed in my mind. We had been talking about some of the "unhappy geniuses" of the 19th century—from Keats to Van Gogh. Cunningham said: "No man will ever be entirely great until he has succeeded in declaring himself entirely and completely *for* life, with no doubt anywhere in his being. In spite of death and misery and the apparent cruelty of nature, he has to declare his complete and total trust, without any misgiving." I was so impressed by this that I went into the lavatory and wrote it down on an envelope.

Later. Writing in these long bursts is exhausting. Cunningham makes it necessary; it is impossible to write about him briefly. Anyway, let me jump ahead of my story. Last night I ended by sleeping with Diana, and I still tingle all over when I think of it. And this again as a direct result of Cunningham's intervention. I must confess that my original suspicion of him has changed into fairly undiluted admiration.

Before we left the room to go down, I stopped to shave;

he asked me, grinning, if I wanted to get Diana into bed. I said
I did. At this, he said that he'd make sure that I possessed her
before the night was over. *I knew immediately that he was not
joking,* but asked him how this was possible. He said: "I'll
make sure you get left alone with her. Whip her dress above her
waist and shove it in." I said I doubted whether this technique
would work. "Balls," he said. "Make it a bit more subtle if
you're frightened. Grab her in your arms and ask her if she
loves you. If she says no, tell her she's mistaken—she does.
But she won't say no if you ask her belligerently enough.
Make it sound like an ultimatum, that's the secret."

He then told me gleefully about one of his earliest conquests. When he was at Oxford, he spent a holiday in Paris.
He went to a ball where a dazzlingly beautiful princess was to
be married to a Greek millionaire. As soon as he came into
the room and saw her, he felt that he had to have her. He
said: "I knew that if I didn't have her, I'd spend the next ten
years dreaming about her, and turn into a lovesick poet. I decided I'd rather be horsewhipped than meet with such a horrible fate. So immediately after the first dance, I walked up to
her and asked her to dance. While I was crossing the floor
towards her, I felt an awful sickness, and wanted to rush out of
the place. But the moment I began to speak to her, I re-
gained confidence; I stared at her, and *willed* her to agree to
dance, although I knew her future husband was standing behind her and glaring at me. She said yes and stepped out onto
the floor with me. After pressing her against me for a few
moments, I had a monstrous erection. I deliberately pulled her
close to me so she was aware of it, clenched my teeth, and
muttered in her ear: 'Listen, I've got to screw you tonight or
I'll go mad.' She looked horrified and said: 'That is impossible.
There is my fiancé, and I am still a virgin.' 'That can't be
helped,' I said, 'I am the man who is destined to take your
maidenhead. Come outside now.' She kept muttering: 'No,
no, it is impossible.' I tried to steer her out on to the lawn, but
she wouldn't; she said she had to be back at her table to meet

someone. So I said: 'I'll wait along the corridor, in the room next to the library. If you are not there in ten minutes, I'm coming to get you.' Then, without finishing the dance, I turned and left her. Sure enough, after ten minutes, she came out to the cloakroom. By that time, I'd spied out the house and found a way upstairs to the bedrooms. I grabbed her wrist, pulled her upstairs, and as soon as I'd got her in the room, threw her on the bed, ripped off her panties, and bit halfway through her lower lip. Within less than two minutes I'd stripped off the rest of her clothes and had her."

"Was it pleasant?" I asked. "Not very. She was frigid." "She doesn't sound it." "No? You don't understand. People can be hypnotized by conviction and purpose. They possess none themselves and the idea of coming into contact with it excites them." I asked him what had happened to the girl afterwards. "I don't know. She looked in a mirror and started to cry, because her bitten lip was impossible to hide, and half her clothes were torn. I simply dressed and walked out of the room. I read later that she married her millionaire, so I suppose it must have been all right. But years later, a friend of mine met her in the south of France; he happened to show her a photograph with me in it, and she recognized me. She gave him a message for me: 'Tell him I love him, and that if he wants to come for me, I will go wherever he likes.' " I asked, "Why didn't you?" "I had other things to do. Besides, as I said, she was frigid."

With anyone else, I would dismiss this story as wish fulfillment; with Cunningham, I am certain that it happened—or that something fairly close to it happened.

I should also mention that I finally got around to asking Cunningham about the library episode. I even went so far as to show him what I had written about it in my journal. Perhaps this was a mistake—I should have asked his version first. At all events, he confirmed what I had written. He said he had never seen the girl before, and had not seen her since. He declared that certain women, when frustrated, give off a kind of invisible distress signal. This signal is not visible to all men—only to those who are capable of a satisfactory response. He said that, like me, he had immediately felt a powerful desire for the girl, so strong that he was tempted to grab her in front of everyone in the library. Instead, he came into the corner where I was sitting—the only spot not visible from the central desk—and allowed his own desires to expand until they became a kind of "disturbance of the ether." He claimed that all the time the girl stood at the bookshelf, with her back toward us, she was conscious of him and was already responding actively to his desire in the usual female way. He said that what he was afraid of was that he might give her an orgasm before he had a chance to touch her.

He claims that when he spoke to her, he simply said: "I wish to see certain books in your special collection." I asked him why this caution was necessary; he said because she was a "respectable girl" who might easily take fright at her own responses. However, believing that he wanted to see the theology section, she took him to some damp room in the basement. There, he says, he unzipped her skirt without further ado, and possessed her on a table. He says she made no attempt to resist, but kept moaning: "You're hurting me." Afterward, he said, she got all intense and said: "What are we going to do?," and he realized that she was one of those girls with an awful ability to cling. He said: "These are the moments when I abandon the superman role. The only safe course is flight." He has taken care to avoid the library ever since then.

Diana interrupted us; she came up to ask me what time Cunningham would be arriving, and was disconcerted to find him there already. She muttered something about a makeshift supper, and Cunningham immediately declared that we were all to be his guests, and that we'd go and have a Chinese meal. So we went down and joined Kirsten, who refused a glass of wine, and looked wretchedly embarrassed and stood twisting his hands and mumbling. Cunningham offered to play one of his own compositions on the piano; when he announced the title: "Kratakoa," I suspected it was going to be noisy and discordant, and suggested that it would be better to hear it later when we'd eaten. (Afterwards I explained to Cunningham about Kirsten's dislike of "modern music," and that it might have driven him further back into his shell.) Diana agreed to have a drink (out of embarrassment, I think) and Cunningham and I behaved as if Kirsten weren't there, and continued our discussion. I expounded my theory of the indifference threshold, which fitted in fairly closely with what he'd been saying earlier, then told him my project of an opera libretto on Major Weir. Just as I expected, Cunningham declared that he knew all about Weir, "the inside story." He dismissed my theory that Weir was simply oversexed and repressed, and assured us that Weir really had intercourse with the devil. I noticed immediately that Kirsten looked interested, and began to brighten up.

We took a taxi down to a Chinese restaurant in Limehouse, ordered lager from the pub next door, and had an excellent meal. Meanwhile, Cunningham talked at length about sex and Major Weir. The essence of the thing, he explained to us, was Weir's bestiality with horses, sheep, etc. He declared that there are two types of sexual energy, heavenly and diabolic, and that the sex act is *not* a physical act, but actually a symbolic conjuration, exactly like raising demons. The orgasm does not spring from a reservoir of sexual energy called "the libido," but comes from *beyond the body,* in exactly the same way that the electricity in our houses comes from a power station that may be twenty miles away. Otherwise, Cunningham said, how can you explain the fact that the sexual energies cannot be exhausted? A man can keep on having orgasms indefinitely—20 times a day if he wants to. Admittedly, a man might feel sexually drained after the first orgasm, particularly if it happens to be with a wife or someone who excites no desire for conquest. But this is not real exhaustion, only the refusal of the erotic energies to reveal themselves in response to such feeble conjuration. The exhausted man can be roused to excitement five minutes later by the thought of a *strange* woman or something forbidden.

Hence the importance of sex in all diabolic orgies. For what could be more blasphemous than summoning energy from the divine erotic power house, and pouring it into the anus of a donkey? It is literally dipping Christ into hell. The devotee of the Black Mass who agrees to use his powers of sexual conjuration in this way receives a "bonus" from the devil, an extra load of diabolic sexual energy. This energy, Cunningham said, is admittedly not of the same power or quality as the divine article—its quality is like methylated spirits compared to Napoleon brandy—but *added* to the divine article, it makes a mixture of unparalleled kick. The only trouble is that it is habit-forming, like a drug, and finally sets up a perpetual torment, a kind of unquenchable thirst. This is the explanation for the fact that all sex maniacs have to commit their crimes with increasing frequency, and are often driven by an inner compulsion to be caught. The torment is unbearable; the more they commit their crimes, the worse it becomes, like trying to satisfy a burning thirst with petrol or corn whisky. They are also driven further and further from a sense of contact with other human beings, until they feel alone in the outer darkness with the devil. This is why their sadism increases. Cunningham instanced a case of sexual murder that took place in Arkansas when he was out there just after the war. The murderer preyed on young lovers at the time of the full moon. His first crime only involved knocking out the man and raping the girl. Subsequently, he got into the habit of shooting the man, and then torturing the girl before he killed her. In the last of these cases, the killer tortured the girl horribly, mutilating her with a knife, for six hours after he had murdered her lover. But now he was nearly insane with remorse; he tried to confess to a priest, but the devil drove him out of the church before his turn came. Finally, knowing that he would be driven to even greater lengths next time, he decided to hand himself over to the police. At this point, the devil intervened, and put the idea of suicide into his head, knowing that suicide is the ultimate sin for which there is no forgiveness. The man threw himself under a train.

At this point, Kirsten asked how Cunningham knew all this, since the man had never been caught. Cunningham said that he had access to all details in these cases, but that he could not, at present, tell us more. Diana asked if he had known the identity of the murderer before he committed suicide. Cunningham said yes, he had.

At this point, I asked Cunningham if he knew the identity of Jack the Ripper. He smiled and said he certainly did: the Ripper was a rich nobleman who inherited a certain type of insanity from his grandfather; he had died of syphilis in a mental home near Ascot. He then leaned over and whispered the name in my ear*

Cunningham told me that he could present me with definite evidence at any time I wished.

Diana now asked him if he knew anything about the Whitechapel murderer. I watched Cunningham closely to see if he'd look at me. It is probable that Oliver has told him about Austin, even though Oliver was never certain. But Cunningham said cautiously that he only knew certain details; since the man was still alive, he was not allowed to speak of it. Kirsten pressed him to tell what he knew. Cunningham shrugged, and answered that the killer was a rich homosexual, who, like Jack the Ripper, had inherited his degeneracy from a line of alcoholics on his father's side. He said he could not tell us any more, and was not allowed to reveal the name. Naturally, both Diana and Kirsten were seething with curiosity, and asked Cunningham why the murders had stopped so abruptly, and whether the police knew the killer's identity. He said yes, the police knew his identity, but that nevertheless the killer was not now in prison. Naturally, I suspected that Glasp had

* For various reasons, connected with the surviving relatives of the man named, it has been thought advisable to suppress the next sentence. *Editor.*

told him everything. (It is strange, incidentally, that Oliver hasn't asked me any questions about Austin, almost as if he had some secret reason for keeping silent.)

Now there was a curious event. Cunningham stared at Diana very hard, and she stared back at him, her eyes very wide. Kirsten and I simply watched; both of us felt that we shouldn't interrupt. Finally, Cunningham smiled and asked her what she was thinking. She looked at him in a very puzzled way, and asked if the murderer was a woman. He said no, and asked her why. She said that a name had come into her head—"Anne." Cunningham only smiled; then he told Kirsten that his wife had definite psychic powers. He said that as she was staring at him, he was suddenly aware of a definite psychic pressure, as she tried to read his mind. He had therefore looked at her, and given her a chance to read it; this was why they stared at one another.

Diana admitted that she had been staring at him, trying to force him to tell them the name of the murderer, and that when he had looked at her, the word "Anne" seemed to come into her head.

As she said this, I suddenly realized that "A. N." are Austin's intitials, and my hair stirred; I felt as if I'd accidentally sat in an electric chair. For some odd reason, all three of them looked at me, as if they were aware of something. I muttered: "Strange," and took a long drink of lager, to cover up my confusion.

After this supper, there is no doubt whatever in my mind that certain people possess the rudiments of curious powers. Well, why not? We know, for example, that the sense of color is a fairly recent development in human beings. The ancient writers never mention colors. Tests on animals prove that they have almost no color sense; they see the world in a kind of monochrome. Color sense is an evolutionary luxury, and it has not developed until fairly recently (over the past two or three centuries, I suppose). Well, why should there not be still further senses in a stage of early development? Again,

Cunningham admitted that sadism is a sign of degeneracy—i.e., the opposite of evolution. A more sensitive person is *too closely in contact* with other people to be able to inflict pain. Surely it is not fanciful to suppose that evolution will move toward a universal sense of community, constant telepathic contact between human beings? Perhaps Cunningham's ability to see around corners is an example of this new sense. What puzzles me is that it should be a man like Cunningham, who definitely strikes me as a kind of fool. (In many ways, he is strangely like Austin.) He undeniably has powers—remarkable powers, and a kind of genius, but it is on an animal level; he lacks the real self-discipline of the mystic or man of genius. Hence, I suppose, his interest in magic and other offbeat subjects. I find this possibility of developing new powers immensely exciting; it gives the world a new meaning for me.

After supper, we took a taxi back to Kirsten's, now in a very friendly mood. Cunningham easily induced him to drink more—we stopped at a pub to load up on spirits—and he became talkative. It was the usual kind of think—the world of the spirit, the empyrean, etc. Then he wanted to tell us about an opera he'd written, based on a novel called *Varney the Vampire*.* The plot sounded excruciatingly funny, but both Cunningham and I kept a straight face. Kirsten explained that the heroine symbolized Heavenly Virtue, renunciation, unselfishness, etc. He then sat at the piano, and insisted on playing us the overture and leading arias. Kirsten would insist on singing the words—his own, of course—and interrupting the playing to shout things like: "He seizes her in his arms; they reach a transport of ecstasy," and more thunderous bangs on the piano, with Kirsten yodeling like a dog.

After half an hour of this, Kirsten was in such a state of alcoholic emotion that he was hardly intelligible. Cunning-

---

* By Thomas Prest, one of the earliest and most famous of vampire novels. Printed in 1847, it was reprinted dozens of times until Bram Stoker's *Dracula* eclipsed it. Prest also wrote *Sweeney Todd, The Demon Barber*.

ham now asked him about his invention, and said he'd like
to see it. Kirsten forthwith leaped to his feet, and told us to
follow him. Diana, looking oddlly subdued and tired (or perhaps it was only the gin she was drinking), followed after us.
She was so bewildered she even left the door wide open and I
(who was last out, since I'd gone up to get an overcoat) had
to close it. I walked with her behind Kirsten and Cunningham,
and as she showed a disposition to stumble, had an excuse to
put my arm around her waist. She didn't seem to mind in the
least. To my surprise, I realized that she was wearing only a
thin dress under a short jacket, and apparently no underskirt.
The zipper at the side of the skirt was partly open, and her bare
flesh underneath it was icy cold. I immediately insisted that she
wear my overcoat; she agreed, although she protested that
she wasn't cold. Kirsten's workshop is half a mile away, behind
Hanbury Street, a room in a freezing warehouse that smells of
leather. I was surprised that his "invention" looked less weird
than I'd supposed it would. I'd expected a kind of Heath-
Robinson* contraption; instead, it looked like a theater organ.
He said that it was an idea he'd got when he saw an invention
of Maelzel's as a child, on exhibition at a fair; it was called
an "Orchestrion," and produced noises like violins, flutes and
horns all from one machine. Kirsten himself had also noticed
that a combination of piano and organ sounds impressive, and
had started designing the machine simply with the intention
of uniting piano and organ in one instrument. Soon it came
to him that all kinds of noises can be produced by pipes and
strings, properly combined, and he began to design his own
"orchestrion."

It was icy cold in the damned shop, and poor Diana was
now shivering, in spite of my overcoat. I was pretty chilly myself. However, Kirsten insisted that we hear his instrument,
and announced that he would play us some more extracts from
Varney the Vampire. At this, my heart sank, and I began to

* An English cartoonist who specialized in drawings of strange-looking
machines tied together with string.

make excuses; but Kirsten ignored them and sat down, remarking that we must remember that the machine was still un-
finished. He then proceeded to play his overture. To my utter
amazement, it now sounded quite different. What had sounded
absurd and tinny on the piano now became tremendously impressive. Some of his effects were astounding; for example,
there is a quiet passage, played by a thing that sounds like a
flute or a high violin, where the piano suddenly chimes in with
a weird effect like an old barrel organ; then the organ notes
take over again, rising to a tremendous, jarring climax. (I
don't know why Kirsten professes to loathe modern music;
he's an expert in the use of discord.) There is now no doubt
whatever in my mind that Kirsten is a musical genius of the
first order. While his conversation is precise and pedantic and
somehow lacking in vitality, his music shows evidence of a
mind of great agility. There seems to be no effect in which
he is not an expert: passages of Miltonic dignity are followed
by distorted strains of Hungarian violins or cockney street
music, giving his music a completely unique flavor, as tart as
unripe apples. When he went on to play us the heroine's final
aria, it was now sublime and tremendous; it was everything
he had said, a climax of sweetness and poignancy that actually
brought tears to my eyes. In spite of the cold, I could have
gone on listening for hours. However, it was now after midnight, and Diana was shivering convulsively and protesting
that she wanted to go home. But Cunningham grasped Kirsten's hand, called him a universal genius, and asked him to
come back to his place and talk. I also tried to express what
I felt to Kirsten, and he looked as if he was going to burst into
tears. Suddenly he cheered up and shouted: "Let's go and
have another drink." Diana said firmly that she had to be up
early and wanted to go home. He tried to dissuade her, but I
could see she was tired, and strangely sharp with him, in the
way that women are when they think their menfolk fools. Finally, she said she would go home alone; I said I'd go with
her. At this, Kirsten said: "Good, in that case I'll go back with

our friend Caradoc." (He was already using Cunningham's Christian name, which I can't bear to pronounce.)

Diana had already walked out of the place; I hurried after her and caught up with her in the street. She said I needn't spoil my night on her behalf; I didn't tell her that I was hoping she'd *make* my night for me. She let me put my arm around her, but walked back very fast (we were both frozen). As we went up the stairs, I was wondering what excuse I could use to get her to come up to my room, but I didn't need one; she opened her door and asked me if I'd like a cup of tea before I went to bed. So I went in with her. Her gas fire had gone out (she had left it turned on) and neither of us had any small change. Her gas stove was also out of action. So I suggested we go up and use mine. At first I thought she'd refuse and go straight to bed; but she came up docilely enough. In my room, I lit the fire and turned it up high; she huddled over it. I also put the kettle on the ring in the hearth, to warm the room quicker. For five minutes she sat with my overcoat on, until the heat became too great. Then she threw it off. The zipper on her dress was now completely undone, but she didn't seem to care; there was a strange abandonment about her as she sat there, as if she were drunk and tired. (But we'd been listening to the orchestrion for an hour, so she'd had time to recover from the gin.) I was full of enthusiasm about her husband, and said that I thought he'd be a great musician. At this she looked a little more interested, and asked me if I thought he would ever be a success. I said that I would be very surprised indeed if he wasn't, and that I couldn't understand why he hadn't made a success already. She shrugged, and said that he'd ruined all the opportunities that had presented themselves so far. People who showed an interest in his music were put off by his conversation—this is, by his abuse of all contemporary composers, his contemptuous sneers about "compromise," and his proposals to write symphonies that would go on for three hours, or operas longer than the Ring cycle. They all ended by thinking he was a crank, and sneaking away.

The tea seemed to make her more lively, and as the room was now stiflingly hot, she moved over to the bed and took off her shoes. For half an hour now, I'd had a curious feeling with her. It was not that she was willing to give herself to me, or was offering herself; it was just a *certainty*. I found myself looking at her as if she was already mine. For example, when she removed the overcoat, and I saw the zipper was undone, I was surprised that the sight of her bare flesh, and a bit of garter belt, aroused no desire, any more than they would in a husband. Yet it wasn't that I'd lost interest; I was tingling with need for her, and longing to pounce on her like a wolf. And yet it was as if I had already possessed her once. She went on talking about him with a curious bitterness, and I began to wonder if she secretly resented the fact that Kirsten could never *need* her as much as a "normal" man could.

When she'd finished her tea, she lay back against the pillow, her shoulders on the wall, and closed her eyes. At this moment, we both thought we heard footsteps on the stairs, as if Kirsten were returning. I was certain it was Kirsten, and immediately gave up all idea of making love to her. We didn't speak about it, but just sat there, waiting for him to come up or call to her. Five minutes went by, and there was no sound, so we went on talking. Then, with a feeling that the evening was almost over (and in any case, I wanted to go down to the lavatory, which I suspected would break things up), I went over to her as she lay with closed eyes, moved her shoulders so she was lying on the bed, and kissed her. She lay there as if she was unconscious; I knelt beside the bed for a few minutes, kissing her face and throat; then the bursting bladder got the better of me, and I went out of the room. After I came out of the lavatory, I saw that her door was slightly ajar, so I pushed it open and called "Robert?" Then I looked inside; we had obviously been mistaken in thinking he'd come home. It was probably the tenant on the floor below coming up to the lavatory. There was a bunch of keys on the table, which I recognized as Kirsten's, so I reasoned that he had probably gone out

without them, and would have to ring the bell to get in. I
then went down and confirmed that the front door was closed.
Finally, I went up to my room, and found that Diana now
appeared to be asleep. I turned off the fire and the light and undressed in the dark (my heart thumping, afraid she'd wake up
and protest, or that the doorbell would ring). But nothing
happened, and I climbed into bed; she stirred and moved
over. But as soon as I started to kiss her and raised her dress,
she woke up and struggled. I tried to hold her, but she refused.
She said: "No, don't. What if Robert comes back?" I told her
about the key on the table, and that he'd have to ring the
doorbell to get in. By this time she was sitting up, and had got
out of bed. I accepted the idea of defeat, and lay down again.
She opened the door, picked up her shoes, and went out of
the room. I said "damn" and turned over. However, before
I could fall asleep, she came back into the room and closed
the door; then I heard her clothes falling on the floor. A
moment later, she slipped into bed. She left me finally at half
past seven this morning.

Now it is over, I feel my usual persistent desire to anat-
omize the event and examine my own feeling. The most surprising thing is this: I am certain that I'm in love with her. As
I write this, I can hear Kirsten's piano below; the thought that
she will sleep with him tonight is unbearable to me. And for
the first time in my life, I want a woman so completely that
I'd be happy to marry her, or agree to take her off to the other
side of the world.

I try to understand how this feeling came about. It may be
connected with my feeling of *protectiveness* about her. I've
pitied her since I met her looking so tired on the stairs. I had
spent the evening with her, and watched her shiver in clothes
that should have been thrown away last summer. But the
certainty that I was in love with her came on me quite suddenly when I was kissing her, immediately after she got into
bed. A man in bed says "I love you" automatically; the strange
thing was that I didn't want to say it, because it would seem
a simplification of what I actually felt about her. This was

partly physical excitement, no doubt. She seemed unsure of herself, and lay on her side, facing me. So I didn't try to force her; just kissed her, and let my hands move over her body. She has an exceptionally pliable body—more soft than anyone I've ever known. She lay against me, her thighs caressing me, and it was then that I wanted her—I mean that I wanted to marry her. Finally, I had to ask her: "Would you leave your husband to live with me?" She said "I don't know," and sounded frightened. I said: "Supposing I gave you a baby?" "I don't know." I said: "Then let me give you a baby." When she didn't reply, I asked her: "Is it possible for you to have a baby at present?," and she said yes. At this, I started to make love to her like a demon. I had a violent climax inside her; she felt it, and tried to twist away, but I held her tight. I felt that she had to be bound to me somehow. There was the feeling of urgency, in case Kirsten came home, so I made love to her again and again, and after the second time she no longer tried to make me withdraw. Before she left, I had made love to her eight times. At one point, we heard someone on the stairs, and assumed it was Kirsten. Yet she made no move to get out of bed; on the contrary, she put her arms around my neck, as if she wanted him to find us together. For my own part, I didn't care; I'd prefer him to find out quickly, so that I'd know where I stood. However, no one called, so I suppose it was one of the tenants going to the lavatory.

And yet we spoke very little; I didn't even say I loved her. At dawn, she slipped out of bed, pulled on her dress, and went out, carrying her clothes. I didn't want to sleep. I had to overcome a temptation to go down and join her, but reasoned that Kirsten might come in suddenly. Finally, I got up and began to write in this journal. At half past ten I met Kirsten on the stairs; he told me he'd spent the night talking at Cunningham's, and that he thinks Cunningham a great man!

Now I should try to use all my insight to try to focus this problem of sex—but now is the very moment it seems most elusive. And yet one thing came to me clearly last night: sex depends entirely upon the idea of the *violation of identity*. It is like banging two eggs together in your hands so that they both break. (The simile fails because only one of the eggs breaks—still, it holds my meaning.)

Yes, we are all lonely, "each in his prison," all automatically grasping for freedom as a moth flies to the light. And there, yesterday afternoon, was a desirable but inviolable Diana, a separate identity, who might be "an immense world of delight, closed to my senses five." Then, like peeling the skin off an onion, I strip away the outer layers of her identity, and plunge into her center as a bee plunges into a flower. I, of course, am the same for her. A shell is cracked.

What I am suggesting, of course, is an "illusion" theory of sex, a neurosis theory. Sex, then, depends upon our being sick enough to want to smash the shell. A madman might believe that the whole world is against him, that there is a conspiracy to defraud him of his reality. The sexual illusion is on precisely the same level—a false notion that the being of the other person conceals a reality that you lack. It is like a child who, asked to choose between two apples, can never believe that he has not chosen wrongly. No wonder the ancients were inclined to summarize human existence in such legends as the myth of Tantalus.

The odd thing is that I'm not at all pessimistic about this. The illusion is only harmful if you allow it to be. For example, it might reach a stage of Don Juanism where you want simply to ravish every pretty girl you see in the street. But the real danger would only start if you began to calculate how this could best be done (like the West End rapist with his ether pad). Frustration is bad; failure of self-control is worse, the swiftest descent into hell. Meaning vanishes. This is surely the reason that all the most spectacular series of lust murders have ended either in the suicide of the killer (as in the Ripper case, or the Arkansas murderer), or in the murderer walking into the police traps like a somnambulist, as with Kürten and Heath.

I wish I had a language in which I could describe this

failure of "meaning" that must come to the sexual killer. I can *focus* the idea, yet cannot express it. I think of the Texarkana murderer, who began by merely attacking a couple in a car, knocking the man unconscious and raping the girl, and ended by torturing his victims to death. But even if he was an exceptionally stupid man, completely unreflective, he must have felt an awful sense of panic after each of these murders, an anticlimax worse than a bad hangover, a sense of having been cheated by the gods he was obeying. Such "hangovers" must have produced the idea of devils in the Middle Ages. The devil whispers "Rather murder an infant in its cradle than nurse unacted desires. If you want sex, go and grab it. If you envy the man in the car, with one hand up her dress, go and knock him out and take the girl yourself. Do that and you will eventually be free and godlike and wise." But all that happens is that each time, he has to go further, until, in an effort to grasp the girl's innermost reality and violate her separateness, merely penetrating her body is not enough; he has to torture her, destroy her completely. And after each crime, he knows that he has sunk lower, and the fairy gold still glitters and lures him—further down the pit. And the slope above him is so steep that only a spiritual giant could find the courage to climb back. There is no answer but self-destruction.

Now I want to rest in Diana, to sink into her, make her my terminus and goal. Arbitrarily I say "I love her," and it is true.

It is half past eleven; I shall go out and meet her for lunch.

Later. There are times when I feel driven to destroy illusions —my own and the world's. The reason, I suppose, is that I want to know just how tolerable life would be without illusions—or if Andreyev and Artsybashev are right when they say that life would be revealed as it really is—loathsome, naked, ugly, intolerable.

One thing I know for certain—it is damned hard work

being a human being. When they are handing out the parts in heaven—"You go to Mars; you are to be reborn on Saturn; you are to be a salamander and live in the center of the sun"— Earth is regarded as the "tough assignment." "You are to be born as a human being on Earth." "Oh no, not that filthy dump. Why, everybody knows that to be a human being is the lousiest deal in the universe."

These thoughts occurred to me on returning from lunch with Diana. She seemed tired, and talked to me casually, without intimacy, as if last night had never happened. I left her, feeling irritable, resentful. When I got in, I thought: "The hell with it; so you spent a pleasant night in bed with somebody else's wife, and now it's over, so why worry?" It is true that I sometimes wonder if I *can* ever be in love; I have made a habit of examining every emotion too closely, analyzing it into its constituent parts. Love I see as part egoism, part possessiveness, part need for security. And I wish I could explode this sexual illusion. Is there any hope that man might be a little more godlike without it? The world seems to me so full of illusion. Cunningham is a good man, vital and intelligent; yet all his talk of magic and evil is an illusion with which he keeps himself going. There is no evil, only stupidity. There is no magic; magic never works, never, at any time. So we are left in a rather unglamorous universe. The mainstay of the entertainment industry—romantic love—is another lie. Centuries have built codes of ethics on this idea of romantic love— knights on horseback, killing dragons and giants for the sake of a lady's glove, and it is all a lie to conceal the truth—two dogs copulating in an alleyway.

No, I'm good at seeing through illusions, but what is the truth underneath them? That I can't see at present. We are so closely enmeshed in illusions that the explosion of one or two of them makes no difference. On the street corner below, a crowd of teddy boys stand most evenings and whistle at the girls who go by. They have probably all had sexual experience; yet every girl who passes represents a taboo that they long to break. Illusions. I put on a record—it is Tchaikovsky's *Pathé-tique*. More illusions, another poor devil who thought the universe owed him love. A self-betrayer, as Bill Payne would call him. Give us love, give us illusions. These cinema posters —"Escape to Happiness"—desert islands, golden sands, hand-some men, "Beyond the Blue Horizon," beautiful girls in motorboats on the Riviera. But someone has carefully dec-orated the girl's bathing costume with a vagina and pubic hair. This is what horrifies me. The entertainment industry de-pends on giving the public "what it wants," and what it wants seems to be a symbol of kittenish innocence—Brigitte Bardot and Marilyn Monroe. But a lot deeper, there is this violence, the desire of a starved tiger for flesh.

And this is something, at least, of the reality that Cun-ningham wants to cover up with his talk about Grimoires and unutterable secrets.

Nov. 17. I was interrupted yesterday by Carlotta. My first re-action on seeing her was irritation; I thought I'd got rid of her when Cunningham took her home. However, she wanted to talk to me, and she asked me if Cunningham might turn up while she talked; when I said I wasn't sure, she insisted on going to the pub on the corner. There we found a quiet table and I bought beers; she leaned over and asked me solemnly if I thought Cunningham was sane! I replied that, on the whole, I did. She then said: "I think he is perhaps the most dangerous man I have ever met." From the way she said it, I knew ex-actly what she meant: that she was somehow terrified of him, but that he fascinated her. For some reason, I suddenly felt sorry for her. Yes, I think I know why. She sat there, looking so solid and German, with her attractive, squarish face, excel-lent nose and lips and high cheek bones, and her eyes looking absurdly tragic, and I suddenly thought of Cunningham's story about seducing the princess; I imagine the princess as the op-posite of Carlotta (although perhaps I'm being romantic)— slim, rather pale and with the curious self-confidence that generations of money and servants can give. And I know Carlotta hasn't a chance anyway; I imagine she'd excite a slightly sadistic element in Cunningham. However, I couldn't tell her this, so I simply asked her questions. First of all, she asked me if I was jealous of Cunningham. I asked her why I should be. She then said dramatically: "You know I stayed with him the other night?" I said yes, I had expected that. It's easier to tell a girl that you don't object to her infidelities than to tell her you don't care about her; yet they amount to the same thing.

She then went on to tell me what had happened. She described again her sensation on first meeting Cunningham— the strange feeling that she was being violated by him without any physical contact. This feeling continued to obsess her for the rest of the evening. She said that she had a sense of being dominated by him. I can't convey the way she said all this. She evidently takes herself very seriously; I can't take her half so seriously. She explained it with her eyes downcast, in a low voice, as if we were talking about great mysteries. At the same time, I sensed that she didn't look at me because she was afraid I'd be laughing at her—which I suppose I was. She declared that it was "horrible," that she hated it, and yet wanted it. I felt this was partly untrue, but couldn't be bothered to try and get at the truth.

When they went back together, she was in a state of excitement, for she felt that something awful might happen to her. Cunningham remarked that it was too late to get her home, and that she could have the spare bed. She took this to be an excuse to persuade her to stay, and made no objection. However, to her amazement, Cunningham took her into a room upstairs, made up the bed, and left her almost immediately, warning her sardonically to lock her door in case Oliver tried to get in! When he had gone, she locked the door. (She claims she did this because she didn't want him to come in; I think she did it out of pique, or perhaps to force him to knock and beg her to open.) Immediately, she felt oppressed by the room. There were several locked trunks in it, and a table on a raised platform was covered with black cloth. She said she felt instinctively that there was something *wrong* with the room. She even pulled one of the trunks aside to see if by any chance it concealed another entrance to the room. She then undressed and got into bed. She woke an hour later and was aware of someone making love to her. (I pressed her to be specific, and she said she felt someone lying on top of her, actually having sexual intercourse.) She wondered how Cunningham had got in, but nevertheless kept her eyes closed. Suddenly, something made her open them. Immediately, she realized she was alone in the bed, and that the sense of weight on her body had vanished.

She found the room oppressive—it smelt of some scent or incense, and she suspected that this had induced the illusion. So she got out of bed, and opened the window. It was a windy night, and she had to cover her face with the bedclothes to avoid the draft. She then felt "safe," and went to sleep again, this time lying on her stomach. Some time later, she was awakened by the sensation of someone in the bed again. This time she kept her eyes closed for about ten minutes. All the time, her visitor continued to make love to her, while she lay perfectly still. Suddenly, tempted no doubt by her position, he tried to make love "in the Italian manner." By this time, she was quite certain that her former experience had been a dream, but that Cunningham was now definitely in the bed. So she opened her eyes and said "no." Immediately, she was again aware of being alone. This time she lay awake for more than an hour before she went back to sleep.

It happened a third time. She kept her eyes closed and let her "visitor" make love to her. "He is a pervert," she said. I pressed her to explain, but she refused to be more specific. However, I gather that this went on for some time—no doubt she didn't want to risk having him vanish by raising objections—and it wasn't until he hurt her suddenly that she opened her eyes. Immediately, she was alone in the bed, although she said that the state of the bed convinced her that she had not been alone a few minutes before. She lay awake, and the dawn came through the curtains. She then got up and hurried off to the tube station. She did not see Cunningham. She left a note on the pillow saying "Thank you," then was struck by its ambiguity, and tore it up. On arriving home, she said that she was suddenly stricken with the most awful stomach cramps, and had to lie down for an hour. I asked her what she thought had happened, and she said that she supposed Cunningham had waked up, found her gone, and somehow projected his rage to Kentish Town!

I find all this interesting, simply as a demonstration of human gullibility. I don't believe for a moment that Cunningham really possessed her in the night. But I *am* convinced that he somehow induced her to believe that he would.

The next problem is: Why should he? If he wanted to sleep with her, why didn't he go ahead and do so? The only reason that seems plausible is that he intends to use her for some other purpose in the future, and wants to make her feel thoroughly dominated first. If I know Carlotta, a night in bed with Cunningham would have left her slightly contemptuous, again mistress of herself. This wouldn't matter if he only meant to sleep with her once. But what other purpose could he have?

I asked her what she intended to do—if she meant to avoid him in future. She said she would like to, but couldn't. Then she said—this impressed me—"I think he is capable of doing something terrible to me." It didn't impress me because I thought it true—I don't. It impressed me because she wants to believe it true.

I didn't want Carlotta on my hands for the rest of the evening, so I advised her to go and see Cunningham, telling her that I thought he would be alone now. She accepted this idea immediately, and went off with a predatory gleam in her eye. I then went to my room again.

Kirsten was still playing the piano, but he stopped occasionally to talk, and I could hear Diana's voice. They, of course, could hear me moving around. I started reading about Major Weir again. Then, to my surprise, my door opened and Diana came in. I was still annoyed and resentful—in fact, I'd accustomed myself to the idea that there was no longer anything between us. So I got up, grabbed her and kissed her. She talked in a whisper, said Kirsten (who was still playing) thought she had gone down to the shop, and that she wanted to ask me if I would try and keep Cunningham away from him. She said she was certain Cunningham was an evil influence. I wanted to quarrel with her, so I said I thought she was wrong, and that Cunningham could probably get Kirsten's music published. Then I asked her directly to come to bed. She said she hadn't time. I said of course she had—Kirsten wouldn't know that there wasn't a long queue in the shop, and pushed her onto the bed. I expected her to rush off, and verify my feeling that last night meant nothing to her. But to my amazement, she yielded immediately, and let me possess her without even taking off any of her clothes. When it was over she stood up, smoothed down her dress, smiled at me in a funny way, as if to ask: "Are you satisfied now?," and went out. I became convinced that I shall never understand women. Diana is a puzzle to me. Why is she so undemonstrative? Is she capable of caring about anybody? And how can anyone who seems so shy and demure give herself to that bookmaking type?

I've given up worrying about these questions.

Half an hour later, Diana came up again and asked me if I'd like to come down and have something to eat. I said I'd eaten, but went down with some wine anyway. Kirsten, however, wouldn't drink. He only wanted to rave to me about Cunningham again, and to say that he was sure that, with Cunningham's help, he'd manage to get *Varney the Vampire* presented. Diana showed herself more practical than I'd expected, and asked me what I knew about Cunningham's relation to Oliver. I told them frankly what I knew, including the finances of the matter. Kirsten asked me directly: "Do you think he hopes to make money out of me?" I said I didn't think it unlikely. Then he laughed and said: "Well, if he can make money out of my work, there's no reason why he shouldn't. I've been trying for ten years, without success."

I was struck by Kirsten's proprietary air about Diana—a thing that hadn't struck me before. It is obvious that he wouldn't dream of mistrusting her, any more than he'd mistrust his own right hand. And yet, as she demurely made coffee, I kept realizing that I had only just possessed her.

We sat and talked for two hours. I find Kirsten a sympathetic man, although his lack of discrimination is disturbing —he should have been born a hundred years ago, when his flowery language and cranky idealism were fashionable. Then he played me Schumann and Brahms until late. I heard someone go up to my room, but I decided not to show myself—it was probably Carlotta and I didn't feel like playing confidant any more. I drank most of the wine myself.

Nov. 18. I spent last night at Cunningham's place. He is undoubtedly one of the most amazing men I have ever met, and I think I now begin to understand what he's after. Until I met him, Austin was probably the most remarkable person I'd ever known. (I'd still like the two of them to meet.) And in some odd way, Cunningham reminds me of Austin. Both have an intelligence and sensibility well above average; and yet both somehow strike me as "wrong." I cannot explain what I mean at the moment. Perhaps later.

At mid-afternoon I went over to see Cunningham, sick of trying to write with the noise of Kirsten's piano. Oliver told me that it was Cunningham's meditation period, but I went up to see anyway. Sure enough, there was Cunningham, wearing a voluminous yellow robe, sitting in the lotus position and contemplating his navel. He didn't seem to notice me, and I was sure that he'd make it a point of honor not to be disturbed by me, so I sat down, picked up a book—it was one of Suzuki's volumes on Zen—and read for an hour. Cunningham's position brought a certain nostalgia, for I remember when I thought that I was cut out to be a Hindu ascetic sitting cross-legged on Mount Meru. Why did I give up the idea? Because I suspect that *that* kind of sainthood can only be developed to a certain extent, and then becomes redundant, like an over-blown rose. When the idea first comes, it is tremendous, a great revelation. You've become accustomed to seeing things through a mist of emotions and desires and motives; suddenly, you see it through the eyes of the ascetic, and it is no longer confusing; it is strangely pure and simple, like a Japanese paint-ing—like Hokusai's picture of Fujiyama and the wave. It suddenly seems that all people are wasting their lives and their time in their silly preoccupations, while you have stumbled on the *only* thing that matters, the answer to life itself, the need to seek "salvation," the need for truth and intensification of con-sciousness and the way to become a god. But as soon as you try following this new way, it becomes more complicated; you promptly lose sight of what you were after, and realize that your simple attempt to reach out and grasp it was like a child reaching for the sun. It remains an aim and an ideal, but there's no point in sitting cross-legged. You can stare at your navel till you burst; you don't get any freer.

At the end of an hour, Cunningham "woke up," and greeted me as if he didn't know I was in the room—even asked me how long I'd been waiting. We then got into a discussion of Zen and meditation, and I made the comments I've written down here. This immediately led us into what now seems to me the most exciting and fruitful discussion I've ever had. We went out for a walk, had a meal, and Cunningham was completely frank with me. Now I begin to understand his plans, I see their audacity, and realize that he has more than a touch of greatness. And yet I'm also aware of some weakness in him, some flaw, that I find difficult to describe.

We didn't get around to discussing these plans until late at night, but there is no point in detailing our other talk. All the same, it was obvious that he felt I understood him completely, and that he could be completely frank with me.

He began by asking me if I thought it could be chance that had brought the four of us together—Kirsten, Oliver, Cunningham and myself. "Let us not be modest about this. We are probably the four most remarkable men in London. How is it, then that we have come together like this? I believe there is some strange destiny that brings together men who will have a great effect upon the age. Think of Nietzsche and Wagner, Schumann and Brahms, Goethe and Schiller. . . . The great men gravitate together." I was so flattered by this remark that I didn't point out that most great men meet when they've become sufficiently famous to be able to seek one another out.

What he then went on to say—and I was struck by his penetration—is that many such men have no capacity for making their own way independently, and he instanced Kirsten and Oliver. He might have added himself. A man of genius is often helpless on his own; banded with one or two others, his strength increases hundredfold.

I now began to see the nature of his idea. He himself, he explained, is one of these people who are fated to *be* rather than to do. His poetry, he said modestly, is fine, but not for the present age. On the other hand—as he has already proved with Oliver—he has a capacity for getting himself noticed. So what could be luckier than the four of us meeting like this? Plainly we are predestined to help one another.

He then went on to explain that he owns a small island off the coast of Sardinia—only a few acres, with a deserted farmhouse. Why should we not move there, with our respective women, and form a community that would live together on completely anarchic principles? Everything would be shared, including the women. We would put into action Rabelais' precept: "Do what you will." His problem so far had been lack of money. Oliver's painting and Kirsten's invention would probably supply us with money. As soon as our community became known, we would attract great artists from all over the world, and rich women would beg to be allowed to give us money.

Cunningham is a good talker, and I must admit that he had me enthusiastic after ten minutes. But at this point, I interrupted him to ask what he had in mind for the two of us; I have so far never made a penny from writing, so can't contribute much. Cunningham asked me about my private income; I explained that it was only a few pounds a week. He wanted to know if it wouldn't be possible to get access to the capital; I said no, it wouldn't, since this was against the terms of the will. (It isn't—although I doubt whether I could get the money as easily as that. I wasn't going to tell Cunningham, who is a first class shark where money is concerned.) Cunningham then said that I could probably sell my annuity for a lump sum; I cautiously agreed. But if Cunningham's plan involves losing my narrow margin of independence, I shall drop out of the scheme. I think he guessed my thoughts, because he said suddenly that perhaps it would be a better idea to keep my money in reserve, in case the whole scheme failed and we were all on our uppers. In that case, the £3,000—for which he seems to think we could sell my annuity—would get us out of trouble.

I was attracted by the idea, but thought it cranky. Besides, I hate travel, and think I'm probably too much of a lone wolf to commit myself to living in any "community." But now Cunningham became fiendishly persuasive. He said that we needn't think about going to the island until we'd made sure that we can make the community "work" by experiments in London. He then hinted obscurely at "masters" somewhere in the East—men from whom he derives his "powers"—and who, if they could be persuaded to support the venture, would guarantee its success.

I must admit that by this time I was sceptical, but was taking care not to show it. It was beginning to sound like a confidence trick. Then Cunningham astounded me by seeming to read my thoughts. He got up and carefully closed the curtains, brought out a bottle of Chartreuse, produced black coffee, and then said: "Now, we can get down to discussing the *real* problems, and the real nature of our work together." (He has this habit of talking as if the two of us were conspirators.) "Now, Gerard, tell me what it is that you want most in the world." I said that I didn't particularly want anything, since I had enough money to live and work. "Yes, I know you don't want to be rich. I wasn't referring to that kind of need, anyway. You know what I mean. What do you want out of life?"

Since I'd been brooding on this, I was able to reply immediately: "Some way of intensifying my consciousness tenfold; some way of living more completely." He nodded, and said that he knew I was going to make this reply. (The funny thing was that I felt he was telling the truth, and that he knew in advance exactly how the conversation would go.)

I want to try to record the next part of the conversation as accurately as I can, because I think it proves that, no matter how much of a charlatan he may be, he undeniably *has* some deep insight, some unusual knowledge of psychology, that he couldn't have learned in England. (I dismiss the possibility that he thought it out for himself; although he is intelligent, he doesn't strike me as a creative thinker.)

First of all, he pointed out to me that I am basically dissatisfied with myself. I have all the things that I once believed would make me ideally happy—I mean "a room of one's own" and five pounds a week, music and books, and a fairly interesting love life. And yet I'm bored and unfulfilled. Why? "Human weakness," I said. "Quite. You are right. But what is the exact nature of this weakness?" "Low intensity of consciousness." "Precisely. Your consciousness is trimmed low, like a tiny candle flame. It doesn't *embrace* the things you ought to be grateful for. Consider what happens if you go into a bookshop and find a book you've always wanted to own. Your consciousness puts out a kind of arm, a pseudopodium, and envelops the book. For a few hours—or perhaps days—

you are intensely aware of the book. You keep saying to your-self: 'I've got it at last.' Then your consciousness relaxes; the arm is withdrawn. You get used to the book and no longer feel grateful that you possess it. Am I not right?"

I admitted he was. All this, he said, is a result of the low pressure of our conscious minds. It is like a terribly low gas pressure that won't boil a kettle. "You have many things that you would hate to lose, and yet you are in the strange position of not being at all glad you possess them. Have you never bought a book and forgotten about it? Then someone borrows it from you, and your interest in it revives. As soon as it's re-turned, you plunge on it and read it from cover to cover. The consciousness has to be constantly stimulated into gratitude by loss."

I reminded him of Chesterton's novel about a man who keeps leaving his wife and going off around the world, because it's so nice when he comes back to her. He said: "Precisely. Can you imagine a more terrible indictment of human beings? They exalt love and romanticism as the greatest thing in the world. All their most moving poems and epics are about the tremendous importance of love. And yet when a man is mar-ried to a woman he is in love with, he is promptly bored by her. He is not actively and violently bored; he doesn't want to poison her or push her out of a window; but he can't help taking her for granted, and losing the first intensity of posses-siveness."

Cunningham then proceeded to the question of the in-tensification of consciousness, and the achievement of what he called "cosmic consciousness." There are various methods, he said. Drinking, for example. This relaxes us, fills us with a certain spirit of acceptance, intensifies the power of affirma-tion. But it causes deterioration. The same is true of drugs.

At this point, he asked me if I'd ever tried drugs. I said I hadn't. "Then you must start immediately. It will lend point to what I'm going to say." I protested that I didn't want to try, but I must admit that I felt curious. Cunningham opened a cupboard, came back with a tiny packet, and poured a small amount of a grayish powder on the back of my hand. I sniffed it through my nose as he instructed me. He also took some—about three times as much as he gave me, I noticed. He wouldn't tell me what it was—said that he only wanted to demonstrate it to me, and didn't want to get me "hooked" on it. He denied that it was cocaine, although he admitted that it contained cocaine. It made my nose very sore and made me want to cough. I drank some wine to clear my head. After five minutes, it began to take effect. Cunningham was right; it was like turning the control on a gas jet; my consciousness seemed to light up, to expand. The curious thing was that it had no other effect—didn't give me a pleasant sensation, like alcohol, and didn't have any effect at all on my mind, except to make my thinking rather clearer.

"You see," Cunningham said, "there *are* quite simple means of intensifying consciousness. But I may as well be frank with you. Their disadvantages are exactly like those of alcohol, only more so. You noticed that I had to take three times as much as you. This is because I have been using it for several years. I'm not hooked on it. I could give it up within 24 hours. I am the only person I have ever known who can *use* drugs without becoming their slave."

He then became very mysterious. "There now remains only one great method that we haven't mentioned—sex. This is in some ways the most important. To begin with, it has no harmful effect on the body. A man who has spent a lifetime having sexual intercourse is unaffected by it, unlike a drug taker or alcoholic. Moreover, sex *can* sometimes produce an intensity of consciousness far greater than anything that can be attained through drugs. The main trouble with the sexual orgasm is that it is too brief. There is no way of prolonging it, and whether we like it or not, the intensity vanishes immediately afterwards."

The effect of all this talk, with my mind abnormally brilliant from the drug, was indescribable. I had a feeling that I was on the dge of a revelation that would change my life. And Cunningham finished by saying: "I have discovered a means of prolonging the sexual orgasm for a slightly longer period—about a minute. But this is not enough. And I need two things: leisure to experiment, and an intelligent helper. And I think you could be the helper."

Up to now, I had been fascinated by him, and convinced that, even if he had no "supernatural insight," he possessed a psychological knowledge that went beyond anything I'd ever met. And yet, just as abruptly, he began to speak in a way that made me think that he was either a fool or a charlatan. I naturally pressed him to tell me more of his method of prolonging the sexual orgasm. He appeared to hesitate for a while, then finally went out of the room, and finally came back with a book bound in leather. The title page read: *The Book of Ceremonial Magic of Abrahamelin the Mage,* translated and edited by Caradoc Cunningham. "Take this away with you and read it—particularly my introduction. You won't be able to gather much about the text itself without a certain amount of help." I glanced at it, but couldn't see anything that seemed particularly profound. I noted a few sentences: "Among the smaller birds, the magpie is talkative and forctells guests," "Moreover, the elements themselves teach us fatal events." There were various tables giving details about the Tarot pack, the Kaballah, etc.

I said, "I don't want to jump to hasty conclusions, but some of this stuff looks like the mumbo-jumbo you can buy in fortune-tellers' booths for a half crown." He defended it by saying that much of it was symbolic, and required long study. I asked him if he had ever obtained any positive results by magic and he said gravely: "Many times." "But what *kind* of results?" "I hesitate to tell you. I don't want to hurry you into this thing too fast. You are naturally sceptical, and your scepticism has to be dissipated little by little. You see, it isn't a question of some totally new revelation, but of getting you to place slightly different emphases on many things. This will make everything appear to you in a completely different light."

He refused to say anything more, but whenever I looked into the book, I couldn't help feeling that anyone who could translate so much nonsense must be simple-minded. Cunningham plied me with a lot more drink. I took some of it, but soon realized that I'd regret it in the morning, so refused to drink more, and said good night. There are no clocks in Cunningham's room, and I'd left my watch behind. So I was startled as I came out into the street, and discovered it was already dawn. I came back here and slept for a few hours. Since eleven o'clock, I've been sitting in bed drinking tea and reading Abrahamelin the Mage. Cunningham's introduction, and his notes on the various sections, seem to me more interesting than the text itself. But what really astounds me is that he claims in print that it is possible to raise demons, kill people by black magic, cause storms, etc. To do this Abrahamelin bloke justice, he seems to be more of a Jewish mystic than a magician; he includes long prayers to be repeated before the invocations, declares that a man will lose all spiritual power if he attempts to do evil with the magic, and includes a set of rules of "preparation" that include fasting and praying for a week.

After reading most of Cunningham's own original work in this book, I am disappointed. He strikes me as a romantic who'd like to believe in all this trash. But as far as I can see, the main thing that's needed is a capacity for self-delusion. It's all very well talking about magical experiments, but the main trouble about all magic is that it doesn't produce results. I suppose it was an early form of science. But how can anyone attach any seriousness to a formula for making gold with the dried blood of a newt, two hairs from a witch's cat, and a number of incantations in Hebrew? The stupidity of the whole thing lies in the desire to make gold in the first place. If gold could be manufactured easily, it would be as worthless as iron. I'm forced to the conclusion that Cunningham has no spiritual perception.

I took the trouble to write out on a sheet of paper a summary of my own aims, which I shall give to Cunningham when I return this book. It will explain my rejection of magic more clearly than any number of criticisms. I copy it out here:

"I am perpetually aware of the feebleness of my consciousness. I have only one aim: to learn to 'pump up' consciousness in the way you can pump up the pressure in a primus stove. I agree that the sexual orgasm, alcohol and drugs can momentarily raise the pressure of consciousness. But this is like pumping air into a tire with a hole in it; within a few minutes, it's flat again. I am horrified by the instability and inconsistency of human beings. We seem to have virtually no values that don't change minute by minute. If time could be speeded up fifty times, we would be able to see this amazing lack of direction. This is how it would look: A man groans with hunger; he grabs food, but before it is halfway to his mouth, throws it away and complains of indigestion. He starts to kiss a beautiful girl, but suddenly lashes out and blacks her eye instead, then immediately bursts into tears and begs forgiveness; within a few seconds he is laughing hysterically and jumping up and down. . . . And so on. Scorpions stinging themselves couldn't be more absurd and inconsistent than human beings. Even the greatest of them talk nonsense, and all philosophers contradict themselves before the end of the book. They preach universal love, then admit that there is often more vitality in conflict, or declare the need for freedom, and end by admitting that men are disgusting idiots who need to be bullied. Nothing we can say about life cannot be negated by another statement that appears equally true. Our moods and mental climates are more changeable than England's weather.

"I admit that we have a few *negative* values that are far more solid and consistent than our positive ones. Waste of life always strikes us as a stupidity, whether it is a man engraving the Lord's Prayer on a pinpoint, or a man who commits murder for a few shillings and is hanged for it. Cruelty seems to excite a fairly uniform revulsion throughout mankind. But compared with the few things that we *know* to be bad or worthless, there seem to be millions of contradictory things that we think good.

"All this feebleness is the outcome of our fluid consciousness, which is too passive. It merely photographs things, and loses the photographs almost as quickly as it takes them. The consciousness never seems strong enough to see meanings in things; all it can do is just observe blankly. It is like staring at a page of a book in a foreign language. We seem to be crippled; there is an awful paralysis in our feelings, our values. A man can return to a place he has longed to see after ten years, and experience absolutely no emotion; his feelings are paralyzed. A soldier returns from the war; he has been dreaming of home for years and rereading every letter fifty times; within a fortnight he is quarreling with his wife and going out to get drunk to forget his boredom.

"I am perpetually aware of this, and I realize that the only answer is an internal strength so enormous that certain values would be quite permanent. A man with such strength would love life with an unimaginable intensity, and his love of life would provide a stimulus for striving after still greater strength. Only this paralysis of consciousness stops us from marching down the road toward the superman."

That, I think, is as clearly as I have ever expressed my central obsessions. At least Cunningham has stimulated me to that extent.

Later. After writing the above—it was about two in the afternoon—Cunningham arrived. I immediately showed it to him while I went to make tea. When I came out again, he was excited, said that I had proved myself to be one of the "new men," and asked me if he could use it in his new book on magic. Naturally, I said I'd be delighted. He then insisted on taking me out for a meal (I hadn't eaten since getting back this morning). We took a taxi to Fleet Street, and went to Cunningham's club for a drink. Here, a great many people seemed to know him, and I got the impression that he was

popular. Only one thing struck me as odd. We went downstairs
to eat, and Cunningham went out to the lavatory. Immediately,
a small, dark man who was dining with a platinum blonde,
came over to my table and bent over me in a conspiratorial
manner. He asked me if I knew Cunningham well. I was surprised, and said that I'd known him for a week. At this point,
he thought he heard Cunningham coming back down the stairs,
and thrust a card into my hand, asking me to telephone him
later. He then rushed back to his own table. However, it
turned out that it was only the waiter coming downstairs. He
sat there for another five minutes; still there was no sign of
Cunningham. So he plucked up courage again, darted over,
and asked me if I'd give him my phone number. I told him I
didn't have one, but managed to tell him my address as Cunningham reappeared on the stairs. He went back to his table
and I saw him writing it down immediately. I don't know
whether Cunningham saw him, but if he did, he didn't mention
it to me, and I didn't speak of it either. Ten minutes later, as
the little man got up and left, Cunningham noticed him and
stared after him rather hard; however, he said nothing. He
seemed to be in a talkative mood, and very gay. He drank
lager instead of his usual wine, and explained that he'd been
drinking too much wine recently and that it was impairing his
clairvoyant powers. I asked him about these, and he talked
with a quite new candor. I set it down here because I've never
encounterd any similar case.

Cunningham explained that when he was about ten, he
was at a private school. His mother came to visit him one day,
and said: "Guess what I've brought for you?" Cunningham
replied: "Wait, don't tell me. Let me tell you. You've brought
me an antique ring, and you bought it in that shop in the Old
Brompton Road where we both stopped last time I was in
London." Cunningham said that he hadn't consciously "read
her mind"; it was simply that he had a sudden strong impression that he *knew* what she was going to give him, and could
see where she'd bought it. His mother was astounded; she had,

in fact, bought him a curious ring in the shape of two snakes twisted together, since she knew he was fascinated by snakes. ("Symbol of forbidden wisdom," he explained.) After this, Cunningham said, he found a book by Rudolph Steiner in the school library about the development of "occult powers," which explained how the soul should be sent into "outer space" every night on the point of falling asleep; it also explained that the drinking of wine was ruinous to these powers. Now it happened that at this time, Cunningham was anemic, and was always made to drink a glass of some "tonic wine" before he went to bed. He knew it was no use explaining his reasons for refusing wine to the housekeeper; but he contrived things so that he could manage to pour the wine away without her seeing. He also practiced the method explained by Steiner. Within a few days, he was aware that his powers were developing. When the boys set out to go to play cricket with another school, he suddenly knew for certain that one of them would not return that night; he told this to one of the boys. The boy laughed, but nevertheless told various others, who began to tease Cunningham about "ghosts." However, they were all greatly impressed when, in fact, the boy did *not* return to school that night; he had been hit on the head by the cricket ball and was taken to the hospital with a slight case of concussion. Cunningham, however, was clever enough to realize that he would only awaken a lot of tiresome curiosity if he paraded his powers too openly. He was therefore the first to declare that the whole thing had been coincidence, and took care not to say anything more about his second sight. But from then on, it functioned fairly regularly for several years. Only one evening, he inadvertently gave himself away to a friend. They had a gramophone in his room and were playing a Beethoven symphony. The friend started to look through a pile of records, when Cunningham said unthinkingly: "No, it's not there. I lent it to Smith." He realized when he'd said it that his friend had not actually said he was looking for the Mendelssohn violin concerto. His friend looked startled and said: "What?," and Cunningham tried to retrieve his mistake by saying: "I thought you said you wanted to hear Beethoven's Fifth, so I assumed you were looking for it." His friend was satisfied—until suddenly Smith walked into the room with an album and said: "Here's your Mendelssohn violin concerto back." The friend said later: "You *did* know what I was looking for, didn't you?," but Cunningham insisted that he had only made a lucky guess. All the same, he developed something of a reputation at school for spooky powers, and found this a nuisance when boys kept approaching him about the results of the next football match.

These powers disappeared when he went up to Oxford and began to drink heavily, but, he explained, he was already interested in other aspects of occultism, and did not regard the loss of his second sight as very important.

While Cunningham told me all this, I had the impression that he was being quite frank and honest; he told it humorously, with no attempt at mystification, as if second sight were a curious disability like a tendency to seasickness.

Since he was in this frank mood, I asked him about Carlotta. (He had already asked me about Diana; some of his questions were so personal that I blushed, but I felt he had a certain right to know, since he played such a part in the affair.) He asked me what Carlotta had told me, and when I repeated her story of the "incubus" in her bed, he was delighted. He told me that as soon as he had seen her, he realized that Carlotta was an exceptionally good subject for his type of power. She possessed a great store of vital energy that had been frustrated and bottled up for so long that it was easy to "use her." (He didn't explain what he meant by this.) I tried to press him to be more specific, but he only said he would tell me more later. He *did* say, however, that he had not been in her bed that night—astrally or otherwise.

This puzzles me. Do I have to conclude that Cunningham can somehow influence people at a distance? It is hard to believe—even though I saw him cause that man in the street to stumble. What is more likely is that he somehow took advantage of Carlotta's hysteria to make her believe in his "powers."

At the end of the lunch, Cunningham explained to me that he felt I was ready to be introduced into the "mysteries." I possess, according to him, an unusual degree of psychological perception; my mind makes persistent attempts to get beyond the façade of the everyday world into the realm of the occult. But I still see things in their "natural" light; I seek a natural solution to the problems. I have no inkling of the concealed mysteries. He became very confiding, placing his hands on mine and leaning over until his face almost touched me; the waiters must have thought we were a couple of queers. "Do you think it coincidence that you have met me at this point in your life? Don't believe it. The Powers have been preparing you. The Powers arranged that you should meet me. And the Powers ordained that you should help me to bring my work to fruition." He also hinted that he had been "told" about me several years ago, warned that he would meet a co-worker, and told how to recognize me. However, he refused to talk about this.

When we left, he told me to prepare myself for two more days, with thinking and meditation—and prayer, if I feel so inclined. I am to meditate on the problem of human boredom. This will prepare me for the revelation he proposes to make.

When we got back—it was after five o'clock, and I was sleepy from the wine—he told me that he intended to take Kirsten out this evening to meet someone who could help him with his invention. I knew what he meant—that I could spend the evening in bed with Diana. I delivered his message to Kirsten, then went up to my room and fell asleep. I woke at about half past seven, took another half hour to wake up fully, and heard Cunningham going out with Kirsten. I went downstairs and knocked on her door. She was alone, but I somehow felt in no mood to take advantage of Kirsten's absence. We sat and talked for a while about Cunningham, then she said she'd like to hear music, and we came up to my room and played records for a couple of hours. It was a curious situation. I wish I could read her mind. Sometimes I suspect that she doesn't quite trust me—thinks I'm out for a casual love affair. Anyway, we both felt rather tired and subdued, and I didn't feel like drinking again. When Kirsten came home, just after ten, I hadn't even kissed her. I called to Kirsten that we were in my room; he came up, and didn't seem in the least surprised to find us together. He was full of talk about Cunningham, who had introduced him to a Jewish music publisher; the man was coming back tomorrow to hear the Panharmonicon.

It amused me to notice that Kirsten's presence seemed to create an intimacy between Diana and myself that had been absent when we were alone. I caught her looking at me several times with a kind of tenderness, and when she finally left, she found an opportunity to touch my hand for a moment.

Now, alone, I think about her, and realize that my feelings of the other day haven't changed at all. I was afraid then that it was my usual sense of gratitude for a woman who gives herself to me. But it still seems preposterous that she should go off to sleep with another man. I actually feel married to her, instead of feeling that we're deceiving her husband. Yet I like Kirsten. I wonder if he'd care much if Diana left him? He seems a cold blooded fish. . . .

Nov. 21. Yesterday was a crowded day, and I realize it will take me several pages to write of it in detail. And yet when I read back over the past few weeks, I'm not sorry that I started to describe my life so fully. Even if Cunningham vanished out of my life tomorrow, I'd be glad of the notes I've made about him. He puzzles me; I want to get to the bottom of him. There's definitely something wrong. Power and weakness, knowledge and delusion, are so oddly mixed in him that I'd like to take him to pieces and make a minute analysis. For example, I can't quite believe that my "natural" vision of life is only a preparation for some occult insight. In another journal, I had written: "Unless the world is richer, unless it has other depths and dimensions, I loathe it." Cunningham would use this as evidence that I await some "revelation." Yet I want my "richness" to be natural, not supernatural.

Anyway, to return to what happened yesterday. This morning, I got a letter, addressed simply to "Gerard," at this address. It was from the man I'd met in the restaurant the day before, and whose card I have somehow mislaid. His name is Steve Radin, and he works for the *Daily News,* doing mostly celebrity interviews. I hadn't, of course, told him my name when I gave him my address, but he overheard Cunningham calling me Gerard, so relied on his letter reaching me. The letter simply said that he would like to talk to me, and would I ring him at his office during the morning. I was curious, and went down to the phone immediately. His secretary said he hadn't come in yet, but had left a message for me: if I rang, I was to say what time during the day it would be convenient for Mr. Radin to call. I said any time. The secretary then said: "Mr. Radin said he would like to see you alone." So I said I'd be alone all morning, but couldn't guarantee the afternoon. The truth was that I was curious to know what it was all about, and wanted him to come as soon as possible.

He arrived an hour later—at about 11. The first thing he said was "Are you alone?," and then, "Is there any chance we might be interrupted?" I understood he was asking about Cunningham, and I admitted there was a faint chance he might turn up. Radin promptly insisted that I go out with him to talk. He had a car there, and took me to a club in Soho. As we passed Farringdon Street, a taxi stopped alongside us, and to my astonishment I saw Father O'Mahoney* sitting in the back. He's been in Italy all this year for his health, and I never expected to see the poor old boy alive again. We managed to wave before the lights changed.

* A Catholic priest, friend of Austin Nunne and Gertrude Quincey. At the time of Nunne's murders, he was seriously ill and thought to be dying.

The club was one I didn't know. It was almost deserted. Radin had refused to talk about Cunningham on the way there—only told me that he used to be a free-lance reporter, and now worked for the *News*. Then we talked about Bill Payne, whom he seems to know quite well. But as soon as we were settled, with drinks, he plunged into the subject. He asked me if I realized that Cunningham was regarded by some people as a highly dangerous man. When I said no, he said: "I'm going to take a chance with you. I don't know why, but I got the impression the other day that you're not yet very involved with Cunningham. So I'm going to talk frankly to you about him, and rely on you to make sure it never gets back to Cunningham." I promised him—I'd have promised anything, I was so curious by this time. I asked him in what way Cunningham is dangerous—whether he's a criminal, a madman, or what. He said: "No, I don't think so, although I wouldn't like to swear to either. But he's a professional corrupter and wrecker."

What he then went on to tell me was almost as interesting as what Cunningham had been saying the day before. Radin claimed that, as a journalist, he had a curious way of anticipating stories. For example, he had known a man in various pubs around Chelsea, and as soon as he met him, had a conviction that this man would one day be "news." The man was Neville Heath, and a few months later he murdered a woman in a Notting Hill hotel room. Radin said that this was not second sight, but just the instinct of a good journalist. (I seem to remember that Bernard Shaw once saw the murderer Haigh in a South Kensington hotel, and predicted that Haigh would be hanged one day; Haigh had lost his temper over a child.) Anyway, Radin said that he had had the same feeling of "news" ever since he'd met Cunningham. I asked him if he thought Cunningham would commit a murder, but he said no.

Before he would say any more, he asked me to tell him how I'd met Cunningham. I didn't see any harm in it, so I told him pretty well everything—except the "sex magic." I think the association with Oliver and Kirsten rather reflects credit on Cunningham anyway. I didn't know how far I had a right to tell him Cunningham's plans about the island, but he finally wormed it out of me.

In exchange, he told me everything he knew about Cunningham, which was a lot.

Cunningham was apparently at Oxford for a while, where he caused considerable scandal by publishing volumes of pornographic verse; one, called *Slimy Weapons*, got him into the trouble that led to his being sent down. There was also some talk about his having curious sexual tendencies; a local girl who became infatuated with him got badly beaten up one night and had two of her teeth knocked out. As she served in one of the cafés, this was rather noticeable. However, she refused to say anything against him. She was apparently fairly obviously pregnant when Cunningham had to leave Oxford. And yet—this surprised me most—it was general knowledge that Cunningham had homosexual tendencies; he hung around with a queer set, and apparently once boasted that he had committed sodomy with a choir boy on the altar in one of the chapels. He was then very rich, and was noted for extravagance. He hung his rooms with expensive tapestries, and made a habit of wearing jewelry—particularly rings. But he was also apparently pretty tough. One night, a group of football-playing hearties decided to break up his rooms. He got wind of this, and pretended to go out. Actually, he waited in the room. When they broke in, he waited until they were all inside—about a dozen beefy lads—then went for them all with a heavy stick. (Radin told me this story with admiration, and apparently the exploit gave Cunningham a great reputation in the college.) He closed the door and switched on the light, and the hearties thought they were in a trap until they realized they only had Cunningham to deal with. Then he went into them like a whirlwind, and the dozen of them couldn't master him. I gather he broke several heads and managed to bruise pretty well all of them. When one of them managed to twist the stick away from him, he immediately grabbed a short club which he'd concealed, and went on. After five minutes of this, one of them managed to get the door open, and they all made a break for it. But a persistent rumor got around later that Cunningham had taken something—some kind of drug—that acted as a temporary stimulant. (I must ask him about this one day.) They said he was like a demon. Actually, I suspect that one violently angry man is more than a match for a dozen sheepish louts, particularly with a stick.

Radin wasn't sure about the "scandal" that caused him to be sent down, except that it involved the book *Slimy Weapons,* and pretty open flaunting of the rules. There was also a story that he'd gotten his tutor drunk and inflicted some indignity with a can of paint, but this was never confirmed.

Apparently Cunningham spent the years just before the war traveling abroad and mountaineering. He is known as an excellent mountaineer, and a man with unusual physical endurance. When he was in India with Sir Harold Clunn, they broke a mountaineering record on one of the peaks, and Cunningham saved someone's life by some extraordinary bravery. However, he apparently set out with his own team of climbers a couple of years later, and the whole thing was disastrous. Radin said that he thought Cunningham had no gift for command—he was too much of an anarchist and a wild man. Everyone quarreled, the party split up, and finally three men of the splinter group fell into a crevasse and were buried by a landslide. Cunningham stood by and refused to help them, because he said they deserved whatever they got for rebelling against him. Two of them died before the others could dig them out. This caused something of a scandal at the time, and Cunningham was denounced in the papers, and thrown out of some clubs. There was talk of a prosecution, but he hurried off to South America and stayed there for a couple of years.

There, apparently, he went in seriously for this black-magic lark. He went searching around New Mexico, in the Lawrence country, to find tribes who still practiced human

sacrifice. But again, I gather he made some pretty startling dis-
coveries about Aztec and Mayan remains, and I'm told that
some things he discovered in the jungle are now in a museum
in New York and are regarded as priceless.

This helps me to define what I find so hard to understand
about Cunningham. Half the time he behaves like a spoiled
child, and shouldn't be allowed into civilized society. Yet he
appears, under certain circumstances, to be genuinely capable
of extraordinary self-discipline. Without this freakish element
in his character—this tendency to raise hell and thumb his
nose at society—I think he could easily be a great man. But
he seems to need external challenges to get the best out of
him. This makes me wonder whether a combination of my
sense of purpose and Cunningham's vitality couldn't achieve
something worth-while. . . . Is this perhaps why he wants my
help?

To return: he had to leave Mexico, again after a scandal
involving a death, and he returned to England just before the
war. He professed to find politics vulgar and boring, and was
quoted as saying that he didn't object in the least to Hitler's
cruelty, but couldn't bear his commonplace mind.

When war broke out, he apparently served in the army
for six months—as a private, oddly enough—and was then
discharged on medical grounds. Radin met him in Fleet
Street shortly after this. Radin himself was a conscientious
objector, and was about to be sent to some awful labor camp
in Wales. Cunningham told him that he ought to have spoken
to him about it, and hinted that he knew of drugs that could
produce the effect of a disease that would lead inevitably to
discharge. Cunningham wasn't specific, but Radin thought he
had "worked his ticket" in this way.

He didn't see Cunningham again until after the war.
Cunningham apparently spent the war years in the north of
Scotland, where he bought himself a large house, gave himself
a title, and divided his time equally between drinking and
practicing black magic. His house got itself such a bad name

among the villagers that even ten years later, when Radin visited the place on another assignment, he was told that it was haunted by demons, and that no one would go past it after dark.

His only other news of Cunningham during the war came from a Sunday newspaper that revived the controversy about the Loch Ness monster. Cunningham wrote an article for this paper in which he declared that the monster was not a survival from the Jurassic era, but had been "conjured up" by the witches of Boleskin in the time of Charles II. Cunningham pointed out that there were no references to the monster before this time, and hinted that he had some inside knowledge that confirmed his suggestions. He also hinted that there still were active witch cults in remote parts of the British Isles— and again let it be understood that he had some secret knowledge. His article created an unusual amount of controversy— considering its nonsensical nature—and Cunningham gained a kind of overnight notoriety.

This led to his acquaintance with Lord Belmont, who was supposed to be mostly concerned with archaeology, but who was actually studying witch cults and magic. Radin covered the scandal when Belmont's daughter Clara ran away with a Mediterranean smuggler, and was caught just before they got to Gretna Green, so met her on several occasions. He described her as a very pretty girl, but with an extremely weak mouth and chin, and a fancy that she was an intellectual and a defender of women's rights. (Her elder sister got herself half killed by some American soldier during the war, and Belmont was perhaps stricter with her than necessary.) When she met Cunningham, she was drinking heavily and sleeping around as much as she could. For some weird reason, Cunningham agreed to marry her—Radin thinks it was misplaced chivalry. At all events, they managed to get married in Edinburgh before Belmont found out about it. He threw a tremendous tantrum, went out looking for Cunningham with a revolver, and wrote his daughter letters saying that Cunningham was insane and a pervert. It was at this point that Radin met Cunningham in London; Cunningham consulted him about whether he thought he could get heavy damages from Belmont for defamation of character. Radin said he thought not because on the one hand, the court would probably sympathize with the father whose daughter had eloped for the second time; and on the other, Cunningham's character might easily be blackened by the defense lawyer if he took the trouble to read up old newspaper reports of the mountain-climbing incident. It was at this point, Radin said, that he suspected Cunningham was losing his money and was getting worried.

The next thing that happened was that the wife had a baby—a daughter—and Cunningham dragged them off on some peculiar trip across Africa, apparently to learn about tribal magic. Radin is not sure of the details, but it seems that the three of them got abandoned by their servants when they were about two hundred miles from the nearest town. Cunningham then deserted his wife, made his own way to Durban, and sailed for England. The wife managed to get to the coast, but the baby died on the way, of some fever.

I must admit that this story shook me. A man can be forgiven for many things, but deserting his wife and baby in the middle of a strange country is not just weakness or even wickedness, but a repulsive kind of selfishness that disgusts me. However, I'd like to hear Cunningham's version of the story. I felt that Radin, in spite of his "lack of prejudice," actually hates Cunningham's guts, and is looking forward to the day when the "scandal" breaks. Even so, the facts look pretty damning for Cunningham. His wife returned to him in England, and lived with him for a time. Then he left her again, and was seen around London with another woman—an actress. The wife had some kind of a breakdown, and ended up in a mental home. Radin says he believed this was the effect of drugs, alcohol, and the sheer craziness of life with Cunningham, who spent half his nights trying to raise the devil by long incantations. He also asked his wife to believe that he was the latest avatar of the World Savior, sent to create a new age. (I gather that his wife is now living again with her father, but is a chronic invalid; she has divorced Cunningham, and has refused to talk to Radin about him.)

This summarizes all that Radin told me about Cunningham. We went out and had lunch in the Gay Hussar, and talked until well after three o'clock. Radin says that he lost touch with Cunningham about five years ago. He has no idea how or where he's lived since deserting Clara; all he knows is that Cunningham spent all his money, and had to sell his property in Scotland.

I found all this fascinating, but difficult to believe. Radin assured me that it was all true, and that he would introduce me to someone who would verify it all. I was, to tell the truth, pretty sleepy and anxious to get home, but didn't feel I could rush off since I owed Radin a lunch. I tried to find out exactly what Radin wanted me to do, but he wouldn't be explicit. I imagine that he was simply curious to find out what I knew about Cunningham. He also, I think, relies on my future co-operation, and perhaps hopes that I'll be a source of inside information about Cunningham's plans.

He insisted that we call on someone in Soho, but the person was out. He then said that we could at least walk past the British Museum and see if we could find his friend there. So we went in, and Radin looked in the reading room, and came out a few minutes later with a man I remember having seen there many times. His name is Frederick Wise, an authority on heretical sects. He's a curious old man with a mop of white hair and an awful looking goiter that gives him the appearance of a toad. He was rather brusque, declared he was too busy to talk at the moment, but finally came outside with us. However, he became more talkative when we sat down, and, as it was bitterly cold there, agreed to come across the road for a cup of tea. Radin explained to him that he'd been telling me about Cunningham, and that he thought I was in danger of coming under Cunningham's influence; he asked the old man's opinion. Wise said: "There's only one thing I can say for sure about Cunningham—he's one of the few really evil men I've ever met. Keep away from him." He then told the story of Cunningham's marriage, but in a slightly different version from Radin's, and, if possible, even more damning. But what interested me most was that Wise is plainly a believer in magic and witchcraft himself; this came out in several things he said. Finally, he jumped up and said he had to go and work, and vanished without further ado.

Radin said: "It's a pity he's in one of his bad moods. When he's talkative, he'll go on for hours. He could tell you some astonishing things about Cunningham, and what's more, he understands these things." I pressed him to explain himself, and he said: "What I really wanted Wise to tell you was his theory that Cunningham was always doomed to fail and to be unlucky in anything he attempted." Wise believed that Cunningham had taken various solemn oaths when he started to study magic—oaths binding him to use his power only for good, to keep his eyes fixed on the highest ideals, etc. It is also a part of these oaths that a man calls down upon himself the most awful maledictions in the event of his breaking them. I can easily imagine Cunningham taking such oaths and believing in his own sincerity; but I can also imagine that a character as mercurial and weak as Cunningham would forget them a fortnight later. Wise, apparently, believes that this is what happened, and that Cunningham has exposed himself to "formidable spiritual reprisals" by breaking his oaths. He has definite knowledge that Cunningham found the disciplines prescribed by Abrahamelin the Mage too binding, and that he went off to Egypt (this was before the war) searching for a new "Bible for the Supermen" in the museums of Cairo, and probably in certain tombs. At all events, he sent communications to various occult groups in London and Paris, declaring that he had received some revelation direct from the Egyptian god Anubis, and that he had been ordered to proclaim himself the new leader of all such groups. Naturally, this caused a great deal of trouble; nobody was willing to accept his leadership at such short notice. At the meeting Wise's group called to discuss the matter, a black raven flew into the room and blundered against the light bulb, causing it to blow out. Afterwards, they verified that there had been no window open to admit the bird, and concluded that it was a sign that Cunningham's claims were to be taken seriously. However, Wise had the idea that all members should be searched before they left the room—he seems to have been shrewder than the others—and in the pocket of a man who was known to be friendly to Cunningham they found grains of corn and some feathers! This ended Cunningham's hopes of becoming leader of the group, and also convinced everyone that he was to be treated as a charlatan who only wanted power.

I finally left Radin at five o'clock and came back here. I think he'd gained what he wanted—to keep track of Cunningham's exploits. As for me, I can't drink during the afternoon without feeling fit for absolutely nothing in the evening. So I lay down and tried to sleep. However, after a quarter of an hour or so, Diana came and woke me up. I pulled her down on the bed and said: "Listen, I want to ask you something. Do you love me?" She said: "How can I love you? I've only known you for a few days." "But you've slept with me." "That's not the same." "You mean you don't mind sleeping with a man you don't care about?!" "I didn't say I don't care about you." "What *do* you mean, then?" "To love someone, you have to be absolutely sure of him. So you have to know him well. I haven't known you long enough." She looked at me so honestly as she said this that I was touched. I said: "Do you love your husband?" Again she looked doubtful. "In a way . . . but—" "But what?" She shrugged. "I can't talk about him to you—yet." It seems to me that she has an extraordinary honesty. It would have been so easy for her to say: "No, I don't love him any more." Finally, I asked her: "Supposing I asked you to leave him and come to me?" She looked surprised. Instead of refusing, as I expected, she said: "Do you want me as much as that?" I nodded and kissed her, and said: "Don't you believe me?" "It's not that. But . . . I don't think you're the sort of person to stay with one woman. I think you like women too much." It took me some time to convince her that she was wrong, and that I really wanted her to come away with me. I pressed her about it; she temporized and said she couldn't tell me immediately. Then she lay down on the bed, as if to say: "Make love to me, and excuse me answering any further questions." It seems that Kirsten was out again with Cunningham, so I decided it would be a pity to waste the opportunity, and undressed her. As I was making love to her, I said: "Supposing I give you a baby. You'd have to leave Kirsten then." She only nodded, her eyes closed. Half an hour later, she said she had to go out to get food, in case Kirsten hadn't eaten. But when she'd gone, I lay there and thought it all preposterous. I don't want a love affair with her. I want to marry her. She seems to me the sort of girl I could live with for the rest of my life without getting tired. I am analytical enough to realize that this is because she's curiously yielding and quite unegotistical—and this is necessary for an egotist like me. She'd put up with me. I don't think it's success she needs in a husband, although I have never doubted that I shall achieve immense success one day, but simply affection and need for her. I feel that Kirsten doesn't offer her much affection. A kind of need, perhaps, but nothing very personal, just the same thing he feels about his supper. I realize that I'm giving up my independence, and yet this makes no difference. I never valued it that much. Besides, I might never meet anyone like Diana again. But I wish I knew how much Kirsten needs her. . . .

Nov. 22. I spent most of yesterday filling in my journal, which exhausted me. However, I didn't finish. Kirsten returned with Cunningham again, and Cunningham came up to ask me out to supper. I told him I'd already eaten, and didn't feel like another meal. (Luckily, he didn't use his second sight to find out about Radin!) But he persuaded me to go back with him.

He was only slightly puzzled that I wouldn't drink; I said I had a headache.

The truth was that the things Radin had told me had affected me; they made me see him in a different way, as a weakling. He could sense this, I think. He said something about magic, and I said that he should realize that I am, at present, one of the unconverted, and feel a slight derision when I hear the word. At this, his manner became rather quiet and serious, and he said: "But you must realize, Gerard, that magic is perhaps the *only* thing in the world really worth doing. Because in its broadest sense, magic means trying to summon up forces greater than your conscious self. Don't you believe in such forces?" I said I did, but not in wishful thinking. He said: "Is it wishful thinking? White magic is supposed to be a means of invoking the gods. Black magic means summoning up devils. Well, I can tell you now that these forces exist—forces for evil or good."

He's a cunning devil. He knows I can't resist intellectualizing, and that the surest way to gain my attention is to say something intelligent. I told him that religion means trying to summon the god inside you—in the subconscious or superconscious or whatever you want to call it. Magic seems to mean trying to summon gods and demons from outside you. And they just don't exist. Cunningham said: "Don't think I'm trying to quibble. But it depends very much on what you mean by inside and outside. I could take you right now to a room half a mile away where you would be convinced of the reality of spirit-mediumship. I could introduce you to a woman who could tell you things about yourself and your life that she couldn't possible have learned from anyone. And she's no charlatan. She doesn't know herself how she does it. She doesn't try to use her powers to get rich—although she makes a living by them. Where does she gain this power? From inside herself or outside? Most of her congregation at the Spiritualist church will tell you it comes from outside, from the spirits of the dead. I don't think it necessary to accept this idea. I believe it comes from some unknown, untapped resources that we all contain."

I must admit that Cunningham has a brilliance that makes it impossible to dislike him for long. I wish I could have asked him outright about the story of abandoning his wife and daughter, but I didn't want to tell him about Radin—partly because Radin made me promise so solemnly. (I almost suspect that he's afraid of Cunningham.)

When I said that I'd like to study a case of "genuine mediumship" before I made up my mind, Cunningham looked thoughtful, then said: "I might be able to do better than that. I wonder. . . ." Then he said suddenly: "Wait here for a moment while I telephone." He went out, and came back ten minutes later. "Would you like to see a haunted house?" I said cautiously that I might find it interesting. He said: "All right. Come on."

By this time, my headache had disappeared completely. We went down to Whitechapel High Street and got a taxi, then drove to Hanover Square. On the way, Cunningham explained that he couldn't promise any manifestation, but that if there *were* anything, it would convince me far more than any case of mediumship. Then he explained that we were going to a house near Hanover Square. "Have you ever read Lytton's *Haunted and the Haunters?*" I said yes. "This place is the house that Lytton was supposed to have based the story on. It was empty for a long time. Now the ground floor has been turned into a flat, and the upper part is used as a storeroom for paintings. I know the son of the man who owns it." As we went along, he told me the story of the house—the usual thing about a wicked Victorian who beat his wife to death and let his niece starve because she wouldn't marry the man of his choice; the niece committed suicide by jumping out of the window— which is on the second floor—and the wicked uncle died in his sleep, after living alone in the house for some time. Thereafter, the room in which the niece had been starved and the wife had died was haunted, and the story has it that people who stayed in the room have been driven insane. Cunningham agreed that all this was unauthenticated, and that the story about people going insane and dying of fright and delayed shock sounds like the usual exaggeration. However, there are a number of reports from people who testify to a definite "presence" in the haunted room, and the house *did* remain empty for ten years or so—in spite of its position in the middle of the West End—until a firm of art dealers bought it.

We called at a house in Hanover Square, and Cunningham collected the key from a servant, then we walked around the corner to the house itself.

There is no point in going into detail about this. The room didn't strike me as in any way peculiar, except it was hellishly cold. We switched on a large electric fire, and it gradually warmed up. It was pretty uncomfortable, having only one chair and a mattress in it; it was full of dust, smelled very stale and depressing; the light was also very weak; I think a decent 150-watt bulb would completely dissipate its spooky atmosphere!

When we were settled, Cunningham declared that we ought to have brought some booze, and insisted on going down to get some. I think this may have been a ruse for leaving me alone there and trying to get me into a state of nerves. However, the room didn't impress me, and I sat there until Cunningham came back (loaded with drink) without noticing anything that made me nervous.

We sat there for a couple of hours. Cunningham said that we would leave at one in the morning if we saw and heard nothing. We drank whisky out of tooth glasses we found in the bathroom next door, and talked. I must admit that Cunningham showed no disposition to try to "set the atmosphere" by talking about ghosts. Instead, he went into a quite brilliant discourse on logical positivism. Some of it struck me as so sound that I note it here. He attacked the position that philosophy must confine itself to what can be proved or tested. He said that many propositions of vital importance are unprovable. For example, someone once said that no man dies until he has accomplished whatever he has inside him—that if Schubert and Keats and Wolf had lived thirty years longer, they wouldn't have added substantially to their achievement. Now this proposition is plainly of the utmost importance; a man of genius who accepted it and believed it implicitly would be freed of the usual gloomy fatalism and would work twice as hard. There is not a single human being who wouldn't derive some benefit from believing it. And yet how is it possible to test it? Not that it has to be swallowed blindly. But you can only apply to it the test of your own intuitions and experience, and they may be quite uncommunicable to another person.

Cunningham's talk always excites me, and I drank more than I intended to. Before very long, I noticed it was after midnight. It was then that I observed that the room was horribly cold. At first I thought the electric fire had gone out. But it hadn't, and I got up, went over to it, and warmed my hands. Yet even as I sat there, the back of my neck was freezing. I suddenly shivered, and had an awful sense of foreboding, as if something had crept up on us without our noticing it. Cunningham was smiling oddly. Then he said: "Well, how do you account for that?" "For what?" I said, my teeth chattering. "This cold. It wasn't like this half an hour ago. He pointed to the fire, which was large enough to warm any other room, and I saw his point. However, I commented that it was, after all, after midnight, and probably the temperature outside had dropped a great deal. The creepy feeling had quite vanished. We drank more whisky—I wasn't feeling too good, not because of the cold, but simply because it doesn't suit my stomach to get slightly drunk twice in one day—and I tried not to be sick. Suddenly I felt a great deal of pity for the poor girl who had starved in this room. It was a hell of a room to be sick in. The wallpaper—mid-Victorian and pre-Morris— was the most depressing I've ever seen. In fact, I wouldn't be surprised if the "evil influence" of the room hasn't something to do with the smell and awful pattern on that lousy wallpaper. Finally, I suggested we go. Cunningham said all right, and we went out. Then I got a surprise. Although the rest of the house smelled musty enough, it was nowhere near as cold, and when we got outside, the night seemed warm compared to that room.

Cunningham took me home and let me go to bed without further talk. I still cannot explain the cold in the room. But this doesn't mean that I accept the idea of ghosts; after all, it could be due to physical causes—a draft down a chimney or something.

Thinking about it all, I feel badly puzzled. Oh, I can see already what Cunningham is driving at. He wants me to admit that, since I reject this boring world of my everyday experience, I may as well take the plunge into the occult world. But I am as ultimately unconvinced by it as I was by Father O'Mahoney's Catholicism. I agree that the answer *fits* the questions; but that still doesn't guarantee that it's the right answer. Cunningham has already dropped hints of the direction in which he wants to lead me. We are to form a society who will "dare anything." For example, he asked me questions about Christine that make me suppose that he is thinking of her as a possible subject for his "sex magic." (I don't know what Oliver would say!) Oh, I can see it all with complete clarity. Cunningham has not yet succeeded in impressing the world, in getting the world to take him on his own terms. He is now approaching 50; he has published a couple of dozen volumes of various kinds (so he tells me) and yet he is completely unknown. He becomes especially bitter when he talks about Auden, Isherwood and Spender, whom he knew in the thirties, and it's easy to see that he feels he's been left behind. He ought to be the dominant figure of his generation, and instead of that, he has only a certain amount of newspaper notoriety. He thirsts for fame, for recognition that he is an extraordinary man. Now he feels he might be able to do it. But not merely as the patron and impresario, a role that doesn't suit him at all. So he wants to bind his own destiny to that of Glasp, Kirsten and myself, to be the leader and mentor, the man who provides the ideas, the philosophy. We are to form a little Thebaid in the desert of modern civilization, bound together by esoteric knowledge and probably by sexual orgies.

I don't object to this—I sympathize. There is no doubt whatever that Cunningham has helped Oliver unselfishly— (because I don't count the pocketing of Oliver's profits as real self-interest; Cunningham feels he has earned it). If he can get Kirsten's music performed, or my books published, I have no doubt he'll do it just as unselfishly. But will he ever be accepted in his own right? I almost think Wise was right when he said that Cunningham had "incurred heavy spiritual reprisals" for some loss of integrity.

But where is the point in proving to me the existence of spirits, or anything else of the kind? I don't doubt that the house in Hanover Square *is* haunted, in some sense or another. There is definitely a presence in that room. But so what? There are tigers in India and polar bears at the North Pole, but they don't make any difference to me.

All this stuff about sex magic worries me. The orgasm isn't everything; it's only a part of it. I know the sexual act *can* be supreme, bringing immense insight and triumph, a sense of godhood. This I experienced that first night with Caroline, and again the other night with Diana. But I never experienced it with Gertrude, or Madeleine, or Carlotta. What is this elusive power that can make sex an astounding experience? It is a kind of life, freshness. The early days with Caroline had a real magic about them, even though I wasn't in love with her. She was intensely exciting, as fresh as the heart of a young lettuce, and I felt as if she were my *reward* for a long period of hard work and refusal to be distracted. *I felt that the powers of life were in the ascendant.* We normally work in the face of defeat, always aware that things may get worse, and that death is the final end. But in the best moments, we cease to be slaves; defeat vanishes, and there seems a chance that death may be ultimately defeated. Nijinsky's wife said that the first time he made love to her, she felt as if she were making a sacrifice to the goddess of love. This I understand—in bed with a godlike man, the greatest male dancer the world has ever known; they must have felt like gods on Olympus. This is what sex *ought* to be.

Of one thing I am sure. *So far, the human race has always worshiped death and defeat.* I am sickened and irritated when I read the Bible, with its talk of "man's final end," or the respected classical writers declaring solemnly that even the greatest men must end in death. It strikes me as being nauseating flattery of a tyrant, like that ballad that talks about "good King John" when everyone knows he was the rottenest swine who ever disgraced a throne. I know this is supposed to be a part of human nature, but it's time it stopped being so. Only stupid savages adore a tyrant because he is cruel and destructive. There are times when I catch a glimpse of a state of consciousness, only slightly higher than our present one, when all the blacks will turn into white—or at least into gray. At present, a writer can say: "We all agree that life is a long-drawn-out defeat, ending in death," and no one raises the slightest objection. But a day will come when such a statement will be greeted with yells of derision. Life is meaningless unless death can be finally defeated. And I don't mean "eternal life" in the religious sense. (If we have to choose between that kind of nonsense and total pessimism, give me total pessimism any day.) I mean a life in which consciousness is no longer a feeble flame, like a gas jet that takes an hour to boil a kettle. I mean a life in which men no longer *feel themselves slaves,* when every one of us will feel like Paris, "that first dawn in Helen's arms."

Can Cunningham show me the way toward this state? I remember reading once that magic is just a bastard form of mysticism; well, I prefer mysticism to magic.

Nov. 24. The Diana business has come to a head rather absurdly. I was reading in bed yesterday morning when Kirsten knocked on my door. He looked rather odd, and I suspected that he'd found out about Diana. He sat down, stared gloomily at the carpet, then said he wanted to ask my advice. Then, with a rush, he said: "Sorme, I think my wife is being unfaithful to me." I asked him cautiously what made him think that, and was glad he didn't look at me, because my heart was thumping and I was probably red. He then held out to me a handful of letters, all scrawled in a semi-illiterate handwriting on tiny sheets of a sixpenny notepad. I said I didn't think I had any right to look at letters addressed to his wife. He assumed from this that I was reproaching him, and asked me what he should do under the circumstances—after all, his wife's love affairs *were* his concern, and he felt completely inadequate to cope with the situation. So out of curiosity, I took the letters and glanced through them. Most of them were not dated, but one that *was* was over a year old. The early ones began "Dear Di." This changed into "Dearest Di" and "My Darling Di," and finally into "My Darlingest Own" and other endearments that made me wince. I glanced at Kirsten as I looked through them, and saw that he was trembling, and looked as if he were about to burst into tears. I couldn't help feeling irritable with him; after all, if his wife's unfaithful, why doesn't he black her eye or throw her downstairs instead of confiding in his next door neighbor? I finally said that there was no evidence that she had been unfaithful, and he snatched them from me, turned to one of the later ones, and read aloud to me a passage that began: "My dove, I shan't ever forget last night and the feel of your thighs pressed against mine." I pointed out to him that the last letter began by mentioning that she had refused to go away with him, and accused her of ceasing to care about him. I suggested to Kirsten that the affair was probably now over, but he said that *if* it was over, why hadn't she burnt the letters, instead of keeping them carefully concealed under some old magazines on top of the wardrobe? Then, to my embarrassment and astonishment, he said that he had been observing her recently, and had suspected that she was in love with somebody else—that he had suspected it was me! At this point, I was tempted to break it to him, but found I couldn't.

Kirsten went on to say that the letters indicated that she often met this man for lunch or after work, and that he wanted to go down to the factory and see if his suspicions were correct. I said I thought this was an excellent idea—being fairly certain that she has stopped seeing her bookmaker type. Kirsten then had to ask me if I knew where the factory was. He didn't even know! (He claimed that he'd been there, but had forgotten.) It was at this point that I had my inspiration. I told him that I believed it was in Clark Street, which is actually where the back entrance of the factory is situated. He asked me if I would go with him, but I said that I didn't feel I had any right to spy on his wife, and he finally went off alone. As soon as I was sure he was out of the house, I rushed off to the telephone in the pub next door, and rang the factory. They refused to let me speak to Diana on the phone—said it was against the rules to allow employees to use the office phone (lousy bastards, may they rot in hell), but that they'd give her a message if it was urgent. So I told them to tell her that her husband was ill, and would like her to come home at lunch time.

My ruse worked. Half an hour later, Diana came running into the house, and had not seen Kirsten, who was probably waiting by the back entrance. As soon as she saw me, she asked "Where is he? Is he all right?" and I explained quickly that nothing was wrong with Kirsten except jealousy. We decided we'd better leave the house, in case he came back when he discovered she wasn't there. So we walked to a café in Commercial Street.

I couldn't make up my mind whether this was a tragedy or a fortunate accident. I wanted Kirsten to find out about Diana, but we were still as far from my real goal—telling him about Diana and myself. Diana didn't seem as upset as I expected. She said: "Oh, that. It's all over." I had to explain to her that this might be the opportunity we wanted. If Kirsten should throw her out, we could live together. She said: "But he won't throw me out." "Why?" "Because he's too reliant on me." "But if he's reliant on you, why were you unfaithful to him?" "He was only reliant on me in *some* ways. Not at all in others."

Nevertheless, I felt that this was the time to make changes, if we intended to make them. So I told her that she couldn't go back to work, and that she didn't have to go back to Kirsten at all. We could simply find ourselves a room somewhere else, and, with a little care, I would have enough money to support us. The idea obviously appealed to her. (I'm sure that her life with Kirsten is beginning to ruin her.) But she finally said that she couldn't simply leave him without talking to him. And in spite of my persuasions, she insisted on going back to work (even though she hadn't eaten anything). However, she agreed that she would try to bring things to a head with Kirsten, and try to get him accustomed to the idea that they should live apart. I managed to persuade her to take a few sandwiches back to work with her, and she went off.

I immediately felt a sense of anticlimax, so I walked up to see Cunningham to tell him what had happened.

When I got there, I saw something that surprised me. Cunningham was still in bed, drinking lemon tea. Oliver was also in the room in a dressing gown. This would not have struck me as in any way peculiar, except that Oliver became violently embarrassed when he saw me, made some excuse, and hurried out. Cunningham looked after him ironically. I also noticed that Oliver didn't look his usual self; his eyes seem partly closed up, or perhaps they simply looked "faraway"— I didn't have time to observe him closely and make up my mind. I'd be startled to hear that Oliver had turned homosexual, but I wouldn't blame him particularly. I can hardly put any other interpretation on his embarrassment when I appeared, unless he was simply embarrassed at being caught in his dressing gown at one in the afternoon. And I doubt this.

Yet when I remember some of the scathing things he once
said about queers, I find it difficult to accept it. As to Cunningham, I'm sure he's bisexual anyway; it's impossible not to tell,
from the way he treats me occasionally, that he's had some
homosexual experience.

However, I didn't raise this matter, but told Cunningham
what had happened about Diana. He didn't seem to understand me at first. He said: "But my dear boy, why not let them
work it out for themselves?" I explained that I thought this
was as good an opportunity as any to get Diana to break with
Kirsten. "But why? Why shouldn't you simply continue as you
are?" When I explained that I'd like to live with Diana, he
said, in a slightly shocked voice: "You're not in *love* with her,
I hope?" I said that I simply found her very attractive, and
thought it a pity she should stay with Kirsten. Cunningham
then got out of bed. (I have yet to see a more repulsive sight
than Cunningham naked; he has a lot of surplus fat, large,
almost female breasts, and is covered with hair; he also
smelled abominably of sweat and some musky kind of per-
fume.) He insisted that I come up with him to the bathroom,
and he talked to me while he took his shower. After this, he
powdered himself elaborately with talcum, sprayed himself
with scent, and rubbed some kind of spirit into his genitals.
(He gave me a short discourse on the health of the penis, explaining that it is, after all, almost the only part of the body
that never sees the light of day, and never has a chance to
get sunburned; then declared that savages who live naked
are twice as potent as men who wear trousers; hence Cunningham devotes special attention to his member, "toning it up"
with pure alcohol and various other stimulants!) Meanwhile,
I could tell that this new development struck him as interesting. But his only concern was whether it would upset Kirsten.
When he'd finished dressing, he said: "Look, my boy, leave
this in my hands. I will go to see Kirsten this afternoon." I
asked him to be tactful, and he promised that he wouldn't
mention what I'd told him.

I went back home, meeting Oliver on the landing—he wouldn't look at me. (I thought this a good opportunity to mention that I'd seen Christine, but all he said was: "Oh good, give her my regards" as he vanished into his room!) When I got into my own room, I found Kirsten waiting for me. He said that he'd waited there all through the lunch hour, but that Diana hadn't emerged; I said that she probably stayed inside eating sandwiches. Kirsten was by this time in a pretty emotional state; I could see he'd been crying, and I felt miserable. I even decided that, if necessary, I would give Diana up, and persuade Kirsten to forgive her. He began to reproach himself, said he'd never paid her enough attention, and that it was disgraceful to allow her to work in such a place. (Evidently the squalor of the neighborhood had impressed him.)

After twenty minutes of this, Cunningham arrived. We heard him knocking on Kirsten's door. I quickly asked Kirsten if he wanted to see Cunningham, and he shook his head. However, Cunningham bounded up the stairs. I must say he's an excellent actor—started to talk about some business, then stopped and asked: "Is anything wrong? Have I come at a bad time?" Kirsten looked sheepish, and I explained that he was upset about his wife. Cunningham got the cue immediately: "Why? Has she left you?" Kirsten didn't need much encouragement to tell him the whole story. I then saw a remarkable piece of "persuasion." Cunningham listened gravely, looked at the letters, and finally said: "My dear chap, I sympathize with you. It must be rather a shock. But—don't mind my being frank—I can't help thinking that you're lucky." Kirsten looked surprised, and Cunningham went on: "Don't think that I dislike Diana—I don't. I think she's a delightful girl. But is she the woman to share the life of an artist of your stature?" I could see immediately that he'd struck the right note. He went into the question of the wives of men of genius —Mozart's Constance, Haydn's Maria, Wagner's Minna— and pointed out that most of them were catastrophic, or at least thoroughly unsuitable, declared that Bach and Schumann were the only two great musicians to have made suitable marriages, but still declared that Beethoven, Brahms and Schubert had been wisest in remaining single. It was, I suppose, a fairly obvious form of flattery—to keep comparing Kirsten to Beethoven, etc.—but it worked like magic. Kirsten's eyes began to sparkle, his head lifted, and he looked like a war horse at the sound of a trumpet. Then Cunningham went on to speak about the essential loneliness of greatness, to say that Beethoven could never have written the Hammerklavier and the Ninth symphony if he'd been happily married, and to declare his belief that men of genius must learn to accept their destiny, which is all arranged in advance by providence.

Then, having got Kirsten into a state of exaltation, Cunningham said that he'd come to tell him that the representative of a famous Washington opera society was in London, and was anxious to hear the music of *Varney the Vampire*. This, of course, completed the work of making Kirsten forget his upset. He mentioned that he had just put the finishing touches to a *Fantastic Overture,* which he was thinking of using for the Weir opera (when I supply the libretto!). Cunningham immediately demanded to hear it, and we all went on to see the orchestrion (although apparently Kirsten had made an arrangement not to use the warehouse during the day, when his music is likely to distract the workmen). He collected up sheets of disarranged music paper from all over the room, and we went. Luckily, the warehouse was empty, and I took the precaution of putting on two pairs of trousers and a woolen scarf, so the next hour was very enjoyable. The *Fantastic Overture* wasn't entirely a success—partly because Kirsten couldn't read his own writing, and often had to stop and work out what key he'd intended, partly because he put the music in the wrong order, and also because parts of the overture were supposed to be played on keys that he hadn't yet installed on the instrument. However, Cunningham demanded to hear pieces of *Varney* again, and Kirsten needed no encouragement. I must admit that it sounded even more impressive than last time. I cannot see how the opera can fail, once it's decently performed. After this, Kirsten went on playing of his own accord—a sonata for piano and violin which sounded excellent on the orchestrion, and then some fragments of a witches' sabbath that he'd written for *Weir*. We both praised them lavishly. At the end of an hour, someone came into the warehouse, and Kirsten decided we'd better go. On the way home, he was singing us fragments of his compositions, outlining his plans for a three-part opera on the life of Buddha, and talking about going to America to conduct *Varney*. When Cunningham mentioned Diana, his face fell, and it was obvious that the memory hurt him. Cunningham immediately began explaining that what he needs is a woman who is entirely devoted to him, who loves his music and cherishes his genius.

As we turned the corner to go into the house, we saw Diana coming from the other end of the street. We waited for her, and she and Kirsten went up the stairs first. She looked so nervous that it was obvious that she knew something was in the wind, but I don't think Kirsten noticed. Cunningham and I watched them go into her room, and then went on up to my room. I expected to hear raised voices, but not a sound came from their room. Cunningham looked absurdly pleased with himself.

I produced some wine—not very good stuff, but standing it in a bowl of warm water for five minutes improved it slightly—and we sat and talked. Cunningham lit a cigarette, and said: "It's strange, my dear Gerard, how easily our emotions can be influenced." The way he said "My dear Gerard . . ." and threw away the match reminded me of Austin, and I must have stared at him in an odd way, because he asked me what the matter was. I said he reminded me of a friend, and mentioned Austin's name. He immediately asked me to tell him more about Austin, saying that Oliver had mentioned the name several times. I felt embarrassed about this; I didn't want to be drawn into speaking about Austin. (His father spent half an hour impressing on me the importance of absolute and total silence about him, and since he concluded the lecture by handing me the check, I feel under a certain obligation to keep my word.) Luckily, as soon as I mentioned that Austin was homosexual, Cunningham was sidetracked; he evidently thought this was what I meant, and said quite openly: "But then, I'm not completely homosexual, of course." I assured him that this wasn't what I meant, but the discussion then turned to homosexuality, and I was glad to have gotten away from the subject of Austin. He asked me if I was bisexual; I said no, and admitted that I have so little homosexuality in my composition that I'm totally baffled by the phenomenon—I simply can't imagine how a man could find another man attractive. Cunningham declared that this is so in a few people—their sexual impulses are like a river that runs in a very narrow and deep gorge, and can never overflow in any other direction, no matter how high they rise. His own impulses, he said, have always been for the most part heterosexual, but if he ever reached an intense peak of sexual frustration, he could satisfy himself on man, woman, child or animal.

By this time we'd emptied one bottle of wine and opened another, and it was obvious to me that he was in the mood for self-revelation. So I kept firing questions at him. The story of how he first developed a taste for homosexuality strikes me as interesting. When he was 18, and had only just gone up to Oxford, he fell violently in love with a waitress—a small girl, not conventionally pretty, but with lovely eyes and a boyish body. For several weeks he pursued her with gifts and poems, and she finally gave herself to him. He was so crazy about her by this time that he decided he must marry her as soon as he could get permission from his guardian, or when he was 21. She declared that she would never leave him, and allowed him to take a cottage for her just outside the town, where he spent all his free hours with her. For six months they were ecstatically happy; then one day, he discovered that she was in the habit of betraying him. She was a nymphomaniac who had to keep having sex as often as she could get it. As a waitress in a café, with a cottage of her own and a lover who could only call at certain hours, she had plenty of opportunity, and even slept with the milkman. In fact, it was with the milkman that Cunningham actually caught her in the act. They were not even in bed, but in the kitchen, against the table. When she knew there was no point in lying, she was completely frank, and admitted that on one occasion, she had even had sex with the baker in the outside lavatory while Cunningham was lying in her bed, waiting for her to bring him a cup of tea! The need for haste and the possibility of being caught only made her enjoy it more.

Cunningham was overwhelmed; he wanted to kill her. He was insanely in love with her, and her infidelities made no difference; in a way, they only made her more desirable. Yet he knew he could never bear to stay with her. It was the end of term; he went to Scotland and tried to forget her; it was impossible. He went to London and tried sleeping with prostitutes; he found them loathsome, although this was by no means his first experience. He said that he found the majority of women detestable because they were so unlike her; but when a girl reminded him of her, this was even worse, because it brought back her infidelities.

For weeks he was tormented. Then one evening, at a friend's party, he looked across the room, and met a pair of large, dark eyes in a pale face. Instantly, he felt weak and shattered; he knew that he was in love again. The eyes had looked at him in a way that told him that nothing could prevent their coming together. He finally gained enough strength to push his way across the room, and found the beloved talking to their host. And it was a man. Cunningham said that at first he was horrified. (His upbringing had been strictly religious, and although he thought himself "emancipated," he was still easily shockable.) But as soon as he began to talk to the stranger—whose name was Roddy—he realized that this made no difference. Two hours later, they left the party together. Roddy had a cottage at Stratford; they drove there through the night, arriving at dawn, staggered into the house, and immediately tumbled into bed. They stayed there for a fortnight, with brief visits to the local shops for food! Roddy was also at Oxford, and they returned together the following term. His nymphomaniac waitress was still working in the same café and living in the same cottage; two months before, he would not have believed it possible that he could return to Oxford and be indifferent to her presence. But he was. The affair with Roddy lasted only a few weeks, but when it was over, Cunningham was completely cured of his earlier love affair.

I asked Cunningham if he had had any exclusively homosexual periods since then. He said only one, just after the war, in London, when he had suffered a great disappointment. (He did not specify what this was.) He suddenly decided that he would wash it out of his system with a period of promiscuity, and for a year had frequented homosexual clubs and taken satisfaction wherever he could find it. He said that he found most satisfaction when it was unexpected and in completely unsuitable surroundings, and suddenly was able to understand his nymphomaniac waitress in Oxford. He said he soon discovered that there were a large proportion of homosexuals among taxi drivers, railway porters and window-cleaners. He found that a completely frank approach was usually best. For example, one day a young window-cleaner was washing the outside of the windows, sitting on the windowsill with his legs in the room. Cunningham started to unbutton his trousers, and when the man looked startled, said: "Look, I'm awfully sorry, but I have an irresistible impulse to make love to you." The man said cheerfully: "That's all right guv, you go ahead," and went on cleaning the window!

It had been about an hour and a half since we left Kirsten outside his door. Now Kirsten came in, looking very pleased with himself, and announced: "She's gone." "Gone?" I asked.

"Where to?" "The other man." He said that it hadn't been an angry meeting; she was very quiet and reasonable, and told him that she found him too distant and detached, and that when another man had showed sympathy, she had found it irresistible. She felt that he didn't need her. (All this, of course, was exactly the right approach—to confirm Kirsten's feeling of being a "man on his own," a genius with his head in the clouds and no time for women.) Finally, Kirsten said generously that he was willing to let her go, if she was sure the other man loved her. She admitted that she wasn't sure of this. Kirsten then rose to heights of unselfishness, and told her to go and see "the other man," explain the situation to him and ask him if he was willing to marry her. If he refused, then she could return to Kirsten, and he would take her back without recalling their past differences. (This made me smile. Since Diana is virtually supporting him at present, his gesture loses a lot of its effect!) So Diana had gone out.

Cunningham immediately proposed that we should go back to his place, but I said I felt tired and would stay behind. Kirsten and Cunningham went off, and I lay on the bed, and tried to restrain my impatience. This was almost impossible; I was in a fever to find out what she intended to do. Finally, after an hour, she came in and came up to my room. She looked very tired. I made her take her coat off and get into bed—not from sexual motives, but because the poor child looked so miserable. She told me she had been walking around in the park, hoping that Kirsten would go out so she could talk to me. I made her tea and cooked her some frankfurters and eggs, and she began to improve. (She hadn't eaten all day, having been too upset during the afternoon to eat her sandwiches.) It seemed to me that everything was now very simple. She can see that Kirsten isn't going to be broken-hearted about her; her affair with the bookmaker type is at an end. There's nothing to stop us from simply living together. She seemed unhappy and unsure, but too tired to make any resistance. So when she'd eaten, I locked the door securely, turned off the lights (in case Kirsten should try and come in) and got into bed with her. We lay there with the electric fire on, the radio playing a Bach concert very low, and not even making any attempt to make love. I said: "This is your first evening as my wife instead of Kirsten's." She said there were a lot of difficulties ahead, and I said it didn't matter if she really wanted to live with me. Then suddenly I realized I was on the point of saying: "If you don't betray me as you betrayed Kirsten," and had to stop myself. I understand now what Cunningham meant about betrayal. When Diana was Kirsten's wife, I didn't give a damn about the bookmaker type, and when she slept with me, I felt pleased because I was making her unfaithful to two men. Now I feel she's mine, and immediately feel uncertain. But there's no point in thinking too much about this.

So that is what has happened. Diana insisted on getting up and going to work this morning. She says she'll work until the weekend, to get her paycheck, but will give notice today. I tried to make her see that the miserable two or three pounds she'll draw are unimportant, and that it doesn't matter if she doesn't bother to collect them. But years of half starving have made her cautious, and she went off at half past seven this morning, going downstairs in her stocking feet in case Kirsten should recognize her step. And I am now left with the problem of what I intend to do. I wonder if Cunningham could persuade Kirsten to move out of his room? It is obviously impossible for Diana to move in here with Kirsten in the room below. On the other hand, if we could manage to avoid Kirsten for a few weeks, something might be done. . . .

Nov. 25. Things are, in fact, working out unexpectedly well. Cunningham has offered Kirsten a room in their place—they have an attic above Cunningham's room. Kirsten has already given notice and has started to move his things out. We had a tense moment last night when Kirsten knocked on my door after Diana and I had gone to bed. He had a message for me from Cunningham, so I had to let him in, and Diana had to rush into the bathroom in case Kirsten looked into the bedroom. The message was to tell me that an old associate of Cunningham's was in town, and to ask me to go and meet him today. Kirsten had spent the evening with him, and been much impressed by him as a sincere and honest man.

Kirsten then went on to talk about the room that Cunningham had offered him, then about Diana (whom he presumes to have gone back to her bookmaker, since he hasn't heard from her). He was evidently inclined to stay all night, but as Diana was sitting uncomfortably on the edge of the bathtub with no clothes on, I had to be fairly brusque, and tell him that I had a headache and wanted to get back to bed. At this moment, unfortunately, Diana managed to knock the plug into the tub. Kirsten looked startled, then smiled knowingly, said "My apologies," and left. I immediately felt an utter swine. However, I want Diana so badly that I don't let this worry me too much.

I'm amazed when I examine my feelings about her. In a quarrelsome mood, Gertrude once accused me of being incapable of any deep feeling for anyone. As far as Gertrude is concerned, this is true enough. I think that my feeling about Diana may be partly protective—she seems to have had so little out of life, and to deserve so much. And yet ever since I've known her, I've had an instinct that told me to grab her, as if I instantly recognized someone I could live with and spend a lifetime with. How far this is a real perception, I don't know. It's a fairly new experience for me.

Later. I went to see Cunningham, as he suggested, and was directed to phone his friend, who is called Tim Wedmore, at the Regent Palace Hotel. I did, and he immediately asked me if I could come and have lunch with him. I didn't much want to: I've started to work on the Weir libretto, and wanted to spend the day on it; but he sounded so friendly that I agreed. He is on his way to California, flying tomorrow, so there wouldn't be another opportunity.

He turned out to be a big, well-fed man in his fifties, with a craggy bald forehead, very pale blue eyes, and a sensuous mouth. He's a Scot who went to New Zealand to farm sheep, and made a decent lot of money. During the war, when he was in the army, he read a book by Cunningham, and immediately wrote to him. The result was that he went to live with Cunningham immediately after the war on the "island," and became a fervent disciple.

On my way to the hotel, I wondered about Cunningham's motives in introducing me to Wedmore; I soon found out. Wedmore also worships Cunningham; and since he's a shrewd and intelligent man, his enthusiasm is contagious. We had lunch up in Wedmore's room—he wanted to be able to talk without interruption. He began by saying that he had heard I was a great writer, and would probably be able to make Cunningham's work known to thousands of people. I modestly disclaimed all this, but it was obvious that Wedmore was determined to regard me as a friend and ally.

The story he told me while we ate was as startling as anything in *Varieties of Religious Experience*. The trouble, Wedmore said, was that he was a man of strong feelings and instincts, quick tempered, highly sexed, but with a background of Scotch Presbyterianism that gives him a naturally gloomy and mistrustful outlook on the world. As a sheep farmer, he read Plato and the Upanishads, and meditated on the problem of why God made the world with so much evil in it. He had a half-caste girl on his farm with whom he had sexual relations when he was at home, but during the weeks when he was riding over distant parts of his land, he admitted to a strong temptation to use the sheep to satisfy his desires. He was horrified by this streak of bestiality in him. He did not care for the half-caste girl, but found her physically exciting. On the other hand, he knew a schoolteacher who attracted him, and often thought of marrying her; but he was reasonably certain that she would not satisfy him physically, even if she would make an excellent wife in other ways. It was at this point that he read a book by Cunningham (called *The Voice*

of Baphomet) in which Cunningham spoke about techniques
for being able to see into one's previous incarnations, and declared that no man could ever understand himself or be completely free from self-division unless he knew about past incarnations, and learned exactly how he came to develop his
present characteristics. He wrote to Cunningham, mentioning
that he was a fairly rich sheep farmer. The result was an
irregular correspondence that led to an invitation to Cunningham's island off the coast of Sardinia.

Wedmore said he was in a pretty bad way when he accepted the invitation. He had spent the last year of the war in
a Japanese prison camp, and seen some pretty awful things.
He felt a consuming hatred of the Japanese for some of the
atrocities he had seen, and was obsessed by the idea that the
whole Japanese race must be destroyed before we can hope for
world peace. Yet his religious ideas made him feel that this
thought was evil. So he was pitifully self-divided when Cunningham met him at the boat and arranged the trip out to the
island.

At first, he was shocked by Cunningham's farm. To begin
with, Cunningham made no secret of having sexual relations
with two young Indian boys who acted as servants, as well
as with a skinny American girl. The walls of the house were
covered with designs of erect phalli, and marijuana cigarettes
and dishes of cocaine lay around the place for anyone to take.
Cunningham was engaged in magical researches which involved killing a cat, and hanging crucified toads on an in-
verted crucifix. At first, Wedmore was completely bewildered,
and thought that he had fallen in with a madman. Soon after
he arrived, more visitors came—various eccentrics of the
international set who seemed to be out to throw off all restraint.
Cunningham declared that his true disciples would be willing
to prostitute their bodies to anyone who should ask; most of
the guests promptly declared themselves his true disciples, and
made this an excuse for a sexual orgy. Wedmore himself was
attracted to a slim, quiet girl who had come as the companion

of a Greek banker, and one afternoon he possessed her on the beach after they had been bathing. That evening at supper, heated by wine and drugs, some of the guests proceeded to have sex at the table, declaring that the pleasures of food and of love should be mixed. Then, to Wedmore's horror, his "quiet, slim girl" tore open his trousers, and proposed that they should perform various sexual acts on the table while the others ate. Wedmore rushed out of the room and went to the beach; he wanted to leave the island immediately, but could not find a boat.

Late that night he was sitting on the beach, shivering, when Cunningham and his mistress arrived. Cunningham came over to him, and told him that he now proposed to initiate him into some of the great secrets. Cunningham then explained to him that his trouble was simple: he had always been afraid of his subconscious mind, not realizing that it contained the dark mystery of his true self. Cunningham expounded his views for about five minutes, declaring that the conscious self is nothing more than the upper layer of the subconscious being. The conscious cannot have any will of its own, and it is impossible to be good or virtuous from purely conscious direction. The problem is to relax and allow the subconscious to encroach on the conscious, bringing its life-giving forces, and revealing its will. At the bottom of the subconscious, Cunningham said, is the meaning of all life, the purpose that drives us and grants us life. It must be encouraged to rise and express its will.

Cunningham then proposed that they go for a swim, but Wedmore was too excited. He stayed where he was, and watched the others swimming in the moonlight. They then came out of the water and copulated openly on the sand. Suddenly, Wedmore said, he understood the full grandeur of Cunningham's conception. Cunningham *wanted* to shock people like himself and arouse doubts in their minds because truth itself is a paradox; he took an ironic pleasure in seeing them struggling with despair when he himself was in permanent contact with the truth, and knew that they could reach it too with a very slight effort of will.

That night, Wedmore said, he felt as if he was being torn in two. He tried to kneel down and pray, but thought he heard a voice shout: "Don't do that, you fool, or you're lost." He went out and walked over the island, cutting his bare feet badly on the stones, but not even noticing this. Something inside him kept saying: "I have discovered the truth, but perhaps it is too late. I have already destroyed too much of myself." He realized that his religious training—even though he had been an avowed atheist since his fifteenth year—had given him a tendency to believe that only the conscious motives mattered. He felt that if, on the day of judgment, he were accused of being a sink of filth and lust, he would be able to reply: "But I fought it with all my will power." He had developed a very considerable will power for suppressing his "lust." Now, quite suddenly, he was told to try to listen to the voice of his lust and all the other obscure impulses from "down there," to decide how he should live. But years of repressing these feelings had made him incapable of treating these impulses as friends; he had been regarding them as enemies for too long. This knowledge made him feel as if he were suffocating.

For two days he went through a great crisis, sometimes praying, sometimes thinking about his past problems and how easily he might have solved them if he had known about his "true self." Finally, the squealing and giggling of the other guests drove him to the other side of the island (which I gather is only a few hundred yards across), where he had a sense of tremendous greatness, of standing on a mountain top. He realized that Cunningham was the only one who shared this greatness with him. All the others were there from base motives. Their orgies were not the prompting of their "true will," but self-conscious titillations that were only a temporary escape from their littleness. He felt that he had released something in himself that made him feel as great as a mountain or a giant; he was aware of subconscious powers as vast as the sea. This sense of his own limitlessness—that he had never before recognized—took away his breath. He said that he suddenly realized he had been living in a tiny, cold room when he had a whole palace at his disposal.

He now began to feel feverish excitement. He took advantage of the lax rules of the place to have sexual intercourse with every woman there. He even tried the two boys. This aroused the resentment of the Greek, and one of the Rome playboys insulted him and tried to get him to fight a duel. But he felt so superior to them that he only laughed, and pulled their girls into bed again. The Greek left in a rage with his girl (who was most reluctant). Wedmore now had a tremendous reaction of disgust and bewilderment; he begged Cunningham to initiate him into the innermost mysteries, but Cunningham laughed and said that he was an ignorant peasant. He decided that he must return to New Zealand. But on his last evening there, Cunningham projected his astral body so that it shared Wedmore's body, and Wedmore was aware of being able to read all Cunningham's thoughts and his past history, and also of revealing himself completely to Cunningham. That night, he had an exceptionally vivid dream in which he was a London paper merchant on his deathbed. The dream seemed to progress backwards in a series of scenes, and when he woke up, he was dreaming that he was witnessing the coronation of Queen Victoria. He knew, even before he spoke to Cunningham, that he had now penetrated into his last incarnation, the London businessman who had always had an urge to enter a monastery, and who died of cancer at the age of 50. When he told Cunningham, Cunningham replied that he was now beginning to gain control of his subconscious impulses, and would eventually learn about all his previous incarnations.

Wedmore went back to New Zealand, but now he was a disciple of Cunningham. He sent him money regularly, had established a Cunningham society in Auckland, and was now going to California to preach the Master's doctrines there.

What amused me was that Wedmore was still the shrewd

and wide-awake Scotch businessman. He had sold his farm, and invested the money in such a way as to ensure that he would have enough to last him for the rest of his life, which he would devote to spreading Cunningham's ideas. Cunningham had tried to persuade him that he would do better to stay in New Zealand and continue to farm. Wedmore winked, and said: "I know what he's after. With things as they are at present, I need all my money for travel and living expenses. If I stayed on in New Zealand, I'd have money to give Cunningham, and that's what he'd prefer. But *I'd* rather travel!" So in spite of his enthusiasm, he has no illusions about Cunningham!

What interested me most was all the talk about magical ceremony. This is obviously an aspect of Cunningham that I have yet to see.

Wedmore told me, incidentally, that two of the women in Cunningham's life had committed suicide, having increased their mental instability with drugs. Drugs apparently do not affect Cunningham, and he claims he can use them and give them up exactly as he pleases.

I told Wedmore something about myself, my ideas, my ambitions. He seemed puzzled; evidently I am too much of an "intellectual" to appeal to his temperament. He finally said: "Well, you must have some remarkable qualities, or Cunningham wouldn't have spoken of you as he has." I didn't know whether this was flattery or an expression of disappointment.

I ended by saying that I thought magic was nonsense. Then Wedmore said, ponderously: "Magic is only an attempt to invoke the force of life. All life is magic already." This struck me more than anything else he said to me.

As I left, I told him Wise's idea that Cunningham has exposed himself to spiritual reprisals for breaking some oaths. I expected him to deny this, but to my surprise, he nodded, and said: "I have sometimes thought the same. He is dogged by the most appalling bad luck. Still, all great prophets have to go through trials and torments. . . ."

Nov. 26. Yesterday evening was curious, but I am too tired to write about it at length. I must stop this writing; it leaves me exhausted, and I sometimes feel as if I'm writing my life instead of living it.

Kirsten met Diana on the stairs when she came home from work. Naturally, he thought she was coming to see him, and she didn't want to disillusion him. She told him that she was coming to collect some of her clothes, and that she was living alone for the time being. Kirsten told her he was moving, and she finally hit upon the excellent idea of storing her clothes in my flat until she finds a permanent place of her own. This means that she can be seen coming into my place now without arousing suspicion. So Kirsten and she moved several bags and suitcases up here, and now the place is littered with all kinds of women's belongings. She let him understand that the liaison with the bookmaker is continuing, and this seems to satisfy him, although I think he is now permitting himself the sentimental pleasure of imagining that he's unhappy about it.

Later we went up to Cunningham's, and found him in a most weird mood. I think he'd been taking drugs. As soon as Diana came in, he declared that she was giving off "psychic vibrations" and that he suspected her of being a medium. He made her sit down, gave her a large gin, then made Oliver bring up one of his paintings—an abstraction which looks as if its central object is the sun. He set this up on an armchair, illuminated by a table lamp, and made her stare at it, while he slowly stroked her forehead. In about two minutes she seemed to be asleep. Then he asked her where she was. She answered, in a rather monotonous voice: "Here, in this house." He said: "Have you any message for me?," and she said: "No message. This house is full of evil." I felt myself shivering—there was something oddly impressive about it, although it wasn't at all theatrical—in fact, it seemed somehow as commonplace as asking her questions while fully awake.

Cunningham said: "What is the evil?," and she replied: "It is the evil of displaced energy." (I saw Cunningham look puzzled at this; he asked her to elaborate, but she didn't reply.) I can't detail all the questions and answers. Some of them seemed meaningless to me. He would ask something like: "What is the meaning of Seven hundred and twenty-six?," and she would reply: "I see two men clothed in red." I strongly suspected her of pulling his leg and only pretending to be in a trance.

Finally, Cunningham asked her again: "What is the evil?," and she replied: "It is the force of Seven hundred and twenty-six who intends to destroy your work." At this, Cunningham went unexpectedly pale, and sat down. This made me realize that, at least as far as he was concerned, the thing was no joke. Then he asked, rather shakily: "Can I do anything to prevent it?" and she replied: "Not unless the forces have forgiven you." "Can I do anything to hasten this?" "Yes. Learn to live from your center." He asked her for further details, but all she would say was: "There is one in the room who understands."

Cunningham seemed strangely upset by this. He said: "I am going to awaken you now. When you are awake, you will remember nothing of what you have said." He started to make passes over her forehead, when Kirsten interrupted him, and asked if she were bound to tell the truth in her state of trance. Cunningham said yes. Kirsten then asked if he could ask her questions. I wanted to interfere—this seemed to me unfair—then realized that my indignation arose from a sense that Diana was, in some sense, mine, and that I could hardly expect Kirsten to understand this! So I had to keep quiet. But all he asked her was: "Are you in love with someone else?" She answered immediately: "Yes." He asked, "Have you betrayed me with him?," and again she answered, "Yes." I was now on tenterhooks; it seemed impossible that he would not now ask her the name of her lover. But Kirsten simply sat down gloomily, and said to Cunningham: "That's all I wanted to know."

Cunningham's face surprised me; he looked more downcast than I've ever seen him. He made passes over her forehead, and she woke up and didn't seem at all curious about what had gone on while she was asleep. Then Cunningham asked us if we'd mind going downstairs to Oliver's studio for a while, as he wanted to be alone. So we went. Oliver was working, but didn't seem to resent the interruption. He asked: "Did it work?," and when Kirsten said (rather unhappily) that it had, he looked pleased with himself, and said that he'd painted the picture upstairs to Cunningham's specifications. I asked him how Cunningham could "describe" an abstract painting as complex as the one we'd seen, and he replied: "He didn't describe it—he showed it to me. He made me close my eyes, placed his hands on my head, and suddenly I saw exactly what he wanted." Kirsten shook his head and said: "That man is a black magician." Then, to my amazement, Diana gasped, and went horribly pale. We helped her into a chair. She looked at Kirsten and said: "What you said . . . it reminded me of something." Then she looked around, shivered, and said: "There is evil in this house." Oliver said cheerfully: "Oh, I don't think so. I find the atmosphere helps me to work." I could see his point. His new paintings were very powerful indeed, full of that quality of atmosphere that Oliver has always possessed, which seems to have nothing to do with anything specific *in* the painting, but almost to have been added afterwards, like the varnish.

Cunningham called to me to go upstairs. I found him sitting in the chair, now looking definitely ill. I asked him if I could get him anything, but he shook his head, and said: "This is not a physical illness. That girl has made me realize that I've got a hard fight ahead." I tried to make him explain himself. But all he would say was: "There are forces that want to kill me. They won't succeed." This all sounded to me like nonsensical superstition. He sat there, staring at Oliver's painting, and wouldn't talk, so I helped myself to a gin and sat down. Then he said: "It's a great pity. One imagines that one has broken through at last . . . into the daylight. Then the darkness comes again." Then, for another quarter of an hour, he didn't speak at all. Finally, he said: "Gerard, perhaps you can help me. That girl's a bad medium. Her own personality gets mixed up with the message. But if I could hypnotize you, you might be able to tell me how to defeat them." I said. "All right, if you think it's worth trying." He said: "No, not now. At midnight." He then became more cheerful and we went down and joined the others. He suggested that we go out for a meal, and all five of us walked out toward Whitechapel High Street. On the way, we passed the end of our street, and to my amazement I saw Gertrude's blue Consul parked outside my door. I explained to them that I thought I had a visitor—this was out of a sense of duty, for I shrank from the idea of meeting her at the moment. So we all went up to my room, and found Gertrude sitting in the armchair, reading my book on Weir. Apparently she'd seen Father O'Mahoney during the afternoon, and he had mentioned seeing me in a taxicab with Radin and—believe it or not—said I looked unhappy! (How the devil you can see unhappiness through two panes of glass, I don't know.)

I introduced her to everyone; as soon as she spoke to Diana, I felt that she smelled out her connection with me—or at least, saw her as a rival. Even introducing Diana as Mrs. Kirsten made no difference. (On second thought, no doubt it was the presence of Diana's suitcases that made her suspicious.)

She was obviously pleased to see Oliver again, and put herself out to be nice to him. I suggested that she should join us for a meal, and we all went off in her car to the Chinese restaurant. She didn't ask me why I hadn't been to see her, and I had a feeling that she hadn't wanted me to go. One thing she said made me curious. She mentioned that Father O'Mahoney seems to have made a remarkable recovery and is now moving around a great deal. I asked her innocently why she'd been to see him, and she colored. Oliver said cheerfully: "You're not thinking of becoming a Catholic, are you?," and to my surprise, she said: "Would that be so strange?"

Cunningham took this up immediately, and began telling her that she couldn't take a better step. This startled me, coming from him, but it evidently delighted Gertrude, who immediately launched into an intimate conversation with Cunningham—as intimate, that is, as a dinner table will permit. They sat at the end, and talked as if the rest of us weren't present.

We left at about eleven. I insisted on paying for Kirsten and Diana, for I'm tired of taking meals off Cunningham (and realizing that they're paid for with Oliver's money.) Gertrude then said she should go home, but Cunningham persuaded her to come back to his place to have her fortune read in the Tarot pack. She explained that she didn't believe in it, but came nevertheless. We all went into Oliver's studio again—it is bigger, and has more chairs than Cunningham's—and Cunningham shuffled the Tarot cards, selected one that was supposed to stand for Gertrude, and laid out ten cards. He then read the interpretation of the cards out of a book by Eliphaz Levi. I could see that Gertrude was impressed. She looked embarrassed and confused when Cunningham claimed that the cards revealed an element of sensuality in her past life (Diana shot me an odd look—I wonder sometimes if she's clairvoyant). But the card that represented her future was—the Pope! Cunningham then declared that they would cross-check the results by consulting the *I Ching,* and brought out three Chinese coins with holes in the middle, which he made Gertrude throw down six times. Each time she threw, he drew a line—either broken or unbroken. He then looked up the result, and again produced a result that was weirdly close to the reading in the Tarot. The book said that Gertrude was to be "given in marriage," which symbolizes a religious commitment, and gave various other details of her past and future, including "loss of maidenly virture," all of which startled her.

Diana very sensibly slipped off, saying that she had to go home; I had given her a spare key to my flat, so she was able to let herself in. Gertrude and Cunningham got into a discus-

sion of magic, in which she expressed herself strongly about
the wickedness of such superstitions. This had the effect of
rather spoiling the pleasant rapport between them. She finally
left, but told me that she might come and see me soon; I got
the impression that she had something on her mind. Finally, as
midnight struck, Cunningham asked me to go up to his room.
The first thing he asked me to do was to consult the Tarot for
him. I did this under his instructions, and the results did not
reassure him. The card representing his future was a tower
collapsing, with people falling out of it. The card representing
himself was—the Devil! And the card representing his "final
end" indicated absolution and repentance, followed by a
restoration of grace.

Cunningham became extremely depressed, and said: "It
seems that the time of revelations has arrived." He said that
there are certain times when the future is completely opaque,
and others when it can be divined to a certain extent. The
present, he said, was the opposite extreme from the opaque—
complete clarity—and it would be necessary to take advantage of it while it lasted.

He then said that he proposed to try to hypnotize me,
and that I should do my best to help him by relaxing my will
completely. He also offered various other instructions, which I
can't be bothered to detail. At all events, the whole thing was
a failure. I was tired enough—I could barely keep my eyes
open—but staring at the illuminated picture of Oliver's only
seemed to make me more awake. Cunningham tried swinging
a bright silver medallion in front of my eyes, and stroking my
forehead from behind, but it made absolutely no difference.
My mind had never felt clearer and more sceptical. At one
point, I thought I was "going off," but I was only getting
sleepy, and suddenly woke up with a start. After half an hour
of this, Cunningham looked very tired. He said it was obviously
no use going on, and that perhaps he might be able to hypnotize Oliver. He said he was puzzled about me—that he had a
definite feeling I would be an excellent medium, but that there

was something in my personality that he had left out of
account.

So I went home, leaving Oliver with Cunningham. Kirsten walked back with me; he was wide awake, and talked nonstop about music being the first of the magic arts, etc. He wanted to come up to my room, or me to go into his, but I said I was too sleepy.

In fact, Diana was fast asleep when I got in, and I simply climbed in beside her, and went off to sleep myself. But two hours later I woke up in a fever of desire, and made love to her several times. I was startled by the intensity of my own need for her—it was as if my mind had been cleared of all distractions so that I could suddenly grasp how much she means to me.

Nov. 27. Strange things are happening over at Cunningham's. I helped Kirsten move some of his stuff over there this afternoon. We didn't intend to disturb Cunningham, but the door of the upstairs room was locked, and Oliver was out, so there was no alternative but to knock on Cunningham's door. We could hear someone moving around inside. Finally, he opened it, and the most awful smell came out—incense mixed with burnt meat—and Cunningham himself was wearing a peculiar black robe with a hood. Either his eyes were very tired, or he was under the influence of some drug. He handed me the key without looking at me properly, and slammed the door again.

Later. I was writing the above when Gertrude arrived. She seemed to be in a strange mood, and said casually that everything was now over between us. I had a feeling that she wanted me to deny this, give her reasons for making her change her mind, but that she was unable to say so. When she's with me, I realize that she has a curious power of exciting me sexually—far greater, in its way, than Caroline ever had. This I suppose to be due to her air of separateness, a kind of inner reserve that she couldn't abandon no matter how hard she tried. Diana lacks this; I sometimes feel that when she gives her body, she has no awareness of giving something of importance; it is something she hardly values. Consequently, sex with Diana never produces a feeling of violation, of overcoming obstacles; Diana has a capacity for giving herself so completely that she seems to dissolve into oneself. This satisfies me emotionally and gives her an absolute hold over me. Gertrude can never give herself to the same extent; but the consequence is that she arouses far more straightforward animal lust in me.

Still, it was obvious to me from the beginning that Gertrude has nosed out what is going on with Diana. I naturally felt reluctant to talk of it to her—it would seem too much like gloating over a new mistress. She asked me bluntly why Diana's clothes were all over the place. I explained that she and Kirsten had broken up. She then asked me why Diana's stockings were on the bathroom floor, and I had to admit that she was staying here. She then said rather coldly: "You don't have to lie to me about these things; what about her husband?" When I told her the story of Diana and the bookmaker type, her nose wrinkled with disgust. It was obvious she had difficulty in preventing herself from saying: "Oh, she's *that* kind of a woman, is she?" (Women have the most phenomenal capacity for seeing other women as they want to see them; their capacity for distortion is so great that it's a good thing there have never been any women philosophers.)

I was interested in her indignation about Diana. I wanted to ask her about her standards of morality, that allowed her to go to bed with me, yet condemned Diana for escaping from an unsatisfactory marriage. But she steered clear of this, and said that she thought Kirsten needed to be taken care of. Thinking that this might give a new direction to her interests, I started to talk about Kirsten, said that I was convinced of his genius, and then gave her a brief character sketch, emphasizing that Kirsten is too abstracted and otherworldly to make a satisfactory husband. Then Gertrude suddenly declared that she was convinced that Cunningham was an evil influence; I wasn't prepared for this, since they seemed to get on perfectly last night. When I pressed her to be more explicit, she said: "I haven't met many evil persons in my lifetime, but I have a feeling that he is actively evil." This gave me a sense of despair—it is useless trying to talk to Gertrude about certain things; she has an absolutely closed mind. I couldn't make her see that Cunningham is probably much like the rest of us—a man who doesn't really feel very much at home or very secure in the world, who has an unusual amount of vitality, but is strangely weak in purpose. This now seems to me to be the truth. I understand what Diana meant in her trance when she said that he doesn't live from his center. I myself am uncertain what I ought to do with my life—I call myself a writer because this seems about the most plausible of my notions of myself; but I feel no sense of destiny as a writer, as I think Shakespeare and Dickens probably did. And yet I undoubtedly have a kind of magnet at my center which, whether I like it or not, draws all my energies into a knot, so that all my living seems to me a constant effort in a certain direction—even though I couldn't define that direction. I believe this also applies to Oliver and Kirsten. But I feel it does not apply to Cunningham, any more than it applied to Austin. I feel there is something oddly pathetic in all this talk about magic—even if there *is* something in it. I find this difficult to express—but it seems to me like the way that very young animals try to suck at any object that reminds them of the mother's teat, but don't succeed in getting milk! I think Cunningham is right to be jealous of Spender, Isherwood and the others. He possesses as much talent as anyone of that generation; the only trouble is that he has never learned to keep it concentrated on one purpose. The result, I think, is that he has come to compromise more and more as he's got older, and many of his compromises have probably been bad—in the moral sense. But I don't find *evil* in him; only weakness.

Of course, I suspect that Gertrude is aware of the at-

mosphere of sexuality that he exudes. This is something I
have become steadily more aware of over the past few days—
almost as if he wanted to drop the concealments and show
himself to me in full. But this only deepens my sense of his
weakness. He is a victim of the sexual confidence trick. It is
obvious that every girl represents a challenge to him, a privacy,
a self-enclosed identity, and that his immediate desire is to
tear off her clothes, drive his assault weapon into her, and say
"There, take that, you bitch." Then, with a satisfied grin, he
can make another entry in his book of sexual conquests. I
sympathize with this; I recognize the same urge in myself. Yet,
carried on in this spirit, it is finally a self-frustrating activity,
like killing flies in summer; no matter how many you kill,
there are still billions left in the world, and they are in-
eradicable; they've existed for millions of years, and will probably still exist when the world comes to an end. So this continual conquest is like drinking vinegar to quench your thirst.
Wedmore told me a story that didn't strike me as important
at the time. Cunningham had sex with every woman in the
house during the period that Wedmore was there; many of
them obviously wanted to continue sharing his bed, but he
asked Wedmore to help him in evading them. He did this by
playing them off one against another, and by making use of the
menfolk to whom they were supposed to be attached. After
one complicated maneuver, Wedmore remarked that Cunningham would have done better to avoid these women in the
first place. Cunningham replied: "That's true, but I had to possess them *once*." This is significant; it indicates, I think, his
compulsive need to keep "possessing" different women, as if
to prove something to himself. This also struck me about
Cunningham's story of seizing the princess in the middle of
her engagement party and rushing her off to bed. I can imagine
him, afterwards, saying to himself: "I did it. I am godlike.
How many other men could have done that?"—and yet somehow not *feeling* any different. And this brings me to another
point about Cunningham: his constant need to thumb his
nose at society. He is *too aware* of society.

Nov. 28. Things get crazier. Diana and I were eating supper last night—peacefully and happily, because she had left that filthy factory for good, and Kirsten had moved into Cunningham's (two men spent half the afternoon wrestling his piano downstairs). There was a knock at the door; we thought it might be Kirsten again, and she rushed into the bedroom; but it was Cunningham, looking completely exhausted. I offered him some wine; he poured himself half a pint of Medoc, drank it straight down, then vanished into the bedroom and closed the door. We left him to himself. Diana and I wanted to celebrate, so we took a bus out to Woolwich, had some beer in a pub, went across on the ferry, and then back. I felt absurdly happy, although it was a raw, misty evening, and there was an icy wind on the river. On the way back, I asked her point-blank about Tom Drage, the bookmaker type—she once told me that she had never "given herself" to him. Now that I pressed her, she said that she *hadn't* ever given herself to him. To begin with, she had more than a suspicion that he already had a wife, or at least a permanent mistress. He once tried to persuade her to go with him to a hotel, but she thought it too sordid and refused. I asked her about the night I saw her coming off the waste ground; she said that he had been trying to persuade her to go away with him for the weekend, and had been particularly persistent. She admitted that he'd gotten her half undressed and had a determined attempt at raping her, but claimed that he didn't succeed. I asked if he changed his mind and abandoned the attempt; she looked embarrassed and said: "No, something else happened." I didn't press her, but gathered that his enthusiasm was his undoing.

This pleased me, even though I'm not sure whether to believe her. Although I had gotten used to the idea that she had been Drage's mistress, it faintly disturbed me. . . . Anyway, we went into another pub to celebrate, and I drank two pints of black and tan, and Diana drank sherry, and we arrived home at ten o'clock feeling tipsy and very happy. I think if we'd met Kirsten, we would have made no attempt to conceal what is happening.

Cunningham was still asleep when we got in, but he roused himself and joined us. The first thing he did was to drain another glass of wine, then he lit a cigarette with an abominable smell. (He smokes very little as a rule.) Then he said: "Ah Gerard, I begin to wish I'd introduced you to this earlier. Now I need your help, and you don't even understand what's going on." I urged him to explain to me. He said: "I've suspected for some time now that my enemies are trying to kill me. I felt fairly sure of it the other day when someone tried to push me downstairs." He explained that it wasn't a *person* who had tried to push him—just an invisible force. He then went into a rambling story about some magical order in Paris, which was headed by a German, an Italian and a Hungarian, and of how they had expelled him after a quarrel about publishing certain secrets in their magazine. The Hungarian swore to kill him, and Cunningham had one night become aware of a presence in the room, and a hand that hovered around in the air, waiting to grip his throat! For three days, he said, he performed a ceremony to invoke certain destructive forces under the command of his guardian angel. On the third day, the Hungarian died—apparently of heart failure, as he walked down the steps of the Bibliothèque Nationale. The trouble with black magic, apparently, is that a competent magician can redirect all your curses back on your own head!

Now, Cunningham said, he was convinced that the other two had decided that they were strong enough to attack him. To begin with, they had somehow learned where he lived; this enabled them to direct a continual stream of some malevolent influence at the house. He asked me if I had mentioned his address to anyone. I felt rather guilty, and said that I had spoken to Radin, who had come and talked to me while Cunningham was out of the room. I didn't tell him that I'd actually had lunch with Radin. Cunningham said: "Ah, that explains it. I know that man is an enemy. You shouldn't have given him my address. He must have sent someone into the house to pick up some article belonging to the house—otherwise it is impossible to direct a psychic stream accurately." I had drunk so much beer—and in any case, gotten so used to Cunningham's eccentricity—that I didn't even suspect him of being dotty. However, this explains why Cunningham had come to sleep at my place—there was no "psychic stream."

However, the next problem was to thwart the enemies, and this demanded that he should find out where they were, and what they were planning. He said: "I must have a clairvoyant," and looked speculatively at Diana. She immediately said: "I don't want to be hypnotized again." "Not even when your refusal may cost me my life?" She looked so miserable and undecided that I asked him if we couldn't get anyone else in her place. "Oliver's no use. He's an even worse hypnotic subject than you. That child Christine might be the answer if we could get hold of her." I pointed out that, at half past ten at night, there was no hope of getting hold of Christine; she'd be fast asleep in bed. Then I thought of Carlotta, and suggested her. He said: "Yes, she *might* do, although I'm afraid she'd let her own personality get in the way." However, we agreed to try Carlotta; I hastened downstairs to phone her, and Diana came with me, claiming she wanted to buy cigarettes. As soon as we were in the street, she said: "I don't want to let him hypnotize me again. He wants to gain power over me." I asked her what she meant, and she said: "He wants to rape me." I said I was sure Cunningham wanted to rape anything female and presentable, but she wouldn't change her view.

I rang Carlotta, and she immediately agreed to take a taxi over—evidently my talk about Cunningham's needing her help excited her. She didn't even ask questions. When we came out of the phone booth, Diana said: "I wish we could get away from him. He wants to eat up our lives."

Back in my room, Cunningham casually asked Diana if she had a cigarette, and she had to admit she'd forgotten to buy them; she got an ironical look. Cunningham then went and took a bath, and borrowed my razor to shave. Carlotta took nearly an hour to get over—said she couldn't get a cab—

but she finally arrived around midnight, and we went up to Cunningham's.

I hardly recognized his room. He had draped the walls with black curtains, had a skeleton in one corner, and had set up a kind of altar where the bed used to be. Although the window was wide open, the awful smell of incense and burnt meat still lingered. I noticed in the corner of the room a large cage—the kind of thing that pet shops sell for guinea pigs or hamsters—and presumed that this is where he got whatever animal had been sacrificed. I only hope that he killed it quickly.

Cunningham then—rather to Diana's dismay, flung off all his clothes in the middle of the room, and pulled on his "robe" —which was rather like a black dressing gown. Many of the signs on it unmistakably represented erect phalli. He then ordered Carlotta to strip. He said it so seriously and peremptorily that she began unzipping her skirt without even asking questions. I hastily said that Diana and I would leave the room; Cunningham said he would need me for the actual incantation. So I said I'd come back in five minutes. I opened the door—and immediately closed it again, for I saw Kirsten coming up the stairs below. Luckily he didn't see me. Cunningham told me to lock the door. A moment later, Kirsten knocked, and Cunningham told him that he would be engaged for the next hour, and asked him to come back later. We heard Kirsten going up to his room, and shortly afterwards, the piano started. (This annoyed Cunningham, who was afraid that it might interfere with his hypnosis.) By this time, Carlotta was naked. Cunningham started to rub her body with some kind of oil, and announced that she would have to prepare herself with a sex ritual. I guessed the nature of the ritual, and said we'd be back in five minutes. Then Diana and I unlocked the door and crept downstairs.

Oliver's door was locked—possibly he was asleep—so we went down into the street, and walked around the block. Diana asked me if I took all this magic seriously; I said I didn't know, but it was obvious that Cunningham took it seriously. Finally, we went back up to the room. Carlotta was now dressed in a white garment that covered her from head to foot, and was drinking what looked like a very large gin and orange. (I gathered later that this is what it was.) Cunningham had inscribed a pentagram on the floor, in front of the "altar," and a smaller one in the far corner of the room. He presented me with a piece of parchment with various letters on it, and short sentences in Latin, Greek and Hebrew. He spent about five minutes coaching me in the correct pronunciation of these. He then made Diana take off her dress, and put on a red garment—but allowed her to keep on the rest of her things, even her shoes. I was the only one in the room who was normally dressed, but Cunningham said that his ceremonial robes were in Paris, and I would have to take the risk of irritating the "powers" by appearing in everyday clothes. Since I was fairly sure the whole thing was imaginary, I made no objection.

Carlotta was obviously in a very strange mood—whether this was autosuggestion or something in her drink, I don't know. But her eyes were glowing, and she was as pink as a baby.

Cunningham gave Diana a black vase full of some powder, and told her to throw it on the brazier whenever he raised his hand towards her. He then announced that everything was ready, and made me take up my position inside the pentagram. He made Carlotta lie on the couch, and pulled up her robe around her throat. I expected Carlotta to raise objections; instead, she lay with her eyes closed. He then kissed her on the navel and on both breasts, and proceeded with the "sexual invocation." I must confess that I now felt no desire to leave the room; I also noticed that Diana was staring, fascinated. As for Carlotta, I'm quite certain that her pleasure was intensified by the knowledge that the whole thing was being watched by us. She lay there while Cunningham covered her like a great black bat, with his face and shoulders suspended over her face, looking down on her, and making love as impersonally as if he were an animal. It suddenly came to me that this was the truth of "black magic"; by destroying all taboos, it appeared to release forces that were completely beyond the experience of the participants. I can easily imagine what would happen if this room had been full of men and women, and a Black Mass in progress; within minutes it would turn into a sexual orgy.

After five minutes of this, Carlotta began to moan and shudder; then she suddenly grabbed Cunningham's hair and began to writhe like a madwoman. With the light on the top of his great round head, and his eyes in shadow, Cunningham looked like the devil.

Finally, she quieted down, and Cunningham stood up, his robe now wide open—as it remained for the rest of the ceremony—and made her stand in the middle of her pentagram. He then began chanting formulas in Latin and Hebrew (although some of it was in English), and I called the responses as he had explained. It went something like this: Cunningham intoned, "I exorcise thee, creature of ink, by Anston, Cerreton, Stimulator, Adonai . . ." I had to call: "Abrachay, Araton, Samatoi, Scaver, Adonai." Then Cunningham would drone on: "I exorcise thee, creature of the feather kind, by Etereton and Adonai . . ." I have taken the above from Abrahamelin the Mage, but it sounds roughly like what Cunningham said, and the kind of thing I had to reply. He also scattered a white powder from a dish—probably salt—and burnt some feathers. After ten minutes of this, he stroked Carlotta's forehead, while I had to stand to one side and swing the gold medal on its chain in small circles in front of her eyes. She went off very quickly, and Cunningham started asking her questions:

"Where are you?"

"In front of a door."

"Open it and go in."

"I can't. There is some obstacle."

"Push it aside and go in."

"I have pushed it aside. But the door won't open."

She then declared that a man in silver clothes was standing behind her, and Cunningham told her to ask his name. The man apparently replied: "Ashtiroth."

I cannot detail what went on in the next two hours. To me, it sounded mostly mumbo-jumbo. At one point, Carlotta said that she saw two men lowering an effigy of Cunningham into a coffin, and driving a knife through its heart. Cunningham then began to repeat all kinds of strange sounding formulas (which he told me later were ancient Egyptian), and Carlotta described how one of the men had cut his wrist quite badly on the knife. She then said: "They know you are working against them." Cunningham said: "Tell them I will hunt them down and kill them." She said: "I can't speak to them. I can only watch them." "Then tell Ashtiroth to tell them." "He says he can't speak to them either."

Unfortunately, the room was now getting horribly cold, and instead of thinking about the magic, I began to wonder if Carlotta wasn't frozen stiff under the thin white muslin; poor Diana was definitely cold, and kept blowing her fingers, then trying to warm her hands at the brazier, which was filling the room with a curious odor, containing a definite component of vegetable decay.

It was quite an ordeal standing there—at least, after the first half hour. But Cunningham showed no sign of letting up. After a while, he made Carlotta lie on the bed again (she seemed to be still in a trance) and repeated the whole magical ceremony, making me repeat the responses. This woke me up temporarily, but as his chanting went on, I found myself sleeping on my feet—waking up as I were about to fall. Added to all this, I wanted to get down to the lavatory. The room was so full of blue smoke that my eyes were watering. Suddenly, Cunningham grabbed Diana, and called: "Into the circle," pushing her in so that she stood beside me. This woke me up for a while, but I could see nothing, except that the room was now so smoky that it might have been a pea-soup fog. When he paused for a moment, I hinted that my bladder needed relieving, but all he did was whisper "Keep still." So I stood there for another half hour, getting colder and more fed up, although it was a consolation to have my arm round Diana—we helped to support one another. Suddenly Diana gripped my hand, and I opened my eyes. In the corner over the empty cage, there was a definite disturbance of the smoke, as if a draft were coming through the floor. I then had the impression that I was being looked at from the same spot. There was not, as far as I could gather, an actual figure there, although the smoke gave something of this illusion. Cunningham had his back to it, and didn't seem to notice it. I closed my eyes again, prepared for another hour of discomfort, when Cunningham suddenly stopped chanting. The room was now almost empty of smoke. Cunningham said: "Good. They've gone." He then said: "Thank you, Gerard. You've been a great help. You too, Diana." He woke up Carlotta—I suspect that she had only been fast asleep—and told her that she could now go to bed. I said that Diana and I would go home immediately, and we left. As we went out of the door, Cunningham asked me: "Did you see anything?" I was feeling so irritable—and also rather taciturn—that I answered: "No. Not a thing." He asked Diana, and she said: "I don't think so." But on our way home, she agreed that she thought she had seen a shadowy figure above the cage, and also had a sensation of being looked at. But we both agreed that, after two hours of chanting, incense, sex magic and cold, it would have been very easy to make us think we'd seen ghosts.

Nov. 29. Romain Rolland once called artists "the masters of the world, the great defeated." This, I suppose, is one of my central problems and preoccupations, and the reason that Cunningham interests me, because he plainly has no intention of being defeated. And yet for all that, I am aware that he has no hope. Why? I can't explain it. I simply sense it. Still, that's a poor admission for a writer, so let me try to be more specific. What he lacks is a desire for the simplicity of self-conquest. What is at issue here is our idea of *success*. For Cunningham, success means power and fame, a life like a procession of an Indian Rajah, noisy success, success that no one can deny. My own vision of success is completely dissimilar; it is a state of sudden illumination that is entirely subjective, something closer to Wordsworth's vision of that dark hill above the lake and "unknown modes of being." But I'm sick—utterly, miserably sick—of this narrowness of my consciousness, this inability to see or think beyond the present moment. My body has never been so heavily oppressive, my spirit never so totally bound, as at present. My brain is like the engine of a car with a completely dead battery; no amount of effort can stir it into life; I only exhaust myself. My spirit twists and wrenches to bring forth its solution, for I am convinced there *is* a solution.

All these gloomy thoughts come to me after having spent the afternoon with Oliver. Luckily, Diana had gone out, knowing that Kirsten would finish his moving today, and afraid he would come in and find her here. Oliver arrived just before she'd gone; he was in a worse mood than I'd seen him in for a long time. When he saw Diana, he was about to leave again, but she forestalled him and said she had to go. When she'd gone, he said: "So it was you who robbed Kirsten of his wife?" His tone irritated me, but I said that I thought it might prove to be best for all of us. "For Kirsten, at least," he said, "Gertrude has been tidying his room all morning." As soon as he began to gossip about Gertrude, he cheered up. I told him that I was pretty certain I'd marry Diana, as soon as Kirsten divorced her, and he became cynical again: "And how long do you suppose it will last?" I couldn't be bothered to contradict him. I said that I thought his disappointment over Christine had given him a pessimistic outlook. He said: "That's another thing. Christine. She's found out where I live. I saw her standing watching me when I went out yesterday." I asked him what the point was in bearing a grudge against a thirteen-year-old girl. It was pointless, as I should have realized. It wasn't Christine's fault. It was Oliver's fault for imagining she embodied some ideal. And yet I'm sure that, given a chance, she could give Oliver what he needs—love and admiration and loyalty. I sometimes wonder if he doesn't enjoy torturing himself.

I offered him something to eat, and made myself a ham sandwich. He refused, but finished by eating two large sandwiches anyway. This seemed to improve his temper, and he told me he intended leaving this place as soon as possible. I asked why (thinking that perhaps he wanted to avoid Christine). But he said: "Because that man [meaning Cunningham] is driving me mad."

As soon as he started talking to me, his confidences came out in a rush. It struck me as peculiar that Oliver should think of me as his best friend. (He actually said this at one point.) He's so given up to extremes of emotion that I can't imagine him feeling anything as positive as friendship. However, it was obvious to me that he'd been under great emotional strain, and needed badly to talk to someone.

He told me first of all how Cunningham had prevented him from committing suicide. Amusingly enough, he'd decided on this after reading a pessimistic novel by Artsybashev called *The Breaking Point,* which paints a grim picture of life and declares that suicide is the only dignified way out. (I read it myself years ago and found it bad and depressing—and also a fake, because if the author had really believed it, he'd have committed suicide instead of writing a book.) However, Oliver read it at a time when he was feeling very low, and its Buddhistic pessimism seemed to him an accurate account of the human situation.

His account of how Cunningham stopped him corresponded pretty closely with Cunningham's own account. For a few days after this, he felt happy and exalted, and was sure that Cunningham was going to provide him with a solution to all his problems. There was only one fly in the ointment. (It obviously took Oliver a tremendous effort to tell me this, and I found myself admiring a strange, despairing honesty in him.) Cunningham preached the need for destroying all sexual taboos, rooting out all sexual shame, in order to discover one's "true will." He asked Oliver what he found most repulsive in sex; Oliver admitted that he had always loathed the idea of homosexuality. He hadn't expected Cunningham to take this so seriously; but in fact, Cunningham returned to the subject again and again, told Oliver it was due to repressions instilled by his parents, and that the total destruction of his suicidal impulses depended on his coming to terms with homosexuality. The result of this was that after a week, Oliver gave way. First of all, he consented to sleeping with some silky-haired little fairy whom Cunningham picked up in Lancaster, and finally slept with Cunningham himself. He said he did all this in a genuinely ascetic spirit. (I can believe this, remembering how he used to sleep on the bare wires of his bed and indulge in other forms of self-torture.) But the result was the discovery that, contrary to Cunningham's expectations, he had no repressed homosexual tendency at all; he found it rather boring. (I could have told Cunningham this; if he really wants to release Oliver's deepest repression, he should get him into bed with Christine.) In spite of this, Cunningham periodically insists that Oliver should overcome his revulsion— hence the scene that I witnessed the other morning. (I was pretty sure at the time that something was going on between Oliver and Cunningham, and yet simply couldn't imagine Oliver as a queer.)

But the major shock, according to Oliver, was the matter of his exhibition. I remember that he always refused even to try to exhibit his work, saying that he didn't want impertinent busybodies telling him how he ought to paint. When Cunningham said he would get his paintings exhibited, he hardly took him seriously. But the result of being written about by various art magazines, and even bombarded with requests to give lectures in art schools, was that he lost all sense of privacy. Luckily, the gallery refused to give people his address; but even so, he got letters from enthusiastic art students who wanted to come and admire him—all of which he took care not to answer—and requests to talk about his painting on the Third Program.

In any other person, I would have suspected these complaints of lacking sincerity; but I know Oliver too well to suppose anything of the sort. I remember the passage in Rilke in which he advises young poets to take care to remain unknown as long as possible, because fame will destroy their sense of privacy; he must have been thinking of people like Oliver.

He says that he has now begun to find the constant presence of Cunningham oppressive. Cunningham has been sensible enough not to try to influence Oliver's painting, but he still makes comments, and generally gives Oliver a feeling of being under some kind of an obligation.

I failed to sympathize with a great deal that Oliver said. After all, he's better off now than he was a year ago; he can always go and hide where no one can find him, and he's now in no danger of starving.

Oliver complained that all money is paid direct to Cunningham, who is his "agent," so that he has no money of his own. I told him that if he was really determined to move, I would lend him enough money to find himself another place. Besides, all he has to do is go to the gallery and say that in future all money is to be paid direct to him. But, like myself, he is a moral coward when it comes to offending anyone (or else he's afraid that Cunningham might put a spell on him!).

I promised to raise this matter with Cunningham—tactfully, without letting him know that Oliver has spoken to me. When he left, an hour ago, he seemed more cheerful. But I then began to think that he doesn't know when he's well off. I wouldn't object in the least to having my work known. And if he hadn't met Cunningham, he might have committed suicide—although, having heard Oliver's version, I am doubtful about this. Then, having reflected that Oliver is a kind of spiritual hypochondriac, who is simply constitutionally incapable of allowing himself to be happy, I realized that I have no right to talk. I have everything that should make me happy —my freedom, the books I need, a girl I'm in love with—and

I still feel this inexplicable oppression of spirit. Perhaps I need to escape. . . . I don't know. Where should I go? I always had a romantic notion of living in the Aran Isles, imagining a misty land where the soul would confront the bareness of the sea and sky and throw off all its civilized boredom. But when I read Synge's book about them, I realized that they are simply cold, wet and fishy, and not nearly as convenient as London from the point of view of libraries.

It's so easy to agree with De L'Isle-Adam's Axel—that the world is nothing but disappointment, that life is an indignity. Yet somehow I can't believe this.

Sunday morning. I am writing this in the bedroom, while Diana irons clothes in the other room. Cunningham told me last night that he has a publisher interested in my *Methods and Techniques of Self-Deception;* he borrowed the manuscript two weeks ago—the hundred pages I typed out in Kentish Town —and sent it to a James Curzon of Lloyd and Rich; yesterday he got it back with a letter that says: "I feel this book shows a remarkable and original talent, and if the second part maintains the same standard, we shall be happy to publish it." The letter goes on to say that I can't expect a sale of more than a couple of thousand copies, and that they would like to see a novel if I decide to write one.

This is why I can't make up my mind about Cunningham. He agrees that I'll be lucky if I make a hundred pounds out of the book, and that the publishers might easily lose money. So what possible motive can he have for trying to get it published?

On the other hand, the whole business is rather strange. He didn't tell me about the Lloyd and Rich offer until I had begun to talk about Oliver. I went over after supper, and found Carlotta installed, laundering his clothes. I got him to come out to a pub for a drink, and then told him that I'm worried about Oliver, and that I think he wants to go away. Cunningham immediately became slightly indignant, and asked me if I thought he was interested in Oliver solely for the sake of the money. I assured him I didn't. But he then told me he had a surprise for me, took me back up to his room, and produced the letter. Naturally, I was overwhelmed, and decided to go home immediately and settle down to typing the rest of the book. Remembering my complaints in my journal a few hours earlier, I felt guilty. However, Cunningham said it would be a good idea to keep them waiting for a while. It was then that I recalled that the date on the letter was the 24th— four days ago. Of course, it may simply have been waiting around the publisher's office for three days, or been delayed in the post. This seems very odd. I also had a devil of a job persuading Cunningham to return the first half of the type-script—he said he had left it upstairs somewhere. At this point, Carlotta said that she had seen it in a cupboard, and went and fetched it. I caught the expression on Cunningham's face—it was murderous exasperation. (From several things he said, I gather that he is already wishing that he hadn't in-vited Carlotta to act as his medium last night; she actually behaves as if she's married to him.)

Finally, Cunningham settled down to a fairly frank dis-cussion of Oliver. Most of it struck me as nonsense. He told me that he had been forcing Oliver to undergo homosexual experiences to "learn his true will," and had concluded that he was originally mistaken in supposing that it was repressed homosexuality that was Oliver's trouble. At this point, I said: "I can tell you Oliver's trouble," and told him about Christine. As soon as I'd spoken, I regretted it. He said slowly: "Ah, I see. I think you may have found the solution." I quickly told him that Christine's father is a difficult character, who wouldn't hesitate to accuse us all of violating his daughter if he thought he could get us into jail.

As I left him, he told me that he intended to get Carlotta into a trance again at midnight, to find out how successful he has been in defeating his "enemies." I immediately said that Diana had declared that she wouldn't take part in any more magical ceremonies. He said: "I hope you don't feel the same?"

I said no, although I realized that I was being a coward. There's nothing I want less than to have to spend another two hours listening to Cunningham deceiving himself with gibberish and imagining he's conjuring up spirits. However, he said he wouldn't need any help tonight, as he only proposes to hypnotize her.

When I left, I noticed that Gertrude's car was parked around the corner, so I presume she is still nursing Kirsten's genius.

Dec. 1. Odd things happening. Yesterday I had a visit from Radin, who asked me if I would go with him to see a man in St. Johns Wood. Out of curiosity, I agreed. On the way there, Radin offered me money—five pounds a week—to keep him informed about Cunningham. Naturally, I refused.

The interview was brief. Wise was there, and a tall, skinny man in a Scotch kilt, to whom I took an instant dislike. The skinny man—whose name is Doughty—told me that he had reason to believe that Cunningham intends to publish various secrets of his magical order, secrets that Cunningham had once been pledged not to reveal. I suppose this must be the order that Cunningham once tried to dominate. I said I had no idea what Cunningham intended. (The man's bullying manner annoyed me.) He then asked me—as if he were a prosecuting counsel and I were in the dock—if I had had any experience of Cunningham as a "mage." Since I had already told Radin something about our experience the other night, I didn't try to deny this. He immediately began to ask me questions about the ceremony. I hadn't told Radin about the "sex magic" part, but it now slipped out—to Radin's evident delight. Doughty shouted: "Just as I thought—he's deliberately distorting our ceremonial with his filthy abominations." By this time, I was just about ready to explode. So I said that, if he wanted to know, I thought Cunningham's magic was all self-deception and mumbo-jumbo, and that I thought anyone who took magic seriously should be put in a lunatic asylum.

At this he smiled very thinly and very wickedly, and said: "Thank you, sir. You have told me what I wanted to know. Good day to you." I strode out without even speaking to him. But I was also in a filthy temper with Radin, who was bursting with curiosity about the "sex magic," and obviously wanted to flatter and propitiate me. So he began by saying that he thought it was all rubbish too, and that Doughty was a bit mad—however, he had a great deal of money and influence in certain circles, and no journalist could afford to ignore the possibility of a good story, etc. By this time, I was almost bursting with loathing. So I said: "Look here. I don't care if Cunningham *is* mad, or even if he's a crook. But he's given me no reason to sell him—either to you or Mr. Doughty." By this time, we were near the Baker Street tube, so I insisted on getting out and taking a train—claiming I had other things to do before I went home. Radin refused to be offended, said that he would keep in touch with me, that I wouldn't regret being frank, etc. —and drove off.

Dec. 3. I've been working hard on my book for the past two days, and so have had no time for keeping this journal. Cunningham has been around several times in high good spirits. He certainly knows a tremendous amount about magic and its history. I am adding a chapter on the great charlatans— Cagliostro, Saint Germain, etc. I intended to include Nostradamus, and for that purpose got Laver's book on him from the Whitechapel library. I'm amazed to discover the almost creepy accuracy of his prophecies. I was glad to have a chance to discuss all this with Cunningham. His view is that concentration on *any* faculty will develop that faculty, even if it had not existed before. He cites the case of the Fox sisters, the founders of spiritualism—how, as soon as they made table-rapping fashionable in the States, the craze spread all over America, although it was almost unknown before.

Nostradamus predicts the end of the world for 1999. I hope he isn't as accurate about this as he was about the date of the French Revolution, etc. The only consolation is that he seemed to be most accurate when predicting things in the near future, and became less so with more distant epochs.

I have also decided to include Crowley in my charlatan chapter. Cunningham knew him well in the thirties, and is of the opinion that Crowley definitely possessed certain powers, although most of his magic was wishful thinking. This is the thing that startles me about Cunningham—that he can be so detached and sceptical about magic, while apparently holding the most fantastic beliefs. He criticized a sentence of mine in which I said that a kind of mental blindness is necessary to swallow the extravagances of Cagliostro. He said: "My dear boy, you need hardly any credulity to become interested in the occult. The minimum working hypothesis is very simple. The first thing you *know* is that you're bored and tied hand and foot. Everybody agrees about that. The only other thing you need to accept is that there *are* great powers in the universe, outside yourself, and that in rare moments you can make contact with them and feel like a god. As soon as you study the methods of making contact, you become interested in magic."

The magicians are the ideal subject for the last chapter of my book, because they stand in the way of a simple, wholesale solution of the problem. It is tempting to agree with Schopenhauer and the Buddha that all men are adept at self-delusion, and that there is no reality except death. But the magicians make it apparent that this would be an oversimplification. They represent such a strange blending of illusion and reality. Is it possible to believe in illusions so fiercely that they turn into realities? I am sure it is. By the power of total belief, we summon up powers we didn't know we possessed. This must be the answer to all magic, spiritualism and the rest. It is the summoning of the unknown life forces from our own depths.

Later. Was seriously distracted from my book when Cunningham met Radin on the stairs, and threw him all the way down.

Radin was on his way to visit me. He went off swearing to sue Cunningham for assault and battery; I expected him to return with a policeman, but he didn't. Cunningham claimed that he had received a sudden "psychic message" to the effect that he must hurry to my flat to prevent some serious mischief. I wish I could believe everything he tells me; half the time I suspect it's wishful thinking.

But later on, he showed me an interesting trick. Diana came in very tired after doing the shopping, and I persuaded her to go and sleep. Cunningham came about half an hour later, and I heard him throwing Radin downstairs. We made tea, and sat talking about magic, fairly softly, so as not to wake Diana. He suddenly offered to give me a demonstration of "psychic force." He took off his shoes, and crept into the room where Diana lay asleep. He stood at the side of the bed, stretched out his hand over her head, and concentrated on her. After a few moments, she rolled over on to her back, and her lips parted. Suddenly, her hips began to move, and it was quite obvious to me that she was having a sexual dream. Cunningham concentrated more, bending over her, and she began to look worried. Then she woke up, saw Cunningham bending over her, and shrieked. It took me about five minutes to calm her. Cunningham went out of the room, smiling to himself, and I explained that he had offered to give me a demonstration of psychic force. (As a matter of fact, I felt embarrassed, and wouldn't have been surprised if she'd lost her temper and walked out on me—I wouldn't have allowed it if I'd known what Cunningham intended to do.) However, when she calmed down, she said that she had been dreaming that she was being embraced by a tall, blond man who reminded her of me. Suddenly, he began to change into Cunningham, and at this point she woke up.

Cunningham told me that this was a simple trick of thought transference and suggestion, that anyone can master with a little effort. He claims that people can communicate on several different levels, besides ordinary conversation. We all have the potentiality of becoming telepaths. He thinks that, in the next stage of evolution of the human race, certain "magical" faculties will be quite common—intuitions of danger, seeing around corners and through walls, etc.

All this strikes me as of immense importance. Even in my family—about the least psychic I've ever known—I've heard of odd things that can't be explained except by some kind of thought transference—for example, my father suffering my mother's labor pains, although she was a hundred miles away, and the baby wasn't expected for another fortnight—so he could have had no idea when her labor would begin. This kind of thing is fairly common, I believe, and supports Cunningham's contention that all "paranormal phenomena" like second sight, clairvoyance, precognition, etc., are simply examples of faculties that will seem perfectly ordinary to our remote descendants. I also remember examples in Jim Corbett's books on tiger hunting—how he would suddenly be quite certain that a tiger was waiting for him on a particular stretch of road, although there was no concrete evidence to account for his certainty. This, I think, is also fairly common—that a man who spends a great deal of his life meeting certain kinds of danger develops a "sixth sense" about the danger. This sixth sense is partly unconscious observation; but I do not think this accounts for all such instances.

The thing that irritates me is that these faculties lie so close to us, and yet I remain encased in this stupid, insensitive body, and there seems to be no way of escape.

Dec. 4. The talk with Oliver about boredom seems to have crystallized something in me, and I have been sitting around all day in a curious state of depression; no, the right word is *oppression,* a sense of gathering storm. I walk up and down, look out of the window, read a few pages of a Moravia novel, and feel my senses coated with a thin, sticky boredom. No doubt Moravia is not the ideal person to read under these circumstances, since his favorite topic is boredom, and he writes about his dyspepsia as if it were a universal condition or a mystical insight. This is the trouble with all these apostles of suicide and nausea—they all write with a naïve egoism, assuming that their weakness is universal.

And yet my misery alternates with moments of intense certainty, when it seems to me that, like Arjuna, I was born to conquer.

I understand, I understand it all—the unfulfillment, the meaninglessness, the ennui. I know that our basic experience of the world is of pointlessness, matter leading back to itself, denying the reality of mind. I contain in myself all the most suicidal pessimists of the past 150 years, from Werther and Childe Harold down to the latest hero of Moravia or Beckett; yet in spite of all this, I am the most incorrigible optimist I know. The men who can do something for this age will recognize one another; the others do not matter. I know that we shall finally create a race of men who are incapable of boredom, men in whom values and vitality are synonymous, who never find their appetite for life diminishing, negating the values of yesterday.

But I am tired. And this tension oppresses me. I wish it would rain.

Jan. 15. (Shannon Cottage, Galway.) It has been more than a month since I last wrote in this journal. It arrived this morning in a parcel, together with proofs of the extracts that will appear in the *Sunday Star*. The extracts they have chosen are stupid and unrepresentative, but at least they might counteract some of the stupidities that have been quoted in the other newspapers. So much has happened in this last month that I've had little time for writing, although even so, I managed to post off the manuscript of *Methods and Techniques of Self-Deception* four days ago, and this morning received the hundred pounds advance that Lolyd promised me. Also, the local representative of the *Sunday Star* tramped out here last night to tell me that Cunningham is definitely in South America, and to get my comments.

The day after my last entry, Gertrude came to see me. She told me that she had seen Cunningham with Christine, and that she was convinced that his intentions were definitely "wicked." I dissuaded her from going to see Christine's parents, and said that I would speak to Cunningham myself about it.

Cunningham wasn't at all pleased when I went to see him. He looked as if he were suffering from a hangover. (Actually, as I discovered later, he was waiting for a delivery of drugs, and was in a state of tension because they were delayed.) He had a violent outburst about interfering women—about Diana as well as Gertrude. He said: "I will tell you frankly, Gerard, I'm disappointed in you. It's one thing to steal another man's wife to sleep with her, but quite another to decide to marry her. You'll be unfaithful to her within a fortnight of being married. Why can't you be like Oliver, and remain a lone wolf?" I told him Gertrude's suspicions about Christine, and he readily admitted that she would consider his intentions wicked. His intention was—quite openly—to get Oliver to overcome his inhibitions about Christine. What is more, he had carried out the first part of his plan—had Christine in to tea, and told her that Oliver was actually romantically in love with her, and hoped to marry her as soon as she was old enough. He said she was obviously overwhelmed and delighted, but pretended not to believe him. She was too shy to see Oliver again, but had agreed to come back to tea the following day.

I had to agree that this didn't sound too wicked. I know Oliver well enough to be sure that he wouldn't take advantage of the child; on the other hand, to see her again would probably have an excellent effect on his work, and I could see no reason why he shouldn't marry her in five years' time if she still wanted to. So I agreed to do what I could to help. That is, I went down to see Oliver, and told him that Christine had been to see me and wanted to see him again. His first reaction was rage—he stormed and swore, and called the poor child names that made her sound like the whore of Babylon. I then laid it on thick—told him about her devotion to him, how she had tried to contact him through me, and finally pointed out that the fact that he had returned to live in the same area proved that he subconsciously wanted to see her again. The result, as I expected, was to calm him down. He asked me to go away so he could think about it, and I left him in an obvious state of excitement and perplexity. I didn't tell him that she was invited for tea the following day. But Oliver came to see me the next morning, saying that he had thought it over, and could see no reason for refusing to be friendly with the child, although he had no intention of assuming their old relations.

There was, however, a delicate situation that had to be faced. Christine's father had separated from her mother—she got sick of his drunken rages, and called in two of her brothers to bully him. It ended in the father's stamping out of the house, with his wife suing him for maintenance.

But although this apparently simplified Christine's life— it was her father who had had Oliver arrested on a charge of raping her—it actually made things more difficult. He was alleging that his quarrels with his wife were about the children's morals, and that she was no fit guardian for them. Christine was his favorite child, and he was trying to get her away from her mother. This idea horrified Christine. If her father found out about Oliver and Cunningham, he would probably use it to prove that she was under "dangerous influences." So it was important that she should be on her best behavior until her father gave up the idea of having her live with him.

At all events, Christine came to tea—I wasn't there, but Cunningham told me about it—and finally went downstairs to see Oliver. I gather there was a great reconciliation scene that ended with Christine sobbing on Oliver's shoulder, and Oliver promising that he would never leave her again. Cunningham was delighted by all this. He obviously expected that a Lolita situation was the next obvious development. I didn't disabuse him of this idea.

The next important development was that Kirsten found out about Diana. I hadn't seen much of him for several days —I was working hard, and I gather that he was working on his opera for the Washington opera group. (I note from this week's *Radio Times* that some of his chamber music is being done in the Thursday concert.)

One day, I met him on the stairs at Cunningham's, and asked him how things were going. He gave me a most odd look, and then said quietly: "You don't have to try to deceive me any more, you know. I know about Diana." I felt embarrassed about this, but since he knew, decided I would rather explain it to him. So I asked him if he'd let me explain, and we went up to his room. I noticed immediately that he wasn't angry. And when I saw the state of his room—incredibly tidy, with a neat pile of newly laundered washing on the table, and not a speck of dust anywhere—it wasn't difficult to guess the reason. Not that I believe there's any romantic relation between Kirsten and Gertrude; I'm sure she feels that she is helping a great musician as impersonally as Nadezhda von Meck helped Tchaikovsky, and is reveling in the feeling of selflessness. Still, this made it all much easier; I told Kirsten about the bookmaking type, and this seemed to please him. He was very bitter about Diana. When I said I wanted to marry her, he asked me how I could ever be sure she wouldn't treat me as she had treated him. Finally, he ended by admitting that he now felt better off than ever before, and that he was glad it was all over.

I was glad of this. I didn't want Kirsten to feel compelled to break with me. We parted on good terms, and he referred to Gertrude as his "guardian angel."

Cunningham was beginning to feel that he was losing his hold over all three of us. Oliver's association with Christine had temporarily solved *that* problem—Oliver no longer talked about getting away—but Cunningham was aware that both Diana and Gertrude were using their influence against him. So one day, he asked me to come and see him. He told me that he had decided to leave for his island immediately after Christmas, when the signs of the heavens would be propitious, and wanted me, Kirsten and Oliver to join him there. He realized that Kirsten wanted to stay in London until his opera was revised, and that Oliver would probably not want to leave Christine, but he was relying on me to go with him and prepare the place to become a great cultural center.

I was naturally dubious, being happy enough where 1 was, especially since finishing my book was a full-time job, and I needed to be within reach of the British Museum reading room.

Cunningham said: "I realize why you hesitate. You are not convinced that it isn't all self-delusion. Weren't you convinced by my last demonstration?" (meaning the long conjuration in his room). I agreed that both Diana and I *thought* there had been another person in the corner of the room, but that neither of us could be certain.

He said: "In that case, you need more demonstrations. Suppose, for example, I could prove to you that the sexual orgasm can be prolonged for several minutes—perhaps even as long as half an hour?"

The end of it all was that I agreed to help him in a series of experiments that would last about a week. He explained to me that there are drugs that can produce an impression like a sexual orgasm for a long time—at least an hour—but that these drugs are dangerous. They burn up the body as a candle flame consumes the candle, leaving no inner resources of energy. On the other hand, if a man could learn to tap his inner reservoir of power, this intensity would leave him completely unaffected. This, Cunningham said, was the only safe way. The other way usually turned into some dangerous disease in a matter of weeks—usually consumption. He pointed out that this is true of sex generally. Sometimes an act of sex can leave you completely exhausted and drained; yet under different circumstances—or with a different partner—the appetite seems to increase in a curious way, as if it is fed by some inner spring of power, rather as a well continues to remain at the same level no matter how much water is taken out of it.

All this intrigued me. I have already noted my belief that the whole key to human existence lies in the sexual orgasm.

I have always felt that if only it could last longer—minutes instead of seconds—I would have the whole secret of human existence. Someone once wrote a novel about men trapped in a bunker, with enough food and drink to last for years, but no hope of escape, and about how they turned into animals.* On the other hand, someone once wrote of the Tarot pack that a man who was kept in solitary confinement with nothing but these cards would be able to acquire the whole sum of human knowledge through them. Well, if human beings are still half animal—as pessimistic philosophers never tire of pointing out—it is because we have all been confined to a huge bunker, with enough hardship to keep us wide awake, and enough amusements to occupy our leisure, but no inspiration to prevent our becoming worthless and lazy. Civilizations have developed on the human need for self-assertion, and have collapsed when that need wore itself out; religions have been created to explain the mystery of man to himself, and have died when the ignorance and prejudice that sustained them has been dispersed. But still man is basically in a meaningless universe, with no guide but a bundle of instincts which civilization dilutes.

And yet again and again, in the sexual orgasm, I have felt that the solution is nearer than we think—that if that intolerable light would only persist for ten minutes instead of dying in a few seconds, man would know every secret of his own being, would fuse into a united whole instead of living as a mass of divided emotions and half-completed insights. The first man to achieve such a vision would be as distinct from all other men as man is from the gorilla. Light would shine from his head; his whole presence would radiate a power that could be sensed in all his neighborhood. The wave carries us to a height, poises us there for a moment, then swoops down again; but how if we could cling to some ledge while we are up there, and be left on it when the wave subsides? Man would be permanently on a new plane of being.

* *The Blockhouse*, by Jean Paul Clébert.

Then, I realize, men who have become more godlike than others sometimes fall from their ledge and die insane—like Nijinsky. But that is because they lack the strength to be god-like in this world without purpose, in this enormous bunker where bored men play cards and spit tobacco juice.

It seemed to me that if Cunningham knew some technique to increase that intensity, he might provide me with my "key," even if he possessed no real power or knowledge of his own. (It is obvious to me that, in spite of his intelligence, his mind has no concentration; it lacks the analytical toughness to think for long distances and to keep a tight hold on its results.)

Carlotta was still ostensibly living in Kentish Town, but in fact she spent most of her time at Cunningham's. It soon became obvious that she was getting on his nerves; I saw her several times in tears, and one day she appeared with a swollen cheek and a partially-black eye. This did not seem to affect her feeling for him; I have an idea that when he wasn't blacking her eyes, he was spending hours in "sex magic," and that even in hitting her, he was only responding to her taste for being dominated. I have always felt sorry for Carlotta. There are certain women who seem born for lives of vague dissatisfaction. Too strong to make a man their whole center of gravity, and yet too weak to stand alone and create, they invite unhappiness. And when they choose, they choose the worst possible man, as if out of a deliberate perverseness. I doubt whether Carlotta responds deeply to anything in Cunningham; she is fascinated by his confidence, his apparent certainty of purpose, but her feeling is as irrational as a moth's attraction to light. And she's puzzled when the glittering thing that attracts her shows its dark side and blacks her eye.

I stopped going to Cunningham's because of the possibility of meeting Gertrude. Not that I felt any dislike for her, but I felt guilty about her. My absence had the effect of making Cunningham anxious to show me "results" that would turn me into a full-time disciple. Also, he didn't like the way that I was settling down with Diana—quietly and unexcitingly, without quarrels or even disagreements. I have always felt that it makes very little difference to Diana whether she's married to me or Kirsten—or anybody else, for that matter; she's a quiet, good girl who takes life as it comes, and wants security. I sometimes find this passiveness exasperating—but then it fits in with my own methodical character.

Finally, on the 10th of December, Cunningham told me that I was to prepare for a revelation on the following night. He told me that ideally I should fast for two days—but that if I didn't want to fast completely, I should at least confine myself to bread and butter and milk—on no account meat or alcohol. He also advised me to read the Marquis de Sade, explaining that although Sade is a fool who lacks the capacity for thinking clearly, his belief in a total freedom from morality is a good mental preparation for magic.

I was more than dubious about all this. To begin with, I was now working in the British Museum during the day. After three hours of reading and writing, I would find myself getting tense and nervy, and the ideal remedy was a beef sandwich and a pint of bitter in the pub across the road. But apart from that, all this talk about leaving England to live on an island bored me. I realized that I owed the acceptance of my book to Cunningham, but now I was working on it, the idea of going on a wild goose chase to Sardinia was intolerable. Besides, I had Diana, and in many ways felt more contented than I'd been for years. So I suppose I was unconsciously *willing* Cunningham's "magic" to fail and release me from my obligation.

On Thursday (the 10th), I met Radin and Wise in the Museum. I wanted to let Radin know that I was not a party to Cunningham's roughness the other night—in fact, I'd been feeling guilty about it ever since it happened. But he didn't seem to bear me any grudge, and immediately asked me to go and have a drink. I said I couldn't—that I wasn't drinking. I didn't intend to tell them the reason, but Wise asked immediately: "Are you fasting for some initiation?" I admitted that Cunningham wanted to impart certain secrets to me and wanted to get me into the right frame of mind. I thought I was being tactful, but my remarks seemed to drive Wise to a fury. *"Our* secrets!" he said, grinding his teeth, "the secrets he swore never to reveal." I tried to smooth things over, but it was hopeless. I finally agreed to go to the pub with Radin simply to get away from Wise. (I drank orange squash.) I tried hard to convince Radin that I thought he was on the wrong track with Cunningham—that Cunningham had no real magic powers, and was only a harmless crank. To convince him, I told him in detail about the ceremony of the other night, feeling that, since he knew half of it, there was no point in trying to hide the rest. But I also tried hard to convince him that Cunningham's main interest was in feeling himself "in charge" of a situation—arranging things for his friends and arranging their lives. I told him about Kirsten's opera, about my own book, and finally, about Christine. I took care not to mention Cunningham's expectations about this Christine situation, but simply told him that he had brought them together again in a thoroughly disinterested way. Then I noticed that he was listening with his eyes on the tabletop, as if completely bored, and I knew this to be a danger signal—that he was not looking at me because he didn't want me to see that he was mentally recording every word. So I dropped the subject, and refused to start it again. I left Radin—on friendly terms—an hour later.

I spent part of my time reading Sade, but found him boring. All his gleeful talk about incest, rape and murder struck me as schoolboyish. But here again, I was made aware of elements in Cunningham's character that he is clever enough not to show. For example, his disregard of other people, his capacity for cruelty. I had only seen this briefly, or been left to infer it from his treatment of Carlotta, his "sacrifices," etc. But I am unobservant, and always think the best of people until the worst is too obvious for me to miss. But reading Sade made me aware that my own habit of mind is completely foreign to Cunningham—a rather cautious and scientific approach, a deliberately cultivated manner of bourgeois living to counterbalance my tendency to lose myself in dreams or abstractions. There is something of Nero about Cunningham—a desire to set the world on fire with a torch and then watch it burn. I became aware of all this as I read Sade. It is extreme romanticism—impatience with all restraints, the desire to reach the stars with one leap, and a muddled way of thinking that concludes that the reluctance to commit murder and rape is only another form of slavery.

I didn't tell Diana too much about Cunningham's plans, hoping that he wouldn't expect her to take part in the ceremony. But early on Friday evening, he came up to our room and told me that I shouldn't eat anything for the rest of the evening. As Diana was cooking supper, I found this tiresome. However, I ate a few water biscuits with cheese when he'd gone. He said I could drink now, as it would be a suitable preparation for the ceremony, but I decided not to, since I hadn't eaten much all day. Cunningham also said that he wanted Diana to come; I knew she was unwilling, but that she didn't like to oppose him openly. Finally, we went over there at about ten o'clock. On the way up, I met Oliver on the stairs, and he asked us to go into his room. Christine was fast asleep in bed. Oliver was worried; he said that Christine had been to Cunningham's for tea, and that Cunningham had offered to hypnotize her. She had gone to sleep and answered some questions—rather incoherently—but when he tried to wake her, she went on sleeping. Cunningham said that this was common in cases of suppressed hysteria: the subject has a subconscious desire to stay in the hypnotic trance because certain deep inner forces are allowed to escape. I immediately suspected a more simple explanation—that Cunningham had put some kind of drug into her tea, and used the hypnotism business as an excuse. However, I didn't tell Oliver this—he was worried enough already about how to get her home. It was long past the time when she was supposed to leave, and he couldn't take her himself, for obvious reasons. He had tried ringing Gertrude, to get her to take Christine in her car—Gertrude could fabricate some excuse, and Christine's family knew her as a social worker—but got no reply.

I suggested ringing her again; I went down to a public

telephone; but I also got no reply. What puzzled me was Cunningham's motive in drugging her. It was Diana who saw the explanation—that a scandal about her might compel Glasp to leave the country—especially since he had already been accused of assaulting her by her father. Even so, this explanation seemed to me rather far-fetched, because probably all that would happen would be that Christine would return home late, get into trouble with her mother, and perhaps not be allowed to see Oliver again. This wouldn't necessarily make Oliver willing to go to Sardinia.

We decided to ask Cunningham if he couldn't get her out of her "trance." I even suggested to Oliver that he should promise Cunningham to go out to Sardinia for a few weeks—after all, he couldn't be compelled to stay. So I went up to Cunningham's room, and found him sitting with Kirsten and Carlotta, both pretty high. I persuaded Cunningham to go down to see Oliver. I felt pretty constrained with Kirsten there, and it was obvious that Diana didn't like the situation any more than he did. Finally, she came in and sat down in a corner of the room, then whispered to me: "I'm going home soon." We helped ourselves to gin, having nothing better to do. After 20 minutes or so, I decided to go down and see what Cunningham was up to, and warn him that Diana wanted to leave. I found Christine sitting up in bed, looking quite happy but very dazed; she said she felt wonderful. Cunningham had apparently produced this effect by stroking her forehead and reciting incantations. We got her out of bed and asked her if she could walk, but she promptly sat down and began to giggle. She said she wanted to stay in Oliver's bed, and she put her arms around his neck and began to kiss him—to his obvious embarassment. Then she got back into bed. Oliver talked to her about her mother, but she only said: "I don't care." We made two more attempts to get her to walk, but the third time, she simply went back to sleep. I suggested calling a taxi and sending her home, but this was obviously no solution. Glasp was in despair—was afraid that the police were probably already searching for her, and that this would provide her father with a perfect excuse to get her away from her mother. Finally, Cunningham said he could suggest only one thing: that they should take her upstairs, and he would try to bring her back to consciousness by "magical means." Glasp didn't like this idea, but finally agreed, and Cunningham made various passes over her forehead, to guarantee that she wouldn't wake before the ceremony was over. It was only his assurance that Christine wouldn't know about the ceremony that made Oliver agree. Cunningham picked her up and carried her upstairs. There she was laid on the bed, and Cunningham explained the situation to Kirsten and Diana. He then asked Diana to undress Christine. Oliver immediately said that he couldn't allow this. Cunningham said that he couldn't perform a magic ceremony if Christine were dressed—it might bring her into great danger. In that case, Oliver said, they wouldn't perform the ceremony at all, and he started to shake Christine and try to wake her. I could see Oliver was getting hysterical, so I joined Cunningham in persuading him that it made no difference if Christine was asleep. So we left Diana and Carlotta to get her undressed, while Cunningham got out his black robes, drew pentagrams on the floor, lit candles on the altar, and started to burn incense. He also told me that I would have to take off most of my clothes, but that I could keep on my trousers and shirt. He then dropped a small quantity of some brown powder into a glass of gin, and told me to drink it down. Oliver refused to drink his, until Cunningham told him that he would either have to participate in the ceremony or go out of the room. He then agreed to drink the stuff. I noticed no immediate effect except a burning sensation on my tongue. But within a matter of minutes I felt as if I'd drunk a quart of whisky—this may have been the effect of gin on an empty stomach.

Cunningham now told Diana that she would have to strip and put on the red robe; she was unwilling, but by this time the atmosphere was so electric that she didn't make much objection. I noticed that Carlotta made no bones about undressing in the middle of the room, and putting on her robe. Glasp looked quickly in the opposite direction when he saw her, and said: "I say, Cunningham, I hope there's not going to be any sex?" Cunningham said grandly: "Of course there's going to be sex. The ceremony couldn't be performed without it." But he pointed a sort of black wand at Christine and said: "Don't worry, she won't be touched." This seemed to reassure Oliver, and he even took off most of his clothes until he was also wearing only a shirt and trousers. Cunningham then gave us both short silk jackets to wear—they were bright blue and yellow, and looked as if they'd been used in a pantomime of Aladdin.

Carlotta was helping herself very freely to the gin, and also to the brown powder. This had an almost immediate effect of plunging her into a condition of ecstasy—she sat on a chair, stretched out her arms, and looked as if she were being carried up to heaven by angels.

Cunningham said: "I can feel evil currents. We must hurry." He gave me the same parchment as before, and Oliver another copy of it, instructing us to call the responses alternately.

It was now about midnight, and Oliver was obviously anxious about getting Christine home as quickly as possible. He asked Cunningham if we couldn't hasten the ceremony, and Cunningham agreed. He warned us all that we must stay inside our pentagrams whatever happened. Diana, who had been changing in Oliver's room, came in with her robe on, and was given the same task as before—keeping the tripod fed with incense. Cunningham poured her gin, then looked into the jar containing the brown powder, and said; "Who's been taking this?" I pointed to Carlotta, and he said: "Oh Christ, why didn't you stop her?" I said I didn't know anything about it and asked him what it was, but he seemed too worried to reply. He asked her if she felt all right, and she said (without opening her eyes): "Oh, beautiful, BEAU-tiful!" So Cunningham said: "We'd better begin." I thought he looked anxious.

Since Christine was on the bed where they usually practiced their "sex magic," he spread a kind of quilted blanket on the floor, and made Carlotta lie on it. Kirsten had fallen into a drunken doze by the fire; he was waked up, made to take off most of his clothes like Oliver and myself, and given one of the blue jackets to wear. He wasn't given anything to read, but was told to repeat a formula in a loud voice if any evil influences appeared. (It sounded like: *"Omfalu gadoris tvasem abishthu"*—a language I don't recognize—but I wouldn't vouch for my accuracy here.)

They then proceeded exactly as before, with the chanting, the kissing of Carlotta's navel and breasts, and the act of "sex magic." I now suspected that the brown powder was a sexual stimulant, because I found myself sexually excited in a way that I cannot describe. But it was not the normal excitement that I can control. There was less of a cerebral element in it; it felt unpleasant, as if I was being excited against my will, like being tickled so that it hurts. But it undoubtedly produced quite new sensations in me. I find this difficult to explain; but it felt as though my brain was like a permanently opened eye. Half an hour before, I had felt sleepy; now I had a strange, naked sensation inside my head as if I could never again hope for sleep, and a realization of what it would be like to get more and more tired and yet be unable to fall asleep. I also felt an unpleasant sensation as if I were on waves. I usually associate this with getting drunk and feeling sick, but in this case, there was no sensation of physical sickness—just a weird feeling of being in a boat at sea.

It was getting so dark in the room that I could barely make out the responses; besides, the fumes from the censer were choking. When Oliver's voice repeated the responses, it was very tense, as if his throat had contracted. (He told me afterwards that he felt someone was trying to strangle him; this may have been because he was too close to the censer.)

Then Cunningham stood up, leaving Carlotta lying there, looking as if she'd fallen from a great height and broken all her limbs, and went over to the corner; when he came back, I saw that he was holding a black bird—I'm not sure what kind of bird it was, but it looked too big to be a crow. He carried this to the altar, where poor Diana was completely enveloped in smoke, held its head against a metal plate, and cut it off with one blow of a heavy knife. This shocked me; I hate the idea of killing animals (although I suppose its death was quick enough). Cunningham then allowed its blood to run into a chalice, made various passes over it with his hands, and drank it down in one gulp. I now began to feel ill, and my forehead was sweating. Cunningham then went back to Carlotta, made her sit on a stool, and started to ask her questions. I was not listening carefully this time. I heard her say that she was in a stone room, and she thought it was in a pyramid. He pointed to Christine and asked: "Who is holding her captive?" Carlotta said: "No one. She is asleep." "Who *was* holding her captive?" "He who is dressed in black." (It didn't strike me until afterward that Cunningham was dressed in black.)

Cunningham then went over to Christine and began to repeat all kinds of formulas over her, and I got the impression that currents of air started to stir the smoke in the room. Cunningham suddenly said: "Something is going wrong." He looked around, and saw that Diana had sat down on a chest that stood behind her. He said: "Quick, stand up and get back into your circle." She dragged herself to her feet; I could see she was very tired. I said: "How much longer is this going on?" Then, as I spoke, both candles suddenly flared up, sputtered, and went out. The room immediately filled with a smell like burnt hair, and I felt dizzy. Carlotta's voice started to sing a song in German, and Kirsten began to repeat the formula that Cunningham had given him. Something brushed against me, and I felt I had to sit down, so I cautiously lowered myself on to the floor, and sat with my head between my hands. Cunningham's voice was droning on with his incantations, and he suddenly called: "No one is to move out of his circle. There are evil spirits in the room." Carlotta's voice started to moan: "They are hurting me," and then there was a sound as if she were vomiting. This time, I had no sensation of something strange in the room; although I felt so dizzy that I couldn't tell anyway. I heard Oliver's voice say, very sluggishly: "What are you doing, Cunningham? What about Christine?," and Cunningham said: "She's still asleep." Christine's voice came out of the darkness: "No I'm not." At this point, a strange languor came over me, and a feeling of well-being. I stretched out on the floor and let myself fall asleep. The last thing I remember was the sound of Carlotta moaning and being sick.

When I woke up again, I was in the same room. I looked at my watch; it was four o'clock. Only Cunningham was still in the room. I said: "Where's Diana," and Cunningham answered: "I think she's asleep on Oliver's bed." I dragged myself to my feet, feeling very ill and faraway, and saw that the floor was an awful mess of vomit and broken glass. (I didn't find out where the latter came from.) Cunningham said: "Quick, help me to clean up. I've sent for a doctor for Carlotta." I asked what was wrong with her, and he said: "She's being sick. She took too much of that powder." (Later, I discovered that the main component of the powder was cantharides—Spanish fly—as well as some cocaine. No wonder it knocked me out!) I asked about Oliver, and learned he'd taken Christine home in a taxi.

I went downstairs, and found Diana asleep in Oliver's bed, still wearing the robe. I woke her up and helped her to get dressed. At this point, the doctor arrived, and went up to Kirsten's room, where Carlotta was apparently in bed. Cunningham then rushed in, and said in a whisper: "Go away quickly, and deny that you've been here this evening." I didn't need telling twice; I helped Diana downstairs—she seemed very shaky, but the night air woke her up. When we got home, she said: "Promise you'll have no more to do with him." I promised—I'd already made up my mind that this was my last experiment in magic. We then fell into bed, after I'd taken several asprin.

As we were falling asleep, she turned over and said: "Gerard, why did you get into bed with me when I was asleep?" I immediately knew what had happened. I asked her: "Did I make love to you?" She said: "Yes. . . . didn't you?" I said: "No, but I know who did." I asked her if she was quite certain that someone had climbed into bed with her, or whether it was possible she dreamed it. She got up, and went into the bathroom without a word. A moment later, she came back and said: "No, I didn't dream it."

There seemed nothing we could do about it, so we went to sleep. I could see no point in being angry. It wasn't Diana's fault—I suppose it was mine, if anybody's. And I remembered what I'd written in my journal about Cunningham's obsession with sexual conquest—with the actual possession of as many women as possible. And after all, I suppose it makes no difference to anybody, provided there are no unpleasant consequences.

In the morning, I woke up at ten, still feeling ill and drunk, and immediately had to rush to the lavatory. I noticed that my diarrhea caused a burning sensation at the point of evacuation, exactly like the feeling in my mouth when I took the brown powder in the gin. I have since discovered from a book on toxicology that this is another sign of cantharic poisoning.

In spite of feeling ill, I was anxious to find out if Carlo was all right. Diana didn't want to get up, so I left her in b while I walked around to Cunningham's. As soon as I arrived saw the police car outside. At first I was tempted to go ba home; then I went in, reflecting that I hadn't done anythi illegal. I knocked on Oliver's door; he opened it, and imme ately signaled me to be quiet. I asked him what had happen and he told me that Carlotta had been taken to the hospital, and that the doctor had notified the police—as apparently he was bound to.

As we talked, we heard the police coming down the stairs, and Cunningham's voice with them. They went out, and we heard the car pull away. I asked about Christine; Oliver said he hadn't heard from her yet; he had taken her home at three in the morning, and she had thought up some excuse about a schoolfriend of hers. He hoped her mother believed it. At all events, she seemed none the worse for her experience. Oliver asked her if she wasn't frightened to wake up in the dark with strange incantations and the sound of someone vomiting; she said: "No, because I heard your voice and knew it was all right." We talked for a while about what might happen to Cunningham, but it obviously depended on Carlotta's condition. Besides, both Oliver and I had seen her helping herself to the powder, so there was no question of blaming Cunningham. I also asked Oliver how Diana had got into his bed. He said Cunningham had carried her down, and that he had left Cunningham alone with her when the taxi came.

I went back home, feeling horribly sick and tired, and wishing I'd stayed in bed. I was sweating, and my whole body was prickling as if I had ants under my clothes. I was afraid I'd collapse in the street. The Saturday morning crowds made me feel awful; I felt I'd never have the strength to get home. However, I arrived—and found Radin's car outside the door. And when I got up to the room, he was just on the point of leaving. His eyes were glittering, and he called me "my dear Gerard." I told him I felt too ill to talk to him; he asked me what was the matter, and as soon as I mentioned the symptoms, said; "That sounds like cantharides poisoning. You should see a doctor." I said I only wanted to go to bed and be left alone. I pulled off my clothes and collapsed into bed, feeling horrible. Radin was persistent. It was soon evident to me that Diana had given him an accurate and minute account of the proceedings, omitting nothing. I could only nod as he reeled off the whole story and asked me to confirm it. He even mentioned Christine. At this, I remembered Oliver, and asked him to try to keep her out of it as much as possible. As he left, I asked him how he'd heard about it, but all he would say was: "We have our sources." But I gather that newspapers automatically check with all police stations to find if there's anything happening, and Radin must have told his night editor to let him know if there was any news item involving Cunningham.

I slept for the rest of the day, although Diana went out and brought a doctor. He simply gave me a sedative, said he thought that I was suffering from a hangover, and went away. Diana seemed better than I was, and looked after me. But she made me promise that if Cunningham came I wouldn't admit him—just pretend that I wasn't at home, and keep the door locked.

By evening, I was well enough to get up, and sat around reading, feeling very weak. We went to bed at ten o'clock. I was awakened hours later by the sound of my bell ringing. Diana woke up and said: "Don't answer it." I didn't need any encouraging; I wasn't going to tramp down three flights of stairs at two in the morning. It went on ringing, and finally, we heard someone coming up the stairs, and knocking on the door. One of the other tenants had opened the front door. Someone's voice called: "Mr. Sorme, could I speak to you?," and I realized it wasn't Cunningham. So I got out of bed, pulled on my dressing gown, and opened the door.

It was a reporter from one of the daily papers. He was carrying a first edition of the *Sunday Messenger* (which is the Sunday version of the *Daily News*). Its headline read: BLACK MAGIC BY CANDLELIGHT: NEW CARADOC CUNNINGHAM REVELATIONS. I had to invite him in—besides, I was curious about the story. It was a full spread, and Radin had done what he had always hoped to do—get a scoop on Cunningham—There was even a photograph of Christine. There were one or two exaggerations: it declared, for example, that all the women present were naked. But it hinted very plainly that Diana had been raped, and ended by declaring that Cunningham should be arrested and charged with impairing the morals of a minor.

I am told that the article was flagrantly libelous, and that Cunningham might have sued them for heavy damages. It dragged up all kinds of things in his past, and even hinted that he had sacrificed babies. It said that Carlotta was on the danger list, and that he had poisoned her. (Both statements were untrue—she spent a week in the hospital and recovered; but then, Diana hadn't seen her helping herself to the brown powder, and assumed that Cunningham had given it to her as he had to the rest of us.)

I could see that Cunningham might be in serious trouble, so I gave my own account of it, toning it all down greatly, emphasizing that Christine's morals had been in no danger, that he hadn't given Carlotta the poison, and that he wasn't practicing black magic but white magic.

The reporter spent nearly an hour with us; when he asked Diana if it was true she had been violated, I gave her a warning look, and she said No, she didn't think so. When we finally got rid of him, I disconnected the bell, and we managed to get a good night's sleep. But the following day was hopeless. First the police came—I gather they were upset by the allegations that they were allowing black magic to be practiced under their noses—but at least they confirmed that Carlotta was in no danger, and that Christine had been examined by a doctor who verified that she had not been assaulted.

After that, a stream of reporters turned up. By midday, I was exhausted, so I hailed a taxi, and Diana and I drove over to Gertrude's in Hampstead. We found Kirsten already there —also hiding from reporters. Gertrude was magnificent in the crisis—no reproaches or anything of the sort; she simply let me go to bed and sleep until evening, and treated Diana with perfect courtesy. (Caroline came in the evening, bringing the actor she's going to marry, but I was fast asleep and didn't see her.)

The Monday morning papers were also full of the story, and added the information that Cunningham was nowhere to be found. We stayed at Gertrude's for two days, until the thing died down of its own accord, and then went back home. (Gertrude firmly put Diana in a separate bedroom, though!) We also saw something of Father O'Mahoney, and although Gertrude has not said anything more about it, I gather she has every intention of becoming a Roman Catholic. Even Cunningham's approval didn't put her off.

That is pretty well the end of the story, as far as I'm concerned. We have heard no more of Cunningham. Presumably he had no need to go to America; I can't imagine what charges the police could press against him; as far as I know, practicing magic isn't a legal offense.

Diana and I had a great deal of unpleasantness; abusive letters through the post, and someone even chalked on our door: "Get back to hell where you belong." The local tradesmen all regarded Diana with suspicion, so that she moved further away to do the shopping. The owner of the flat came to see me, saying that the other tenants of the house were complaining about the publicity, and I immediately offered to let him have his flat back for the same amount I'd paid for it. A week later, he found another tenant. By this time, it was Christmas, and there wasn't much to be done; we spent it with my family, then came here, to Ireland, leaving most of our belongings to be sent after us. Diana had relations in Galway, so we came here, and almost immediately found ourselves this cottage, which we rent for seven shillings a week. It has its disadvantages: I have to get drinking water from a well in the garden; I am doing my best to poison the rats, and the local council wants £50 to connect us to the main electricity supply. But it is quiet; I've started to work on a novel, and never cease to congratulate myself on getting away from London. Oliver has promised to come and spend some time here later in the year. He is still living in the same place. I gather that the publicity has made the Christine situation difficult, and he has been asked not to see her until the court proceedings about her mother's separation have been completed.

Poor Cunningham. I didn't dislike him, and I can't bring myself to agree with Diana's resentment. I wonder where he's living now, and whom he's driving mad. . . .

AUTHOR'S NOTE

* * * * * * * *

I have omitted the final pages of the fifth notebook, since it has no relevance to the subject; besides, the final sentence quoted above gives the book an artificial appearance of coming to an end.

In my prefatory note, I did not mention the most serious result of this diary falling into the hands of the press—I mean the consequences for the family of Austin Nunne. The press had no idea of my whereabouts for several weeks after I left the Whitechapel flat, and I had no idea that my journals were not still in a locked box, waiting with the rest of my books to be sent on to me when I found a permanent address. Consequently, I had no idea of my sudden leap to notoriety until, in Galway, I saw a newspaper headline: IDENTITY OF WHITECHAPEL MURDERER DISCLOSED IN SEX DIARY. Radin's paper had another "scoop." There were also photographs of Oliver and of Austin Nunne's father; the article talked about a "plot to evade justice" and about the serious consequences for all who knew that Austin was the Whitechapel killer. These stories died out two days later when it was revealed that the police had always been fairly certain of the identity of the Whitechapel killer, but had dropped the case for lack of sufficient evidence, and because Austin's father had undertaken to ensure that he would be permanently confined in a private mental home with no possibility of escape. Later, Austin was examined by a number of doctors, who found him to be suffering from a venereal disease that had affected his brain tissue, so that he would be completely unable to understand the proceedings if he should be brought to trial.

In the meantime, I took care to keep my whereabouts a secret. I found myself a cottage and then, when I was certain that there was no further possibility of proceedings, wrote to my former landlord, and arranged to have my belongings sent on. In the following weeks, I was interviewed by a great number of reporters, and by the police. Like most press sensations, this one was dead and forgotten in a matter of weeks, and I was able to work quietly on the final chapters of my book. I was later attacked by Radin for allowing extracts from my journals to be printed in a Sunday newspaper, and for accepting a large sum of money from the newspaper. I have already, in my prefatory note, explained my reasons for doing this.

When *Methods and Techniques of Self-Deception* appeared in the autumn of 1957, I was startled by the amount of attention that it attracted—out of all proportion to the number of readers I expected to interest. At first I congratulated myself on the size of the audience it had reached, and it took several months for me to realize that it was being bought on the basis of my dubious notoriety, but was not being read. In spite of its sale, both here and in America, it had no audience—for the readers I had originally hoped to reach were put off by the publicity the book received. All this became very obvious to me when my second and third books were published, and were attacked and praised in a way that appeared to have no connection with the content of the books themselves. This provides me with a further reason for publishing these journals without any attempt at editing. I am told that some of the aims and motives revealed in them are hardly creditable, and that some passages are extremely damaging. I feel that this is preferable to the present tangle of misunderstanding. There is nothing here that I think worth concealing.

Caradoc Cunningham was recently deported from the United States, after the latest "Cunningham scandal" in Los Angeles was given wide coverage in American newspapers, and was taken up in England by the newspapers who were so prominent in attacking him six years ago. I am told that he is at present living in Mexico City, supported by members of various Cunningham Societies in the United States. I also hear that his books are regarded as having scriptural authority, and that he is the founder of a new religion.